PRISONER

ROSS GREENWOOD

B
Boldwood

First published in Great Britain in 2021 by Boldwood Books Ltd.

Copyright © Ross Greenwood, 2021

Cover Design by Nick Castle Design

Cover Photography: Shutterstock

The moral right of Ross Greenwood to be identified as the author of this work has been asserted in accordance with the Copyright, Designs and Patents Act 1988.

All rights reserved. No part of this book may be reproduced in any form or by any electronic or mechanical means, including information storage and retrieval systems, without written permission from the author, except for the use of brief quotations in a book review.

This book is a work of fiction and, except in the case of historical fact, any resemblance to actual persons, living or dead, is purely coincidental.

Every effort has been made to obtain the necessary permissions with reference to copyright material, both illustrative and quoted. We apologise for any omissions in this respect and will be pleased to make the appropriate acknowledgements in any future edition.

A CIP catalogue record for this book is available from the British Library.

Paperback ISBN 978-1-80048-462-7

Large Print ISBN 978-1-80048-464-1

Hardback ISBN 978-1-80162-814-3

Ebook ISBN 978-1-80048-465-8

Kindle ISBN 978-1-80048-466-5

Audio CD ISBN 978-1-80048-456-6

MP3 CD ISBN 978-1-80048-457-3

Digital audio download ISBN 978-1-80048-458-0

Boldwood Books Ltd
23 Bowerdean Street
London SW6 3TN
www.boldwoodbooks.com

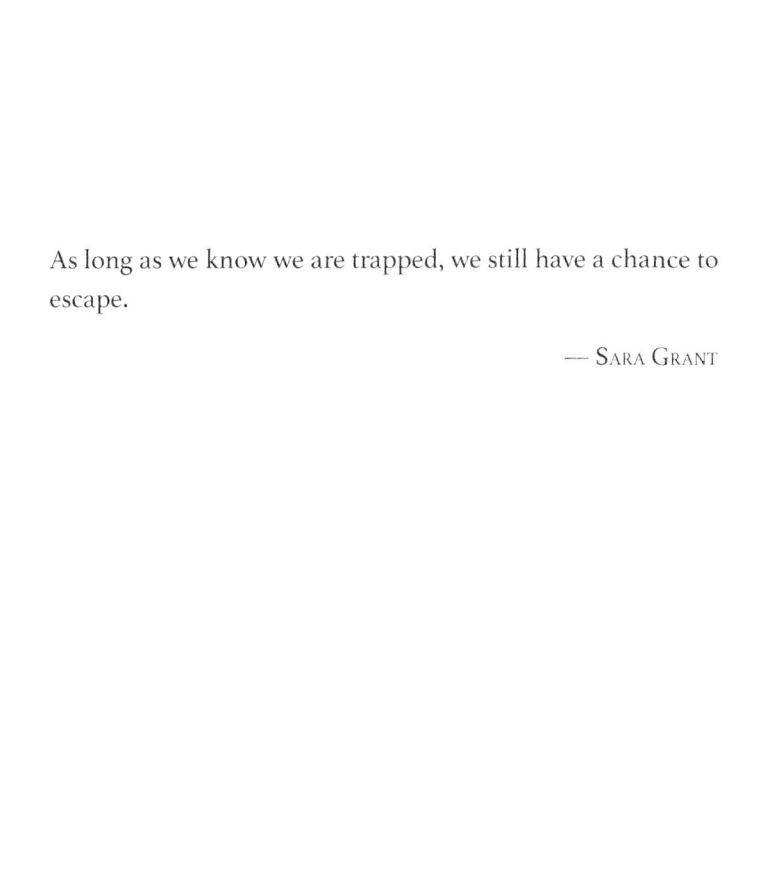

As long as we know we are trapped, we still have a chance to escape.

— Sara Grant

In memory of
Prison Officer Pat Phillips – 1947 – 2021
Senior Officer John Veitch – 1960 – 2018
Prison Officer Adam Jarvis – 1987 – 2018
Legends.

A TALE OF TWO JAILS

HMP Peterborough is the only purpose-built prison in Britain to accommodate both sexes. It holds approximately one thousand men and over three hundred women. They are housed separately and kept out of sight of each other at all times.

Prison officers generally work either the male side or on the female estate, because, even though you might think they would be the same, they are very different places.

Call signs and locations have been changed, and the characters and events in this book are purely fictional, but the dangers behind bars are real.

1

NOVEMBER LAST YEAR

I've watched movies where people get shot or stabbed, then stagger and drag themselves for miles to safety. Until this evening, I imagined that was possible, but it isn't. Not for me. Instead, my eyes begin to close.

A cool breeze rustles the branches. It chills the sweat that covers my body, except for where the sticky warmth runs down my left hip and leg. My left hand rests on the hole in that side, but it lacks the strength to staunch the flow.

Twenty metres away, through the treeline, occasional cars roar past. I blink back tears. Perhaps, there is still a chance. I manage to shuffle forwards through the damp leaves, gasping through gritted teeth. A sharp, intense spasm in my stomach forces me to arch my back and look skywards. Through the canopy overhead, the moonlight bathes me. I sense part of me drawing upwards, and my face relaxes.

My weak legs give way, and I slump to my knees, then topple forward over a felled trunk at the side of the path, but any pain has left me now. As my vision blurs once more, there's no rush of reminiscences or regrets. Instead, the faces of my children appear in my mind, memories from less than an hour ago. I told them that we would always be a family. Instead, I will die alone in the mud.

And it's no less than I deserve.

2

SIX MONTHS BEFORE THAT

Reaching over, I tap the off button on the alarm clock before it rings at 5.30 a.m. I had the misfortune of seeing the time at midnight and every hour after. It's not uncommon for me to take prisoners to bed, but it's been many years since one kept me up all night. But Gronkowski is different. I understood that the moment I met him.

It's cold in the bedroom even though May Day has been and gone. Abi, my wife, prefers the heating on, but our last gas bill put an end to that. She's buried herself beneath the covers next to me with just her nose and mouth poking out so she can breathe. Asleep, she resembles the woman I fell in love with.

The floorboards on the landing creak as I tiptoe across them, but luckily both my children sleep like the dead. It's their only similarity. I pop my head around the door into eight-year-old Tilly's room. Just a thin blanket covers her lower legs. Her pyjama top has ridden up to reveal her plump tummy. I occasionally call her The Beast because she's warm and toasty whatever the weather, and she's never sick. She doesn't seem to mind.

My five-year-old is the opposite of her, to all children it seems. I step into the box room and stare down at Ivan. A minute I don't have to spare passes. It's hard to leave my boy. There's enough light from the streetlamp outside his window for me to frown at the sheen of sweat on the lad's forehead. Even so, I envy him his fevered rest. I'm at that level of tiredness where you're nauseous. Ivan grumbles mid-dream, so I stroke his cheek to settle him. He has the same dimple on the right-hand side of his face as me and my long-dead father. Seeing it always makes me smile.

'Shh, my boy. It's okay.'

Ivan's breathing settles, so I leave the room. I couldn't be bothered to shower after work yesterday, so I need to have one, but I can't take more than a few minutes or the water will run cool when Abi washes her hair after breakfast. Then she'll want to discuss my selfishness the second I step through the door in thirteen hours, after the resentment has spent all day poisoning her.

After a brief shower, I sneak a final glance at the kids before pulling my uniform on, then go downstairs and fill a bowl with cornflakes and milk. My nose wrinkles at the pungent smell in the kitchen. After three spoonfuls, I slop the remains into a gap in the overspilling bin, despite knowing that the next chance I'll have to eat anything substantial will be in six hours after lunchtime bang up.

Letting myself out of the back door, which I gently close behind me, I undo two thick cable locks on my bike and place them over my shoulders like ammo belts. Then I scoot through the rear gate. It's a still, hushed morning with an insignificant drizzle, and the city holds its breath with anticipation.

Work is five miles away. If it rains, I sometimes take the car, but then Abi is without it, and she'd be stuck in the house with the kids. The buses are too busy, apparently. The prison provides its staff with big waterproof coats for walking the perimeters, but they are so heavy they make you sweat, so I stick to a light officer's jacket.

I cycle hard through Orton Longueville Village, the posh area alongside our estate, and race along the rowing lake. My warm breath steams ahead of me in the cold air. When I hit Atherstone Avenue, near where the prison is, I spot Fats up ahead. He's my favourite officer to work with. We joined on the same day, five years ago. Fats started on his thirtieth birthday, and it was only a few months until it was mine, and we have similar interests. Our first conversation was a clue to how our relationship would unfold:

'Hi, I'm Jim Dalton.'

His enormous hand covered mine as we shook, but he was gentle.

'Tony Domingo. You can call me Fats.'

He bopped his head ever so slightly as he said it. I thought at the time it was to give me a hint on his nickname, but I later discovered he had a habit of nodding when he was nervous.

'Like in Fats Domino?' I ask.

'That's right, sir.'

'Didn't you say Domingo?'

'That's right, sir.'

Fats says that a lot, even to the prisoners. It's incredibly disarming.

His homesick father had returned to Scotland after his birth, leaving his ogre-like mother to raise him. Her family had a slaughterhouse out in the sticks near Spalding. Fats once showed me a picture of the whole clan in between a big barn and a forklift. I'd never seen such huge people, which was saying something if you consider where I worked – Gronkowski would fit in with them. I suspect Fats was raised in the same way as a young bull: by constant feeding. He weighs nearly twice as much as my trim twelve stone, even though we're both six feet tall. He isn't all fat, but neither is he all muscle.

I soon catch up with him and cruise behind his creaking bicycle.

'Is Hitler struggling?' I ask.

Fats laughs and gasps loudly. I'd told him once that if there was a God and such a thing as reincarnation, then Hitler would have been reborn as Fats's bicycle. He mentions it constantly, as though it's the best joke ever.

'You on the wing?' Fats wheezes.

'Yeah, Agony. You?'

'No, just the morning. I've got a nicking today, so hopefully they'll make me GD.'

An Agony is what the staff call an A shift, 7 a.m. until 7 p.m., whereas Fats's morning shift will start at the same time, but he'll leave after lunch at twelve-thirty. A nicking is the adjudication meeting after we've put a prisoner on report for poor behaviour. GD stands for general duties such as providing support for the wings when it's time for medication and methadone, and is much less aggravation than running a landing. We've been so short of officers lately that the chances of Fats getting GD are slim, but he's an optimist.

I asked him if he fancied a beer when we first started, but Fats said he didn't drink. I got the impression that if I'd asked him for a coffee or even water, I'd have received the same reply. It doesn't matter though, because I'm bogged down with family life, so a work friend is all I can handle. Fats lives on the same ropey estate as me with his girlfriend, Lena, whom I've never met.

'You hear about Sandringham?' asks Fats.

'Yes, very sad.'

I realise that I've hardly thought about Sandringham's death since I was told. Does that say something about the person I've become, even if I barely knew him?

'Did you meet Gronkowski yesterday?' asks Fats.

'Yeah, dangerous guy. He arrived late morning. I had an early, so

I only spoke to him briefly. They had better partner me up with someone who knows what they're doing today.'

'I was on his wing at bang up last night. He gave me a mean look when I locked him in, like we were squaring up in a boxing match. Do you know what he did?'

'Grievous Bodily Harm, wasn't it? Beat them to a pulp when he was robbing them.'

We stop talking as we weave through the cars in the prison car park. It's already filling up. If I bring my own vehicle, it's usually the most battered one there, unless Fats has driven, although I think his car recently passed away after many illnesses. I enter the code for the staff bike shed, and we stow our bikes. Fats stands in front of me with sweat pouring down his face as I put the padlock back.

'That's right, sir. Gronkowski was remanded for GBH. They said he beat the couple real bad. The girlfriend is still in Intensive Care but, just before we left last night, we heard that the boyfriend had died. That makes Gronkowski a murderer.'

3

I'm glad Fats told me the latest about Gronkowski. Many officers aren't interested in the crimes of the inmates, but I'd rather know if they've received unpleasant news. They may be prisoners, but they're still human, and a few quiet words might help. Although in Gronkowski's case, I'm more focussed on the fact he is capable of beating someone to death. It's hard to imagine what kind of rage could cause a person to commit such an awful act. You'd think your inner spirit would prevent you from taking a life. I suspect we all have murderous thoughts, but only mad or evil people act on them.

As Fats and I stroll to the gatehouse, I glance up and across at the looming whitewashed walls visible beyond the administration building. There's a red dawn behind, giving them an ethereal glow. It's difficult to believe that each dark, barred window hides a compact room where men live out their days. It has never seemed right to me that humans are treated like this. Much of prison life doesn't make sense, but I've got a job to do, and it pays my bills. In some ways, I'm as much a prisoner here as they are.

'Dalton! Fats!' says Lennox, who is at the front of the queue.

I wave to her and nod to the other officers as we line up to walk through the security scanners. Some officers bring their phones in and put them in the lockers at the gatehouse because having one inside is a criminal offence. Fats is one of them. What can be so important that you'd need to come out each lunchtime and check your phone? I like that nobody can get hold of me. Numerous officers get caught and sacked for 'forgetting' their phone is in their pocket, so I leave mine at home. Occasionally, the security team searches us blurry-eyed officers when we arrive first thing, but today's just a normal day.

The jail is awash with illicit items, mostly small phones and drugs. Crooked staff are the main source of the contraband that gets brought in. I despise dodgy officers. The role is hard enough without wondering whether the guy next to you has your back. An officer recently got caught bringing a knife in, which is terrifying. Prison weapons, shanks as they are called, tend to be constructed with razor blades and are for slashing and scarring, not for killing. Deep, puncturing weapons are much more dangerous.

We reach the front where we collect our radios and keys. I glance down at the detail, which shows everyone's work location for the morning. Fats has his wish and is GD. I frown, then lean towards the holes in the plastic screen that separates the gate staff from us.

'Delta Eight, please.'

The Operational Support Officer, or OSO, drops a set of keys in the chute and a radio follows soon after. I pick them out, realising that I'd been praying for a miracle that would place me on a different wing and away from Gronkowski, but no such luck today. At least I'm working with a solid guy called Bishop. I step to the side and wait for Fats.

'Delta Eleven,' says Fats with a smile.

Grim-faced, I stare down the long line of queueing officers. There'll be over a hundred of them on shift before unlock. It's a tale of two jails. The bigger, older men, some ex-forces, stand with expressionless faces. They will usually be on the male side of the prison. Most of the female officers and a few of the younger lads, some only twenty years old, look relaxed and joke among themselves. They'll work the female side.

Fats and I wander to the electronic security door and press the button to request clearance from Comms. The door clicks, and I open it. Then we trudge across the sterile area, our footsteps echoing around the high walls, through two big metal gates and finally towards more double doors. I plug in my radio earpiece, hook the mould over my ear, and squeeze the talk button.

'QP, this is Officer Dalton, taking call sign Delta Eight.'

There's a crackle from my radio, but nothing more. Everyone is signing on at once so it often takes a few attempts. I repeat the words and receive a reply.

'Officer Dalton received. Taking call sign Delta Eight, please confirm First Response.'

'Delta Eight confirms First Response.'

First Response means that when an officer presses his or her personal alarm, First Response come running. That's the idea anyway. Most days, we're down to two officers on a wing of eighty. If the other officer is doing meds or in the toilet, you can't leave the wing unmanned to help. Assistance for the officer in need might be a while coming, so in the meantime, they will have to fight.

Fats opens the heavy doors and the heady waft of hundreds of caged men drifts over us. It's a unique smell that sticks to the back of your throat. It reminds me of a men's changing room after a competitive football match but with the added bitter sting of fear, resentment and regret.

'After you, sir. Don't worry, Dalton, I got your back this morning.'

We enter the hub, which is a central octagonal room about four metres wide with the wings coming off it like the spokes of a wheel. Sometimes it's messier than the wings. Only Officer Claire Lennox, whom I saw at the gatehouse, and Senior Officer John Bowell are present. Oddly, Lennox looks exactly like her namesake, Annie, except her cropped hair is black and she has a thick Welsh accent. Bowell is ex-army and has an enormous belly and grey hair. Lennox once asked him if his first name was large, which he laughed his head off at. He's a much-respected SO. We might need a man like him today.

'Welcome, ladies. I have some good news and some bad,' says Bowell.

'What's the good?' I ask.

'I got four numbers on the lottery last weekend. The bad news is Bishop and Sharpe have rung in sick with flu.'

'Shit,' I whisper under my breath. 'Put Lennox on with me.'

I'm pleased some females choose to work on the male side. A few of the older officers don't like it because it riles up the women-haters among the prison population. Naturally most females also have less upper body strength, and prison violence often comes down to power and weight.

But I've been here long enough to know a balance works best. Women can defuse situations that men can't. The quality I need backing me up is guts. If necessary, I can provide the violence. After Fats, I'd take Lennox over anyone else. Despite being just twenty-two, she grew up on a tough estate with three brothers. She's wise to male bullshit, and has a razor mind to match her sharp tongue.

'No can do, they're sending two over from the female side,' said Bowell. 'Lennox is running Bravo wing today. You and her get one each.'

'Who are they?' asks Fats with a barely suppressed grin.

'Peasbody and Sheraton,' replies Bowell with a raised eyebrow.

'Aren't they cartoon dogs?' jokes Lennox, who then pauses. 'Shit, I think they're both off the last training course.'

My skin contracts. 'No fucking way. That course finished a month ago. You can't put me on there with a newbie.'

Bowell leans back in his chair with his hands out. 'I'll give you the biggest guy.'

The rest of the shift filter into the hub. I check my cheap watch — cheap because they often get broken. Ten past seven. Five minutes to unlock. The buzzer sounds for one of the emergency buttons in the cells. Lennox picks up the phone.

'Please state your medical emergency.'

She listens, says, 'Five minutes,' and puts the phone back.

'Fats, mush, that was cell forty-eight. He reckons you didn't give him a goodnight snog last night.'

Fats doesn't miss a beat. 'That's bullshit. I kissed the entire bottom landing.'

Everyone laughs except me. I've heard it all before. Apart from Fats, the rest of the officers only have about a year's service each, although it will still feel like a lifetime, and they will have already changed. The person they were before they joined the prison service is gone. If you can last six months, you can last forever, is the saying, but it's not true. Officer Sandringham lasted three years on the female estate.

Few walk the male landings for more than two years. Those that do often have a short retirement or, like Sandringham, never get there at all.

The door of the houseblock clangs open, and I shake my head as I look out of the window at the approaching officers. Their dark-blue trousers are a tight fit, but nothing compared to their dazzling white work shirts, which look as though they've been painted on.

Their sleeves are rolled up, revealing sleeve tattoos. With their slicked-back hair, they could have stepped off the cover of a teen magazine. But they aren't swaggering now.

Fats stands next to me and rests a meaty paw on my shoulder.

'Relax, the cavalry is here.'

4

I turn to SO Bowell, who's smiling at me. The sneaky sod knew they'd sent a couple of kids over.

'Come on, John,' I urge him. 'I've got Gronkowski and a traveller gang on there, not to mention Scranton. It's not training day.'

'You can have the ginger one, Peasbody. All them redheads are feisty, although I will accept Peasbody's not the best name for a screw.'

The two young officers open the hub door and stand awkwardly in front of us. The allegedly feisty ginger lad looks as though he shaves once a fortnight even if he doesn't need to, but at least he's holding eye contact. The carpet fascinates the other guy.

Bowell's phone rings. He picks up and listens.

'Bollocks, another one with flu. Okay, I'll send him up.'

He gently places the receiver back in the cradle and tuts.

'Fats, they're one light upstairs, off you go. Everyone else, get them unlocked. Be careful today – we're short-staffed and there might be trouble.'

I nod at Peasbody. 'Follow me.'

When we reach the wing, I let Peasbody open the heavy gates

and keep an eye on his hands. They don't tremble, which is a surprise. I stand still and listen while Peasbody relocks the fire hydrants and hoses. It's silent otherwise, but on the other side of all those doors are unhappy people caged like rats. As the saying goes, this is the calm before the storm.

I open the door to the office, which is the same size as a cell and contains only a chair, a desk and a cabinet. On the wall there is a whiteboard with fifty-six boxes and seventy-nine spaces. All of them have a name in them. I write five cell numbers down on a piece of paper, and hand it to Peasbody. I talk as I write our names in the observation book. Dalton and Peasbody on duty. Roll count. Seventy-nine.

'Have you worked male side before?' I ask him.

'No, well, a few hours on the detox wing with the service users when I was training.'

I glance up to see if he's joking. He isn't. That's not what I call the residents of Bravo wing. The inmates there can be mouthy with withdrawal, but weak and skinny. It's one of the easier wings to work as long as you don't mind a bit of moaning and thieving.

The sheen of sweat on Peasbody's forehead, despite the cool hour, makes me think of Ivan at home. It's much worse for Peasbody, though, because he's awake for his nightmare. I have to try to pass on five years' worth of jailcraft to him in thirty seconds.

'Look, Peasbody. It's different over here, so stay calm. Open the wing workers up, then the rest of the cons two minutes later. Stop puffing your chest out, or someone will do it for you. This is a remand wing, and it also includes immigrants awaiting deportation. Quite a few have been with us over a year. There's a lot of anger here. It's not far below the surface.'

Peasbody looks at the list of names as if it will tell him who's going to be trouble.

'Many of these men are looking for a fight or answers to their situations – it's not for us to provide either, but be polite. Anyone gives you any hassle, let me know. Anyone has questions, tell them I said to see me. Do not provoke anyone, or be provoked. Your job today is to ensure the inmates go back in their cells at lunchtime in the same condition as when they left them this morning. Do not be a hero.'

'Okay, I'll do my best.'

'That's the spirit. A fifth of the men on here could beat one of us up, but none of them can take us both. Remember that.'

I think of Gronkowski and suspect I've just lied.

'Keep away from Scranton and Gronkowski. Cells forty and forty-three.'

'Right.'

'And don't worry about being new. They'll know the moment they see you and will try to push your buttons or take advantage. When I shout bang up, start at the bottom and lock the doors one by one. Don't worry if they're not inside. Close the door. They'll soon come running.'

I watch him lick his lips.

'And breathe. You'll never forget today. Try to enjoy it. When you walk out of here at lunchtime, you'll be a new man.'

Peasbody's Adam's apple hammers up and down his throat like a faulty elevator. He nods, then runs up the stairs with the list to get the wing workers out. They tend to be time-served prisoners who will serve meals and clean the wing. They are desired positions because they are out of their cells for most of the day. The other workers will leave the houseblock to attend industries or education. Five minutes later, the servery has a queue of tired-looking men. Sleep doesn't come easy in a prison, especially for those on this type of wing where they have an uncertain future yet to be decided by the courts.

'Queries!' I shout from the office door and prepare myself for the arguments that will shortly commence.

One of the travellers is first, but he's barely got warmed up about his clothes being at Reception still, when a big hand grabs him around the neck and yanks him out of the office. The traveller turns with a snarl, but, having looked towards a heavily muscled chest, and then upwards into what must be a daunting face, he decides his interests lie elsewhere. Standing outside the doorway in just a pair of shorts is Gronkowski. I recognise his chin, which is prominent, to say the least. His nose is out of sight due to the giant's height. Gronkowski bends his back and edges his head under the doorway and into the room. The walls shrink in.

'I want answers,' he says in accented English.

I step behind the table to keep some distance between us, even though he could probably reach right over it and grab me.

'Fire away.'

There's a tut, and a 'come on' from behind the huge inmate. Gronkowski turns and bellows something in Polish and the remainder of the queue vanishes. His eyes are blazing when he returns his gaze to me.

'I am innocent. I kill no one. Please, I just saw me on the news. Who do I talk to?'

I'm still processing the size of the man. He reminds me a little of Ivan Drago in *Rocky IV*, but his chest is much more pronounced. With his shaven head and trimmed beard, it feels as though I'm being scrutinised by a Greek god, although now he leans towards me, the eyes are bloodshot and watery. I've dealt with lots of Eastern Europeans in this place, and they're often easier to deal with than the local guys as they seem to have more common sense. Honesty is the best policy with them. Even so, my mouth is dry.

'The only person who can get you out of here is a judge, unless the police drop the charges, which seems unlikely. You'll have to wait for a plea hearing. To be honest, that might take months.'

'I didn't do it, and I must be home.'

The volume of his voice is rising, so I speak slowly and quietly.

'I'm sure it won't surprise you, but half of the people on here say they are innocent when they first arrive. They soon realise that my job is to keep everyone in here safe. Nearly all of them return from court with a sentence and proudly tell me that they were guilty anyway. Ring your solicitor before lunch and see what he has to say.'

Gronkowski slams a fist on the office table. Everything on it jumps an inch off the surface. I'm glad I haven't had time to make a hot drink.

'I must speak my girlfriend. She make baby.'

'Ring her, then.'

'I use phone. It say number not allowed.'

I don't fancy explaining to him that prisons run as reliably as cheap Chinese toys. Sometimes they work, sometimes they don't. Gronkowski's permitted telephone numbers might get updated this morning, or it could take weeks. I hear a shout of, 'Delta 1, medication.'

'I have meds to do. Ring your solicitor, and try to stay calm. Everything takes time here.'

'You not understand. My girlfriend make baby today.'

I'm used to hiding my emotions, but my face falls. It's hard to imagine a more deadly combination of circumstances to make a man anxious and desperate.

'I can't promise anything,' I say, 'but I'll see if I can get you a phone call from the office.'

Gronkowski's eyes have dried and he sizes me up.

'Tak,' he says and backs out of the room.

I follow him, locking the door behind me. When I turn around, Gronkowski waves a thick finger in my face.

'Do not let me down. I want phone call in one hour or I break everything. And everyone. I know prison. The timid mouse eats no cheese.'

I step past him, thinking I'll process that titbit later. Scranton is lurking outside the office and follows Gronkowski up the fifteen metal stairs to the top landing where both their cells are. Scranton is a career criminal who's spent more of his adult life in jail than out. Prison doesn't faze him because he knows the rules and nearly all the other inmates. It's his school, and he's the headmaster. Scranton's wiry strength and ratty features reflect his true nature. There's always a prisoner who runs the wing, and at least Scranton isn't generally violent. He is mischievous though, and a real shit-stirrer.

Peasbody and I soon get the men who have prescriptions out to the med hatch and back on the wing. I stand between the pool table and ping-pong table and bellow.

'Gents, behind your doors, please.'

I nip up to the top landing to lock the last few cons away. Scranton is at Gronkowski's door. Gronkowski seems to consider something Scranton has said, nods, steps inside his cell and pushes the door to. I lock Scranton in, then swing Gronkowski's door open to check he's alone.

'You have to wear a shirt when you're out of your cell,' I tell him.

'That not important.'

'It is to me.'

He smiles, grimly. He does know the game. I bang his cell door shut and lock it.

Peasbody has done well getting everyone out for medication and then locked up again. He's shown grit and pushed back the right amount when necessary. Confidence is the key to being a prison officer. The officers don't need to be hard nuts; men like that are often a liability. The service needs strong men and women, mentally, and then only physically when someone erupts under the strain.

Even so, I look through the thick bars of the wing gates down the line of cell doors, softly cursing. It's quiet. Too quiet.

5

All the officers gather in the hub, where I get the printout that lists which workers are to leave the wing at 8.30 a.m. We spend ten minutes pulling each other's legs, then we're back on the wing unlocking those prisoners with jobs or education. When the inmates have left the houseblocks, the prison officers have their daily meeting back in the hub. SO Bowell runs through the usual messages and asks for any other business. I raise a hand.

'The murderer on our wing, Gronkowski, says he's innocent and that his girlfriend is due to give birth today.'

'Ooh, nasty,' says Lennox.

'Yes, and his phone numbers aren't on his pin. I said I would try to get him a call in the admin office. That's okay, yeah?'

Bowell quietly clicks his fingers as he considers his reply.

'No, I don't think so. One, he's been *accused* of murder, so I'd rather we kept him in his cell or at least on the wing. And two, he might be yanking our chains. He probably ate his last girlfriend.'

We all laugh. The first thing you learn in prison is that most prisoners lie to your face. You can't blame them because there are no prizes for honesty. I'm not happy, though.

'Look, if we give him the phone call, he may calm down. I don't reckon it's his first time in prison, and the wing feels wrong. I'm not sure if everyone's scared of him or it's something else.'

'Okay, tell him I'll come on and have a word with him this morning. That all right?'

I'm not listening though. I've picked up the previous day's visit list.

'It says here that Scranton had a visit yesterday afternoon. Can anyone recall if he went?' I ask.

'Yeah, I remember him leaving,' says Fats.

'Shit. He's supposed to be on closed visits, but there's no mention of it on here. I bet that's what it is. His visitor probably brought in drugs and he's returned to the wing with them stuffed up his arse. The cons are quiet because they all know.'

'We could spin his cell?' offers Lennox.

'There isn't any point. He won't have anything on him by now. It'll have been split up and sold all over the wing or passed through the gates. Did the night staff leave any messages?'

'Yes,' says Bowell, reaching for the night report. 'She said there was a strange smell on Bravo 1 and Delta 1.'

'Spice!' Fats and I say together.

'Right,' says Bowell. 'I'll ring Security and see what they say. Keep the wing workers locked up, but send those with healthcare appointments. I'll check with Visits to see if Scranton's visit was closed. To be honest, I doubt Security will have the staff to do any major searching and we certainly don't, so that means get straight on with your daily cell checks. You know their hiding places. If a cell stinks, tell me, and we'll get it fully searched.'

Peasbody and I walk back to the wing. I pass him the healthcare slips and go in search of coffee. There's no one on self-harm or suicide observations on our wing today, so in theory we have an easy day ahead. No one's nicked my Nescafé, so I fill my cup from the big urn of almost boiling water on the landing. Drink in hand, I sit down at the desk in the office, take a sip, and flick through the day's paperwork. There is a master list for the healthcare appointments. As I glance at the names, the unmistakable aroma of sweet tobacco filters into the room.

British prisons are smoke-free places now, so someone's breaking the rules, but the smell has a touch of herbs about it. I've come across it many times before. It will be tobacco mixed with spice. Spice is synthetic cannabis and the effects, good and bad, are similar to the real thing. Some users feel happy and relaxed, giggly even, and become very talkative. Others just feel ill or paranoid. Neither of the latter states are desirable in a cell. Synthetic cannabinoids react more strongly with some of the brain's receptors and are way more potent. It's easy to use too much and then we're in trouble.

Gronkowski's name is second on the healthcare list. I step from the office and lock the door. I walk forward, looking up to the top landing, mouth open to tell Peasbody not to unlock Gronkowski, but it's too late. Gronkowski towers over a cowering Peasbody with an angry but confused expression.

'Get away from him,' I shout.

The order is directed at Peasbody, not the prisoner. Gronkowski registers the yell, leans over the railings and glowers at me. My mouth opens wider as I stare up into a face of madness. Both eyes half retreat into Gronkowski's head, then flicker back down. It happens again.

'Run!' I shout to Peasbody, but he's frozen to the spot.

Gronkowski shoots out a hand, grabs Peasbody's tie and collar, and pulls him close. He clamps each hand on one of Peasbody's biceps, then lifts him a foot off the floor. Gronkowski turns to me and leers. I run towards them, while pressing the personal alarm button on my radio. When I'm underneath them, I open my arms to catch a ten-stone man, knowing my chances of success are zero.

6

I hear the guy in Comms talking in my ear as Gronkowski's eyes go completely white and he stands like a statue. There's no panic in the clinical voice over the airwaves.

'Personal alarm, personal alarm. Officer Dalton, last known location, Delta 1 wing. First Response, please attend.'

I press my talk button.

'QP, request Officer Domingo attend Delta 1 immediately.'

There's a pause of a few seconds and the world stops spinning.

'Delta Eight, that's confirmed. Officer Domingo en route to your location.'

Gronkowski's pupils roll back into view. He's confused again. Instead of throwing Peasbody over the bannister, he strides to the top of the landing with the officer in his vice-like grip. When he reaches the stairs, he releases a pained roar, and launches Peasbody backwards into the air. For a moment, I think Peasbody will land on me, but gravity takes hold. He lands arse first on the third last stair. His head flies back and I cringe at the sickening impact as the back of Peasbody's head thuds into the wing floor.

The men in their cells realise that there's a distraction to their boring lives. They kick their doors and cheer. I know who they want to win.

Gronkowski steps gingerly down the stairs. Half drunk on chemicals, he resembles a terrifying beast from a fantasy film. His pectoral muscles flex menacingly on his bare chest. Small men on spice often need four men to restrain them. Sometimes just a touch on the arm sends them ballistic. With a gulp, I put my hands under Peasbody's armpits and drag him around the pool table and backwards towards the gate.

Two officers from First Response arrive. One is the officer, Sheraton, who came over with Peasbody. He halts on the spot as he sees Gronkowski, and his face whitens. Fair play though, he takes a protective stance and looks to me for guidance.

'Don't touch him, skirt around him until we have more people.'

The other officer, Taufel, has got too close to Gronkowski. It's the first time I've ever heard an open-handed slap sound like a punch. Taufel flies sideways and is almost cut in two by the leg of the pool table. Gronkowski stands over his inert form and raises a foot. I open my mouth, but Lennox, who is next to arrive with SO Bowell, beats me to it.

'Stop!' she roars.

Gronkowski pauses as he focusses on the female officer, as if seeing one has jumbled his brain further. His eyes flicker again, but his jaw bunches and he places his foot back down next to the injured officer's head. Then he marches towards us. Bowell and Lennox are edging away around the pool table when Fats arrives. I drag Peasbody behind him. Fats slowly walks to stand in front of the freely sweating ogre.

They stand toe-to-toe. Two leviathans, matched in battle. The Polish prisoner has the advantage of nearly a foot in height, but Fats's face shows no emotion. Lennox and I edge behind Gronkowski, who swings a wild fist at Fats's head with incredible speed. If it hits, it takes Fats's head clean off. Instead, Fats leans back just out of the way, then steps forward and grabs the unbalanced prisoner's head.

It's called dropping someone and is a case of simple physics. If you grab the head and pull it towards the ground, the body comes too. If you weigh twenty stone plus and your centre of gravity is between your ankles, as in Fats's case, it doesn't matter if your opponent has a neck like Mike Tyson's. Gronkowski hits the deck face down. I leap on Gronkowski's right arm, clamp a hand around the wrist, and hold the arm straight out while Lennox does the same on the left. That way, the bulging biceps have no power. Bowell lays his belly over the thrashing legs, so the inmate can't get to his knees and use his huge thigh muscles. Then the rodeo begins.

He's incredibly strong and writhes like a python. Lennox and I both struggle with our respective arms. I glance up at Fats. With him holding the head, the prisoner is going nowhere fast, but if Gronkowski gets up, he'll be hard to drop again. Fats can lean forward and put a hand and all of his weight on the inmate's back, but it's dangerous. That will compress Gronkowski's ribcage and could stop him breathing. Even though the inmate wants to kill us, his safety is our primary concern. That pretty much sums up prison life.

Just as we are losing control, two more officers arrive and kneel on the backs of Gronkowski's biceps. Gronkowski must be off his rocker not to scream in agony, but he stops struggling. Big men are extremely powerful, but they use up their energy fast. We relax a little. The banging and shouting from the inmates stops. The only sound is the heavy breathing of my colleagues.

There is a sequence of moves that officers go through that gets a prisoner to his feet but still keeps him secure. Gronkowski has his head and back bent forwards, arms held tight, hands twisted with thumbs pointing out, like a stooping, geriatric Fonz. We're different from the police because handcuffs are only ever a last resort. In prison, they tend to escalate the problem and can cause serious injuries. Raging men who can't use their hands tend to use their heads, or teeth.

Sweating, we shuffle and nudge him to the block. The officers there are ready. I stay as they strip-search Gronkowski while he remains restrained. Ten minutes later, Gronkowski is lying on his bed asleep. As I leave his new cell, I wonder what, if anything, he'll remember. A nurse waits nervously outside to check his pulse.

I make my way back to the wing office, passing a groggy Taufel, who's staggering to Healthcare. I hear Comms asking for the gatehouse to prepare the route for the ambulance. When I reach the wing, two nurses are leaning over Peasbody, who won't be walking off the wing after all.

I glance at my watch. It's not even half-past nine. I put two fingers over my wrist and check my pulse. It's barely changed. An experienced officer who was retiring when I first started told me that when this place stops shocking you, it's time to leave.

7

It's an easier time for everyone in a jail after a shocking violent act has occurred. The prisoners' bloodlust has been sated and they are calm, as if they've had a heavy meal. I open the windows at the end of the wing and the cool breeze seems to blow any remaining tension away. Of course, inexorably it will build again until it boils over once more. That's just the way things are.

Peasbody's replacement is a fifty-five-year-old woman called Trudy Tyler, who usually works on the Mother and Baby Unit. At 6.30 p.m., she and I lock up and count the inmates. There isn't even any dawdling to get behind their doors. Perhaps Trudy, who we call Tex on account of her love of line dancing, has something to do with it.

She speaks to the inmates as if they're cheeky children. The hardened thirty-year-olds receive the same treatment as naughty toddlers, despite her being barely seven stone. Actually, she talks to me in the same manner, and all of us can tell she cares.

After the prisoners are banged up, I return to Scranton's cell and open it, knowing he'll be waiting at the window. We exchange cold looks for a few moments.

'Night, guv. Sweet dreams.'

'That was stupid, even for you.'

'No idea what you're talking about,' he says, failing to hide a smirk.

Scranton gave Gronkowski the spice, and Scranton knows I know. I'm also sure that Scranton deliberately gave him too much.

'Karma can be a bitch,' I say, pulling the door shut again and locking it. I nod to Tex, who came up to stand behind me just in case it kicked off, and slam the bolt into place. It's often at this point in the day that the energy drains from my legs. A peace settles over me with the shift finished and everyone put away. We have a roll count of seventy-eight, one in the block. As I saunter back to the hub in time for roll call, a familiar voice shouts out to me.

'Yo, bruvva! Jimbo. Howzit?'

I blink tired eyes at the young face pressed against the bars of Bravo 1, the detox wing. It takes a few seconds before I recognise my brother-in-law, Wyatt.

'You've got to be kidding me. Wyatt, what the hell are you doing here?'

'It was a rumble. The whole crew's here, innit. No sweat, though. We'll bust case. And call me Colt in here, man. Wyatt's dead, bro.'

With that, he lowers his tracksuit bottoms at the side and lifts his T-shirt. He's only gone and had a tattoo of a pistol pointing at his groin done. I walk towards him at the gates, shaking my head. I stare at the gun. It looks like something that shoots caps, not the deadly possession of a Detroit gangster, which is how Wyatt, I mean Colt, now likes to think of himself. I'm sure one of the hardened cons will point that fact out to him. I must be getting old because I thought Wyatt was a cool name.

He was about nine when I first started dating Abi. There are sixteen years between them. He had too much energy, even then, but was generally lippy rather than naughty. I used to call him Wyatt Earp, and he'd shoot me with his fingers.

His dad didn't expect another child so long after Abi's birth and suggested an abortion, which explains the glacier between him and his wife. Wyatt's father chose golf over any involvement with his new child. Maybe he and I are both to blame in some way for how Wyatt turned out.

Wyatt drifted towards crime and there was no one around to notice and pull him away. I used to joke that he was a little scrapper, but now he's turned into a little fucker. We had to stop him coming around because he'd be looking for money to buy drugs. When his hair was longer, he looked a bit like a young Johnny Depp, but he shaves his head now. There's another tattoo on his neck, a gecko or lizard of some kind, and he has the faraway gaze of a dedicated stoner.

'Take it easy in there, Colt.'

'Forget that, man. Smack rats don't vex me.'

I sense an edge in him from how he was a few years ago. He also has a long scar in his hairline that wasn't there before.

'Keep your head down. When are you at court?'

'Two weeks. Slap on the wrist. No sweat. Some stuff got nicked from a house, they fronted, man got hurt, and the judge panicked because nobody grassed.'

Officer Lennox stands behind Colt.

'Come on, son. Behind your door,' she says.

Colt's eyes finally focus on me and there is fear in them. He's not been inside before. It's a new world, a man's world, and he understands it's a dangerous one.

'Tell my sister not to worry, yeah? And it'd be great if you can find me a few extra sachets of sugar, please.'

It seems little Wyatt's back. I nod at him. He is a scumbag, but he's just a boy. One who's going to learn the hard way. The youngsters arrive as children, but they don't leave as kids, however long they've been in. I watch Lennox give him a few kind words as she gently closes the door. Bowell pops his head out of the hub.

'We haven't got all night, Dalton. Roll?'

'Seventy-eight, just Gronkowski off this morning.'

I let out a deep exhale, enter the hub and ring Security to tell them I have a family member here. It's a heightened risk having a relative in the prison. The temptation to help would be too much for many, never mind the psychological aspect of locking your own family away. I suspect they'll transfer him out in the morning.

I finish the call and wait for the roll to clear. There's a part of me that wants to leave him rattling in his cell, gurning and sweating as the drugs vacate his system, but I've been here long enough to know that doesn't work. He'd suffer for no benefit and he's angry enough at the world as it is. Lennox smiles at me.

'Well done today. You hold this place together.'

The rest of the officers nod and a couple clap, and even Bowell drags his gaze temporarily from his computer to join in.

'Brother-in-law?' asks Lennox. 'He told me when he arrived.'

'Yeah. Got any choccy?'

She always has chocolate and passes me a KitKat before giving me a stern you-owe-me expression. I leave the hub and walk into the Bravo 1 wing office where I grab ten sachets of sugar, which will make his comedown easier. You aren't supposed to open the doors once the roll has gone in, but no one will mention it. They know I'm straight as can be. When I open his door, Colt jumps out of his seat, fists raised to fight. His face and eyes are red, his cheeks moist. I throw the bar and sugar onto his bed. There's no need for words. I lock him in and return to the hub. The radio crackles in my ear.

'The roll has cleared, male side. I repeat, the roll is correct, male side only.'

Everyone in the hub cheers and all of us except for the night

OSO file out of the houseblock. Clearing first means we'll get to the front of the queue at the gatehouse to hand our keys in before the female side officers. We pass the entrance to Separation and Care, where Gronkowski now lives. A big officer leaving from their entrance wipes his forehead. He looks relieved to be heading home, too, but his relief will be temporary. He'll have to come back tomorrow when Gronkowski will be awake. He's their problem now. And I'll sleep better tonight knowing that.

8

After we drop our keys and radios off and exit through the security scanners, Fats retrieves his mobile from the gatehouse lockers, looks at the screen and taps it for a little while. Outside, with us back on our bikes, I follow him out of the car park. I usually say goodbye because he's pretty slow on the way home. He'll be mentally and physically exhausted, as I am. I often push myself to get back to my family, but, when I arrive, I sometimes wonder what the rush was for. We cycle in silence until we reach the path next to the rowing lake, and then I move alongside him.

'Hey, Fats. I just wanted to thank you for responding today.'

'No worries. You'd do it for me.'

I smile but consider the respect I received in the hub after the incident. I couldn't have done it so fast without Fats. We always win because more and more officers arrive until it's over, but a lot of people can get hurt if situations aren't controlled fast. I'm not sure how to express my gratitude, but he's smiling at me. He understands. That's what I like about him.

'Fats, do you enjoy bring a prison officer?'

'No, not really. Do you?'

'I like it when I leave, but I don't like going in, if that makes any sense. I think I'm doing something that most people couldn't do, and that makes me feel good about myself.'

'That's kind of how I feel. I worked for years in our family's abattoir and I was great at it because of my strength, but I couldn't do it any more. It was the way they brought the animals in through pens and corridors, and they'd be scared. The cows' huge eyes eventually got to me. I don't think they knew we were going to kill them, but they were anxious after the journey. The new surroundings, the smell of strange cows and all the different humans unsettled them.'

'So, you left and became a prison officer?'

'No, I worked in a warehouse first. But that was depressing, and every day was the same. My mum was angry at me for leaving and, apart from my sister, the whole family stopped speaking to me. Then I saw the prison position advertised, and the money was good. It's more or less the same thing as my family's business. We take them out of the transport vehicles, process them, herd them along corridors and into the place where they need to be. They are scared as well and can lash out. It's just we don't stun their brains and let them bleed to death.'

It's the most he's ever said to me.

'We could have done with one of those bolt guns this morning.'

'That's right, sir. Maybe more than one for a big guy like that.'

We've reached the path where we go our separate ways. Fats surprises me by stopping. He looks around and then down at the ground.

'Do you want to come in for that beer?' he finally asks.

I decide not to mention he told me before that he doesn't drink.

'Yeah, sure. I haven't got to get back for anything.'

I follow him to his home and I'm surprised. He's not the type to live in a tired bungalow, yet that's what it is. He takes me up a ramp and opens the door. Inside, the décor is modern, but there's very little furniture. A big woman with a bigger grin and twinkling eyes scoots towards us in a wheelchair.

'You boys look like you could drink something cool?' she asks.

'That's right, sir,' I say to her, and she tips her head back and laughs.

So that's why Fats takes his phone. The woman gets us each a bottle of cold Budweiser. There's frost on them, so I suspect they've been in the freezer. Fats must have texted her before we rode home. We sit around the table and chat. Physically, she's similar to him. She's got the same wide shape as Fats and the same nose and mouth, but her eyes and smile are his polar opposite. Her grin is fast to his sleepy one and her eyes are quick and engaging compared to his dopey expression. They're affectionate to each other in a way that Abi and I aren't any more.

'This is Lena,' says Fats, with evident pride.

'I don't get out much, so I look forward to Tony coming home,' she says. 'There are kerbs and cars everywhere here, so it's tricky getting out and about without him. When I got his text to say he might have a friend come with him, I was like, hurray, company!'

Fats's face goes red, so I glug my beer. It tastes damn good. They always do after a hard day, when you feel as though you've earned it.

'Actually, Fats wants to go nightclubbing,' I say.

She throws a tea towel at me. Fats does a little jiggle in his chair.

It's nearly 9 p.m. when I leave. I wheel my bike home, enjoying the buzz of the alcohol after amusing company. I have a sense of satisfaction after surviving another tough day. There's a tinge of regret that Fats and I could have been mates outside work years ago, but life's not easy nowadays. It seems as if having a family has taken me away from my friends and how I lived before. I never even wanted kids.

I remove the locks and secure my bike in the rear garden. Abi is staring through the kitchen window as I approach it. Her jaw is set and she doesn't open the door to let me in. Why do I have to come home to this every day? She sits down at the kitchen table when I step into the room, tapping a fingernail on the surface.

'Evening.'

'Don't give me that. Where the hell have you been?'

'I've been at Fats's.'

'Why didn't you ring me?'

'On what? My magic phone?'

'You're drunk again? I can smell it from here.'

'I had a few beers, that's all.'

'You're so selfish. Don't you think I need a break?'

'Yeah, I'm so selfish, I've just spent twelve hours in a prison so you can sit on your fat arse and do fuck all. The kids are in bed by the time I get home. What's stopping you from doing what you want?'

'I wanted to have some adult conversation, or some fresh air. He's been a nightmare again, and he's still awake now. I'm off out. Start your next shift.'

She's so angry, and for a minute I think she might hit me as she stamps past. She grabs her coat and starts hunting through the pile of shoes. Abi looked like Sheryl Crow when we first met, but she's aged fast these last four years. We both have.

It's not safe to walk around our estate late at night but, in this instance, it's the muggers I fear for. They'll get a nasty surprise if they start on Abi. I'm smiling as I climb the stairs, at the thought both of that, and of seeing my son. He can be a handful, but I seem to calm him most of the time. Ivan's awake and stares up at me as I hover over him. He doesn't say anything; he rarely does. We still have the battered nursing chair we had for both kids when they were babies. It remains in the room next to his bed for us to sleep on when he screams at night.

'Hey, son. You okay?'

No response. I fetch a blanket and pull it over me. Right now, I could snooze on broken glass.

'Do you want a hug, Ivan, or a kiss goodnight?'

He shakes his head.

That's not unusual, but a little hand appears from under the duvet and I take it. His breathing settles within a minute. The front door slams downstairs as Abi leaves. She's always been a slammer. She probably wants me to chase after her and try to get her to calm down, as I used to, but I'm too tired. Tired of work, tired of life, tired of my absent sex life, and tired of living with an angry stranger. The worst part is, when I look to the future, all I can see is more of the same.

9

TEN YEARS AGO

There's a knock on my bedroom door. I'm lying on the bed, staring at the ceiling.

'Come in,' I shout.

'Didn't you hear the doorbell?' asks my mum in the doorway.

'No, I was listening to music.'

There's no music playing in my room. My mum grins.

'More like daydreaming, you little love sponge.'

'Mum!'

'Talking of music, play some loud stuff next time Abi stays over. Or I'll be scarred for life.'

'Mum!'

'Shagger is here, but I didn't want him to just appear, what with you listening to music. Shall I tell him to come up?'

'Yes, please. And let's pretend this chat never happened.'

She walks in and ruffles my hair and pretends to look disgusted at her hand as she leaves, as though she's touched something with fleas. My mum's a real joker, but easy-going. I can't remember anything about my dad, but we have a few pictures dotted around.

She said he wasn't the settling-down type and was a messy sod, so we were better off without him. I have no idea where he lives now.

I've moved in and out of Mum's home many times over the years and she always lets me come back rent free. I'm not sure if that makes me secure, knowing I have a safety net, or flaky because I've always got somewhere to return to.

It wasn't supposed to be like this. When I was at school, I often told her that I would be rich. She wouldn't have to work and she could spend her days floating around our outside heated pool. That tickled her. She never had much time to herself. I hate the thought that she might have bought into my pathetic dreams. Perhaps she brought the Argos catalogue home and checked out the inflatable section. I seem to be making a mess of life. Everything good slips out of my grasp.

Martin is my best mate and has been since his family came over from Cork. We started senior school together not long after he arrived. He's what my mum calls a shagger. He agrees with this and thinks he should have been born a stallion. I used to believe I was the same. He doesn't knock.

'Right, Dalton. I assumed you were drunk when I spoke to you earlier, boy. We're heading to the pub now. Get your dancing shoes on.'

'Come on, Martin. I told you I was seeing Abi.'

He sits on the bed next to me. He's deadly serious, which is rare.

'The runner?'

'You know who she is.'

'Where are you going?'

'Bit of shopping, bite to eat, or a coffee at Caffè Nero.'

'Sounds shite. Woods and Belly want to discuss the holiday in The Dragonfly.'

I've been trying to avoid this conversation. Ever since I met Abi,

I've felt torn in two. She doesn't fit into my hedonistic life, but I need to be part of hers. Plus, I can't afford two holidays.

'Come on, Dalton. Tell me you're still coming.'

'I don't know if I am, mate.'

Martin stands. He's not angry, which is worse.

'It feels like I'm losing you to this running thing, when I thought you were a drunken party thing.'

'Sorry. You understand how it is, though, right? I reckon she might be the one.'

'What? Jet Li is the one. So, what does that make Abi? The evil one? The bewitching one? Or perhaps just the horny little one.' He's smiling now, but I can see he's hurt. 'Or is that you?'

'Both of us, I guess.'

'Looks like you're not budging, then, so I'd better go,' he says. 'Ring me in the week.'

I nod and wave, but it's easy to forget when you're so distracted. I've felt as if I've been punched in the gut since the day I met Abi, and it's been brilliant. It wasn't a thunderbolt or mad raging lust, even though there was attraction when we first met. The best way I can describe it is that I immediately felt as if we belonged together. I knew I could spend the rest of my life with her, whatever that might entail, and be happy.

For me, the search is over. Mostly, that's a wonderful feeling but, just on the odd occasion, I wonder if I'm enough for her.

10
PRESENT

The tweeting birds wake me up. My mouth is bone dry from the drink at Fats's and I'm disorientated. After blinking a few times, I recognise my son's plain white bedroom walls. Every other room in the house is magnolia apart from Tilly's, which is pink. I spent an entire Saturday wallpapering Ivan's room with some Disney paper after he started watching some of their cartoons with me. He seemed peaceful and distracted, especially by Buzz Lightyear. Ivan was three then, and the phrase 'terrible twos' doesn't come close to explaining his antics. He screamed the place down that Saturday night, an hour after I'd left him in bed. I had to spend all Sunday taking the wallpaper off and repainting.

It was around then that Abi and I took him to the local GP surgery. Abi explained his behaviour to the doctor with notes she'd made, while I sat quietly with a strange sense of detached reality.

'Sounds like his terrible twos are continuing,' said the doctor.

'And the not talking?' asked Abi.

'You mentioned he talks sometimes.'

'But not much. He rarely likes to be touched, and he gets ever so angry. And not just a tantrum but a really scary rage.'

'The terrible twos cover a range of behaviour that can start as early as one, and may continue for years. All children develop differently but it all sounds perfectly normal.'

'It doesn't feel normal.'

He looked at us both kindly.

'It's possible that he has ASD, Autism Spectrum Disorder, but it's a broad diagnosis and not especially helpful if the symptoms are relatively mild, and your son doesn't seem too affected. From what you've said, he communicates without problems, will let you know if he's hot or hungry. At times, you can leave him alone to draw or play. He tolerates playschool a couple of days per week, and physically he's robust and strong. He isn't significantly impacted like most children with the condition.'

I finally spoke.

'So, we just put up with it?'

'This might seem crazy, but try to enjoy it. Commit to a structured day. Support and encourage him. He may have a few symptoms, but I don't think you need to look for a diagnosis. Work together as a team and give each other breaks. These symptoms are mild in comparison to many, even though it may not seem that way.'

'I could cope, I think, but Ivan's so distant. It feels as if he doesn't like me. Isn't there any help out there?' said Abi.

'Kids change quickly. He's only three. Come back if you have more questions. There's a lot of information about this type of thing on the NHS website. There are groups on Facebook. You aren't alone, but there isn't any funding for therapy at the moment. You'll need to support him yourselves until he goes to school.'

'I've never felt so alone,' said Abi, with no emotion.

The doctor's jovial expression faded.

'And how are you two getting on? Ivan might be picking up on any tension between the pair of you. Are you managing to parent as a team?'

The doctor gestured to our chairs. We'd pulled them up almost as far away from each other as possible without looking rude. Abi and I attempted a smile and left shortly after.

We stopped at McDonald's on the way home and talked properly for the first time in ages. I agreed to be more hands on. She swore she'd try harder. We both had hope, but hope doesn't last forever. Just a few weeks in our case.

Ivan coughs next to me and pulls me from my memories, but he doesn't wake. I gently remove his hand from mine and pull the covers up to his chin. He looks peaceful and relaxed. The floorboards creak as I stand and I freeze. Looking down at Ivan, I hold my breath and watch his eyes slowly open. He scowls, then smiles and closes his eyes again.

It's 4 a.m. Saturday. Outside, I hear distant drunken laughter from people getting home from nightclubs. The prison shifts are different at the weekend. I'm on an eight until five, so there's a chance I can get more sleep before I have to leave.

I creep into our bedroom and slip yesterday's uniform off. Abi grumbles as I slide into the bed, but then reverses a bit so we're almost spoons. I place my arm over her, but it feels unnatural. I've no idea when we last had strong physical contact, never mind sex. Not this year, anyway. I rest my hand on her shoulder and feel her stiffen. She shrugs my hand off, and I turn away.

11

Ivan bursts into our room at 5.30 a.m.

'Come on, Daddy. I'm starving.'

He disappears. I rise how I imagine a ninety-year-old would and follow him downstairs. He pours us both a bowl of cereal as I slump in a seat. More of the food goes over the table than in our bowls so I grab the milk from him to prevent a similar fate. Sometimes he likes me to eat with him. We'll smile at each other in a secret conspiracy. I love it because that often means we have a good day ahead then. He sits on the other side of the table and picks up his spoon.

'Are you going to work?'

'Yes, but I'll be back in time to chomp our tea together and to put you to bed.'

He considers this, judges it acceptable, and begins to eat. God knows what the cereal is. It tastes like crumbled biscuits and will do wonders for my blood sugar.

'Watch *Mermaid*?'

It's a bit early for Disney, but it's nice to see Ivan so relaxed so I set up the movie and sit on the sofa. He usually sits in touching distance, but not actually touching. Today he plonks himself next to me and I tentatively put my arm around him. He tenses, then relaxes. Any stress drops away and my eyelids droop.

The closing credits wake me up again. I glance at Ivan, who still has my arm around him. He waits until the screen goes blank, then coolly looks up at me.

'Again,' he says.

I take the remote off my knee and get it started again. We snuggle back together. After a few more minutes, I close my eyes for a second time, but the lounge door opening wakes me up. Abi stands before me in her Mickey Mouse pyjamas that I bought her as a joke years ago, tears streaked down her face.

'You're going to be late,' she says.

'What time is it?'

'Seven-thirty.'

I kiss the top of Ivan's head and grin because he continues what he's doing. He often shrinks away after affection, as though you've taken advantage of him.

'We need to talk,' she says.

That doesn't sound good.

'Okay, I'll get home before six,' I reply.

'I want to tell you something now, while I feel strong.'

I extricate myself from Ivan's side and stride into the kitchen. My mobile is on the table. I check the time and see a message from my old mate, Martin. It's short and sweet, but distracting. I put the phone down.

'Okay, Abi. You've got five minutes or I'll be late.'

She glowers at me but whispers.

'I think we should split up.'

'What?'

'You heard me.'

'Why?'

She takes a deep breath, but maintains eye contact.

'Are you happy?' she asks.

'No, of course I'm not happy.'

'What's the point, then?'

'I was hoping things would change.'

Her voice rises. 'If you want things to change, you need to change.'

'Me, is it? Just me? Actually, you have changed. Into a nagging grump.'

'You'd turn anyone into that. It's like living with a zombie.'

'I'm tired.'

'And you think I'm not?'

'You can have a nap during the day. She's at school and he's at playschool.'

'Will the washing fairy come over while I'm asleep? Or the hoovering and cleaning fairy?'

My own voice escalates.

'Judging by the shithole we live in, it doesn't look like it.'

'Perhaps if you helped around here, I wouldn't be so miserable.'

'Okay, I'll pop home tonight, pack my bags and clear off. That what you want? I can have both kids every other weekend? Take them to Big Sky with my new girlfriend. Sounds okay to me.'

'You bastard.'

A high-pitched scream stops us in our tracks. Ivan is at the door. I step towards him.

'Hey, sorry. We were just having a little argument,' I whisper.

I reach out to touch him, but he steps back as though I'm a leper. He returns to the lounge and tries to slam the door, but he's too small and it closes slowly. He settles for giving it little kicks on the other side. I shake my head at Abi.

'Great work, you selfish cow. Couldn't you have waited until I got home? Waited until he'd gone to bed?'

I pound up the stairs and quickly pull on my trousers. There are no clean work shirts. I pick up yesterday's and give it a sniff. It smells as if I cycled to my prison job and wrestled with a troll during my twelve-hour shift there, which is more or less true. I put it on and cover myself in deodorant and aftershave. I collect my coat from the kitchen where Abi now sits with her head in her hands. We hear the sound of thrown things ricocheting around the lounge.

I crouch next to Abi.

'Have a fabulous day, sweetie.'

12

I almost slam the front door, but realise in time that makes me no better than Ivan, and I might wake Tilly. The rain is torrential, but getting wet is the least of my worries. I stick a beanie on, unlock the bike and set off in the downpour.

Our next-door neighbour's windows are all open and the curtains billow. Sweet summer rain smells different around our way. My kids will grow up thinking fresh air carries the scent of marijuana. I'm cutting it fine timewise and tear along the streets with a blank mind, just focussing on pumping my thighs. By the time I reach the bike shed, I'm soaked inside and out and my legs are wobbly, but any anger has gone. Fats is securing his bike when I arrive.

'Morning, sir. Another glorious day in the corps,' he says.

'Every pay cheque's a fortune,' I reply.

'Every inmate's really a nice guy.'

'I love the corps.'

It's our take on the famous lines from *Aliens*, one of my favourite films.

There's a big queue at the gatehouse scanners, so we wait at the back. Sheraton, who came over yesterday with Peasbody, is in front of us. He nods at us. I'm sure I detect a newfound confidence.

'Hey, Sheraton. How's your mate, Peasbody?' asks Fats.

'Good. He texted me this morning. They're letting him out later today. No concussion, just a bad bump.'

'That's great news,' I say. 'He did well yesterday, tell him that. You did, too.'

Sheraton grins and straightens his shoulders.

'You okay, Dalton?' asks Fats.

'No, not great. My wife told me she wants to split up as I was leaving for work.'

'No way. I'm sorry, man. Was she serious or just lashing out?'

'No idea. Part of me was relieved. We're both miserable and lonely despite living on top of each other. I can't do anything right and I'm so tired most of the time. All this cycling and walking has put me in the best shape ever, but I feel worse than I've done in ages. Perhaps I should move out for a bit, get my head together.'

Fats looks upset.

'You're going to give up?'

'Yeah, maybe.'

'You should never quit on family. Go home, talk to her. Leaving won't make anything easier, especially not for the kids. Sounds like your boy needs his daddy.'

The queue starts moving through the scanners and, as we traipse forward, I puff my cheeks out.

'You know, Fats, I checked my phone this morning and there was a Facebook message from a mate of mine called Martin. We haven't spoken in years. He sent me a picture of him in Nice at this beach party, surrounded by tanned, slim beauties. Apparently, he's gone there to learn French for three months.'

'That sounds sweet. Jealous?'

'Too right. Look how different my life is. My existence is the polar opposite of his. I'm not sure it could get any worse.'

Fats laughs. 'You haven't seen the work detail yet. You might be in Male Healthcare. There's a nutty guy in there who keeps shitting on the floor. Must smell lovely when the sun comes out. Anyway, snap out of it. You got it all, man. Pretty wife, healthy kids, respect in a hard job. Lot of men would give both nuts to be in your position.'

I smile at him, even though I suspect it isn't true. 'Both?'

'Okay, one of them.'

'I just feel trapped.'

Fats shakes his head at me.

'You're not trapped. Lena's trapped.'

He scans the detail when we reach where we collect our keys.

'Oh, shit,' he says.

I take it off him. They've put Fats in the block this morning and back on the wings in the afternoon, no doubt to help control Gronkowski when he wakes up. Nasty. I can't find my surname in there with him or on the wings. Male or female side. Fats double-checks for me.

'Maybe they think I should have a day off,' I say, only half-joking.

'Are you Jim Dalton?' asks the gatehouse worker.

He's staring at my name badge, so I raise a tired eyebrow.

'Oscar One said to report to him when you arrive.'

Oscar One runs both sides of the jail at the weekends. Being called to his office is rarely good news.

'Did he mention what it was about?' I ask.

'Nope. Didn't look happy, though.'

13

The OSO informs me that Oscar One is in Male Separation and Care, which is the official name for the block. The laughable explanation being that we separate the troubled inmates from main location in there and care for them. I walk over with Fats. Our nostrils flare at the thick stench when we get to Main Street, which is the area of the prison away from the houseblocks where the different specialist departments branch off. It seems the unbalanced man in Healthcare has been busy first thing. We can also hear the rhythmic thud of someone strong kicking the back of their door. That sound is coming from the block.

We open the double doors and the banging is deafening. They've asked before if Fats and I would be based in Separation and Care full-time, but Fats said he felt he was helping people on the wings. He didn't want a job where he only controlled them. The last shift I had in here, a bloke threw a plastic cup containing his spunk at me when I opened him up to deliver his lunch. That put me off the place somewhat.

Fats goes to the office to discuss the day ahead with the other officers. I briefly stare at the line of fifteen cells, which is all they have down here. Some men are in here for months without TVs or visits. What do they do all day? Where do their minds go? I find Oscar One, a grey-haired guy in his fifties called MacStravick, furiously writing in the room where they adjudicate the prisoners who've been placed on report.

'Morning, sir.'

'Sit down, please, Dalton.'

I pull out a chair from under the table and try not to slump in it.

'I thought I'd explain what we're going to do with you.'

'Okay.'

'We can't have you on the landings if your brother-in-law is there. All his co-defendants are here too, and it seems they also know you. They're a challenging bunch. Two of them flooded their cell this morning before unlock. They are both here now. One of them, who said his name was Bumpy, spat at the nurse. The other one is currently kicking his door. He's been shouting for someone to fetch you, for some reason. Do you have any idea why?'

'Who is it?'

'Igualo. Phil Igualo.'

'Yeah, I know him, but haven't heard of anyone called Bumpy. Igualo was Wyatt's best mate at school. I used to play football with them both after they'd finished school when I first went out with his sister. Igualo was awesome. Tall and brilliant in the air. Arsenal wanted to sign him as a kid at one point, but his mum couldn't drive him there for training due to work. He's been angry ever since.'

'Right, you clearly know him well enough. I don't want you over here on this side full stop, then. The Shooter Gang, as Igualo insists they're called, has a trial in two weeks. If they get released afterwards, it's fine. If they receive a sentence, we'll transfer them straight to Glen Parva. In the meantime, you'll work female side.'

I pause for a moment. In the five years I've worked here, I've only done a handful of shifts on the female side, and nearly all of them were in Reception.

'Sure, no problem,' I eventually say. 'Shall I go there now?'

'Yes. Igualo needs to learn that kicking doors doesn't get results. By some miracle, we have a few people spare today, so just do GD on Houseblock One. They'll allocate you a wing after that or leave you floating.'

I stand and open the door to go.

'Dalton, find your feet over there. It's not the same as this side.' He gives me a tired smile. 'Don't get too comfortable though, we'll want you back.' He returns to the report he's writing.

I tell Fats where I'm going. He calls me a lucky bastard, and I set off to the female side. You can walk through two connecting security doors, but it's often as quick to walk outside the prison buildings and through the sterile area that separates the two sides. I'm not in any rush, and it's stopped raining. By the time I open the female houseblock doors, I've missed unlock, so the prisoners are out and about having breakfast and getting their meds.

The first difference that strikes me is the quiet. I can see a lot of women walking around, but there's no shouting. The second thing is the odour, or lack of a stomach-churning one. It reminds me of the smell of a cheap hotel I once stayed in. I let out a big breath and relax. My prison mind doesn't sense any danger. I walk towards the hub, passing a few prisoners on the way.

'Morning, sir,' say two passing inmates, each with a smile.

'Morning,' I reply.

I stifle a grin. I think I'm going to like it here.

14

I head to the hub and pull open the door. It's lovely and cool with two fans moving the air around. We had a fan on the male side for a while, but things like that over there have a habit of walking. I suspect it was 'borrowed' by a wing officer and put in his office. It was eventually found in pieces in the soon-to-be-sacked hub orderly's cell. He'd used the motor to make a tattoo gun.

Only the senior officer, Nasima Khan, is in there. I've only ever said hello to her on a few occasions, but I hear she's popular.

'Morning, Nasima.'

She spins her chair around from the computer and eyes me up and down.

'Oscar One rang to say you were on your way over.'

'Here I am.'

'Call me ma'am, please, while you're here. Not because I'm an arsehole, but because it gives my role gravitas. Then the urchins think they're talking to the person who runs the prison, and the buck stops with me.'

'Fair enough, ma'am.'

She stands up and walks over to me. I tower over her by a foot and I'm twice as wide. She has her hair in a bun and her uniform is spotless. I detect dark bags under her eyes. It's difficult to tell if it's make-up, her natural colouring, or the result of fatigue. She can't be more than twenty-five, yet there is a cold maturity within that stare.

'Well,' she says, 'at the very least you'll be a deterrent. Have you worked much on the female side?'

'No, hardly at all. I did a few shifts in Female Reception about six months ago. I've probably been on a female wing twice in five years.'

'How is it on the male side nowadays?'

'Pretty brutal. There's loads of spice around, so staff assaults happen every day or so. Sometimes it feels like you're working with a target on your back.'

'It's Jim Dalton, isn't it? I heard your name come up when the powers that be were looking for new SOs. Why didn't you go for promotion?'

'The job over there is dangerous. Blood gets spilled, but that's the way it is. I can handle that now and rarely take it home with me. It's a good feeling to leave the prison without baggage. I reckon being promoted would change that.'

She retakes her seat and smiles.

'I have a lot of respect for you guys over there. It must be stressful. I don't think I'd cope with that level of violence in my life, and I've never liked the smell of too much testosterone. The rumours are you were the one who took down that enormous Polish guy. You're making quite an impression.'

I consider telling her Fats was the real hero, but decide it's not important.

'Thanks.'

'If you want to GD for me today, that would be great. Ease you in nice and gently. Usually we have two officers on each wing, no GD, and they do their own meds. At the weekend, we sometimes drop to one a wing if the prison is short on your side. We'll do some urine tests this afternoon, seeing as we have an extra body for the day. How long are you here for?'

'A fortnight at a guess. My brother-in-law and his gang are at court in two weeks. They will plead guilty and, if what he's told me is true, they'll get a suspended.'

'You have to love family. I'll allocate you a wing if you're going to be here a while, then. You might even like it. I've got two gaps at the moment. One with the young offenders and one with the lifers. They've also sent me cover from Mother and Baby. You must know Trudy. You can decide between yourselves who goes where. I'll put you both on the YO wing tomorrow. Trudy knows all the inmates well because we often use her as cover.'

She holds my gaze for a few moments. We're both aware one of the gaps is Sandringham.

'Is it true about him?' I ask.

'That he drowned himself? Yes. Apparently, there's no other reasonable explanation with his shoes placed on the side of the river.'

'Do you know why?'

'Isn't working here enough of a reason?'

'I suppose so.'

'I read some interesting stats about the subject from an American article – 3 per cent of the public have suicidal thoughts, but that rises to 10 per cent for prison officers. For retired officers, it increases to nearly one in three.'

'Wow! I'm not sure I wanted to know that.'

'How are you mentally?'

'Fine. Better for being over here for a while.'

Khan gestures to the door. Just as I open it, she speaks quietly with an expression that's hard to describe.

'Careful out there, Dalton. You're not in Kansas any more.'

15

I step outside the hub and walk to the med hatch through the area that an elderly orderly is mopping. She doesn't complain, just mops up my footprints. The med hatch over here is bigger than on the male side and considerably cleaner. The inmates queue respectfully. Trudy Tyler is at the front with the jug of water.

'Hey, Tex. I'm your GD!'

'F-A-B, Dalton. What are you doing over here?'

'They've transferred me over here until my brother-in-law finishes at court. Apparently, you're here for a while, too.'

'Yeah, Nasima told me. We're both with the young offenders on Whisky wing tomorrow, so we'll chat then. X-ray 1 have had their meds and so have Yankee 1, where I'm working today. In fact, this charming lady is my last victim.'

A bedraggled-looking pensioner gives me a toothless smile and a mock salute as she saunters past. I catch a faint whiff of urine.

Tex hands me the jug and disappears. The way it works on both sides of the jail is the inmates get their meds three times a day from a room with a hatch at the far end. Only one prisoner is allowed in the room at a time, the others queue outside. Some meds are kept in their cells, but overdoses are common, so it's safer to provide them daily under supervision. Drugs with any kind of mind-altering effect, whether it be an upper or downer, have a value in the prison and are easily traded. Things that can kill you are also valued. Those drugs are given out by a nurse in the exact doses prescribed. A prison officer, in this case me, will stand next to the prisoner and make sure the pill goes in their mouth, not their pocket or behind their tongue.

I call it gob watch. I fill their cup with water and they drink the contents. All of it. That way, it's very hard to hide the tablet in their mouths. Loads of them try it on. Many have missing teeth with a handy socket to conceal pills in. The nasty part is that, to check they aren't hiding anything, you need to look in their mouths like a dentist, and dental hygiene is low down on the list of priorities for many within these walls. If capital punishment were the sentence for halitosis, this place would be death row. It's degrading for the prisoners too.

On the male side, it can be a flashpoint, especially first thing. The poor nurse wheels her cart over and then locks herself behind a big, solid, metal door. There's a barred hatch, and a slot to receive the pills. She gets verbally abused many times per shift by those unhappy with their prescription. Drug addicts think they know best. The officer supervising this circus has to judge the line. Moaning is fine, complaining is okay, shouting and swearing is not. Fighting is likely.

I walk to Whisky 1 wing and open the gates.

'Whisky 1 meds,' I holler down the wing.

A young Asian girl walks towards me, holding her jaw. Toothache here is common. I can't think of a worse place to suffer with that. In prison, the nights are long.

It's three prisoners out at a time. Male side, many of them leave the gates and veer towards other wings to pass drugs or messages. When challenged they'll argue as though it's you who's out of line. No such problems here.

The male wings have nearly eighty men on them, on the female wings the maximum is thirty-six, yet meds takes longer over here. It seems as if every prisoner is on something. But there's no real trouble. One girl cries because her sleeping tablets aren't strong enough, but she's not rude. The overriding emotion I sense is one of sadness. Are they beaten down by being in prison, or did life batter them before they arrived?

I have a joke with a few, but they are wary of me. There is a lack of eye contact, which is common to nearly all prisoners. Is that confidence, or a reflection of their upbringing? People don't look each other in the eye where I live, either.

It's nearly 10 a.m. before I shout down the final wing.

'Zulu 1, last call meds.'

A mixed-race woman, a girl really, almost a child, walks past me. She holds my eye from the moment she sees me and maintains eye contact until she reaches the back of the queue. Her black hair is elfin, and so is her size and bearing. A lumbering woman with translucent, greasy skin is last to come out. The grey prison tracksuit she wears looks two sizes too small. She edges by me, leaving a trail of body odour in her wake. I recognise the smell of fear.

When I reach the med hatch, the small prisoner holds out her cup for me to fill with water. She gives me her ID card, which I pass through the bars. She looks young enough to be at school yet she has dead eyes. Her name is Tara Prestwick, which sounds unexpectedly middle class. The nurse rummages in the meds cart. The girl stares grimly at me, yet I definitely detect a sudden crinkle in her eyes.

'What are you thinking? Is it an elf or a pixie?' she says.

I look her up and down. She can't even be five feet tall. It's hard to believe she must be at least eighteen, but it's not easy to tell because, unlike in the picture, she has full make-up on now. It looks professionally done and is a little disturbing in such a grim place. It's as though an assistant from a beauty salon got arrested on the way to work. She has snug pink tracksuit bottoms on and a bright white T-shirt with the word, *Tiger!* in big pink letters on the front.

'I was thinking Bride of Chucky,' I reply.

She gasps. 'You did not just say that.'

With a face of outrage, she turns to the furtive creature behind her, who gives off the presence of someone tiny despite looking nearly as heavy as I am.

'You hear that, Broken? Chucky!'

She can't help laughing, though, and her head tips back, which is a relief. I was wondering if I'd misjudged her. It takes her half a minute to calm down.

'Are you a new boy?' she asks.

'I was once. Old enough now.'

'You're from the male side, aren't you? I can tell. You're too relaxed. First time over here?'

'I've done a few shifts on this side. They must have thought some different scenery and a few fresh faces would cheer me up.'

She edges near me, wafting me with a flowery aroma.

'I bet it smells really terrible over there,' she says. 'But, trust me, it can stink over here, too.'

The nurse rattles the girl's ID card on the dispenser.

'Today, please!' she shouts, with an East-European accent.

While Prestwick returns to the hatch, the other girl passes me her ID card. It feels greasy. Her feet shuffle and she scratches her neck. Her name is Kitty Monroe, which seems remarkably normal for the wheezing creature next to me. She hasn't looked me in the eye once. In fact, she's barely taken her eyes off the floor. The photo of her on the card looks familiar, though. The person in it is enormous with dishevelled, wet-looking hair. Sadly, she reminds me of The Undertaker from WWE. It doesn't look like the woman in front of me, who reaches past me and grabs Prestwick's arm.

'Come on, Ruined. Let's go.'

Confused, I stare at the girl with the Prestwick card and wonder if they've been swapping cards so they can try each other's meds. Something I'm wise to on the male side, but my guard must have dropped.

'Was that Ruined or Ruiz that she called you? If so, where's Prestwick?' I ask the little one.

Prestwick tosses the pill back into her mouth and drinks the cup of water. She shows me a surprisingly white set of teeth and a pink tongue. There's no sign of a pill.

'It's a nickname. I'm Ruined and she's Broken. We know each other from the road. Only one other person calls me Ruined apart from her. It's like our bond. We're sisters. Although a lot of people in here have nicknames. This one in there—' she points to the nurse behind the bars, 'she's called Angsty.'

Prestwick steps past me and waits outside the room for Monroe to get her meds. Out of the corner of my eye, I watch the nurse taking pills from many bottles. She passes them over to Monroe, but then I see the hard-faced nurse's expression change.

'Are you okay, Kitty?'

Monroe nods and puts the pills in her mouth one at a time and crunches them up with her front teeth. She drinks the water with her eyes closed so she doesn't have to look at me. She keeps them closed when she opens her mouth. Her tongue is white and her teeth are brown.

'That's the last one,' I tell the nurse, who grunts at me.

'Okay, ladies. Have a good day,' I say to Prestwick and Monroe.

Monroe was leaving but she stops. She looks at my face for the first time. I'm surprised to recognise intelligence in her stare.

'I remember you,' she says, then strides away.

Prestwick watches her leave with a small frown before turning back to me.

'She never speaks to the male officers. You're an interesting man, sir. Will we see you again?'

I'm not like some officers, who tell the inmates nothing about their personal lives. I tend to be a little vague, or it's hard to build a relationship with the people who will come to rely on you. It's better if they come to me with their problems, rather than letting them fester. Besides, HMP Peterborough's not the kind of place where rich, organised criminals end up. There won't be anyone pulling up behind my car at the traffic lights on the way home and forcing me to bring in things for their criminal boss, so I tell her the truth.

'You should do. I'm here for a couple of weeks, maybe more.'

'Good, this place is tedious, and you've got a spark.'

I'm not sure how to reply to that, so merely smile.

'Bye, sir. Be careful. Not everyone here is who they say they are.'

The nurse has packed her trolley up and stands next to me.

'Can you put a freeze on?' she asks.

A freeze is a security procedure. It clears the route of prisoners so the med trolley can be safely taken to Healthcare, but I haven't got a radio to get everyone behind their wing gates. I glance around. There's no one here who can overpower me.

'It's okay. I'll walk you back to Healthcare.'

The nurse frowns, then pushes the trolley towards the house-block doors. She says nothing on the way there, leaving me to ponder the conversation with Prestwick. Her name makes me think of nobility and she spoke with a middle-class accent despite the slang she used. Even her vocabulary was out of place. I have no idea what angsty means.

I leave the nurse and her trolley in Healthcare and return to the wings. It dawns on me that Prestwick is the third person to give me a warning about this side of the jail.

16

It's probably the easiest shift I've ever had. There were no alarms, no fights, and not even any complaints about the food. Not a single yoghurt was thrown. Time actually dragged this afternoon. Yet I feel eyes upon me. They have dropped when I turn around.

As I'm without a wing, I offer to help the officer, Braddock, on Zulu 1 to lock up. Braddock was left on his own today after his colleague went on an escort to the hospital after a vicious fight on one of the male exercise yards.

'Dalton, you old dog, I see you've sneaked over here,' he says.

'I missed you, Braddock, and wanted to spend more time with you. Did I hear you got your ten-year award?'

'Yes, Christ. Ten years of my life in here.'

'How long have you been with the women?'

'Only six months. I'm moving back to the male side when the next training course goes live.'

'Really? Don't you like it over here?'

'No, not much. Most of the girls are the same ages as my daughters. I find it depressing. My kids are both at university and, thankfully, they don't understand a single thing about the misery this lot have been through. And it's too quiet most of the time. I must admit, I bring the paper in every day, do the crossword, and drink loads of tea. I never had time for any of that shit with the men, but this place gets to you. Mark my words.'

'It's boring?'

'It can be, but the violence can come out of nowhere when you're not expecting it. There are some troubled souls here.'

Braddock and I have a bond. We were working a wing together male side. It was a bad-tempered lunchtime where we hadn't received the right food. I was behind the servery trying to sort out the mess we were in while Braddock was attempting to keep control of the queue of hungry men. I watched an inmate, Pauley, mouth off after Braddock shouted at him to be patient. Instead of rejoining the line, the prisoner walked to the hot-water dispenser. The lad's determined face caught my eye as he returned.

It's true when they say time slows during times of danger. I shouted out a warning but there was already too much noise. Pauley headed straight for Braddock. As his arm came back to fling the near boiling liquid in Braddock's face, I grabbed the only thing nearby, a serving ladle, and threw it at them. It was a poor shot and flew over their heads. Braddock saw it out of the corner of his eye and ducked, which meant the scalding water flew over his shoulder and splashed one of the wing workers behind him.

It nearly caused a riot. One of the cleaners found a tooth on the floor the next day. Braddock didn't thank me. He merely held my gaze and shook my hand very firmly before he went home that night. We never spoke of it again.

'Behind your doors, ladies!' he shouts.

I watch in amazement. The inmates are already standing at their doors. He just walks along the line of cells and locks them in. No aggravation, nobody still on the phones, no one hiding under a friend's bed, not even anyone in the showers. We go around with the clipboard afterwards and do roll count. Nearly all of them say goodnight, despite it only being 5 p.m. It's like a scene from The Waltons.

Braddock is another officer who I have a solely work-based relationship with. He told me his wife left him a few years back and took his car. He said he loved that car. Perhaps it was just bravado, and he was devastated about his wife too. This job changes you. Partners have to adapt. Sometimes they can't.

Braddock and I enter the hub and fill in the form. He has a roll of twenty-nine. The rest of the wing staff filter in and complete their paperwork. The officers are mostly in their early twenties. It seems as though they're all going out tonight. Braddock, who's nearly fifty, rolls his eyes at me, making me feel ancient. He's old school and doesn't bother with an earpiece on his radio, which comes to life.

'The roll has cleared on both sides. I repeat, the roll is clear.'

I reach the gatehouse at the same time as Fats. He looks as though he's just staggered over the finish line of the London Marathon on a hot Sunday afternoon.

'Tough day?' I ask.

'Two barricades. Both my wing. And a stabbing on the yard. Someone nicked my packed lunch from the office, too.' He studies my face. 'You look like you've spent the day at a spa.'

'More a dirty backpackers' hostel than a spa, but still relaxing.'

'Is it different?'

'Yes, very. The YO wing only has nineteen inmates on it.'

'And still has two officers running it?'

'Yep. You not worked over there?'

'No, never. Any pretty girls?'

'Not really. Most of them are in prison greys and are bedraggled. I suppose that's to be expected. We had no fighting today at all.'

Fats looks rueful, but he's not the type to be jealous.

'Good for you. Actually, I have a favour to ask. I was wondering if I could pass your telephone number to Lena in case of an emergency. I know you might be at work with me, but it'll give her a bit of peace of mind.'

'Yeah, sure.'

We reach the bike shed.

'You go on,' says Fats. 'I am pooped. I'm just going to push it for a while.'

Fats waves me off. I feel full of energy. A grin creeps over my face. I set off fast and fly by The Halcyon Pub, which is around the corner from the prison. I'm soon through The Grange playing fields and along Westwood Park Road. It's a while before, as I'm tanking down Thorpe Road, I remember where Kitty Monroe recognised me from. She came in during the shift when I worked in Female Reception six months ago. She hated or feared men at that point, too, but since then, something about her has changed.

17

SIX MONTHS AGO, FEMALE RECEPTION

I check my watch for the fiftieth time. Incredibly, it's now 9 p.m. I walk to the reception desk, where Senior Officer Odom is eating an apple.

'Where the hell are they?' I ask.

'The gatehouse just messaged to say the court van has arrived, and it's being searched.'

'And this is definitely the last of them?'

'Yeah. They were at Cambridge Crown Court. A couple of them received two years, and the other one got eight. The details are a bit sketchy at the moment, but I think the one who got eight killed her toddler. She had a panic attack in the court cells. Hence the late hour, because they were all booked on the same escort vehicle.'

I lean against the desk with both hands, my gaze dropping to the floor, and try to stay calm.

'Okay,' I finally say. 'It seems shallow to complain when shit like that has happened, but my wife is going to kill me.'

'You know you have to forget about outside until the job is done here in Reception. The people on their way in have to be processed before we leave, even if they've made us late and we want to strangle them when they arrive.'

I smile at SO Odom. None of that is news to me, but he understands talking will keep me relaxed. He is an imposing, intelligent guy pushing two metres in height, who initially reminded me of Muhammad Ali, but Odom never needs to fight. I'm not sure if he's gay, but he has a picture of an equally attractive Asian man on his desk. Male prisons might be the last bastions of homophobia, but no one dares say anything to Odom.

'Anniversary?' he asks.

'Yep.'

'Going out?'

I scowl at my watch. 'Seems unlikely now. We have a table booked for nine.'

'I'm sure she'll understand,' he says, but his eyes glaze over. Finishing late is the curse of Reception. It's easier than being on the wings because the prisoners generally come in alone, so there's no pack mentality. A riot is the ultimate fear for an officer. Imagine being trapped on a wing by yourself with a raging mob baying for blood. But in Reception, you can't go home until the last court van or transfer has arrived. Midnight finishes are possible, and it wreaks havoc with your family life and your sleep.

I recall Abi's words when I left.

'You're certain you will be back on time?' she said.

'Yes, I'm only on until seven-thirty.'

She smiled, and I saw a glimpse of excitement on her face. I couldn't remember the last time she'd looked like that. She hugged me.

'Okay, I'll get dressed up and be ready as soon as you get home. The taxi is booked for nine. I love enchiladas and margaritas, yummy!'

She was cold and distant when I rang to say I was going to be late. I said I'd still be back by nine and we'd make it. It's nine fifteen now. Her phone is ringing out. I imagine Abi in her favourite red dress, which she's had for years, sitting on the sofa across from her best friend, Maggie, who will have arrived to babysit. No words, just the smell of disappointment and perfume.

'I hope you got her a good present,' says Odom.

'The meal was the present,' I reply.

'Oops. Look, here's the bus now.'

The vehicle slowly swings alongside the reception entrance. Frost sparkles on the exposed metal bars of the doorway, and I shiver as a blast of freezing air hits me.

The Serco bus grinds to a halt on the tarmac and the two typical transport staff climb from the cab: bald, mid-forties, and losing the battle with the scales.

'Three women,' one of them says. 'One's in a bit of a mess, crying and weeping, and another is barely responsive. Really bad withdrawal for both, I reckon. The other lady is the problem. She went mad when we put her in the van. Started hurling herself around. I thought she might roll us over.'

'Eh?' said Odom.

'You'll see.'

The two addicts stagger off first. They're in a wretched state. They are dirty and dishevelled, thin as rakes in skinny jeans and with only summer jackets to fight the winter breeze. They remind me of ancient hags from distant times.

'Missing dinner for bloody junkies,' I hiss under my breath, not caring that they both hear.

However, their tortured faces contrast with still soft, young skin. They are compliant and, luckily, we have space for them in Healthcare.

It turns out the one who got eight years had left her methadone out at home. Methadone is a liquid substitute for heroin. Same dose, just without the buzz. Her toddler had drunk it, leading to the inevitable and terrible tragedy. She moans as though she is the victim, but her day will come. Reality arrives as withdrawal fades. I'm glad to get her out of my sight.

Now for the last one. It's like waiting for someone to open a lion's cage. The harsh prison floodlights light up the side entrance to the vehicle. One of the drivers stamps up the steps of the van and turns to us.

'Ready? I'll let her out. She was only violent when we touched her.'

Odom and I exchange glances. We're big men. The three female officers we have on shift are mature and experienced, and well used to restraining those who've lost control. The driver backs out and stands away from the vehicle. Then it's quiet. My ears strain for sounds of movement. There's a squeak, then the suspension strains as something heavy moves inside. The van leans towards us and then tips forward as the weight approaches the door.

The woman who comes out is enormous. She's almost as wide as Fats. She thuds down off the last step, keeping her focus on the ground.

'Come forward, please,' says Odom.

She doesn't move. He steps closer. Her knuckles clench.

'Please, we need to process you. Then we'll get you warm with a hot drink,' says Odom.

She opens her legs to assume a wide stance, not dissimilar to a sumo wrestler. The nag of worry deepens. Large people have strong muscles to shift the weight around. Her matted hair hangs down and conceals her face and her intentions.

'It's okay, sweetie,' says one of the female officers. 'We aren't going to hurt you.'

I see the obese prisoner's fists relax. She shuffles forwards and to the side as though to remain a distance from Odom. The female officer cajoles her to keep moving, but she's stopped.

'Odom, come on,' I say. 'Let's take a break. I could kill a cup of tea.'

He realises immediately what I'm suggesting and we both walk along the long corridor and stop next to the prop desk. We look back and watch the other officers quietly check in our new guest.

Odom taps me on the shoulder.

'Good call, mate. You can shoot off now. Maybe you'll still make it.'

I grab my coat and hustle out of the prison. It's 10 p.m. I have to repeatedly smack the front light on my bike to get its beam to work, which reflects off the pouring rain. The puddles on the roads and paths are deathtraps, but I try my best, despite knowing my fate.

I can't seem to do anything right for Abi. We were going to be such a great team, but I keep letting her down. And if she's not happy, the family doesn't work.

My frozen hands struggle with the locks when I reach home. The house is in darkness. I flick on the lounge light and see two wine glasses on the table. The empty one has lipstick around the rim. I pick up the other glass and drain it in a gulp. There's no point in climbing the stairs.

18

PRESENT

I cycle home from my first cushy shift on the female side with the memories of that cold night in Reception at the forefront of my mind. After such an easy day, I've forgotten about the conversation Abi and I had before I left this morning. The air around the house smells of barbecues for a change. I can hear kids giggling behind their fenced gardens, but, yet again, I open the back door with trepidation.

Ivan is colouring at the table next to his sister. They both glance up. She grins, and they return to their tasks.

'Daddy's home,' shouts Tilly.

She leaves her seat and gives me a perfunctory hug. I slip my jacket off and wipe the sweat from my brow. A beer would go down nicely, but the fridge is emptier than usual. Leaving my work boots at the bottom of the stairs, I head for our bedroom. Abi is lying on it in state. Her chest rises too rapidly for her to be asleep.

'Hey,' I say.

'I did a shop,' she whispers, 'but the card declined. I had to leave everything.'

She keeps her eyes closed.

'How have the kids been?'

'I'm not sure. I've been up here.'

'Look, sorry for what I said earlier. I can see you're trying hard. The jail takes its toll on me.'

'Get a new job, then.'

'Where am I going to find one that pays the same? We're struggling as it is.'

She opens her eyes and looks at me for a few moments.

'Do you know what I realised today?'

'Go on.'

'You talk to me as if I'm one of your prisoners.'

'No, I don't.'

'You do. You've changed since you started working there. I don't know who you are any more.'

'Ivan has changed us. Two kids and no money has changed us.'

'The truth is, I *am* a prisoner here. Do you know what it's like to feel trapped like this?'

I sit on the bed next to her, but not touching. She's right. We are prisoners in our own lives. Confined as surely as they are. There are no bars, but there's no escape. There is no point denying it.

'We're trapped together. Things will change. They'll get better.'

A tear trickles from her eye and streaks down her cheek.

'In ten years? Fifteen? I can't wait that long.' She sobs. 'I won't last that long.'

'What can we do? We're stuck, but at least we're together. And they've moved me at work to the female side because of Wyatt.'

She breathes deeply through her nose; I think to stop herself crying.

'Is he okay? Will he be all right?'

'I suspect the other prisoners are the ones who are in danger.'

She lets out a short chuckle and the tears flow freely.

'It's easier on the female side,' I urge. 'I won't be so stressed. I feel relaxed now. I've got twenty quid, so I'll nip to the shop and get some stuff to keep us going until payday. See if they have a four-pack of that cheap cider. I can take the kids to the duck pond, which will get them out of your hair for a bit. After all, we have plenty of mouldy bread.'

Instead of laughing, she turns away from me.

'Come on, Abi.'

I place my hand on her hip, but she doesn't turn around.

19

Abi didn't get out of bed again yesterday. I left Tilly and Ivan colouring and surprised myself by how much food I could buy from the shops by choosing own brand. The cheap bread tasted of sugar, though, so the ducks will be pleased with our next visit. We didn't go for a walk in the end because when I got back, the kids were hungry. After we'd eaten, they just sat either side of me on the sofa.

We watched a cartoon, *The Book of Life*, which was depressing, but they seemed unaffected. Ivan kept smiling at me and cuddled in. I'm not sure if he senses I'm more relaxed, or if he's picked up on the tension in the house and is trying to fix it. He fell asleep, but when I lifted him up to take him to his room, he noticed and slid out of my arms. Both kids went to bed easily though and dropped off quickly. Abi always complains about how traumatic the process is but they're usually good enough for me. I drank the four cans of cider myself and slept on the sofa.

It's 7 a.m. when I wake up feeling completely refreshed, despite sleeping in my work clothes again. I have another eight until five shift today. My clean uniform is hopefully in the bedroom, so I creep up the stairs. To my relief and surprise, Abi washed some shirts yesterday, so I strip, wash my face and armpits, and slip a fresh shirt on. There is even an ironed pair of trousers. Abi's either still asleep or pretending to be. Why didn't I think to wash them myself, seeing as she's struggling?

I skip breakfast, leave the house, grab my cycle, and scoot off. It's a glorious morning. The sun is up and twinkles on the river as I head past it. The paths are full of dog walkers and other cyclists despite the early hour. I feel no tension thinking of the day ahead and it's an intoxicating sensation. Is this how people with normal jobs are on the way to work? I'm early and stop at the petrol station to buy *The Mail on Sunday*.

The front of the paper is always too vitriolic for my liking. It feels as if politicians know nothing about my world, but Abi likes the women's magazine. It also has a great pull-out sports section and a decent TV guide. I often photocopy it for the prisoners on the wing. Some officers think I'm mad to do that, but few of the inmates can afford newspapers and planning a night's TV is something they can focus on. They also have to come to the office to look at the guide, so I can see their mental state and chat to them. Admittedly, it gets nicked when I'm not looking before the end of the week.

I've made good time when I arrive at the prison. There's nobody else waiting for keys, so I'm soon through and join the sole officer in the hub. It's Sheraton, who came over to the male side a few days back. He would have started at seven to relieve the night staff, whereas the rest of us don't start until eight at the weekend. There is something not quite right about him.

'What's going on?' I ask.

'The night staff found a non-responsive this morning when they were doing the handover roll count. Oscar One came down and cracked the door. Stiff and cold. She must have died in the night.'

'No way. Was she old?'

'Yeah, think so. I got here just as they were removing the body. It looks like natural causes. Apparently, she had underlying health issues caused by years of drug abuse. She was on Zulu 1, cell five.'

I log into the prison IT system and bring up the mug shot for Z1-5. My stomach rolls as I recognise the old lady who gave me the mock salute at the med hatch yesterday. She was only forty-six.

The in-cell buzzer sounds for cell W1-14. It's on speaker, so I press the button and answer.

'Please state your medical emergency.'

'Get off me! Get fucking off me, you bitch. Arghh. Fuck! Fuck!'

And then the most ear-piercing shriek I have ever heard in my life, worse than any horror film, screeches from the speaker.

'Noooooooo!' she howls.

And then another scream, which is abruptly cut off.

My nerves jangle and my entire body has goose bumps, but Sheraton is already out of the hub and running to Whisky wing. He opens the gate and leaves it swinging for me. I run through and lock it behind me, just in case it's a fiddle and the prisoner's plan is to dodge past us and run when we open her cell.

Sheraton runs to the laundry room which each wing has for personal clothes and wing kitchen cleaning items, and returns with a towel. I reach W1-14 and open the observation panel, but it's too steamy in the room to see much. I can just about make out a figure standing at the back of the cell facing us. Sheraton stands next to me and nods. I unlock the door, push it wide, and step back.

The door swings open to reveal an average girl in just a sports bra, nothing else, perched against the radiator with her arms outstretched. Her chin is on her chest and her hair is pulled into a ponytail. Her forehead is marble white. Blood surges from a huge wound across her stomach from hip to hip. The cut is so deep I can see the meat and fat of her flesh. A huge puddle of blood has formed between her feet.

Her head rises and her eyes focus on me. She roars and shrieks, deafening us.

'My baby!'

Sheraton curses and presses his talk button.

'QP, this is Whisky Two, calling a Code Red for Whisky 1 wing, Houseblock One. Ambulance required, Oscar One required, Hotel One required, immediately.'

The hotel call signs are for Healthcare and they are definitely needed, but we need to make the situation safe before they can go in. I edge into the room and peer around the door where her attacker must be hiding, but there's no one else in the room. Sheraton strides past me pulling a pair of plastic gloves on and gives me a pair.

'Put them on and hold her right hand.'

The woman's head is down again. I grab her hand at the wrist and Sheraton grabs her left. She doesn't struggle. The razor blade in her left hand glints in the sunlight through the window as he removes it from her grip.

'Jessica. It's okay now. Dalton, grab the towel.'

He picks her up with one arm under her knees, the other around her shoulders, and gently lays her on the bed. I finally recover my senses, fold the towel, and press it hard against the wound. She has seemingly gone into a catatonic state. I shout at her.

'Please stay awake, Jessica!'

'It's okay,' says Sheraton. 'It looks worse than it is. She does this every two or three months. They stitch her up and send her back.'

I hear the houseblock doors bang open and the nurse appears at the cell doorway. She's a small Filipina woman called Rosa who usually works nights. She chucks the big medi-bag on the floor and unzips it.

'Oh, Jessica. What do you do again? Stay calm.'

Oscar One arrives and takes a look.

'The usual?' he asks Sheraton, who nods.

'I've got it covered. You two clear the route for the ambulance.'

We stride towards the hub area. Sheraton has blood over most of his shirt. I point to it.

'Happens all the time over here. I keep a spare uniform in my locker.'

The other officers are arriving now. Braddock asks Sheraton what's happened. I feel superfluous. Braddock tells Sheraton to go and get changed. He'll help sort the ambulance out. I put two fingers on my wrist to check my pulse. It's out of control.

20

It's nearly 9 a.m. by the time the paramedics have left and we start unlocking the rest of the houseblock. Tex and I are on the YO wing and leave the hub together. I unlock the gate while Tex carries the visits list, appointment slips, and the ACCT books we have. These are folders for people at risk of suicide or self-harm. All the prisoners complain about having to wait for their breakfast when we let them out. A small girl with long blonde hair and a mean mouth shakes her head at me when I say we had to wait for an ambulance. She shoves her hands into the pockets of her pilled fleece, which looks desperate for a wash.

'Cut-up should try slicing her throat, not her stomach,' she says. 'I need breakfast early.'

The inmates are like commuters who grumble without thought when someone has thrown themselves on the track and caused a delay. I write the roll count, a miserly nineteen young offenders, into the observation book. The obs book is a blank notebook where officers document everything that occurs on the wing. The SOs expect them to be full of info. The idea being the shift about to start can find out if any prisoners had a bad visit the day before, or if there was fighting that didn't merit a trip to the block. You have little time to update it on the male side, so I rarely bother to fill it in or read it.

Tex, on the other hand, reads it word for word. I raise an eyebrow at her, causing her to chuckle.

'I'm not being cheeky, but you have much to learn about how we do things over here, Dalton. You and Fats are legends to the new recruits over here because of what you do on the other side. Especially the younger officers. But you need to be smart over here, not just brave and brawny. There isn't a YO wing on the male side, is there?'

'No, they tend to keep them on the induction wing with the new arrivals, but if we're full they go on a standard wing with the adults.'

'How's that work?'

'Pretty good. If the young 'uns are too gobby, one of the faces gives them a slap and they drop back into line. Occasionally you'll get one who scares even the faces, and the wing falls apart.'

'Makes sense. Here, we have all the YOs together. We have nineteen of them today. That doesn't seem a lot, but the courts don't send children to adult prison unless every single other option has been exhausted.'

She walks away but stops and turns in the doorway.

'I've worked the male landings enough times to know you guys don't check the obs book first thing, and it doesn't matter too much. That's cos men are simple creatures. They have a scrap and then it's over. The fight settles it, regardless of who wins. It's different here. Women hold bitter grudges, sometimes for months.'

Braddock comes on the wing with two of the orange ACCT books.

'You forgot these,' he says with a smile.

'Really, that means we have nine?'

'Yes, and maybe more on the way.' He speaks quietly then. 'A brutal cut up like the one this morning might well set more off, so be on the lookout. Make sure you double-check the number of obs. Enjoy.'

I read the first book. The picture on the front tells me it's the girl with the long blonde hair and the mean mouth from earlier. Her name is Rose-Marie. I flick through it. Three observations an hour during the day, five at night. That's a lot. On a wing of eighty on the male side, you might have two of these books. Both men would only be on one an hour. Rose-Marie's triggers for self-harm are anxiety and depression following a gang rape, and the anniversary of her sister's death, which she says was her fault. It doesn't say whether it was or not.

I step outside the office and take a sneaky peek at the few prisoners who have bothered to get out of bed. Some are skittish like deer. I recognise the haunted signs of abuse in their eyes. Others stare me down. A sweet-looking ginger-haired girl in prison attire gives me a cheeky sneer.

'What the feck you staring at, Uncle?'

Tex is standing behind her and laughs her head off.

'Don't worry, Dalton. They call me Granny.'

It takes me until lunch to get back on an even keel after the brutal start. I let the servery workers off the wing to fetch the food trolleys and spot SO Nasima Khan leaving the hub. I smile at her and she walks over.

'Morning, Dalton. How are you enjoying your new home?'

'The ladies have made me feel very welcome.'

'I spoke to Peabody yesterday. He's coming back tomorrow, but he doesn't want to be on the YO wing any more, which was where he'd been allocated.'

'I thought it was Peasbody?'

'No, who told you that? Anyway, with Sandringham and him

gone, you and Trudy will be their replacements with the YOs. That okay?'

'Sure, ma'am.'

Nasima looks hard at me, suspecting I'm taking the piss. I'm not, though. It seems I have a bit to learn. All my shifts won't be with Tex, but a fair few will be, and that's just fine.

The trolleys that bring over each wing's food at mealtimes arrive. They look like tall plastic fridges, but keep the contents warm, not cold. The women are a lot more careful with them than the men.

I pull the trolley onto our wing. As I lock the gate, Tara Prestwick, the girl from yesterday, strolls past. She catches my eye.

'Ooh, super screw has graced us with his presence again.'

'Morning, Ms Prestwick. Are you lost?'

'I'm one of the two hub orderlies. I'm trusted, so I get to wander. In fact, I've been here more often than you have, so I can help you. And call me Tara.'

'Fair enough, Tara. How come you aren't on the YO wing?'

'I know I look thirteen, but I'm twenty-two. Kitty is now the same age, too, so we're padded up on Z1.'

I struggle with whom Kitty is until I realise she means Monroe, the overweight girl I saw in Reception when she was brought in.

'Have you met Billie yet?' asks Tara.

'Billie?'

'Obviously not. Chat soon.'

Tara winks at me and wanders back to her wing. The hub orderly is responsible for keeping the area between the hub and the wings clean. We're always sacking them on the male side for dealing drugs through the wing bars. I stare after Tara, wondering what she's in for. I'll sneak a look at her record at lunchtime.

I return to the servery and stand at the door. Mealtimes are a flashpoint on the male side, but the girls queue up respectfully again. Rose-Marie is on duty, serving her first 'customers' with her customary scowl. You need an aggressive con to serve the food, because the meals aren't quite big enough to fill you up. People get the arse and ask for more. That's why many do paid work, so they can buy extra to boost the servery food. Canteen is the term used within prisons for the weekly delivery of items the inmates purchase for themselves.

The food is more than acceptable. They have fish and chips on Fridays, a fry-up on Saturday morning and Sunday lunch with all the trimmings. I'm really partial to the risotto. If the prisoners can't be bothered to choose their options on the consoles the week before, they get a standard meal suitable for vegetarians. That's usually when the arguments start. The beetroot and cucumber baguette causes a lot of trouble.

The officers more or less have the same thing at lunch, although we get bigger portions. Some won't eat it because the male prisoners prepare it, but I do. I can't afford not to. Yet again, I'm not so different from the cons.

It's media bullshit that food quality is rubbish. After all, the little possums have human rights. That said, gravy is very popular from the canteen as virtually anything tastes good covered or dipped in that. Salt intake is low down the list of health risks here.

A door opens on my right. A young girl with a mousey, shoulder-length bob takes a step out of her cell and yawns loudly, arms raised. She has a white vest top on and a pair of baggy jeans. She's curvy for a prisoner, but light on her feet as she steps to the middle of the wing.

'Now!' she bellows, causing her voice to echo around the walls. She stretches out her arms, eyes challenging the other inmates.

'Who's ready for some fucking damage?'

21

The other girls quieten. The late arrival walks straight to the front of the queue.

'Yo, Rose-Marie. Chicken and chips,' she says.

'Piss off, Damage. You're on no choice.'

'I want chicken and chips.'

'I want to screw Prince Harry. Looks like nobody gets what they want.'

I detect the tension change in the air. At least that's the same on both sides of the prison, but the girl with the mousey hair is agile. She leaps up and sits on the counter. Reaching past Rose-Marie's head, Damage yanks her ponytail down, pulling Rose-Marie's face towards the food.

'Enough!' I roar.

On the male side, that would grab their attention, but you'd still have to get in the middle to separate them. Here, everyone freezes. You could hear an ant fart. A girl in the queue whimpers and the people behind her shuffle back while staring at the growing puddle between her legs. Damage releases Rose-Marie's head. They both turn to me. Rose-Marie retreats to the rear of the servery. There is total silence except for the sounds made by two women who were coming down the stairs and who are now swiftly returning to their cells.

Tex comes out of the office with a confused look.

'What's happening?' she asks.

'This lady pulled Rose-Marie's hair,' I say, sounding like a grass.

Tex stands next to the troublemaker.

'Billie?' says Tex. 'Explain yourself.'

Billie says nothing. I realise she's the only one who is still relaxed on the entire wing. She has a slight smile on her lips.

'Who are you?' she asks me.

'I'm asking the questions, Billie. What's going on?' says Tex.

Billie's eyes narrow. She turns to Tex.

'Just getting my lunch.'

Tex looks over her shoulder at me for a reply.

'She jumped the queue, and it seems as though she forgot to make her lunch choices,' I say.

'Back of the queue, Billie,' says Tex.

Billie leans closer to her.

'Keep your crappy food.'

She leans back, spins on her heels and gives me a raised eyebrow. She pushes her hair behind her ear in a way that is so out of kilter with the environment and atmosphere we are immersed in that I can't help staring after her as she walks to her cell and bangs the door shut.

Tex delivers trays of food to the cells of the girls who vanished and the one who pissed herself when I hollered. I'm not entirely sure what's happened. Tex says she'll explain later. The rest of lunch finishes without incident and we lock up for roll count. It takes ten minutes for us to update all the ACCT books. As we walk towards the hub to hand in the figures, I ask Tex the obvious question.

'Who the hell was that?'

'Be very careful with her. She's jailbait.'

I frown. 'I thought jailbait was to do with underage women?'

She looks me in the eye. 'That was Billie. This is jail. She will bait you.'

22

The rest of the shift is uneventful. The girls ask for the pool balls, but they don't play with the same passion and bravado as the men do on the male side. They are polite to each other and don't seem to mind that much who wins. Nobody throws a ball at anybody else. No one hits anyone around the back of their head with their cue or pretends it's a spear. And, as far as I can tell, the players' cells aren't burgled while they're distracted, either.

Tex and I spend most of the afternoon drinking tea and reading my paper in the office. When the roll clears, we walk to the gatehouse together. Physically, I feel good. Sometimes I dread the cycle home after a long day. Mentally, though, I'm a little bruised. Tex picks up on it.

'You did well today,' she says.

'I didn't do anything.'

'That's why.'

'Sorry, I don't get it.'

She laughs. I realise she does that a lot.

'Look at the size of you. There isn't a female inmate who could take you one on one in a fight, even two on one. Not only that, you've worked on the male estate for five hard years. I often see officers come over from that side and throw their weight around. Throw women around. But you haven't when you could have done.'

I'm still not sure what she's talking about.

'Listen, Dalton. When you shouted "enough" earlier, that roar went straight through me and I wasn't anywhere near you. I guess you learn to bellow in that way when eighty cons are causing havoc and the wing is twice as long. But most of these women are victims. I don't see the females on our wings as prisoners. They are mostly exploited girls who've done silly things. Nearly every single one of them has been abused, or raped, or hit, by bigger men.'

'Men like me.'

'Yes, big, angry, shouting men. Then you stopped. They all know what happens when the shouting stops. Most of them were petrified.'

'Should I not roar that loud?'

'Of course you should. They had to be stopped, and no one got hurt. There was no anger in your voice, only control. They learned a lesson today, that not all men are violent when they shout. You earned their trust. Word spreads rapidly around a female prison. But be aware. If you carry on like this, some of them will quickly rely on you for emotional support and a feeling of safety. Most of them never had a father worth shit, but they all needed one. Most of them still want one.'

'I struggle with my own kids. I'm not sure I can cope with another twenty.'

'You made me laugh when you called Tara Ms Prestwick. Do you call the male prisoners Mr?'

'Yes. It shows respect but also keeps them at arm's length.'

'Trust me, you'll be calling the females by their first names before long. You may see them as victims, but I try to view them as survivors as well. You will also come to like them most of the time, warts and all.'

'Like family?'

We've reached the exit and we both throw our keys and radios down the chute. There's a rush of officers trying to leave, and Tex and I get pushed apart. She waits for me outside.

'Just like family,' she says. 'That's the job on the female side. You are more parent than jailer, and sometimes that can be harder, because children let you down.'

'Okay, it was weird though. I sensed that I shouldn't touch them because it wasn't necessary, but I wasn't sure exactly what else to do.'

'It's just the same as the male side in that respect. Send the naughty ones back to their cells. If they don't go, you'll have to handle them.'

She grins and trudges off. She must live within walking distance. I stand and watch her as she walks away. I have always liked her, but I've never really thought of her as being a great prison officer, or, for that matter, a mother.

A meaty whack on my shoulder nearly lays me out on the pavement.

'Spent the day reading the paper?' asks Fats.

It's good to see him. 'More or less. You?'

'Nah, been busy today. We were behind on piss tests, so I've spent all day doing them. I need a shower.'

'You cycling?' I ask.

'Walking. I had a flat tyre last night and was too tired to fix it.'

'You walked all the way to work this morning?'

'That's right, sir.'

I've never looked too hard at my fellow officers. I've got enough of my own problems. But I'm changing. I take the time to study Fats closely. His shoulders are rounded and his face is drawn. I should think a five-mile walk home is the last thing he wants. I think of him as robust and healthy, a real life force, but he's not. He's on the edge and close to breaking. I catch the odd eye, and nod at other officers from both sides as they walk past us and home. Many of them are the same.

'How's Colt getting on?'

Fats chuckles. 'Guns blazing.' Fats shakes his head. 'Wow, he is quite something. He was upsetting everyone on the induction landings, so they brought him over to ours to stop him messing around. My buddy, Taufel, was off sorting queries, so I was on the wing on my own. I watched Scranton wander over to Colt and give him the word. You know, tell him the way things worked on there. Explained that it was him, Scranton, who ran the wing.'

'Yeah, what did Colt say to that?'

'It was mental. Colt was expecting it. He thumped Scranton bang on the nose. Hard. I've never seen a wing go quiet like that. It was as if God paused time. Scranton looked around in disbelief.'

Fats laughs so hard, he has to lean over. He's still chuckling as he rights himself.

'Scranton couldn't believe it. Your boy didn't give him any other choice. Scranton laid into him frantic. He gave him everything he had. You could hear the blows landing, but Colt took them all, and then he sent some back.'

'I didn't hear your personal alarm over the radio.'

'I didn't press it. It was nothing. I just pushed them apart. But there was a scary part to it.'

'Yeah?'

'They were fighting at the top of the landing. I wasn't even that far away, but it took me a while to get there. People kept getting in my way on the stairs. It was only after I'd locked them both in their cells that I realised the ones who kept blocking me were all Colt's little gang.'

'They got stuck in too?'

'No, that's the thing. They did it on purpose to slow me up. Colt planned it. He wanted to fight Scranton and didn't care if he lost, but he didn't want to get killed by him. They knew I'd split them up eventually, but they needed the fight to go on for a while to show the wing what they were about. That is some fucked-up shit. They're just a bunch of kids.'

One of the last officers to leave is Braddock, who walks behind Fats.

'Hey, Braddock,' I shout over to him. 'Haven't you just moved to Hampton?'

'Yeah, want to come around and help me paint?'

'Definitely, let me finish mine first and I'll be in touch. But Fats here is walking home because he got a puncture. You drive past our street on the way to your new place, so can you give him a lift?'

Braddock looks Fats up and down. 'Yeah, okay, but he better not give my car a puncture.'

It's only as I'm cycling along the rowing lake that I realise that when Fats referred to my brother-in-law, he didn't say Wyatt. He called him Colt, and I did too.

23

When I reach home, I open the back door and find the children watching cartoons.

'Evening, urchins.'

All I receive is half a wave from Tilly. I slump on the sofa, but I'm not especially tired. It's warm and breezy outside and it seems a shame to stay indoors. At the commercial break, the kids come and sit either side of me.

'I like it when you get home early,' says Tilly.

'Where's your mum?'

'In bed. She's been there all day.'

'Is she ill?'

'No, she's sleepy,' says Ivan.

'Haven't you had any food?'

This time Tilly answers.

'Dur! She woke up to make us sandwiches and drinks. She played with the washing machine as well.'

'Did you save me any sandwiches?'

'Nuh uh,' he replies.

'Who wants to feed the ducks?'

Neither of them answer. They just run to the door and pull their shoes on. Ivan gets cross with his, but we're soon on the move. I stroll in the middle holding hands with my son. The quick route is under the road, through an underpass, but it's a mugger's paradise. Even the sun doesn't go down there, but Ivan doesn't like to walk too far, so I risk it.

We see nobody at all on the way. The pond is next to a field in the nice bit of Orton Malborne called Stonebridge. Recently, someone hung a swing on the big horse chestnut tree, but it was soon pinched. The ducks race over when they spot us. It said in the paper today that you shouldn't feed them bread, so I've brought a container of porridge oats and most of it blows back in our faces. Ivan copies the ducks' argumentative quacking. The ducklings are so used to humans, they clamber out to peck at the food. Mummy and Daddy duck watch nervously from a half-sunken log.

Going home, the kids want an ice cream. They aren't cheap from the shop, so I buy them an orange lolly and tell them to share it. They don't complain.

When we get back home, I make them beans on toast, followed by vanilla ice cream from the tub in the freezer. Afterwards we watch TV but nothing catches our attention. I nip upstairs to the toilet and find their pyjamas are laid out on their beds. The kids follow me up. Ivan's tired and asks to go to bed, so I help them brush their teeth. Tilly says she'll read for a bit.

'Night, Daddy.'

She gives me a knowing smile, as if she understands I need time alone, or perhaps time to speak to Mummy. I tiptoe into our room. Abi's turned and facing the wall. The kids' rooms are tidy, but ours is a dumping ground. The curtain at the window has come away from the rail. I half fix it and look outside. There's no hiding that the houses are run-down here. Someone's dumped an old brown plastic-looking armchair in one of the parking spaces today, or maybe I just didn't notice it before.

I turn around and listen to Abi as she snuffles in her sleep. This won't have been what she wanted or expected. Her parents are pretty well off. They retired soon after our wedding and when Wyatt turned sixteen and left home without a backward glance, they moved to Spain to play golf. I can't remember much about our special day, seven years ago now, but I'll never forget what I overheard her father say when he didn't know that I was standing behind him.

24

OUR WEDDING

The waitress at the Marriott Hotel takes our dessert plates and cutlery away.

'Any more drinks?' she asks.

'No, thanks,' Abi's father slurs. 'Just the bill, please.'

I smile at him, and he nods back.

Our wedding reception has been a quiet affair. My best man, Martin, is steaming, and he's got the chief bridesmaid, the only bridesmaid, drunk, too. I can see him rubbing her leg under the table. My mum has spent most of the day crying. I think Abi feels the same way, but for different reasons. Wyatt turned up for the ceremony, then said he was going out with his mates. No one thought to challenge him.

I wasn't overly keen on getting married, to be honest. Perhaps it's the thought of being tied down I don't like, but that's stupid, because life has me tied down anyway, and I'm not unhappy. Abi cuddles the reason why we're here: baby Tilly. Abi looks pleased to have something to focus on, apart from our depressing wedding.

I made Abi agree to a small celebration, even though her dad said he'd pay. I couldn't be doing with the aggravation. The only guests today are the two drunks, Abi's parents and my mum. I didn't even tell my other mates any of the details, just that we were keeping to a tight budget.

I've let them slip away. Martin told me that Woods is a research engineer for an airline in Dubai being paid big bucks and Belly has been designing a shopping centre in Australia. I'm not jealous of their success and am genuinely pleased for them. It's myself I'm disappointed in. I was the one with plans and dreams. It was me who would escape Peterborough. Instead I've lived here all my life, rarely leaving even for holidays, and now work for little more than minimum wage as an administrator in a job that might lead nowhere. I wouldn't have been able to look my friends in the eye.

I also realised, at the register office, I had stolen Abi's dream of a magical day, and it was too late to do anything about it. So now we're all just going through the motions. I couldn't even taste my food.

'Let's go,' says Abi. 'Tilly needs a nap.'

It's obvious she can't wait to get out of here. The waitress returns with a silver platter, which she hands to Abi's dad. My mum picks up the uncut wedding cake, while Abi and I kiss everyone goodbye. Her dad can't even be bothered to make a joke about me taking Abi off his hands. My mum says she'll drive us home. The best man and bridesmaid say they're nipping off to have another drink in town. I wish I were going with them. When we reach where we parked, Abi realises Tilly's dropped her little doggy.

I return to the small function room that her dad hired and I'm about to push the door open when I hear him talking on the other side of it.

'My God, what a disaster.'

'Shh, Michael.'

'What? They've gone.'

'It was nice. Abi looked lovely.'

'It was a joke. We have one daughter and I get to hand her over to that loser in a dimly lit room at the register office. I rue the day she met that lad.'

'They're happy and in love.'

'She doesn't look happy and in love.'

'Well, they've got a kid now. No one's happy when they're exhausted.'

She titters a laugh, but he just growls.

'Come on,' he says. 'Let's go home and forget today ever happened.'

'Stop it, Michael. I like him. You've pushed one of our children away already, let's not repeat our mistakes. He is trying hard to make a good life for them.'

'Well, he needs to try harder.'

Their chairs scrape back, so I bluster into the room.

'Oh, hi. You still here? Tilly dropped her doggy.'

I stride to where Abi was sitting, and the doggy is under the table. I manage a grin as I walk to the door. They both look guilty, because they both know I heard. They attempt a smile, but I just leave. There's nothing else to say.

25

PRESENT

A car backfiring jolts me out of a dreamless sleep. Abi also jerks awake. I shuffle up closer to her, but not quite touching. She moves imperceptibly away. It's my day off. Usually I flop around in bed, trying to snooze but failing, but I had another good night's rest, despite the horrific self-harming incident at the prison.

It's gone seven, so I slide from under the duvet and pull a pair of jogging bottoms on. In the mirror, I can see that I've trimmed down so much, my hips and stomach muscles are starting to show. I like it. My body was also something I've let slip over the years.

'I'll wake Ivan and Tilly. Lie in if you want. I'll walk them to school.'

Abi gives me a suspicious frown and rolls back to face the wall. The kids and I eat a bowl of cereal. Ivan gets free dinners at his age, so we only need to pay for Tilly's. It's expensive, but Abi insisted. When I send them upstairs to get dressed, Abi has risen at some point and put their uniforms out.

The amble to school is pleasant. Ivan doesn't want to hold my hand and has a meltdown at the school door and I'm thankful when a teacher whisks him away, but I can hear him crying as I walk past the classroom window.

Abi is drinking a cup of coffee at the breakfast table when I get back. For someone who has spent the last few days in bed, she doesn't seem very rested.

'All right?'

She looks at me through watery eyes. 'I suppose.'

'Kids have been good.'

'That down to you, is it?'

'No, I was just saying. What are you up to today?'

'The same as always.'

'Staying in bed?'

It was a joke, but clearly not a great one.

'No, I'll be cleaning and tidying up after you lot. None of you will appreciate it.'

'I appreciate it.'

'Do you ever say that?'

'I am now.'

'Just after I tell you I want to split up.'

I'm not sure what to say to that. I thought she'd been hitting out.

'Do you still want to break up?'

'I don't know. I've spoken to my parents. They said I can go out to Spain for a few weeks. My dad reckons they have a good school for ex-pats' kids near their villa.'

'Come on. Our children won't want to leave their friends, or their dad.'

She lets out a big breath. 'No, I agree, but neither do they like living here.'

'Look, I'll do all the jobs today.'

'What?'

'The cleaning, hoovering, tidying. You do whatever you like.

Why don't you go for a run? You used to love that, but I haven't seen you in your kit for years.'

'That's because I've always got the kids or housekeeping to do.'

'I'm sure you can find thirty minutes for a quick jog.'

'You'd think.'

'I'm not sitting on my arse either, you know. We need the overtime, remember?'

She goes back to bed and I attack the housework. I'm just done when it's time to pick up the kids. Abi has an early tea made for when we get back. We have the children tucked up by eight. It's a team effort and the kids seem happy. Abi and I sit in the lounge afterwards. Me on the sofa, her perched on the edge of the battered recliner.

'Fancy a drink?' I ask.

'Any of those ciders left?'

'Erm, no. How about the port that's been knocking around the cupboard since Christmas? We can get tiddly and reconnect?'

She jumps to her feet.

'You think it's that easy? Do a bit of dusting and we're all friends? I can't imagine us ever having sex again.'

She stamps up the stairs, leaving me open-mouthed. I hadn't realised how far apart we'd drifted. For the first time, I believe we'll actually break up. And if I'm honest, there's a part of me that welcomes the idea.

26

I wake up the next morning to the sound of thunder. The kids and Abi sleep through the deep rumbles. I arrive at work drenched and trudge to the female side. There is nothing more depressing than a jail under dark skies and heavy rain. The wet metal gates chill your hands and there's little respite from the prison heating. At least Tex is my partner again, and I'm only on an early.

I unlock the wing and get the workers out. Tex distributes that day's tea packs to the prisoners. They call it tea, but I'd rather go without than drink it. We're sitting in the office updating our six ACCT books when they bring back Jessica Smith – the inmate with the self-inflicted stomach wound. Cut-up must be some kind of horrible prison nickname. She is on three observations per hour and breezily says 'hi' as if she's been away for the weekend on a mini-cruise.

A slim, tall woman, who I've heard speaking in a language I couldn't place, knocks on the open door. She has light green eyes and light brown skin.

'Rolls for the bog,' she states.

It's a strange thing to ration, but we have to, otherwise it vanishes. I pass her two and ask if she needs anything else. I get a blank stare in reply.

'That's Billie's roommate, Zelda. Very messed-up girl,' says Tex when we're alone.

'Great, another one to watch out for. Is her English weak?'

'She didn't speak much to begin with, but she's improving fast. I think she came from southern Italy, but I'm not certain. Billie said she'll share with her. I thought Zelda was a loose cannon, but ever since they moved in together Billie's been ordering her around. Scary pair, them. Check out the scars on Zelda's arms when it gets warm, and she only has a T-shirt on.'

Rose-Marie knocks on the door. She's been crying.

'Miss, can you get someone else to do the servery today? I feel bad.'

'No problem,' says Tex. 'What's the matter?'

'My stomach aches and I could be sick. I just want to curl up.'

Rose-Marie's fleece is unzipped. She puts her hand inside and rubs her stomach where the T-shirt has ridden up. There's a bit of a bump. It's something I've never considered: a pregnancy in a place like this. Rose-Marie catches me staring.

'What? Did you think I had wind?'

'How far along are you?'

'About twenty weeks. I just started feeling it move. Easiest pregnancy I've had.'

She gives me a smile, but it soon drops as she turns to go.

'I'll come and talk to you later,' says Tex.

After Rose-Marie's gone, a lot of questions go through my mind.

'How does that work then? Being pregnant here can't be easy. Tex, you're from the Mother and Baby Unit. I assume they have scans at the hospital and deliver there? Will Rose-Marie automatically move onto the MBU here in the prison with the baby when it's born, or do they try to give it to a relative?'

Tex shakes her head. 'You know she's only twenty. She must have fallen pregnant just before she came in. That will be her third kid.'

'Where are the other two?'

'The state has them. Rose-Marie was homeless when she came in.'

'What's she in for?'

'She was shoplifting at Heels Footwear in town and got chased by the security guard. He caught up and had her cornered. She took a needle out of her pocket and said if he came near her, she would give him AIDS.'

'Jesus, how lovely. Has she got AIDS?'

'No, I don't think so. Rumours tend to circulate if they have.'

A few of the inmates have HIV. Nearly always through drug abuse as opposed to prostitution, but they are closely linked.

'So, if we have an MBU and Rose-Marie has her baby, at least she can keep this one with her in prison.'

Tex rubs her face before answering. She looks gaunt.

'It's not that simple. Rose-Marie has been on remand for nearly five months waiting to go to court. Stupidly, she said she wanted a trial, even though there's CCTV of her running away. She reckons she didn't pull a needle on him, but who are they going to believe? Her trial is tomorrow, hence the nerves. If she'd pleaded guilty, she'd have probably been out by now.'

'Why didn't she?'

'That's the thing. We consider this place a prison, but here she is safe. There are three meals a day, scans, healthcare, friends, she's clean from grime and heroin, and there's much less fear than on the streets. It's the safest location for her and her baby.'

'Then why is she so angry?'

'She's not. That's how she's learned to protect herself. Think of her as a hedgehog. If you get too close, it points its spines. You know, be prickly and show aggression to deter threats, but inside it's scared. At the end of the day, she's just a fucking hedgehog.'

Tex rarely swears, but she's riled up and continues.

'Rose-Marie believes she has a hope of keeping her child if she has it here. Say the judge gives her two years, so she does one year inside and gives birth during that time. She thinks they'll put her and the baby in the MBU, then we'll help them both find a place to live when she leaves.'

'That sounds all right.'

'Yes, but it doesn't work like that. She's had both of her kids taken off her for serious neglect. I understand one of them got hurt. The possibility of her being able to look after the child correctly without considerable support is unlikely. The chances of her relapsing are even higher.'

'Can't her parents help? Or the father, or his parents?'

'She has nothing to do with her mum and dad, and she doesn't know who the father is, or won't say. I suspect she was raped, which isn't uncommon for young homeless women, but she will see that as weakness and admitting to it doesn't help her in any way. The state decides whether to take the child away after it's born. It's brutal, but it gives the baby the best chance of a normal life before any permanent damage is done growing up with a chaotic, dangerous mother.'

'Bloody hell,' is the only reply I can come up with. How can I have gone through life not knowing this sort of thing happens? I thought I had a good grip on how awful people's lives can be. 'I see why she'd be nervous about what tomorrow might bring.'

'Yes,' says Tex. 'It's rough to know the worst outcome for Rose-Marie is that she's released.'

We finish the admin tasks and wander the landings. Tex has a quiet word in many of the prisoners' ears. The morning is a peaceful time over here, but I'm starting to be able to sense tension.

Over on the male side, when trouble is brewing there's plenty of shouting and swearing, and slamming doors. It's more subtle here, but the atmosphere still leaches into your bones.

Tex comes out of Rose-Marie's cell after the promised chat. She puts her hands to her face and massages her cheeks, or is she wiping away tears? I know so little about Tex. Is she gay or straight, married or not? Or does she even have kids? There's just the dancing thing that got her that nickname, and it's hard to imagine her togged up in a cowboy outfit, clapping her hands, and moving in a line with a big smile. I feel I should make small talk as we go for the morning meeting, but I'm not sure what to say.

'Do you have kids, Tex?'

She doesn't look at me, but she answers.

'I was pregnant once but there were problems. I couldn't have any more afterwards.'

'I'm sorry to hear that. I won't mention it again.'

'No, that's okay. If we don't talk about these things, then nobody knows, and it just becomes a dirty secret.'

As she strides ahead of me it's painfully clear that she hasn't told me everything. Abruptly, she stops and turns.

'I want to help Rose-Marie, but I can't help thinking of the film *Rosemary's Baby*. Have you seen it?'

'I don't watch old horror films. What happened in it?'

'Let's just say it doesn't end well.'

27

The rest of the shift is fairly slow. If the inmates have a problem, they talk to Tex, not me. I receive a few smiles and some 'morning, sir's. They seem to be getting used to my presence. I hear over the radio that Fats's personal alarm has been pressed. Comms calls for First and Second Response to attend, which means it's serious, while Tex and I are staring out of the window at the prison gardens. I point to two big sheds and a thin wire compound.

'Is that where the chickens live?'

'Yes, just past the vegetable patch.'

'And the prisoners work with them?'

'Yes, about six inmates work in the gardens and a couple look after the chickens. Caring for something, even if it's only some carrots, is really beneficial for their well-being. Most of these kids have very little schooling. It's nice to see them finding pleasure in positive things. Many of them have never been to the countryside for a walk or even to the beach.'

We stand in companionable silence for a few moments. The sun is peeking through the clouds, making the raindrops glisten on the barbed wire.

'It's different over here,' I say.

'Easier or harder?'

'I guess just different. I'm sleeping better.'

Tex laughs. 'Don't worry, that will soon change.'

'It's weird to think we're working on Sandringham's wing. Did you know him?'

'No, not really. I'd say hi, and nod occasionally, but not much more than that. They found his body in the river under a bridge. It isn't clear if he jumped off or just waded in.'

'Any idea why he did it?'

'No, he was a good officer by all accounts. He lived with that Swiss woman who works in the admin building.'

'No way. Not Katrina?'

Everyone knows who Katrina is. She's tall and blonde, and looks as if she spends the weekends yodelling in the Alps.

'Yep, been going out nearly two years. She's pregnant as well.'

'What a snake. He kept that quiet.'

Tex gives me a funny look, and then I remember what happened.

'Sorry,' I say.

Seems as though Sandringham had it all. He was a catch, too, if you liked thin, pretty boys with a good heart.

'It's a damn shame,' says Tex.

'I suppose that's the true horror when people commit suicide,' I reply. 'You often can't understand why they did it.'

28

Just before the workers and trolleys come back for lunch, Tex says she needs to nip to the Details office, which is where they process the shifts, overtime and holiday. All of which they routinely mess up. She's been waiting on a holiday confirmation for a month. I almost ask where she's planning to go, but feel I've intruded too much already.

I have two more cells to check. Each cell is briefly analysed every day to make sure nothing is missing or damaged, from the frame, lights or window, that could be used as a weapon or help the inmates escape. It's also a chance to look for hooch or other contraband. On the male side, there are fifty-six cells so you don't have time to spend long on each one. I barge in whether they are sleeping or eating, only retreating if they are having a dump.

The cells are the same on both sides. Apart from a few bigger ones, which are used for inmates in wheelchairs, they are more or less the same size as a VW campervan. The luxury is similar. The bed is a metal tray bolted to the wall. If the cell is a double, they bolt one above it, but there's no extra room. There's a table, which is a sheet of plastic, also attached to the wall. On this rests the TV and they also eat their meals off it. There are two small, secured cupboards with no doors for them to put their things in.

The toilet sits in the corner, but the room is so small that the other person will hear every plop and tinkle. It has a plastic ridge next to the wall for privacy which is only private if the other occupant stands against the window. There's no escape from the smell because the barred windows don't open and often the vents are blocked or broken. It's a terrible moment for everyone when they get locked in for the first time, often with a stranger.

There are a few new plastic mattresses in the jail, but most are squashed flat by the multitude of bodies that have been lying on them over the preceding years. They wipe clean but it's best not to think about that. The sheets are washed out and cheap. The pillows thin and brown. You may live in the twenty-first century but our prisons do not.

Over here, it feels as if I'm intruding when I enter. There are only twenty-four cells, so I don't need to rush and can wait for everyone to have got out of bed. The last cell, though, has a sleeper in it. With the men, I'd clomp around, but now I'm conscious of what I'm doing. I feel stupid doing the search quietly. When I peer under her bed, the prisoner moves. When I glance up, it's the lairy inmate from yesterday, Billie.

'Morning, sir. Can you put it on the table?'

'Put what on the table?'

'My cup of tea.'

I stand up and laugh.

'I'm afraid breakfast finished three hours ago. If madam would like to come through to the dining room, lunch will be served shortly.'

She grins at me and shuffles herself upwards in the bed. I catch a glimpse of the side of her body and it's clear she sleeps naked. She bunches the duvet up over her chest. My mum used to describe girls like her as developed.

'Well, aren't you the funny one?' she says.

I step backwards to the door, averting my gaze.

'Wait a minute, sir. Are you on this wing permanently now?'

'No, just for a while.'

'Is it different to the men's bit?'

'It's pretty similar really. Obviously there are a thousand stinky men over there and they haven't got any chickens, but apart from that.'

She giggles, and it sounds out of place in the cell. It's light-hearted and free.

'You're a big man, so I reckon you can handle yourself.'

I'm not sure if she's pulling my leg or not. She smiles and does the thing where she hooks her loose hair around her ear. I back out of the room and close it behind me.

The returning workers are collecting at the gate. One of them is the sweet redhead who called me Uncle, who unsurprisingly is nicknamed Red.

'Come on, guv, get a jimmy on. I'm dying for a piss.'

I walk over and let them stream in. The food trolley arrives at the same time, seemingly being pushed by magic. Then I spot a perfectly made-up Tara Prestwick behind it, shoving it in with a grunt.

'Thanks, Tara,' I say. 'Is this what they call child labour?'

'Too right. I'll sue for millions.'

I lock the gates with her on the other side, but she doesn't leave. In the male serveries you need to be present when the prisoners open the food trolley, or the eighty chocolate bars for dessert are liable to go for a walk. Tex says it doesn't happen over here.

'What did you think, then?' Tara asks.

'About what?'

'What I'm in for?'

'I didn't look.'

She has a perplexed expression. 'Oh, I thought you'd check.'

'Did you now? Maybe you aren't as smart as you reckon.' I leave her dangling for a few moments. 'I was planning to, but I forgot in my haste to get out of this place. I'm betting you're a jewel thief.'

'Nope, I'm in for prostitution.'

Now it's me who's surprised. 'Bullshit.'

'No, really. Not what you'd think, but don't forget my nickname, Ruined. And that's what ruined people do. Broken said to tell you what she was in for too. She's in for theft *and* failing to comply with the terms of her licence after she was recently released.'

'Have any of you thought about not breaking the law?'

She smiles her big white teeth at me. 'People like us help ourselves. No one does anything for us. Besides, I've got a plan, and I also have a story...'

The redhead has come to stand next to me.

'Sir, where's the food list?'

'You okay, Red?' Tara asks her.

Red nods respectfully at Tara. 'Sure, Tara.'

'Cool, let us have a moment and he'll get it for you.'

Instead of the attitude I've been getting, Red scarpers.

Tara shakes the bars. 'See you, Dalton. I'll tell you about my plan and my past. Perhaps we'll really open your eyes to our world. Although I reckon you understand more than most.'

'What if I prefer my eyes closed?'

'I think we're going to be good for each other. We all need friends in here and someone to watch our backs, and that includes you.'

29

I cycle home in light rain to find the house empty. The kids will be at school, but Abi has left a note saying she's gone running. No kisses. Regardless, I smile. I feel at a loose end. Normally, I'd just sit around and watch TV or have a few beers, but I'm not tired and fancy doing something.

I get the hoover out, which gives off a strong burning smell after a few minutes, so I put it back where I found it. No point in getting the blame for breaking the vacuum cleaner, too. I used to do a series of press-ups, sit-ups and the like when I was younger and it was such a regular routine that I can still remember it now. Half an hour later, I'm aching, but pleased as I stretch my muscles afterwards. Following a long shower, I wander into our bedroom and find some clean clothes.

There's an opened letter on the table next to Abi's side of the bed. I pick it up and see it has a foreign stamp on it, presumably Spanish. It can only be from one place. I only consider my moral compass for a few seconds before I slide the insides out. It's a greetings card with what looks like a picture of a peaceful Spanish village on it. I sit down on the edge of the bed and open it.

The flowery joined-up writing takes careful reading, but the message is that they are sorry to learn Abi and the children are struggling, but they are more than welcome to come over at any point. There's plenty of room for them in the villa. Abi's dad tells her where the flights are the cheapest from and says to put it on her credit card and he'll send the money over. As far as I know, we haven't got a credit card. He'll obviously pick them up from the airport. My name isn't mentioned once.

We were all invited to their villa last summer, but I couldn't get the time off work, so Abi and the kids went without me and had a great holiday. Abi and Tilly visited the Christmas before Ivan was born, but there's never any chance of getting a week off in the prison at that time of year. Even though I didn't go, at least those times I was invited.

I hear the front door open and close downstairs. Abi must have returned. I slip the card back in its envelope, tiptoe to the steamy bathroom and pick up my toothbrush. Abi runs up the stairs. I turn and smile at her. She has colour in her cheeks, and a spark in her eyes that's been missing for more time than I can recall. Even though her hair is wet and bedraggled and make-up has run down her face, she looks like the woman I once knew.

'You've got to be kidding me,' she says.

'What?'

'I leave you a note to say I've gone for a jog. You know I have to pick the kids up at three. So, what do you do? Use all the bloody hot water just before I get home!'

30

I slept on the sofa. I wasn't ordered to, but it seemed appropriate. It was supposed to be my day off today, but I've come into work on overtime. It's an Agony shift, twelve-hours, but I figure if I'm on the female side, it won't wipe me out. Besides, we need the money.

Sheraton and I are on shift for the morning. Rose-Marie leaves the wing to go to court just as I arrive. There are about ten prisons for women in the country, compared to a couple of hundred for the men, because the judges sentence so few women to prison. The judiciary are very aware that if they send mum away, they are also sentencing her kids to an unstable, uncertain future with the stigma of a parent in jail. Most of the women already have issues with their mental health. Separating them from their children only makes it worse. It's a great way of creating the next generation of prisoners, though.

Sheraton and I get all the work done early, so I sit at the table in the office and finish off Sunday's paper. Billie knocks on the door. She looks different. Then I realise she has make-up on, and I can smell perfume. It's an incredible contrast to the normal aroma of a prison.

'I hope that's not perfume I can smell?' I ask her.

'No, it's deodorant. Do you like it?'

She must think I was born yesterday. It's way too strong for the alcohol-free perfumes they are allowed. That can be an argument for another day as she seems to be in a pleasant, sensible mood, albeit cautious.

'Lovely. What do you want?'

'I feel cheeky asking, but how do you get to work with the chickens?'

I glance out of the window behind me. Myerscough is the officer out there. He walked the male landings for years, then worked in the gym. They seem to be easing him out of here gently with ever more cushy roles. He still looks fit, but he's pushing sixty now. He had a breakdown not long after I started; something to do with his wife. It's not unusual for prison officers' marriages to fail. I may be about to have first-hand experience of that.

I've got no idea who they let look after the chickens. Gardening detail is a sought-after number on the male side, requiring a certain level of clearance, but there's always a screw present, so it's not like the orange bands who roam the prison without supervision.

'I'm not sure, but I'll find out for you. Are you keen on poultry?'

'I have plenty of experience working with animals. I've dated enough of them.'

I laugh, but she doesn't.

'You could get a suntan out there,' she says.

She leans over to read the back of the newspaper that I've folded and left at the end of the table. I notice how tight her spotless white jeans are. She has a dancer's figure, which also seems out of place here.

'Do you have a job interview, Billie?'

I gesture at her clothes and she blushes.

'It's for a visit this afternoon.'

She picks up my newspaper.

'Excuse me. Why are your paws on my paper?' I ask.

'Can I read it?'

With time-served male prisoners, it's well known they often start the grooming of an officer by asking for little bits and bobs, then slowly raise the bar. I'm wise to that, but it's only a newspaper that I was about to bin. Boredom is every prisoner's enemy.

'Go on, take it.'

'Where's the magazine?'

I laugh again. Cheeky mare. 'That's the only bit my wife likes.'

We both turn as the gates rattle. A posh voice reverberates down the wing.

'Cleaning products at the gate.'

I usher Billie out of the office and lock it behind me. With an accent like that, it can only be Tara. Each week, new mop heads, bleach, detergent and wipes are delivered to the wing for the wing cleaners.

'Come on, Billie, give me a hand putting this stuff away.'

I open the gates and Tara nudges the boxes through with her foot. She's also well-dressed with full make-up. She looks at Billie.

'Damage, how's things?'

'Fine, Ruined. How are you?'

Tara smiles at her in the manner of an older sister. Billie, like Rose-Marie yesterday, is respectful. So Billie is the other prisoner that calls Tara by her nickname – Ruined. Billie and I pick up the stuff, nod to Tara, and take it up to the storeroom. We get close as we put it away, and I'm very aware of it.

At lunchtime, I go over to the staff canteen with Sheraton. There's a big queue because it's burgers today. I tap the officer in front of me.

'Nice to see you back, Peasbody.'

'Cheers, Dalton. By the way, it's Peabody, with no S.'

'Oh, yeah, sorry. Why didn't you say before?'

'To be honest, I had other things on my mind.'

He glances around to see if anyone else is listening, but the person in front is moaning to her friend about how slow the queue is.

'Dalton, can I ask you a question?'

'Of course.'

'Are you scared when you go on the male wings?'

Sheraton also looks interested in my response. Normally, I'd just say no, but that's not going to help these guys. At some point, both of them will be called to work with the men again. Understandably that would make Peabody particularly nervous.

'Sometimes. You need to be wary over there. There are big men who are used to fighting and can break bones very quickly. Meaning there's always a level of caution. If you'd been over there longer with me, I would have explained how to manage those wings.'

'Can you explain now?'

The queue's not moving, so I nod.

'It's tough for everyone over there for the first six months, however big or hard you might be. There are so many inmates, many of them looking for an edge, and so many rules, that you have no idea what's going on. When you're new, the cons understand if they push, you'll probably weaken and let them out of their cell to make a call, or whatever they're after, because you don't know all the rules. But that's okay, because that's how you learn. When you arrive, it's their wing. You're the newbie. But any prisoners who arrive at the prison when you're already here will think you're part of the furniture.'

Peabody smiles. 'So, they don't take the piss.'

'Well, not as much, but most of the people who come to jail are nervous and have no idea how it works. They don't know anyone either, so you're potentially the only person that isn't after something. As time goes by, you'll learn who the gits are, who's violent, and who's decent. The best thing is to find an inmate on your wing who you can have a chat with. If the wing is bubbling, go and stand next to them and start a conversation. The other prisoners will automatically assume you're okay. That might be enough to stop any bother.'

Finally, the queue moves. We get to the front and Peabody has the last burger.

31

Sheraton left after lunch and Tex arrives for the afternoon shift. There's not much going on, so we ask the wing workers to clean the stairs. They handle a lot of traffic and get splattered with a variety of substances from food to blood. Billie is one of the wing cleaners, but has spent most of her time talking.

'Come on, Billie, you need to help too,' I say.

'I'm ill. I was sick this morning and yesterday.'

'A little bit of activity will make you feel better.'

'I can't stand the smell of the bleach.'

'If you don't join in, you can go behind your door.'

'But, sir, it's too hot in there.'

She flutters her eyelashes at me and pouts. My resolve wavers. I never had this problem with the men. I suspect she's making it up because she doesn't want to change out of her nice clothes for her visit later.

'Your choice. In or out.'

She gives me a furious glance and stamps off to her cell. I lock her in.

We have four ACCT books today for risk of suicide and self-harm. The idea is that, as an officer, you instigate a meaningful conversation with each person at least twice a day and document it. That way you can gauge their state of mind, but also show them they are not alone and someone cares enough to talk to them. People thinking of hurting themselves often distance themselves from human contact. Having a chat can stop that from happening.

I talk to Red, who is on one observation an hour, in her cell. It's a dirty room. She shares with a small girl who stares at the floor whenever she leaves her cell. They call her Scouse, but, having never heard her talk, even at the servery, I'm not sure if it's because she's from Liverpool or if there's another reason. Scouse is unkempt and has given up any effort to make herself look normal enough to fit in. She looks a little like a cartoon troll and most likely smells similar.

Scouse and Red's cell reminds me of a rubbish tip, which is telling of their mental health. There is not a centimetre of floor that doesn't have discarded clothes on it. A large droning bluebottle fly bumps lazily against the window. Even it has lost the will to live.

It turns out Red has tried to kill herself around twenty times. She tells me this in front of her pad mate as though she's talking about trips to the cinema. She used to work in the library but got sacked for aggressively flirting with the readers. Therefore, she currently spends most of the time banged up. In this weather, their cell is a muggy swamp. It smells as though the previous tenant died in here two weeks ago and they left the body under the bottom bunk.

Red usually wears a lot of clothing, but the hot afternoon sun is baking their cell so she only has on loose gym shorts and a T-shirt. Her arms, wrist to shoulder, and her thighs, knee to groin, are covered in gruesome self-harm marks. By far the worst I've ever seen, and I've seen plenty. There are cuts upon cuts, upon cuts.

It always surprises me how normal these girls sound. You'd

think they would be barking mad to do something like that to themselves, but Red just chats about her home and how she has two cats. She describes them down to their collar colour. It's too much detail and I suspect she doesn't have a cat at all. In fact, from what Tex said, she probably doesn't even have a place to go back to.

Billie's cell is next to Red's. She has her music very loud for someone who's poorly. I sneak a look through her observation panel. She has her eyes closed and her arms are crossed over her chest. She's swaying and slow dancing to Bryan Ferry's *Slave to Love*. Some girls own CD players, but they tend to be the white-collar prisoners. Billie's music is from the prison radio channel on the TV. She moves well, hips sashaying in a dreamlike state. It doesn't feel right to interrupt.

I remember dancing to the same song with Abi, not long after we'd met, at the wedding of one of her friends. It was one of those perfect moments that you have when you first fall in love. Safe in the knowledge that you are with the best girl in the world and your search is over, the beauty of obsession, and the belief that things will never change. But things do change.

I gently close Billie's panel and return to the office. On the male side, when prisoners take the piss, which Billie is clearly doing, you need to let them know you know. Even if they get out of going to work, you should make it an uncomfortable, even stressful, experience. One which they won't be keen to repeat. It's called control.

I have a thought and pick up the visits list for the afternoon. There's only one prisoner with a booked visit – Daisy, a prolific shoplifter from Market Deeping. That's the sadness of these youngsters. Few have family writing to them, less have people visit. We now have a roll of twenty and some, like Rose-Marie, are only on remand. That means they could book a slot for a visit every day if they wished. I suspect they do wish, but nobody comes.

There's also no visit time for Billie. I return to her cell. The song has finished, and she's turned the radio off, so I knock on the door and open it. She seems miles away still, standing next to the window and staring through the bars. Unguarded, she looks different.

'Afternoon, sir,' she says without looking at me.

'I just wanted to let you know your visitor is here.'

Her face is a picture. Her eyes look around the room as if to find an answer.

'Yeah, who is it?'

'Who were you expecting?'

I have to give her credit, she recovers fast.

'Okay, I made it up. If I'm honest, I felt embarrassed that I wanted to dress nice for you.'

'For me?'

She blushes. 'Not in a weird way, but most of the officers are kids, and you're a man. I didn't want to look all horrible and dull.'

I'm not sure what to say to that. To think I thought it was easy over here.

'How about putting your scruffs on and helping with the cleaning?'

'Okay, you win. Not much gets by you, does it?' She smiles. 'If I'm going to take my clothes off, you might want to close the door.' She winks. 'You can be on either side.'

I shake my head and pull the door to. Tex has been supervising the cleaning but has returned to the office to answer the phone.

'Rose-Marie's returned from court,' she says with a grimace.

'Bad news?'

'I assume so. She's bawling in Reception. I've said I'll go and fetch her.'

Tex races off. I sit in the office chair and write in the observation book that Rose-Marie is back, bringing us back to a roll of twenty-one inmates. I haven't made many comments in the book, so I scribble that we've cleaned the stairs today. A pair of shapely legs in tight shorts arrives in front of me as I'm writing. When my eyes track up, they reach an even tighter, cheap, thin T-shirt and a pair of erect nipples on a large pair of breasts. There's no sign of a bra. My eyes continue to Billie's face. She's doe-eyed.

It's lucky I'm sitting at the table, or my chin would be on the floor. Billie stretches her arms out, which jiggles her assets.

'Reporting for cleaning duty, sir.'

It's rare that I'm lost for words. I splutter something indecipherable. She smiles, sticks her tongue out, and leaves. I hear laughter from the other girls and a couple of wolf whistles. The gates clang, which I assume is Tex back with Rose-Marie, so I leave the office to check what state she's in.

Billie runs past me to see Rose-Marie and it's like a scene from *Baywatch*. I wander over and look at Rose-Marie's face, which is now crumpled over Billie's shoulder. Her shoulders heave with sobs and she makes a keening sound. She drags herself away from Billie and staggers towards me. I have a moment of horror where I think she's going to hug me, until I realise I'm standing outside her cell. I quickly open it and she rushes in and pushes the door shut.

When I turn back, Tex has squared up to Billie.

'Did you forget something, young lady?'

'No, miss, not sure what you mean.'

'Very funny. Go and put a bra on.'

'What for? I don't need one.'

'Put a bra on.'

'I don't remember reading in that welcome booklet that you gave me anything about having to wear a bra, so I won't.'

'It's provocative and against the decency rules.'

'Says who?'

'Says me. Now, put a bra or a shirt on.'

'No.'

'Go to your cell.'

Billie shakes her head. I take three steps closer, causing my keys and chain to jangle. Billie turns and glowers at me.

'I'm giving you a direct order, Damage. Now move!' growls Tex.

Billie has murder in her eyes, and my skin contracts at impending trouble. She leans in to Tex and snarls.

'Yes, boss.'

Billie spins on her heels and saunters past.

'Did you mind, sir?'

I keep my eyes on her face but say nothing. I follow Tex into the office; she drops into a seat.

'That girl is trouble,' she says.

'Seems so. Is she often like that?'

'Sometimes, but she can be sweet. I don't think she's had an easy life.'

'You called her Damage then. I thought you said you always used their first names.'

'She is the exception. I sometimes call her Damage to remind me of what I'm dealing with.'

32

I grab two tea bags out of my rucksack to make Tex and me a cuppa and to give her a chance to calm down. While they are brewing, something strikes me. I saunter around the female side with the mindset of not being in danger, but I'm a tall man approaching middle age. Tex is a short, fiftyish woman. If she gets into a scrap, one on one with a young inmate, the result wouldn't be a certainty.

Even though prison officers receive personal protection training, it's pretty basic and is more to do with delaying the fight until backup arrives. If an angry girl from the streets started on Tex, she could get hurt quickly, perhaps by someone like Billie. In fact, maybe that's why they nicknamed her Damage.

I place the cup in front of Tex and I'm surprised to see she's crying. She tries and fails to pull herself together. I stand in the doorway to monitor the wing and block anyone else from seeing her sobbing. After a few minutes, when I look back, she's wiping her eyes.

'You want me to have a word with Billie?' I ask.

Tex releases a snotty chuckle. 'It's not that silly girl, it's Rose-Marie.'

'Did she get years or something?'

'No, that's the thing. The evidence was damning against her. The judge had a word with the prosecution after looking at the details of the case. It's obvious Rose-Marie's had a rough time, and she's also pregnant. He said if Rose-Marie pleaded guilty and saved the state the cost of a trial, he would treat her leniently.'

'Isn't that good news?'

'Rose-Marie's solicitor reckoned on two years. She'd serve one, have the baby here, and be out a month afterwards, hopefully to some place with the kid.'

'Sounds like Rose-Marie's plan all over.'

'Yeah, but the judge was too lenient. She's seen so many women who are also victims that she only gave her ten months. Rose-Marie's served nearly five months already, so she'll be out in a few weeks.'

'Ah, not so great. There's no late checkouts here.'

'No, she's devastated. In a few weeks' time, she will be pregnant, homeless, skint, and more than likely back on drugs.'

'Can't the prison find her a room somewhere?'

'I'll get resettlement on it tomorrow, but it all takes time. There are forms to fill in and risk assessments to pass. She has violence on her record and the hostels are full. The one thing this country isn't short of is hurt women desperate for a safe place to stay.'

'Hasn't she got anywhere or anyone she can count on?'

'No, her dad abused her, so she can't go home. She burned the rest of her bridges. She's threatening to do something terrible. I'm trying to talk her out of it. She's mentioned committing another serious crime just to come back in. I tell you, Dalton, this world is fucking mental.'

With that, she cries again. It is sad, but I'm still not sure why Tex is so upset. Should she be this involved?

After an uneventful mealtime, when Billie stayed in her room and had her dinner brought to her, I push the food trolley out into the hub area. Tara is collecting the ones from outside each wing to take them back to the kitchens.

'Evening, sir, I'm looking for a big strong man to assist me with these trolleys. If you locate one, please notify me.'

'I've been searching for muscular men all day long, but no luck. I'll give you a hand until we find one.'

'Cool, I can give you the details of my plan. Sometimes I'm so thrilled by it that I can't sleep. But first, I should tell you my story.'

'Yeah, I'm interested. You know you talk differently to everyone in here.'

'It's part of the tale. Now, if you're pushing comfortably, then I'll begin.'

I open the houseblock doors and push the first trolley out.

'I had a fairly privileged life. My mother was a headteacher and my dad was a librarian. They met at Cambridge University and were both of the same ilk. Bookish, solitary people who liked helping others. We lived in a nice house in Helpston and they sacrificed many comforts to send me to a private school. My mother's parents were very old and still lived in Africa. My mum came over to study, but fell in love and wanted to stay. My father's parents disapproved of the love match, and completely distanced themselves, eventually retiring to somewhere in Devon. When I was twelve, my parents and I were hit by a joyrider and we ended up in hospital. I was the only one who didn't leave in a box.'

'Shit, I'm sorry to hear that.'

'Yes, being orphaned is quite a shock. I had nowhere to go. I entered the care system and was sent to a posh woman's house. Her name was Lavinia Burford. My mother's keen intelligence and my dad's plummy accent were passed on to me. The comprehensive school was okay, but I got bullied for the way I spoke and how clever I was. I was already struggling with bereavement and not having any counselling to help me through it. Kitty and Billie were already being fostered by Lavinia. They were also angry with life.'

'You fell off the rails.'

'Yes, all of us. They protected me from many who saw me as easy prey. No one messes with Billie, but we got mixed up in drugs and drink. I remember having a whitey and throwing up over myself. Billie undressed me and Kitty held me in the shower. They always looked out for me.'

'At least you had them.'

'Yes, but I was so unworldly to begin with that I didn't know how far I could fall until it was all too late. I still didn't need a bra at that point, but I was about to change. I've always been tiny and didn't have my period until I was fourteen, yet I'd been in front of the magistrates many times before that.'

I'm not surprised by her lack of boundaries. Many in here have either never been taught what they were, or have given up worrying about them.

'Did you ever end up in a juvenile detention centre?'

'No, you have to do something really bad for that. The youth court justices know what they're doing. Kids like us are already falling apart. Locking us away would make it permanent. You could probably argue that sending anyone to prison does that, but anyway.'

'Is that how you got your nicknames, like a gang thing?'

'No, incredibly it was the woman who ran the care home. She was always lovely to me. She did everything for us, too, our washing, ironing, dinners, you name it, but she was weird. Her husband was rich, but he'd left her and lived in London.'

'In what way weird?'

'At bedtime, she'd come to my room and brush my hair. She'd tuck me into bed and say, there, there, I'm sorry it's all been ruined for you. Then she would stroke my back or arm and just softly repeat the word. Ruined, ruined, ruined, and I'd fall asleep.'

We stop pushing the trolley and I open the doors to Main Street. She stares at me to gauge my reaction. I realise who she looks a bit like now. She's a smaller, thinner version of Nelly Furtado, but with brown eyes. Next to the big trolleys, she's so small, but she is strikingly attractive in a reserved way, more handsome than pretty. She's waiting for a response.

'Creepy,' I eventually say, even though that doesn't seem strong enough.

'Yeah, I knew it was odd at the time, but, you know, she was kind to me, and I needed a mother figure. She also bought me a lot of books because I love to read. It was a passion created at private school. I was the best at English by miles just before my parents died, and if you consider the highest achievers tend to be at private school, that's something. As you might imagine, reading is the only way I can tolerate this place. Anyway, Lavinia was doing the same thing to Kitty, apart from she was saying broken.'

'Gross. That's probably worse. What had happened to Kitty?'

'That's her story to tell. She thinks you're nice though. She reckons she can see people's auras sometimes and you have a special one.'

I smile. 'That's reassuring to know.'

'Don't get carried away. Good people still do bad things.'

With that, she rams the last trolley into the others at the kitchen door. I raise an eyebrow.

'Oops,' she says, 'but it makes me fume to remember it.'

'I've met quite a few prostitutes,' I say without thinking.

She nods with a raised eyebrow. 'I bet.'

'On a professional, rather than recreational, basis obviously. You don't fit the image I have. Why do you do it?'

'The money, of course. Are you thinking of skanky crack

whores? What about the posh pros who service the Premier League footballers? They call themselves escorts, but it's no different.'

'Why not just get a job? You're obviously very bright and come across well.'

'Because in the mess our lives became, we missed loads of schooling and most of our exams. I have no qualifications, a very unstable place to stay, no money, no experience and a criminal record. Would you give me a job?'

'Can't you go to college and retake your exams?'

'Wow, I should have spoken to you years ago, you'd have had me sorted out in no time. What would I be living on while I was studying?'

'Okay, smart arse, why don't you hook at night and study by day?'

We're walking back now, and she links arms with me. There's no one around, although there are cameras everywhere.

'That brings us nicely to my plan. I want to own a beauty salon. Nails, make-up, eyelashes, hair, the whole caboodle. A nice place just for women. I don't need qualifications for that. Kitty's going to work for me.'

'As the bouncer?'

'Do *not* be fooled by her appearance. She's actually a nice girl who's been through a terrible time. I'm smart enough for both of us, and she trusts me. All the girls do. I'm clever. I know things, but will the banks lend me any money? Hell, no! But then I discovered small business loans from Barclays. I did a business plan, worked it all out, the figures add up, and the advisor was impressed.'

'And they'll lend you the money? Nice one.'

'Not quite. Nothing's that easy. He said he'll match what I put down. They reckon if the owner doesn't have their own skin in the game, the business is much more likely to fail. We need £40,000 to rent some premises, deck it out, and keep us solvent for the first year. After that, it'll be easy just on repeat customers. Then I can rent bigger units, maybe even multiple places. I'm going to call it Birdies.'

'Ah, as in jailbirds. Nice. So that's why you've been working as a prostitute?'

'Correct! I'm saving up like mad and I'm halfway there, but I was getting impatient and took too many risks.'

'Is that what you do? Footballers?'

We've reached the hub area by now. She's buzzing with her salon idea.

'Those footballers want blondes with pneumatics. Am I anywhere close to that? And Peterborough doesn't have a Premier League team, anyway.'

'What do you do, then?'

'I cater for a specialist side of the market. It's great money, and I don't even need to have sex to get paid, just play a part with the occasional bit of touching.'

'You mean like naked cleaning?'

She leans forward to laugh, flashing those perfect teeth at me. 'Don't pretend to be innocent. You work on the male side. What do I look like?'

With that, she skips off to her wing. A wave of revulsion washes over me as I solve her puzzle. She looks like a boy.

33

For the first time since moving to the female side, I am drained when I leave, but it's not physical exhaustion. Myerscough is in front of me in the queue at the gatehouse. For someone who gets to work in the sunshine all day, he doesn't seem very perky either.

'You okay, Myerscough?'

He turns around and takes a moment to recognise me, despite the fact I worked side by side with him for a year.

'Hey, Dalton. You still alive?'

'Just about, you?'

'I'm retiring next January. That'll be fifteen years I've given this place.'

'Got any plans for retirement?'

'No, not so much. It's hard to imagine a life where I never come back here. Funny to think I'll probably miss it.'

He looks to the side and seems to peer into the distance despite staring at a wall. I notice his nose is red and covered in spider veins. Is that an age thing or a drink thing?

'Once a screw, always a screw,' I say.

'Yes, although whether that's good for your long-term mental health is hard to say.'

'I'll never regret working here, because it's really opened my eyes to what the world is actually like for so many people.'

He turns back to me and focusses his eyes. 'I won't either, but it affects us.'

I can't think of much more to say, not wanting to delve too deeply into that reply.

'Hey, Myerscough. I've got a YO who wants to work with the chickens. How does she apply?'

'Funny you should mention that. I currently have two girls out there. One is being transferred back to a jail near her home in a few weeks so she can have more regular visits and I had to let the other go today. She was just sitting around sunbathing.'

Myerscough has reached the front of the queue and drops his radio and keys down while I grin behind him.

'Prisoners, eh? You give them an opportunity…'

Myerscough gives me a suspicious glance.

'They're laying now, so we're selling the eggs. Half a dozen for a pound.'

'That's not too bad, them being free range and all that.'

'Has your YO got any experience with chickens?'

'It sounds like she's been involved with a few different types.'

Myerscough brightens. 'Ah, well, we have two breeds: Sussex and Rhode Island Reds. It'd be nice to work with someone enthusiastic for a change. It's a decent position, plenty of cleaning, mind. If you're in tomorrow, send her over at eleven. You can buy some eggs at the same time.'

Myerscough slips in front of two officers chatting and puts his index finger on the scanner. He smiles and waves at me as he leaves. I let two others pass through because I see Fats and Braddock clomping up behind me, chuckling together. I smile at them both.

'Happy to be going home, gents?'

'That's right, sir,' says Fats. 'I was just telling Braddock about your boy, Colt.'

'God, what's he been up to now?'

'Him and his gang are doing everyone's head in on the wing. You know what the YOs are like. They've just got too much energy to stay out of trouble. Gronkowski lost his rag today and told them to shut the hell up when they were messing about in the servery queue.'

'Oh, dear.'

Fats's face splits open into a huge grin and he chuckles loudly.

'Yeah, there were four of them. They all attacked him. It was funny really. I was behind the servery counting the food, so couldn't leave because the dessert was Penguin bars. I didn't realise that Lennox was off the wing. It was like *Jurassic Park*, man. You remember the bit where the velociraptors attack the T Rex, and they're too quick, and keep nipping him, and he looks clumsy, until he chomps them.'

I don't really want to know the end of the story but I suppose I should ask. Abi might want to know if her brother has been eaten.

'Are they alive?'

'Colt is. The other three are in Healthcare. That Colt is a crazy mofo, yes, sir. He was on Gronkowski's back, trying to gouge his eyes out. Gronkowski pulled him off and threw him down the wing, but, luckily, he didn't hit anything. First Response turned up and separated them, but Colt was ready for more.'

'He must be suicidal,' I say.

Fats and I share a look. We both know the truth. There's a generation of young men of all colours and creeds growing up who don't value life. Theirs or anyone else's. Everything's a game, and getting respect is more important than losing, even if that means it's game over.

When we get outside, Fats wanders off towards the car park.

'Your bike not fixed?' I ask. 'Want me to come around and help? I've got a spare puncture kit.'

'It's cool, Dalton, sorted, but Braddock offered to give me a lift this morning and I'm a lazy git given half the chance. He said Hitler has paid his dues. Invited me round for dinner tonight, too.'

Braddock smiles at me. 'My sister offered. I think she has a soft spot for his soft head.'

Fats's face reddens, and he scuttles off after Braddock. I watch them leave, feeling like a schoolchild whose best friend is going to another kid's house for tea.

34

Cycling home is a slog. I understand why Fats sometimes pushes his bike, but I force myself to continue pedalling. There's only a slim chance of a nice meal when I get back, but at least I can spend time with the kids. Yet, when I walk through the back door, the only thing waiting for me is another note. I pick it up with trepidation, but all it says is:

Gone to KFC with Maggie.

I take a shower and deliberately stay under the water until it runs cold. Let's hope Abi gets a sweat on with the Zinger burger. I step out of the bathroom naked and pad into our bedroom. Abi has pulled the stuff out from the back and on top of the wardrobes. There are two piles.

I rummage through the pile closest to me. It contains some running medals, a load of the children's school reports and those diary things they give you when they're born. I remember Abi filling in every box for Tilly, adding photos where appropriate, and ticking each milestone achieved. I pick up Ivan's. It's filled in properly at the start, but then tails off, until the entries finally stop. Poor Ivan. We can't help who we are. It's tough to be measured against other people's standards.

The other pile is of my old clothes and under that there's a big box of my knick-knacks and past bank statements. I pick up a few photo albums of the holidays I took before I met Abi. God, I look so young. My old friend, Martin, and I stare at the camera as though to say this is brilliant, but we know there are more good times to come. Perhaps it's better to believe that.

Growing up was tough without a dad. Perhaps that's why I have more patience than most with many of the prisoners who grew up the same way. Mums do a great job, but a man's hand is helpful when puberty hits.

I remember the last year of junior school. Our class had been performing a musical, *Aladdin*, and it was Father's Day. The headmistress thought it would be good to do a fathers-only performance. Ironically, I was one of the thieves. I just assumed that I would have nobody there, but when I stood up to sing my piece, I spotted my granddad at the back. He'd been ill for years with a variety of creeping cancers and had never come to anything before. I belted the songs out. I'm not sure why he made it that day. I never got the chance to ask him because he died a week later, but I've always remembered it. Afterwards, I swore that I would be a good dad, but I'm making a mess of it.

My attention returns to the piles. I pick up the little album of our wedding that Abi's mum kindly did for us. She gave us two copies, but I can't remember why. I think one was for my mum, but she fell ill shortly after. At the time, Abi joked that it was one each for when we split up. I place my copy back in the box.

It seems there's a pile for Abi and the kids, and a pile for me. I pull on a pair of jeans and a T-shirt. The house feels strange, as though nobody lives here. Perhaps they've left for Spain already and told me they were eating out to get a head start.

The fridge is pretty bare, as usual. I turn on the computer and make a cheese roll. There are two very plain-looking yoghurts at the back of the fridge. The type where you need to read the ingredients to find out the flavour. I don't notice how out of date they are until I peel the lid from the second one and get rewarded with a strange smell. I eat it anyway.

That's another thing that pisses me off about Abi. I'm busting my gut doing six or seven-day weeks, and she's out with the kids paying for fast food. We've had more recent yoghurts since these, and they were more expensive. Abi eats those first, chomps the fresh bread before the older stuff, and throws carrier bags in the bin, even though you pay for them now. She even throws food away that's still in date.

It's not a big deal, only pennies really, but it all adds up. I tell her that she wouldn't step over ten pence if she saw it on the floor, but maybe she would. Her family is used to having money. Perhaps scrabbling around for loose change is beneath them. The old laptop beeps and chugs, giving me time to empty the bins in the ten minutes it takes to boot up.

I surf various sites, but my heart's not in it, so I check my bank balance. The prison salary will drop in my account a week on Friday, but there won't be much left after the rent and bills come out. The Child Benefit money goes into Abi's current account but she also has a card for our joint account when that's run out.

I log into Facebook, but no one's interested in my life. Forty-six friends seems depressingly few compared to others. After a few clicks, photos of my friends' lives appear in my newsfeed in front of me. I haven't seen most of them for years, decades even. I've no idea who a few of them are any more. I click on Abi's profile. She has over six hundred friends. I have a look at her page. She used to post loads of pictures of us as a family, but it gradually became just the kids. There's been very little activity these last few months. There are a lot of birthday messages to her, which she hasn't responded to. Surely she's not too busy.

I find my thoughts dragged back to the prison and the girls. It's strange to think they live their lives without computers and mobile phones when the rest of us are glued to them. I picture Tara reading in her cell and remember her using the word angsty to describe the nurse at the med hatch. I grin when the online dictionary reveals that an angsty person is nervous and frustrated. Most of the prison nurses probably feel the same way.

I consider going to see Fats and Lena, but it'd be weird if he wasn't there. No one wants to come home and find their girlfriend and a work colleague sitting on the sofa together. My mind wanders to the jail and the chickens. I know nothing about raising chooks. If you put them in your garden around here, their life expectancy would be shorter than that of a KFC chicken.

I research types of chickens and their lifestyles, and think I'll print it off for Billie at the nick. She can wow old Myerscough with it. Our printer is ancient. I plug it in with the vain hope there's enough ink, and amazingly it seems to work okay. Abi and the children arrive home as I'm folding the piece of paper.

'Daddy, we had KFC!'

'Nice, did you bring me some back?'

'No, you said it was greezy!'

Tilly laughs. Ivan comes in behind her, looking tired. It's nearly 9 p.m., which I think is too late for him on a school night. It's another easy topic for me and Abi to enthusiastically argue over, where we let off steam instead of dealing with the real things that bother us. The kids drop into bed without a story, proving me right, but I keep silent about it. I make Abi and me a coffee while she does the washing up in silence. She must know I'll have seen upstairs.

We sit on opposite sides of the sofa watching the TV. It feels as if there's a force field between us. I don't believe it's up to me to mention the piles of belongings, but I can't be bothered with games any more.

'Are you going, then?'

'I think so. I've been sorting through our things.'

'I saw.'

'Maybe we should just have a holiday there for two weeks. Get our heads in the right place and some distance from our lives here.'

That's unexpected. I turn my head so I'm looking at her, and smile.

'I have enough holiday for a week, and I could pull a sickie for the following week. As long as I didn't go back with a suntan, nobody would know.'

She doesn't turn her head to match mine and the penny drops after a few seconds.

'The invitation to Spain is for three only.'

This time, she does look at me. 'Yes, only for three.'

'Don't your parents want our marriage to work?'

'They want the best for me and it's obvious I'm struggling.'

'What can I do to help?'

'Nothing. You're at work nearly every day.'

'Yes, but for us, for our family. I'm not there because I want to spend every second at work. We need the money. You must know that.'

'If I go to Spain, my parents can babysit and I can get rebalanced. I'm desperate for some space alone, to think, read, walk. Anything but have kids constantly pulling on my arms. I just need a full night's sleep where I wake up naturally, just that would probably save my sanity. I need to do it for me because otherwise I'm going to be no good to anyone.'

'You don't think I want those things?'

'You have a job, a—' She stops when she sees my eyes narrow.

'Go on.'

'I'm sorry, but it's already organised. My dad took charge and booked the kids and me open-ended flights for Saturday.'

'You aren't coming home, are you?'

'Honestly, I don't know.'

After this dismissive conversation, I'm not sure I want her back either, but I have to have Ivan and Tilly in my life. I need them to be with me, or all these years of bullshit will have been for nothing.

'What about me seeing my children?'

'You can use Skype or FaceTime.'

'Well, aren't you thoughtful? Is that forever? Or shall I have them alternate Christmases until they forget who I am?'

'Maybe Ivan will be better in a quieter environment with his grandparents.'

'What? You're kidding, aren't you? If your dad wanted to help, he could send us cash for a deposit on a house instead of paying for the flights to separate us.'

'I might have known you'd bring it back to money.'

'Well, stop wasting it when we don't have any. How was KFC? We had curry at the prison. It was hard to identify the meat, but I ate it because it was free.'

She stands up and scowls at me, but there's a high-handed expression on her face. The horrible cow has set me up. She was waiting for me to mention KFC.

'Maggie paid. She knew you'd moan otherwise.'

'Oh.'

'Apology accepted. I have more good news. I found a big puddle of oil under our shit car.'

With that, she stomps up the stairs. Our bedroom door slamming indicates I will be sleeping in my usual spot. Aren't relationships great? Abi will now use my moaning about her spending to ease her conscience when she clears off with my children.

I need to think. I turn the TV off and sit in the dark. After an hour or so, my mind automatically starts making plans. I could just about afford this place on my own, but it would be tight. I'd be better off saving my money in a house-share. There might even be people like me who'd want to go for a beer or the cinema one night.

It's strange to be in this situation. If this had happened in the past, I wouldn't have given a damn. Screw Abi. I'd have just got my stuff and gone to my mum's, but I have a family now. I can't lose without a fight. What do I do? What can I do?

It makes me think of Mum. Things would be better if she were here, I'm sure of it. But she left me too.

35

FUNERAL

My mother died suddenly. She had a seizure, went into hospital, and a few hours before her bypass operation, her heart stopped. She never regained consciousness. Tilly had just started school and Ivan had started failing to meet developmental milestones. We were already stressed. My mum had been having Tilly overnight at times and had been a great help. I knew we would miss my mum in so many ways.

We weren't sure whether to take the kids to the funeral. In the end, we decided to spare them the experience. Maggie turned up to babysit but Ivan had one of his terrible tantrums and we thought it was best that Abi stay behind. My mum's funeral was the day I realised how selfish I had been towards my mother, but it was too late to make amends. I spent the entire service lurching from sorrow to shame. It was hard not to think of my promises to be a success. Was she proud of me? I'm not even proud of myself.

Her closest friend, Elaine, arranged the wake and funeral with me. Luckily, my mum paid into a funeral plan and with a bit extra we were able to give her a good send-off at the community hall.

Everyone said kind words, and a lot of people came, but I knew virtually none of them. They all mucked in and helped tidy up at the end.

Finally, it was just Elaine and me saying goodbye to the caretaker. Elaine was similar to Mum: overweight, widowed and easy-going.

'Thanks for helping, Elaine. I couldn't have done it without you.'

'Do you want me to meet you at your mum's to sort through her things? We had a chat in case something like this happened, so either of us could sort out the other's affairs.'

'That'd be great. I don't suppose you know if she had much money. I'm about five hundred quid out of pocket for this.'

Elaine shook her head.

'No, Jim, she struggled to make ends meet. Us women from our generation don't have pensions, and when our husbands go first, we often find it hard to get by. You might make a few quid by selling her white goods, but the rest of her stuff is old.'

I knew that she didn't have much, but I'd always thought she wasn't bothered with material possessions, as opposed to not being able to afford them.

'Was she happy?' I asked.

'Of course. Although she missed your dad, despite his uselessness. She talked about you all the time and loved your visits. We often had a laugh about what you got up to. She used to joke that she couldn't wait for you to split up with your girlfriend again because you'd be back at home.'

Elaine kissed me on the cheek.

'Don't feel guilty. You have to go and live your life when you're young. It's the curse of parenthood to be left behind.'

I appreciated her kind words, but they were an ineffective balm to the guilt that swamped me. I'd barely seen my mum in the last few years apart from to drop the kids off or to pick them up. How often did I stop for a chat? Or give her some money for helping out? She was always buying things for the children. I now understood she was going without to pay for them. My poor mother was lonely and poor, and I was too selfish to notice.

36

I have an early shift today and tomorrow, and then a seven o'clock start on Saturday. Abi and the kids' flight is at 10 a.m. on Saturday, so we'll be leaving the house at the same time. I'm dreading it. My sleep is no longer peaceful. My mind churns between thinking it will be good for us to have some space, and horror at the move becoming permanent.

Her father has kindly paid for a taxi for them to the airport, which at least means I have the car, assuming whatever's leaking is fixable.

I'm on the YO wing with Sheraton and I watch him work with a new respect. He still walks as though he's carrying a couple of rolls of carpet, but he's engaged and friendly with the girls. It's clear he's genuinely interested in what the prisoners are saying to him as he talks to them while they are pulling the mops and brushes out.

After the morning meeting, I stand in the office doorway searching for Billie. She comes out of her cell and stretches as if she's just woken up. She doesn't seem to have done any cleaning so far. Her tight T-shirt is too small for her and reveals a few centimetres of stomach that are bright white. She must have been sewn into her black Nike tracksuit bottoms. I beckon her over. She fails to keep eye contact as she steps slowly towards me, as though life has taught her always to expect bad news.

'You have an interview at eleven.'

'To do what?'

'Egg collector.'

'Eh?' Then her face opens up. 'No way, for real?'

'Yes, don't get too excited though. Myerscough is interviewing a few for the role.'

She doesn't look excited.

'Fuck it. There's no chance they'll give me the job. Thanks for offering, but I'll pass.'

I gasp as she walks away from the office.

'Billie, come back here.'

She returns but doesn't look at my face.

'Just go. Someone has to get the position. Why shouldn't it be you?'

'I don't know what I'm doing. I've never had no proper interview before. What do you do at one?'

'You answer the questions.'

'What are they?'

'How would I know? I'm not the chicken master. Myerscough is.'

'Is he the weird old guy or the fat younger officer? I've seen two out there.'

'The older gentleman.'

'All I know about chickens is they like rolling in mud and dust. That's it. Oh, and the Mayo Chicken at McD's is really good. Cheap, too.'

'See, you knew more than I did. Look, I printed this off for you. It's information on chickens. You can knock him dead. It says chickens bathe in dust to get rid of mites and things. Remember it all, tell him you love animals, you're reliable, and you won't let him down.'

She reads the information sheet very, very slowly, especially considering there's only five facts. I wonder about her reading skills.

'The letters c and p are missing on here,' she says.

I take the sheet off her.

'Oh, yeah. Sorry, my home printer is on its last legs.'

'Makes it tricky to read when it's about chickens.'

Finally, she looks at me. The sunlight from the big window at the back of the wing strikes her blue eyes, making them sparkle.

'You did this at home for me?'

I nod.

'Sod it. I'll try. Shall I go dressed like this?'

'They aren't recruiting for ring girls at a boxing match. Just dress sensibly. It's a physical role outside. Don't you have any loose clothes?'

'Tara sent me a load of stuff in before she arrived herself, but I've put on weight since I was here. I go to the gym like mad and do loads of exercise in my cell, but I was skinny when I arrived. You'll have to bring some clothes in for me from Next. I've got a catalogue and marked a few, so it'll be easy enough.'

'Very funny. Take the interview seriously, and you'll be fine.'

Suddenly, she looks focussed. She flicks her hair back and takes a deep breath.

'Thank you.'

'No worries. One last thing, I was just wondering what you were in for.'

'Why?'

'There's a different level of clearance out there. You're next to the gardens, so if you were in for threatening people with a pitchfork, they'd probably think twice about letting you loose.'

'Oh. Well, me and my partner were in the street and some guy walked past with an expensive phone. My partner, impulsively like, pushed him over and grabbed the phone, then legged it. I wasn't hanging around to get caught, so I ran away too, but there was CCTV and they found us.'

It's a rather fluffy explanation of street robbery, which must be a terrifying experience for the victim. It's no wonder Billie got two years for it. I'm not sure what that would mean to Security, but it's not important at this point.

'Go and get ready. I'll walk you down when it's time.'

I spend the next bit of the morning drinking tea in the office while thinking about not seeing my children for two weeks. Sheraton has done all the searching and is on top of the ACCT book observations. The wing is deathly quiet, which would have me patrolling the landings on the male side looking for trouble. Instead, I eat a bag of crisps and flick through *Cosmo*, which Tex must have brought in.

At Billie's interview time, I knock on her door in case she's getting dressed.

'One minute,' she shouts out.

A few seconds pass, then she opens the door but steps backwards to the bed. She's wearing a loose blue shirt and white, three-quarter length jeans. The shirt is completely undone at the front, revealing half of each nipple.

'Do you reckon I'll get it like this?'

'Come on, Billie. Do that up. You'll get me sacked.'

I step outside and pull the door shut. Half a minute later, she glides out of the cell with the shirt buttoned up and I lock the door behind her. We walk along the landing. Rose-Marie, who is half-heartedly mopping the floor, gives her an up and down.

'You at court again, Billie?'

'Yeah, I'm going to tell them you did it.'

Rose-Marie laughs and mimes 'wanker' at her.

We stop at the gate, where Billie takes deep, slow breaths. Myerscough is walking past.

'Hey,' I shout to him. 'I was bringing her over.'

'I just brought one of the other interviewees back, so I'll take her with me. Save you a trip.'

Billie turns to me.

'Wish me luck,' she says.

I just smile because she won't need it. The rest of them don't stand a chance.

37

Billie's away for forty-five minutes and it's Sheraton who lets her back on the wing. She goes straight to her cell. I supervise the servery at lunch, but Rose-Marie does a decent job. Billie and her pad mate are the last to come out.

'Well? How did you get on?' I ask.

'Good. I remembered your research, and I feel confident.'

She smiles mischievously at my raised eyebrows, then picks up her cellophane-wrapped sandwich, crisps and fruit. She takes one glance at the sandwich and lobs it towards the bin. Two Romanian girls, who are nervous and furtive, have just arrived. They look as though their journey over here cost them more than money. Their empty eyes follow the food's arc as it thuds into its destination. They wait for me to leave.

The Italian girl, Zelda, whom Billie shares her cell with, collects her food and gives me a hard stare before walking away. It's the kind of glare that puts you on edge on the male side and has you looking over your shoulder for the rest of the shift. I notice she has the same Nike tracksuit bottoms on that Billie was wearing earlier. I wonder if they're Billie's or hers, although it's not unusual for girls to share their clothes. Even the men do it for special visits from girlfriends and wives.

We've just locked up after lunch when the office phone rings.

'Whisky 1,' I say.

'Hi, is Officer Dalton on there?'

'Speaking.'

'Hi, it's Kennett in Details. You want some overtime?'

I glance out of the window. When it's icy, the prison has a sense of menace. In the sunshine, though, it seems benign. The prisoners dawdle to soak up the rays as they walk between Main Street and the houseblocks. It's not so bad here then, and I've got an oil leak under my car to pay for. But I know how to play the game.

'No, thanks.'

'Come on, Dalton. Time and a half.'

'Overtime is always time and a half. That's like telling me dogs bark.'

'I'm desperate. I've always loved you, Dalton.'

'Ooh, tempting. After all, you are my type.'

Kennett is the hairiest man I've ever met. Neck, arms, you name it.

'Time and three quarters.'

'What's the overtime for, Kennett?'

'It's an escort.'

'And?'

'You want the prisoner's blood type?'

'Spit it out.'

'Funeral escort. It's Glenn Bell, his mother died.'

'Ooh, nice. Those mourners just love us.'

'I'll owe you. It's local, but it starts in fifty minutes.'

I smile. Now I know that fine detail, I really do have leverage. At this brief moment in time, Kennett is the most desperate man in this place.

'I want Christmas Day and Boxing Day off this year. I'll do all of New Year's in exchange.'

'Done.'

'And double time.'

'Don't push it. Get your arse straight over there.'

I put the phone down and quickly leave the office. When I'm striding through the sterile area to Male Reception, I pass Tex, who's on her way in. She's stooped and barely waves. Escorts are two-man jobs unless the prisoner is high risk, then it's more. When I get to the reception desk, I ask SO Odom who's doing the escort with me.

'Officer Flynn from the female gym. I'm glad it's you that's going, Dalton. He's kicking off.'

I find Flynn in a room with Glenn Bell, who has two black eyes. Brilliant. I vaguely know him. He's one of Colt's posse, who messed with Gronkowski.

'Come on, bruv,' he shouts. 'If we miss it, there's gonna be bare trouble. Swear down.'

'Enough, we've got plenty of time if you shut your mouth. Here's the warning. You piss me off once, that's it. You're straight into the taxi, and back here. You say goodbye to your mum when you're released.'

'Okay.'

'Promise.'

'Come on, man. I promise.'

I nod to Flynn. She cuffs his hands together in front of him, then cuffs his right wrist to my left wrist. The SO comes in and checks they are secure. We follow him and he opens the reception gate. A taxi is waiting. Flynn's role is to make notes, carry the mobile phone in case we get jumped, and be in charge. My role is usually to look serious. Funerals are different. There will be a lot of emotions and, ridiculously, some of the prisoner's family will think it's the escorts' fault that their little boy is in handcuffs.

It's hot in the taxi, especially with my jacket on my lap, but I brought it for a purpose. Glenn is, for obvious reasons, quiet. He's a big unit for a young lad, and our shoulders touch as the taxi swings around a corner. The youngsters shave their heads to seem older, but Glenn has a ruddy youthful complexion and acne on his chin. I can feel how tense he is next to me. The church isn't far, so I need to get started.

'Were you close to your mum?'

'Yeah, very.'

'Mums still care, even when everyone else has given up.'

He moves his hands and therefore my left hand to his face to wipe away a tear.

'Your dad about?'

He shakes his head.

'Brothers or sisters?'

'Yeah, two sisters.'

'Okay, the rules are that you don't touch anyone, but, as long as you don't take the piss, I don't mind a bit of hugging and kissing, but not with me.'

He laughs and a little jet of liquid comes out of his nose. I feel some of it land on my wrist. You need to talk to these angry young men as if they are human because they aren't used to it.

'Glenn. Don't worry about crying. There are no cowards at funerals, only sons saying goodbye to their mums.'

By the time we pull up, Glenn is weeping. I almost have to pull him from the taxi. When we're out of the car, I fold my coat over the handcuffs, so you can only see the edges.

'Twenty minutes,' Flynn tells the driver.

Everyone's already in the church. The coffin is at the front. The place is rammed. If it's going to kick off, now will be the time. Especially with the state of his face. A short, elderly lady limps towards us with a sour expression. She stares at me, then grins.

'Oh, thank you for bringing him. Ah dinnae think he was coming,' she says with a heavy Glaswegian accent. 'We really appreciate it.' She roughly grabs a big chunk of Glenn's cheek.

'Come here and give ya Aunt Mary a cuddle, ya wee bastard.'

She smothers him into a big hug, which presses my hand against her ample bosom. Her moist eyes look up at me.

'We've got space for two at the front,' she says.

'I'll wait at the back,' says Flynn, who stifles a smile.

Flynn has worked in the jail for years and is solid. She's an athletic type with many admirers, but another one of those who keeps prison life separate from home. Any hopes of a date are dealt with abruptly. She understands that even if I had Fats here, nothing could withstand a crowd this size. But it's just another task in the day of a prison officer.

I usher Glenn to the front with my head down. The crowd wants subservience and respect. In return, they will act accordingly. Glenn's sisters are scary, bigger versions of him. One of them surveys Glenn with grim fury, while the younger one winks at him.

The service is over quickly. Reading between the lines, the vicar does a good job with someone who has died too early after living a volatile life. Outside, approximately twenty people suffocate Glenn in hugs and kisses.

'Come for a drink at the wake,' says Aunt Mary to me.

'Tempting, but me and Glenn won't be drinking today. Thanks for keeping things sweet,' I reply with a nod.

We get back in the car and return to the prison. When we arrive outside, we sit and sweat for nearly an hour due to an 'incident' inside. It's fine, though. Glenn's almost catatonic, and Flynn and I are on overtime. Finally, the taxi enters through the vehicle gate. Again, I practically have to carry Glenn from the car. The same

Senior Officer opens the reception door for us. Two new arrivals are being processed.

I stand in front of Glenn, so they can't see his face.

'You all right, Glenn? Talk to me.'

'I'm okay. I just can't believe I'm not going—'

His face crumples.

'Try to focus on the good times. Now, wipe your eyes and take some deep breaths.'

He does as I suggest.

'Stand up straight and hold it together until you get back to your cell. Crying is fine at the church, but not so cool inside here. Tell me, did anyone give you anything to bring into the prison?'

'No, guv. Swear down.'

'Okay, step to the reception desk.'

Odom watches Glenn walk towards him, then stares over Glenn's shoulder at me. I give him the nod. Flynn and I have a quick coffee in the kitchen area, then call it a day. We stroll past Glenn as he's being searched by Odom.

'What's this?' asks the SO, holding a small cellophane package up.

'How would I know? My hands were cuffed,' says Glenn.

'Come on, you must have felt it go in your pocket?'

'Have you just planted it on me?'

Flynn and I chuckle as we wave goodbye to Odom.

'Take it easy, Glenn,' I say. 'And well done for being decent today. Can't have been easy.'

Glenn turns to look at me. He's not sure what to say to that. He clenches his fist and bangs his chest twice.

'Whose are the drugs?' asks Odom without hope.

I'm still smiling as I unlock my bike. My guess would be that it was the younger sister who slipped him that wrap. Maybe it was Aunt Mary, wanting the wee bastard to raise a spliff to his old ma tonight. It's another nasty consequence of being sentenced to prison, which no one ever considers when they get sent down. Days like these can't be retrieved further along the line. Glenn has plenty of free time to think about that. Perhaps this will be his rock bottom and he'll decide to change.

I realise that I referred to him by his first name, whereas I'd have called him Mr Bell before. Is working on the female side making me soft? Oh, no. I also remember that I forgot to ring Abi to say I was staying on.

38

I slept well on the sofa last night. I cycled home expecting a big row, but Abi and the kids were out at Maggie's again. They'd left me a doughnut from a pack of four. I realised that in a few days, even that won't happen. I paced through the house, popping my head into the kids' bedrooms. Nearly all their stuff was packed and ready to go. What remained looked unwanted, me included.

My family were still asleep when I left this morning. It's Tex and me on today. We only have a roll of sixteen because of a few releases, and Zelda and two of her co-defendants have gone to HMP Bronzefield for their trial at the Old Bailey next week. They'll stay there until it's finished. I assume they'll be back if they are found guilty. It must be serious for their trial to be at the Old Bailey. I should look up what Zelda's in for, but I've been saying that for loads of the inmates. My motivation for checking on the male side was one of safety. I don't really care what they are in for over here.

Tex started the day's cell searches but hasn't come out of Rose-Marie's cell. It's been an hour now, so I pop my head around the door, where I see them both crying. I tell Tex that I'll finish off the AFCs, which is the official name for the searches; Accommodation and Fabric Checks. Under the last bed, I find a bag of mouldy fruit. It's hard to say if it's definitely being used to brew hooch because it smells so minging and isn't sealed properly, but it's a pretty safe bet it is. I have to say the men are better at it.

It's in the Romanian girls' cell. They look petrified when I hold up the bag.

'Whose is the hooch? Is this yours?' I ask the tall girl, Ana-Maria.

'Sorry, no English.'

'You?' I say to the smaller one, Mihaela.

'No English.'

Neither make eye contact. It's funny, because I heard Mihaela arguing about not getting a banana yesterday at lunch, and her English flowed nicely. I'd be amazed if the hooch was theirs. They haven't been here long enough to accumulate that much fruit or sugar. I pick it up, carry it out of the cell, and throw it in the bin. I catch Laimutė Laurinavicius frowning from the top landing as she watches me do it. There's the culprit, but it would take all day to put her on report with a name like that.

Some of the cons dismissively refer to her as The Russian even though she's Lithuanian, I think, and doesn't speak great English. I've not had any kind of conversation with her yet, not even in sign language. She's nearly as tall as me, but so thin. Her face has extensive acne scars, which detract a little from her prettiness, but she hasn't caused any obvious trouble. It's hard to guess who's running this landing, if anyone. Maybe it's her. The clever ones with their heads down are often pulling the strings.

I write the find in the obs book in the office and fill in a security report about the hooch. The phone rings. It's Myerscough from the gardens.

'Hey, Dalton, just ringing to say that Billie Harding was the successful candidate. She'll work every morning, and the current girl can continue in the afternoons until she leaves. She can start tomorrow.'

'Cool, thanks. She'll be made up.'

'No problem, Dalton. You going to buy some eggs?'

'I will do, mate, but I cycled in today. Do you deliver?'

I laugh as he disconnects the line. Billie is brushing the floor near the office. I call her in.

'I just had a call.'

'Not the police?'

'No, from the chickens. They wanted to say they can't wait to work with you in the mornings from now on.'

'No, fucking, way. I got it,' she whispers. 'I really got it!'

Before I can move, she steps forward and pulls me into a body-length hug. She gives me a huge wet kiss on the cheek. I give her a little squeeze in reply, but grab her shoulders and move her back.

'Well done. Go and tell your mates.'

It's a warm day, but I feel much hotter all of a sudden. Billie runs up and down the wing shouting, 'I got the fucking job.' Tex finally leaves Rose-Marie's cell.

'You okay?' I ask her.

'Don't worry about it.' She gestures to Billie. 'It's nice when they taste a bit of success. That's probably one of the first things she's achieved. Hopefully, she'll learn the value of trying hard for something instead of just taking it.'

Billie is positively bouncing at lunchtime. She keeps attempting to dance with people, so I keep out of her way. It's five minutes to lock up, when I hear loud music from Rose-Marie's cell. Billie comes steaming out of Rose-Marie's cell door, which she leaves open, and the song fills the landing. It's Len Boone's *Love Won't Be Denied*. It's a local classic. There's a kind of line dance called the Peterborough Shuffle that they always do in nightclubs around here. I've even seen the routine on YouTube.

'Come on, Miss,' says Billie, and starts doing the moves in front of her. Rose-Marie stands next to her and joins in.

'Dare ya,' I say to Tex.

Soon, the entire wing is in line, Tex included. Even the Romanians are trying to copy the others. They all move up and down the landing, laughing and singing the chorus. Billie winks at me as she passes. Jessica and Red bump into each other and giggle like schoolchildren. I spot the SO, Nasima, at the gate. I wander over, dodging the prisoners' arms trying to drag me in. I'm laughing when I get to the gate, thinking that the only group thing the male prisoners enjoy with such enthusiasm is rioting.

'Ma'am.'

'All ready for bang up, Dalton?'

'There's one or two out of their cells, but we should be on time.'

Her face has half a smile, but her eyes are cool.

'Take it easy there, Dalton. Don't get too close to them.'

I nod, but I can still feel Billie in my arms.

39

My bike has a puncture when I leave at lunchtime. I got offered overtime again in Male Separation and Care. I'd heard someone is shitting up in there, which means they are smearing their own excrement over their walls, window, and door. Triple time wouldn't tempt me to work in there on a baking hot day like today. I don't mind the walk home. It will only take just over an hour. I need some peace to think anyway.

Abi and the kids fly out tomorrow. I don't know what to say to them, or her. Asking her not to go seems pathetic, because it's only a holiday at the moment. What would I do if I had the opportunity of a break? She clearly needs one. Perhaps if she returns refreshed, we can get through this tough phase. Life was so much simpler before children, but would I trade in what I have? I could tell her not to come back. Draw a line under the whole thing. I allow myself a little grin, knowing my priorities changed the moment I had children. Even forgetting that, from what I've seen of life, if you start another family, the same problems rear their heads again further down the road.

I blow out a big breath as I walk along the rowing lake. The sun's beating down, but there's a breeze here. I think of the girls dancing and laughing on the wing. That's the craziness of prison right there, but it's just a distraction.

When I did roll count afterwards, many were withdrawn. Feeling alive in jail is a double-edged sword. It makes you remember those on the outside and what you're missing. Time slows, and the nights draw out, especially if it's children that you've left behind.

When I get home, I'm dripping with sweat. My mood deteriorates while fixing the puncture in the front tyre. Tilly rushes over and wraps her arms around me as soon as I open the lounge door. Sobs wrack her little body. Abi rises from the sofa with a determined look on her face. I pick up Tilly and press my nose against her neck. She has her very own smell. I inhale deeply, not knowing when I'll next be able to. After thirty seconds, I crouch and put her down.

'Daddy, come with us. I hate your job.'

I glance up at Abi. So that's how she's told Tilly. I'm not sure if that's clever or devious. I suppose telling her the truth wouldn't be very helpful unless she's made up her mind to stay out there.

'Next time, sweetie,' I reply to Tilly. 'Did you tell Ivan?' I ask Abi.

'No, I thought it best to wait until we were there.'

All of a sudden, I understand that this could be it. They leave tomorrow. I drop onto the sofa and put my face in my hands.

'Go to your room for a few minutes, Tilly,' says Abi.

After she's gone, I brace myself for bad news.

'Jim, I don't think we're coming back. Maybe we'll stay there for a few months, but perhaps more. I can't get my head straight here. What will you do if we don't return?'

Finally, the anger arrives.

'Are you fucking mental? That's called quitting. Poor Abi. Is it all too hard for you? Going to ask Mummy and Daddy to look after your children for you because you're not up to it. You're a failure. A disgrace. You're taking my kids away from me because you've given up. If there was any way I could raise them myself, I'd tell you to get on the plane alone and burn your passport at the other end.'

I expect a furious reply from her, but her lack of venom hurts more.

'I'm sorry, Jim. I've left as much money in the account as I could. Hopefully you'll be able to afford to stay here at least until August when the lease runs out, then we'll have somewhere to return to if that's best for us. If I need any more money, I'll email and ask. I won't use the card otherwise, but my dad said he'll pay for meals out and travel until we have a plan.'

'You mean if that's best for you. Do you really expect me to sit around for a couple of months and wait for you?'

'Don't be like that.'

'Don't be like that?' I feel the tension in my face as it curls up with fury. 'We're done. If you come back, I'm off. You've made your choice, and that wasn't me. Do you think you can leave with my kids and I'll be all easy-going and let's see what happens? You're off your head.'

I stand up and close my eyes, knowing I'm scatter-gunning insults because I'm hurting.

'Jim, please have one last dinner with us before we go. I bought burgers and some buns. We've got chips in the freezer.'

My head is ready to explode. I do what many other weak men before me have done in such circumstances. I grab my wallet and head for the pub.

40

I drink four pints of strong lager at The Dragonfly pub, spending nearly twenty quid. I'm too annoyed to get drunk, and it feels like a waste of money. Instead of having another one, I walk to the Spar and buy a six-pack of Stella. With few options, I head to Fats's house and ring the doorbell. After a full minute, Lena opens the door.

'Apologies, I've been painting the bathroom ceiling.'

At my confused face, she smiles. 'Just kidding. I was watching *Friends* reruns on Netflix, and it took me a while to get in the chair.'

'Ah, sorry. I should know that disabled people joke as much as normal people.'

She laughs long and hard.

'It's perhaps more pleasant to say, people with impairments like to laugh as much as non-disabled people.'

I pull a Wallace from *Wallace & Gromit* face.

'Oops.'

'I'm just pulling your able legs, that's all. Are you after Fats?'

'Yeah, is he in?'

'No, he's at Braddock's. I think he's made a friend there.'

'Ah, no worries. I was bored and looking for company.'

'Well, me too! Enter my domain.'

She's backed away and hurtling towards the kitchen before I can respond, so I shut the door behind me and wander in.

'Are those beers cold?'

'Yep, icy. Took them from the back of the cabinet.'

I sit next to her at the table and pass her one over. She takes it, opens the ring pull, and has an almighty glug. She lets out a long, low burp, which reminds me scarily of Fats. I can see what attracted them to each other.

'Come on, doofus, put the rest in the fridge before they get warm.'

'Does Fats see a lot of Braddock now, then?'

'Yep. They're on the same shift pattern, so Braddock gives him a lift in most days. Fats never did like that bike, even after your joke.'

'And that doesn't bother you?'

'Which bit?'

'Him leaving you here while he's having a good time.'

'Hell, no. He has a life to lead. I'm the only one stuck in this chair. Actually, it's helped make my mind up. Before all this, I did the accounts at the slaughterhouse. I liked it, the numbers and all that, but Fats and I left together. Since the accident, I've had rehabilitation, and I did a course in bookkeeping.'

'And passed?'

'Yes, but that was a year ago. I've been dossing around the house, getting fatter, and putting off rejoining the real world. I thought people in chairs were wheelchair-bound and that's how it feels, but I've realised that if Fats can get over his shyness and make friends, then so can I. From now on, I'm a wheelchair user, and I'm applying for jobs.'

With that, she finishes the can, gives a little whoop and throws it in the corner of the room, missing the bin by a good metre.

'And today, I had an interview!'

She spins her chair and heads for the fridge. She grabs two cans and plonks one in front of me.

'Come on, slowcoach.'

'How did it go?'

'Good, I think they like me. I know the system they use. I was worried they wouldn't have ramps and stuff, but it was fine. I was scared the taxi driver would drive off because I haven't got an electric chair.'

'Can't you get one?'

'Probably not. I was lucky and broke my back near the bottom, so I have pretty decent core strength, and I'm not generally incontinent, although I might be tonight.'

She giggles and I join in. With make-up on, she looks a lot more feminine. We chat for a bit, but, as always, the conversation comes back to the prison.

'How about you, Dalton? You leaving that shithole yet?'

'No, sometimes I reckon it's harder for us to leave than the inmates, especially after they put the wages up.'

'I wish Fats would quit.'

'I think he feels the same as me and just tolerates the place. It's stupid but I feel obliged to stay. There are a few bad officers and others that don't care, so I know that when Fats and I are on shift the jail is a better, safer place for everyone inside it.'

'Shall I tell you a secret?'

'Okay.'

'That place is eating him up, I know it. But he does it to punish himself. He doesn't sleep well, and he's quiet. If you knew him when he was younger, you'd see how much he loves to laugh.'

'I always thought that he was a loner. Why does he want to be punished?'

'Because it's his fault that I'm in this chair.'

'What?'

She chuckles again, but it doesn't sound convincing and the laughter soon tails off.

'It wasn't, really. It was black ice on those country lanes. We shot off the road and into a ditch. The van that was following did the same thing and hit us hard. That's what did for my back. Fats says he knows those roads and because of that it was his fault, but if the vehicle behind hadn't been so close, then it wouldn't have happened. It's just one of those things. He believes by helping people in the prison, he's making up for it somehow. Bless him. To be honest, he never was that bright.'

'God, I didn't know. I asked him for a beer once, and he said he doesn't drink, so I thought he was a loner and didn't push, with having enough of my own problems.'

'And what are they?'

I smile, not wanting to put a further dampener on things.

'Well, aren't you quite the nosey one?'

Her booming laugh is back.

'Get my last beer, straggler. You know Fats talks about you all the time. Thinks you're the best officer in the place. He misses you now you work on the dark side.'

'He's always giving me compliments, but he's twice the man I am.'

We pause for a moment, then burst into laughter again.

41

I open my eyes on the sofa and moisten my tongue to get it off the roof of my mouth. It takes a few seconds to recall last night. Lena had a bottle of nasty wine, which we had to mix with Diet Coke to make it drinkable. I staggered home at eleven. All the lights were out, and I realised I hadn't taken my keys, but the back door was unlocked.

Our bedroom door was closed, but the kid's doors were ajar.

I spent about ten minutes at each of their bedsides, listening to their breathing and snuffling, then kissed them on their foreheads. Abi was still moving around in our room, so I raised my hand to knock but, in the end, I just went downstairs. I fell asleep in seconds.

A powerful engine revs and pulls up outside, then a door slams. I leap off the sofa, pull the curtains back, and see the tail lights of a taxi outside our house. It looks top end, and not the normal type of taxi for around here. It can only be for Abi and the kids. I check my watch and see I have five minutes to leave the house to get to work on time. I'm still in yesterday's clothes and shirt, both of which smell as if I slept on the floor of the pub.

Abi, Ivan and Tilly step down the stairs. Ivan and Tilly have little backpacks on and look adorable, but Ivan is doleful, and Tilly, tearful. Despite my state, I pull them both into tight hugs. Ivan doesn't resist.

'Come on, kids. The taxi is waiting,' says Abi.

'Off you go,' I say. 'You'll be back before you know it. Bring me some rock and send me a postcard.'

'Daddy,' says Tilly, 'it's not that kind of holiday.'

By the look on Abi's face, I would have to agree.

Abi opens the door and the kids leave without a backward glance.

'Let me help you with that big thing,' I say, gesturing to the case.

'No, I've got it.'

She bumps it through the doorway, then turns to lock it. Abi holds my gaze for a few seconds, then closes the door.

I listen to the car doors closing and my ears strain at the silence after they've left. I allow myself a few seconds of hope that they might reach the end of the road and turn back. The house feels immediately too big for me. Tears bulge in my eyes but I wipe them away before they fall. I'm in no fit state to think about the ramifications if they don't return. Luckily, I have work to distract me and I have minutes to spare.

I run upstairs and take a high-speed cold shower. There's no one to moan to now, but at least it wakes me up. Abi has hung four work shirts and my spare pairs of trousers on hangers in the bedroom, all freshly washed and ironed. A sickness creeps into my stomach.

I drag my clothes on and head outside. It's warm already at six-thirty, so I leave my coat in the garden. When I push my bike through the gate, I see some arsehole has knocked over two bins during the night. There's rubbish strewn all over. A bag with little teeth marks, cat or fox, has been dragged for at least ten metres. A whiff of fried chicken and rotten eggs has my stomach revolving like a cement mixer.

How can I blame Abi for wanting to get out of here? She comes from good stock and I've dragged her down to my level. Maybe the kids will be better off without me in Spain. No, that's defeatist talk. I need a plan to get out of this place. I've let life happen to me as opposed to striving to do better. Drinking less would be a good place to start.

I cycle off with my backpack bumping around on my back. I can't believe I did that. Who the hell gets so drunk the night before his children go away that he sleeps through and doesn't get to say goodbye properly? They must have come downstairs and had breakfast while I was still snoring. I'm so weighed down with self-loathing that I can barely turn the pedals.

I've been to work with many a killer hangover before and always say never again. The prison is not an environment to feel delicate in. Luckily, all the security doors are opened by Comms as soon as I ask for access, and I arrive at the female hub at eight seconds to seven. Normally you start at eight at the weekend, but I'm relieving the night staff. The guy, whose first or last name is Timothy, gives me a dirty look, as if I'm late, but I return his stare with interest and he looks away.

I need to ensure every person is in their cell on all five wings, not just my own, before he can go, which means looking in the observation panel of over a hundred of them. Then the roll count is my responsibility. My mouth is still Sahara dry as I check what the numbers should be on each wing. When Timothy says he's going to the toilet, I have a couple of big sips of his freshly made coffee. Damn, it tastes good. I lurch to the first wing, which is Whisky 1 where the YOs are.

The feeling of intrusion when doing this has never gone away in five years, although I bet it's the highlight of Timothy's night. It's

7.05 a.m. and most of the cons are asleep. It's easier when it's hot because the cells are mini-ovens and the rotisserie chickens are on display. Each cell gets a three-second glance. A second to find them, one to identify them, and lastly, one to confirm they are alive. In the winter, it's dark, and they're wrapped in most of their clothes and covered by a thin duvet. Then you have to turn the light on if you can't see them move. This is the time of day when you find bodies. It's a well-known fact the darkest hours are just before dawn.

Most of the inmates are asleep, but Rose-Marie is up and staring out of her window like a Salvador Dalí painting, the bump now clearly visible. Billie is facing away from me in her cell and pumping out press-ups in a grey bra and a pair of large, light-blue knickers. Her body glistens with sweat. I count to twenty before closing the metal flap. The metal hinge makes a guilty squeak as I close it. Billie will be able to look through the gaps around the door and see who's doing the checks as I walk about the wing.

I try to be quiet, but jails are noisy places. The gates clang loudly as I shut them. My footsteps thud around the landings like a slow drumbeat. The sun has risen high enough to light up the dust as it floats through the air. I wipe a film of sweat off my forehead and pull the shirt from my back.

On Zulu wing, I find myself staring into Tara's cell. She's naked from the waist up, with an arm hanging loosely from the bunk. Apart from the round, small, firm breast on view, she could be a beautiful, sleeping cherub. I yank my eyes away and glance up to the top bunk. Kitty is awake and stares right at me. It's hard to pull my gaze from her, too.

Everyone is where they are supposed to be and they appear to be breathing. I return to the hub.

'You took your time,' says the OSO. 'Here.'

He points at the handover sheet.

'You don't leave until seven-fifteen, so you can wait until I've had a crap.'

I sit in the toilet knowing it's going to be a long day. When I get back to the hub, Timothy has disappeared.

'Where's knobhead gone?' I ask.

'I said he could go,' says Nasima.

'I've got four missing and thirteen dead, so I won't be signing the handover sheet.'

'Are you okay, Dalton? You don't seem the man who came over a week ago.'

Christ, has it only been a week?

'I'm fine.'

'I told you it's different over here. A lot of these girls are broken and there's very little we can do about it apart from be supportive to them during the day before we lock them up at night.'

I sign the sheet and spin one of the office chairs around to sit opposite her. Not too close, because I don't want her passing out from my breath.

'Come on, talk to me. You came over all clean-shaven and strapping. You look like you've been sleeping here.'

After a long exhale, I tell her the truth.

'I think my wife has left me.'

Nasima leans back in her seat.

'I'd have thought you would know either way.'

'She's gone on holiday for two weeks to her parents' place in Spain. They want them to stay over there.'

'Why didn't you go with them?'

'I wasn't invited.'

'Ah, I see. My folks weren't keen on my choice of partner either.'

She looks at the clock, then turns back to me.

'I came in early to type up and file the appraisals, but I've got ten minutes. Tell me how it came to this, if you want to, of course.'

Everything falls out. I wonder as I'm saying it whether I'd have talked if I weren't so hungover. Afterwards, she looks away from me and chews her lip.

'Do you know what I'd do?' she says after a pause.

'Go on.'

'Enjoy yourself. Have fun. Lie in, get drunk, although you seem to be managing all right on that front already. Go to the cinema, then leave your pants on the bathroom floor. There's not much you can do otherwise. When was the last time you had no responsibilities? If she wants to make it work, she needs to really want it to. Maybe send her a nice email after a week, saying you miss her and the kids. No pressure, but that you're thinking of them.'

It seems remarkably good advice.

'Okay, sounds like a plan.'

'We've got eleven officers in today, so if you fancy being my GD, help me with the filing, then be my guest.'

'Definitely. Do you want a coffee?'

She reaches into her drawer, pulls out a tin of Kenco Millicano and plonks it on the desk.

'Use that,' she says.

She puts her hand back in the drawer, then throws me an Extra Strong Mint.

'And that.'

I grin at her and put the sweet in my mouth. I'm just leaving when she shouts out.

'Dalton. Remember, in many ways, it's still the same over here as the male side. The prisoners will pick up on the fact you're not 100 per cent, and they will seek to exploit it. Be vigilant.'

42

Meds goes smoothly after unlock. Billie comes out for hers and says she's nervous about starting her new job. She also asks me if I have any suntan lotion with me. It's hard to tell if she's joking. Rose-Marie, who was glowing with good health before her court case, looks in worse wear than I do. Saturdays are association, where the prisoners are out of their cells, all day if we have enough staff. It's noisy as hell on the male side, but it's almost totally quiet over here.

There's one incident with the YOs. By the time I get to the landing, Ana-Maria is being held back by Tex. Peabody is pulling a screaming Mihaela away from Laimutė, who has four bright red cuts down the side of her face. Laimutė hocks a wad of phlegm up and spits it straight into the eye of Mihaela, who stops struggling for a moment, then goes ballistic. Even though she's small, Peabody struggles to hang onto her. Trust me, you haven't lived until someone you don't like has spat their thick, warm, smelly spit into your face.

I put on my severest expression, point at Laimutė, then up at her cell.

'Now!' I roar.

Her long legs are up those steps in three big bounds. I follow her so she's not tempted to hurl abuse over the railings. We lock the Romanians away, then take Laimutė to the block. She says nothing through the whole experience. The officers in the female block are stressed. All ten cells are full now. I can hear weeping coming from one of them and doleful singing from another. The air hangs heavy and I'm glad to leave.

I spend the rest of the morning making officer comments on the records of those who had been involved in the fight. Then I fill in two security forms about the tensions on the wing. I'm mooching around before lunch trying to look busy when I catch Tara and Kitty mopping the floor in the hub area.

'Are you helping for the day?' I ask Kitty.

She goes beetroot red, gives me the tiniest of looks, then drops the mop on the floor. She looks changed even from a week ago. Her hair is styled, and she seems to have lost more weight.

'I've just got to go the toilet, Ruined,' she says, and disappears quickly.

'Okay, Broken.'

We watch Kitty scamper away.

'We're both hub orderlies now,' says Tara.

'That's weird, you calling each other the names that a sick woman branded you with.'

'Kitty likes to hear it. She gradually fell to pieces on the out and spent all of her time with bad influences.' She laughs. 'Like Billie, but here, she's found some stability. Strangely, me calling her that makes her try to function normally.'

'I suppose I can understand that. Why is she scared of men?'

'Her looking at you is real progress. I reckon she's practising on you. She doesn't consider you a threat because you're older and work here. You also seem like you wouldn't be easily offended and that will help put her at ease.'

'What happened to her?'

'Let's just say her parents are the epitome of the "c" word.'

'Does that mean what I think it means?'

'Yes. They were evil, twisted, and bad beyond belief. Kitty said it's fine for me to tell you her history. But are you sure that you want to know?'

'Yeah, no worries. I bet I've heard worse.'

'Her father was a convicted sex offender, but he'd been out of prison for a few years before Kitty was born. How this type of thing goes on in this day and age is beyond me. Anyway, she was abused by him for a long time. Eventually one of her neighbours rang the police, then child services took Kitty away, but it was too late. You see, if she was naughty, her dad would bellow in her face, "Go to the fucking shed."'

'Right.'

Tara stares hard at me.

'It wasn't just a swear word. It was a compound noun,' she says.

'I've got no idea what you're talking about.'

'The shed was where her uncle and father did the fucking.'

43

I have a relatively relaxing day, despite the hangover church bells clanging in my head. At 4 p.m., I take Tara and Kitty over to fetch the food trolleys. When we return with them, Myerscough is bringing Billie back from working with the chickens. She looks as if she's spent the day under a sun bed. Tara points at her.

'I never thought I'd come to prison and get lobster,' says Tara.

Kitty, Tara and I laugh our heads off.

'The jobs have to be done whatever the weather,' Myerscough replies without humour.

Billie also looks subdued.

'I can take her back to the wing,' I offer.

'Okay, let the officers know.'

I open the gate to Whisky wing and Billie trudges in.

'You okay?'

'Brilliant.'

'You don't look that happy.'

'The chicken screw is a bit weird, that's all. I did the whole day, too, because the other girl was sick. You know what? There were times it was as though I was free out there.'

I can see Tex and Sheraton are supervising outside the servery.

'One on,' I shout to them. 'I'll change your role in the book and hub.'

Tex gives me a thumbs up.

Billie follows me to the office, where I update the observation book with her return.

'You looked very chummy with Tara,' she says.

'They make me laugh, those two. It's amazing how they can still be so funny after their upbringing. Tara was telling me how they ended up in that children's home and how that weird woman stroked their hair at night.'

'Do you fancy her? Everyone does.'

'No, not everything has to be about sex, Billie. You can just enjoy other people's company without it progressing to anything else.'

'Well, that's not my experience of life. Did she tell you why I was there and what happened when the stroking stopped?'

I detect a sudden tension and the hairs go up on the back of my neck. Billie fixes me with her piercing blue stare.

'No,' I reply. 'She said that was your story to tell.'

'Here it is, then. Let's see if you think it's funny. My mum was useless. She was one of those who blamed everyone else when the shitty decisions she made came back to bite her on the arse. I actually quite liked her. She was funny, really pretty, and – now what was the word Tara used to describe her? – haphazard. She traded on her looks, and it was all about what she could get. What people owed her. What she deserved. Even though she never put any effort in to deserve anything. When she got fired from her latest job, it was because her bosses were a bunch of cunts, and nothing to do with her being late most days, if she showed up at all.'

'That must have been tough for you.'

'Yep. We were always skint, but she always looked fine. There was bugger all for breakfast, but she had the cash to cane twenty fags a day. She met some guy with a load of dough when I was ten and fucked off.'

'What?'

'Yep. I came in from school and found my dad smashing the place up. She'd nicked his wallet, packed a bag, took her jewellery and gone. I don't know where she is.'

'That's awful.'

'I still can't get my head around it now.'

'Was it just you and your dad after she left?'

'Well, as you can imagine, he was no superhero. He knew nothing about me, or my school, who I hung out with, where I went 'til late at night, or how to run a home, or, it seems, anything at all, apart from how to wank his giro on booze.'

Billie wipes a stray tear away with the back of her hand and grits her teeth.

'After a few weeks of me not turning up to class, my teacher rocked up at my house. She was really old, sixty at least, and meant well. Anyway, she arrived the day before he got his income support, so he was skint but sober. He told her the truth. Same bollocks as my mother. Poor him, not his fault, all that jazz. I went to a rough school, and the teacher had heard it before and so gets the social involved.'

Billie wipes her face again, but she's struggling to keep up with the flow and the tears course down her cheeks.

'They turn up the next day, unfortunately mid-afternoon this time, so he's slaughtered. They threaten him with removing me from the house and having to put me in a foster home. I was listening when they told him, more or less, to buck his ideas up. Do you know what his reply was?'

'No.'

'He said he couldn't do it. That I was too much for him. Says if they look after me for a bit, he'll get his shit together and have me back.'

'And he didn't?'

'Well, that was ten years ago, and I'm still waiting.'

'So you ended up with, what was her name, Lavinia?'

'Yep. I was in a right old mess. All that rejection shot my self-worth to nothing. But I thought Lavinia was lovely. I reckoned she was how a real mum should be. She made me feel wanted. When I turned up, Kitty was already there. She said the girl before me had killed herself. I thought she must have been bonkers, because it was a nice little home. Just the couple who owned it in one room and three more bedrooms. I liked Kitty, even though she really was broken. I got my period aged twelve and these bad boys popped up overnight.'

She honks her breasts for emphasis.

'Lavinia's husband left her, and the stroking turned to fondling. The massaging hands became probing fingers, in every hole I have. Messed up, isn't it? But she was all I had. I didn't want her to hate me, so I just put up with it. If I'm honest, I came to enjoy it. That makes me feel dirty now, but there you go. Went on for years too.'

'Jesus,' I say, stunned.

Tex's voice bellows from the servery.

'Billie, come get your sandwich.'

Billie attempts to give me a sweet grin.

'Anyway, that was yonks ago. Lavinia left after a while, and the new couple really were lovely, although we'd all gone wild by that point, so they had a tough time.'

'I'm sorry to hear that.'

'Forget it. I have. Things are looking up now, though. I've got a great job in the outdoors, and I have you to thank.'

With that, she steps forward, rises up on her tiptoes and kisses me gently on the lips. I freeze.

'I can smell alcohol,' she says. 'I quite like it.'

She reaches up again and touches my lips with her fingers, ever so softly, then quickly leaves. I clench my fists.

I should have told her to stop. But I didn't want her to.

44

I have a restless night and feel exhausted in the morning. In my half-dreams, my children's faces become intermingled with those of the prisoners on my wing. I'm tempted to drive in to work, but when I check the car, the puddle of oil has grown. My neighbour comes out at the same time and throws a bag of rubbish in his bin. I don't think I've seen him outside at seven o'clock before. He wanders over, eyes glazed.

'Problem?' he asks.

I point at the edge of the spill, which is visible without getting under the vehicle.

'Nasty. Do you want me to have a look at it for ya?'

I've had a lot of surprises lately, but this is the biggest.

'Are you a mechanic?'

'Used to be. I had a motorbike accident, messed my back up. Pain medication doesn't work either.'

'Well, that would be great, but sure you won't hurt yourself?'

'No, it hurts all the time anyway, so you don't need to worry about that. It's probably something simple, like warped seals or loose bolts. Are you going to work?'

'Yeah, I've got to head off soon.'

'Good on yer. That's a tough job you've got. Leave us your keys. If I can fix it, I will do. Obviously, the engine could be knackered, which would make this scrap. When did you last get it serviced and MOT'd?'

'MOT was January, service, ermm, 2017 ish.'

He laughs. 'I'm Gary.'

I drop the keys into his hand. 'Jim. Will it cost much?'

'If I need parts, you can pay for them, but my hourly rate is zero. I'm pretty bored most of the time, stuck in the house. My wife nags like hell, too.'

I give him a conspiratorial smile.

Gary's kindness gives me a lift and I cycle to work with enthusiasm even though I've only had one day off in the last fortnight. I have an early tomorrow and then a whole day off. It's not until I reach the female houseblocks that I remember the kiss. It's probably best if I just forget it and hope that she doesn't try to do it again.

It's Sheraton and me on duty. He's brought *Men's Fitness* magazine in and takes my jibes about him enjoying looking at oiled men and women with good grace. Billie ignores me at breakfast. She reminds me of a schoolgirl who has slipped the boy she fancies a note yesterday and doesn't know what to do with herself today. She has a blue shirt on and a pair of sensible shorts, both of which drown her. Perhaps she's trying to cover up out in the sun.

Myerscough rings the wing to say the other girl's still ill, so Billie can do a full day. I keep an eye out for when she comes back at lunch and make sure I'm elsewhere. I get Sheraton to open the doors when we do roll count, while I just fill in the tally board, so I don't even need to look at her.

In the afternoon, I do the same. I bump into Tara in the hub area while I'm pretending to be busy.

'Is loitering a crime?' she asks.

'Not since the eighties.'

Billie returns at that point. Her redness has gone a little brown. I see her noticing Tara and me even though we're nearly fifty metres away. You can tell by the way she tilts her head that she's not happy.

'Was that dirty look for me or you?' asks Tara.

'You, I hope. She told me how she ended up in the children's home and how Lavinia's personal service progressed.'

'Did she, now? Did she explain why it stopped?'

'No, she said Lavinia left.'

'I suppose that's true. The real reason is that I hit puberty late. Lavinia's actually what some call a hebephile. That's another one for you to look up. When she touched me down there, I was like, what the fuck? I told Kitty and Billie, and she'd been doing it to them for years. I guess the reasons why they didn't say anything are complicated.'

'Did the police believe you?'

'That's the thing. We didn't tell them. Billie and Kitty had more than enough experience of the police to think they wouldn't be bothered. Billie said let's just tell her if she stops doing it and gives us loads of stuff, we won't tell the police. Kitty and me were too scared, but Billie doesn't mind a bit of aggravation.'

'Ah, so she blackmailed her.'

'Correct! Lavinia stopped interfering with us and we had nice dinners and pocket money. She even took us to the beach for the day, which was pretty weird. Talk about elephant in the room, or car, in our case. I'm not sure that Billie or Kitty had been to the seaside before, so they tolerated the stilted silence. Anyway, a month later, Lavinia abruptly leaves. She tells us she's been diagnosed with terminal cancer. That's God watching, that is. Then that pleasant couple took over.'

'You never told anyone what happened?'

'No one believes orphans. Don't you watch films?'

I study her face for a moment.

'What?' she says.

'Lavinia didn't have cancer. You were blackmailing her. Blackmail never stops. It makes life unbearable. I bet she put up with it for a month, so she could find somewhere else to live and get everything sorted, then said she was dying.'

Tara's face falls.

'Oh, yeah. God, I was so pleased that she was going to croak it that I didn't even think about that.'

'And if you failed to report it, then what's stopping her getting another position in a children's home?'

Tara blanches and looks as if she's about to be sick. I pat her on the back.

'Maybe I'm just being cynical and she is dead.'

Tara shakes her head, looking unconvinced. She walks away staring hard at the floor. I return to the wing and decide to check a few of the usual hiding places for illicit items before the workers return. First off, I check the servery, but it's spotless. Then I go to the laundry room and check the pipes. I shake the vent hose and something rattles in it. Someone's made a split in it and hidden what looks like a biro inside.

I put on my gloves and gently pull it out. It is a pen, but the end has been melted. Razor blades have been attached to it, so it looks a bit like a fletched arrow. It's a brutal weapon, which could ruin a face with a couple of angry swipes. I check the landings when I step outside to see if anyone is looking on, but the wing is empty, even of the cleaners.

I show it to Sheraton in the office. He passes me the security form to fill in from the filing cabinet but doesn't say anything. Our jobs have just become more dangerous.

Dinner on the wing goes smoothy, although Rose-Marie doesn't leave her cell when I shout her name. I take it to her and find her lying on her bed sobbing. Tex would know what to do. A hug would probably help, but it feels as though I would be stepping over a boundary.

'Here's your dinner, Rose-Marie. You need to eat.'

'I don't want it,' she cries out.

I'm not sure what to do with it.

'I'll put it on the side here. It's a no-choice roll and a bag of cheese and onion.'

She doesn't reply, so I creep back out of the cell. Billie is standing next to me when I return to the landing.

'Do you have anything for this?'

She waves a dry red hand at me.

'Ouch, what did you touch?'

'It's not much. My hands go dry every now and again. I only need a bit of moisturising cream, but the nurse won't give it to me without a prescription. By the time I get a doctor's appointment, they're back to normal, but I have a week of soreness.'

'Tex sometimes leaves a bottle of hand stuff in the office. I'll see if I can find it and give you a squirt at bang up.'

Billie raises an eyebrow at me and the corner of her mouth edges up.

I laugh, lock her in, and return to the office. But Tex must take her cream home each night. Sheraton has locked everyone else away, so I hand him the clipboard and I open each door and shout out how many bodies are in each cell. When I get to Billie's cell and crack the door, she's sitting stark naked on the bed. I try to keep my eyes on her face.

'Sorry, there wasn't any cream.'

She smiles.

'That's okay. Thanks for trying, sir.'

I close the door as my blood reaches boiling point.

45

I'm spaced out as I leave the prison and barely register seeing Fats getting in Braddock's car again. I reach home the quickest I've ever done, then pace the house with nervous energy. I try to watch a film, but eventually have to pleasure myself so I can concentrate on it. When the doorbell goes, my first thought is it's the police, even though I haven't done anything. It feels as though temptation is written on my face. I look out of our bedroom window and run downstairs.

'Gary, good to see you,' I say with a big smile.

'All fixed, mate. If you'd had it serviced, they'd have noticed the seals were going. Looks like one gave up the ghost in your parking space. Lucky, because if you were driving, your engine might have seized.'

'That's brilliant. How much do I owe you?'

'My treat. I guess you haven't got loads of cash either, with not getting your car serviced. I gave the whole vehicle the once-over afterwards. It'll run smoother and start easier now.'

'You're right but you know how it is. We missed the service one year to save money because we don't do many miles, then the next year we were skint. I suspect you'd think it's a false economy.'

He nods. 'It's funny. I've always thought you were rude, but you're all right.'

'You're too kind.'

We both laugh.

'I better go,' he says.

'Sure. Hey, do you want a beer?'

'I wouldn't mind a cider.'

'Great. Come over in about thirty minutes, because I have neither at the moment. I'll go to the shops in my fancy new motor. Then we can sit in the garden, have a couple, and laugh at all the potheads living nearby who pretend they smoke it for medicinal purposes.'

'It's for my back!'

He limps off, so I jump in the car and drive to the Spar. My wages aren't in yet, but I've seen my pay slip. There is a big chunk of overtime on it that I wasn't expecting, so I'm feeling flush. I grab four cans of Red Stripe lager, a four-pack of Strongbow, and a multipack of Walkers variety crisps. I pick up a 100g bar of Dairy Milk, which is on offer. As an afterthought, I walk down the pharmacy aisle and find a basic tube of moisturising hand cream. It's two pounds. I can say it's mine if anyone asks.

46

I wake up the next morning with a fuzzy four-can head. The alarm clock gets snoozed twice until I'm pushing it for time. Then I remember the car's fixed. I shower, dress, then trot outside. I can't help smiling when the car roars into life. Even though the exhaust sounds throaty, it's a real joy to arrive at work not dripping in sweat.

Gary and I had a really good chat last night. He's great company, but he's trapped in the house most days because he can't walk far. No wonder I rarely see him. Sounds as if his wife works hard to pay all the bills. Luckily, they only had one kid, and he's currently backpacking around Peru. Spawny git, Gary and I said in unison after he mentioned it.

After the third beer loosened our tongues, we had a good moan about married life. As we chatted through things, it became obvious that our wives might irritate us, but they are doing their best, and perhaps we ought to mention that we appreciate them more often. Gary reckons Abi will come back, but I'm not so sure. I'll take Nasima's advice and send Abi an email when she's been gone a week though.

I almost told him about Billie, but didn't. It would have been helpful for someone to tell me to steer clear. Colt should be due at court this week. I'm going to check with him to see if he has a confirmed date. Once he's left, I'll be straight back to the male side and away from temptation.

I arrive at work and typically the first prisoner to come out of her cell is Billie. She's wearing a white T-shirt and baggy jeans for the gardens today. She must be one of those people who tan easily, because she looks so brown, she could be Mediterranean. With her blue eyes, it's hard to tear my gaze away. She gives me a brief wave over breakfast but doesn't come near me and heads off to work quietly. With the rest of the workers gone and quite a few off the wing at court, we have a peaceful morning.

I find myself flicking through the observation book. It's way more detailed than on the male side. I can see where Peabody has struggled to control the wing. There are verbal and written warnings for many of the youngsters. He wrote that Billie Harding is a nightmare on one of the days. Sheraton's comments are more clinical. I wonder if they looked at this book after Sandringham did what he did. Sandringham's scrawlings are almost unreadable. His only note one day is 'STUPID!' It looks as though he was struggling for a while, but lots of men act like The Great Pretender. They present as chilled and in control, but beneath the surface, they are in turmoil.

At eleven, Nasima comes over from the hub and walks onto the landing, which is weird as she would usually ring. She scowls when she sees my feet up on the office desk, but doesn't mention it.

'Dalton, we need one of you two to go on an escort to the hospital. You've got a low roll, so one officer should be able to manage the wing until lunch.'

'Sorry, ma'am, I'm only on an early.'

'Ah, shit. I was hoping you would do it.'

I frown. 'Why, what is it?'

'It's a hospital appointment.'

'And?'

Nasima looks behind her to see if anyone else is in listening distance. When she turns back, her face is pained. It's not like her to struggle for words.

'The hospital visit is for Rose-Marie.'

'The pregnant girl? Why?'

'It's for an abortion,' she whispers.

'What? You've got to be kidding. She's twenty weeks or something.'

I glance down the wing at Rose-Marie's closed door. Now I understand all the tears, both hers and Tex's. I recall Tex's own history.

'It's her choice,' says Nasima quietly.

'But why? She said herself the pregnancy is going well. In a couple of months, she could give birth and just get the baby adopted if she doesn't want it.'

'Dalton, these things happen over here. It's hard to wrap your head around, but think of who Rose-Marie is.'

'Being a fucking drug addict does not mean she can kill a baby.'

Nasima gives me a sad smile.

'Technically, it's a foetus. Rose-Marie's out in a week. She knows what her life is like. The moment she gets out, she'll use again. She's said that herself. She can't keep it, because on the out she's too chaotic. If she has it, she has to carry it to term, then the trauma of giving birth, holding it, then she'll have to give it up. She says she doesn't think she can go through that again. If she's on drugs, she'll be drinking, and she'll probably damage the baby anyway. At the minimum it will be born an addict.'

I hold my head in my hands.

'This is medieval. There must be another way.'

'I'm afraid not.'

'Do you know Tex's history? You can't make her go.'

'Can't make me go where?'

Tex has come up behind Nasima. She looks at Nasima, then to me, then back to Nasima.

'Is it today?' she asks Nasima.

'Yes, it's all booked in. I'm looking for someone else to go on the escort with Flynn. The woman from MBU who was supposed to be going has this flu bug that's floating around. The rest of the staff have an average age of about twenty. We need a mature person who can handle the emotions of it.'

'I'll go,' says Tex.

'No, I'll go,' I say.

'Dalton, you finish at lunchtime,' she replies.

'I'll stay on.'

Tex reaches over the table and holds my hand.

'I want to go. I've been with her the last few weeks, talking to her, trying to understand her. I've been there myself. Only I can relate to what she's going through.'

And that seems to settle it. Nasima nods and leaves the wing. Tex walks back to Rose-Marie's cell. A minute later, she and Rose-Marie walk out together. Rose-Marie has a carrier bag with her things in and holds the fluffy rabbit I see on her pillow when I check her cell. Her jaw is trembling, and she avoids my glare. I can't breathe.

Braddock comes on the wing to help me do roll count. He knows where Tex has gone and shrugs when I ask him what he thinks. He says it's prison life. I understand that you have to separate yourself from the brutal reality of it all, but how can you when it comes down to killing, what I think of at least, a child? How can she do this when she felt the baby moving?

Everyone's quiet in the hub at roll count and I feel part of me has broken. It's hard to drag my mind away from the horror of what's going to occur in a few hours. I don't know how they abort after nearly five months, and I don't want to. Braddock is stone-faced. A couple of the younger female officers have red eyes and wet faces.

The hub phone rings. Nasima picks it up.

'Houseblock One.'

She listens for a moment.

'No problem. The officers are still here. I'll get Dalton to let her know.'

She puts the phone back in the cradle and looks up at me.

'That was Myerscough. The girl who does the chickens in the afternoon has quit because someone told her she has bird flu. Can you tell Billie Harding to go to the gardens again this afternoon?'

'Okay, I'll tell her now. My bag's still in the office.'

I walk down the wing, trying desperately not to look at Rose-Marie's cell door. To think I thought it was easy over here. I was wrong. The girls get to you. They're mostly likeable, good people, fun even. That they can still laugh after the terrible things that have been done to them is testament to their spirit.

My radio comes to life.

'The roll is clear on the female side. Female side only.'

There are no cheers today from the hub. I grab my rucksack from the office and wave to the officers as they trudge to the gatehouse. It's only then I recall the moisturising cream. Fuck the rules, Billie can have it. Life's too short.

I tap my keys on Billie's door and open it. She's sitting on the bed with a photo in her hand. The curtains are only open a touch and a thin strip of sunlight lights up her face as she looks up, giving her an otherworldly glow. Her expression is unguarded and I'm reminded of how young she is. Too young to be surrounded by this place's miserable hopelessness, and too young to be locked away.

'Hey, Dalton. I don't remember ringing for room service.'

'Cheeky. What's the photo?'

'It's me, Tara and Kitty in the garden at the children's home. I was just thinking how serious we look.'

She passes the picture to me and she's right. That's what abuse does. It hollows out the soul.

'I'm sorry, Billie.'

She gives me a quizzical look. 'What for?'

'Life being unfair.'

'That's okay. I can take it. I'm going to be a success, you see. I don't quite understand why, but I know it somehow. Is that crazy?'

I smile at her and shake my head.

'Here, I got you this. Don't squirt it in anyone's eye.'

She stands and takes it from me, then spends a few seconds looking at it.

'That's very sweet,' she whispers.

I nod and look away.

'Are you okay?' she asks. 'You seem down.'

'Kind of. This Rose-Marie business is pretty awful to think about.'

She takes another step towards me. I can feel the air crackling.

'For some of us, this is the safest place to be pregnant.'

'It shouldn't be like that.'

She pushes the door shut behind me. 'Come here, I'll give you a hug.'

But we don't hug. We kiss, and, just for a moment, all my problems disappear.

47

Time seems to stand still as our kisses harden and our hands roam, but the wing gates clanging has me jolting out of her arms. Wide-eyed, we stare at each other. I wipe my mouth and back out of the cell with my breathing still deep and my heart pounding. I step outside and stare down the landing. It's just the little guy who delivers the prisoners' recorded post, which is usually cheques or postal orders from family. He comes on the wings when everyone is locked away, but he needs an officer to open the cell doors for him. He looks hopefully up at me, but I shake my head.

'Sorry, mate. I'm finished.'

'Oh. The SO said you wouldn't mind helping me on this wing.'

I can see Nasima in the window of the hub with an inane grin and both thumbs up, and I let out another heavy breath.

'Go on, then. Where's the first one?'

Five minutes later, I'm out of there and walking towards the men's side to visit Colt. It's a scorching day with a totally blue sky. Bright sunshine reflects off the steel gates and barbed wire, and hammers down onto the shimmering concrete. My mouth is dry and my feet sweat freely in my boots. I look up at the four lines of eighty cell windows on the building on my right. They are in the full glare of the sun. It must be hot to the point of panic inside.

I bump into an officer from Visits. He has one of my favourite prisoners with him. Crispy. His actual name is Chris Patterson, but we had two wing workers called Chris, so I named them Chris P and Chris D. The other one became Crusty. It suited Crusty because he was a foul, grumpy creature who sadly drowned in the pond of a house he was scoping, with industrial levels of cider inside him, the day he was last released. Crispy, on the other hand, is funny.

'Crispy!'

'Guv!'

'You had a legal?'

'Yeah. The police want me to take the blame for six commercial burglaries. Told my brief to tell 'em to piss off.'

'Did you do them?'

'Not all of them.'

I laugh, even though it wouldn't have been funny if I'd owned one of the builders' merchants where Crispy enjoys letting loose his acquisitive nature.

The officer is a new guy called Ben Patel. I only know this because the prison somehow got his name badge wrong and put Petal on it. Obviously, everyone started calling him that, until HR told us not to. He was cool about it though and is a top bloke.

'I can drop him back if you want, Ben?'

'Sweet, Dalton. I'll then owe you one very small favour.'

'You mean like giving him a hand job?' asks Crispy.

'Correct. Sadly, I have another legal visit to escort from Houseblock Five, so you, Mr Crispy, will have to provide the favour for me.'

As Ben heads off, I pull open the door for Houseblock Three, I realise I've missed this banter. I haven't missed the aroma, though.

It's hard to describe the smell of a thousand men cooking in their cells. You can bite on it.

'Are you in your usual kennel?'

'Yep, C-39.'

'You've been in there so often that we'll have to retire it when you give up your wicked ways.'

'Or I could move in permanently.'

'Don't you get tired of being in here?'

'To be honest, I got a two this time and it's been hard. My first grandkid was born just before I came in, and I feel like I'm missing out on a special stage.'

He's on the side facing the sun. A solid draught of warm air envelops me when I open his door.

'Ever thought about working for a living?'

He cringes. 'No!'

'Okay, take it easy. I'll be back this afternoon for my hand job.'

'Okay, cool. I'll make it a blowie if you bring me a cold beer.'

I chuckle as I shut him in, then stroll to the hub and pop my head in. Only SO Bowell is in there.

'All right, boss. I'm just confirming when my brother-in-law's court case is. What cell is he in?'

'D-26.'

I raise an eyebrow with him knowing Colt's location without checking.

'Yes, he's a nightmare,' Bowell says. 'Can you have a word, tell him to calm it down, or someone will get hurt?'

I'm not sure if he means Colt or someone else, but I give him what I hope is a reassuring nod. It sounds as if there's fighting in his cell when I reach it. I flick the observation panel open and peer in. Colt is shadow boxing, while one of his weasel friends looks on adoringly. I rattle my keys and open the door.

Colt is topless, and all pumped up. He freezes while empty

prison eyes assess the danger. For a second, I think he's going to attack, then he recognises me.

'Jimbo!'

'Colt,' I say, hoping not to sound sarcastic. 'Your sister was worried and wanted to know your court date.'

'Sweet, will she be there?'

'It depends when it is. Obviously, she won't take the kids.'

'Got ya. We're changing our plea.'

'Why? You said they have witnesses who saw it all.'

'Yeah, but we know who the witnesses are, so they're going to have a little visit from my mate, Magnum, to make sure they forget to go to court.'

I can't help shaking my head. 'When's the trial?'

'It's a floater, so any day.'

'If you take it to trial and get found guilty, they'll hammer you for the time and the expense of the trial when you previously admitted to doing it.'

'Yeah, who knows, man? You gotta roll the dice.'

I throw the Dairy Milk bar that I bought for him, which he catches. He nods appreciatively and shows it to his mate. Wyatt always loved Dairy Milk. I assume Colt does too.

'Sweet, bruv. Perfect.'

For a moment he reminds me of the cheeky little boy who pestered me to play football, but that innocent lad is long gone.

48

Since having children, I imagined a day to myself in an empty house would be on a par with a trip to the Seychelles, but instead I feel listless. It's a shame I don't have to pick the kids up later. I force myself to get out of bed at 9 a.m. so as not to squander the opportunity of a day to myself. I'm still tired, though, because I struggled to nod off last night. Forefront in my mind, and my groin, was the kiss with Billie.

I attack the housework with vigour, even man-cleaning the bathroom. It doesn't look or smell the same as when Abi's spent all morning on it, but it's an improvement. Scarily, the time is already nearly 1 p.m., and that's without having to deal with the kids' constant demands. I take the rubbish outside and it's a glorious day again. I was going to watch a film on TV, but my mum taught me not to waste the sunshine.

Raised voices come from Gary's house. I've never been impulsive, but maybe all the changes of late have affected me more than I thought. After knocking on Gary's door, I wait, feeling nervous. A woman in a housecoat answers the door. She's tall and willowy with a severe bob, speckled with grey. I receive half a grin.

'Yes.'

'Can Gary come out to play?'

The smile blossoms, which transforms my impression of her completely.

'As long as you don't go too far.'

'Actually, I was wondering if he fancied a trip to the coast. Wells is only about an hour away. It'll probably do us some good and get him out of your hair.'

'Okay, but he's a bit tired and grouchy with his back from messing with your car. Honestly, says he can't use the hoover because of the strain, then I find him crawling over your engine like Spiderman.'

'I'll look after him. We'll breathe some fresh air, see the sea, maybe have fish and chips.'

'Sounds good, got room for one more?'

'Of course, but you have to sit in the back.'

'Just kidding, I have work later, but it'll be great for Gary to get out. He sits in the house, moaning about not having anything to do, but only he can change that. Nobody's going to come around and whisk him away to somewhere fabulous.'

'Did I tell you we were going to Wells-next-to-the-Sea?'

She laughs loud, head tipped back so I see her fillings.

'Gary said you had a dry sense of humour,' she says when she's recovered. 'If you've been stuck inside for years on end, Wells is excitement enough. I'll send him around in a few minutes. You'd better get a move on because that road will be busy. Now, is it a date or a day out?'

'Ah, good call. You'll need to know so you can put him in the right underwear.'

Gary limps around ten minutes later. He has shorts and a T-shirt on and a little rucksack. Incredibly, his legs are whiter than mine. We drive off in silence, but there's an air of excitement.

'Thanks for asking me.'

'No probs. Nice to have some company.'

We reach the A47 and the traffic snarls up, but I just get comfortable in my seat. It's good to leave the city. Everywhere is in full bloom with green fields stretching out around us. About fifteen miles from Peterborough, we grind to a halt. I glance suspiciously at the car's rising temperature gauge, although having Gary with me is reassuring. I wind down the window and peer up at the sky where the odd wisp of cloud scuds by.

When you're young, you don't look at the horizon. You're too busy with what you're doing. I love The Fens now. It's so flat out here that the views are panoramic and the sky seems enormous. It makes me feel insignificant in the scheme of things, but that relaxes me, instead of adding to any panic. Problems are smaller out here.

'Did you know,' says Gary, 'that most of the land around here is below sea level? They use sluices and drainage at high tide to enable it to be farmed so heavily.'

'That doesn't sound promising when global warming cranks up,' I reply.

'You'll have to scrap this crap car and get a crap boat instead.'

We tootle along in the line of vehicles, but progress is slow. Gary gets his mobile out and there is a thirty-mile traffic jam to the sea. When we reach Elme Hall, I make another impulsive decision and swing into the car park.

'Shall we just have dinner here? My treat,' I say.

'You sure? It might be a bit pricey.'

I get out of the car and stare up at the huge building. It looks like a stately home to my untrained eye.

'It can't be that swish. It says two meals for eleven quid on the sign outside.'

We cautiously step in. It's quiet, but a waitress greets us and we have fish and chips from the lunch menu while sitting in a conservatory. The food is good value and neither of us fancy a heavy pudding after. The drive home isn't as arduous, but I stop for petrol and buy two ice lollies. We sit in the garage forecourt and watch the traffic thunder past as we eat them.

'Your wife seems nice,' I say.

'Yeah, suppose.'

We both chuckle. There's been a giggly-schoolboy feeling to the whole venture.

'When I first had the accident, I was angry and sullen. It wouldn't have been a surprise if she'd left me, but she hung in there. I used to complain about her being distant and cold, but she was just exhausted. I bet your wife's the same. Us blokes do a full day's work, then think we can come home and lie on the sofa as heroes. The women's day never seems to be done, especially with children. There's constant washing and ironing and feeding, followed by settling them when the kids have bad dreams.'

I ponder his words for a few seconds. It's true. Abi never stops when she's at home, apart from lately when she closed in on herself. But even then, she still made sure Tilly and Ivan were fed and clothed. I tend to come back from work and collapse, but how tired am I really? Would it kill me to peg out the washing, or nip the kids to the park for thirty minutes so she can have a cup of tea on her own?

'I get what you're saying,' I finally reply. 'But I think my wife could try harder with me. She's lost all interest in any physical contact and is liable to fly off the handle at the smallest thing, which then gets my back up, so I make nasty comments to hurt her.'

Gary grins. 'It's called raising a family. Nobody warns you about it. If you can get out the other side, you're fine. Communication is the key.'

'Ah ha! Man's strongest point. No wonder we're having problems.'

'Write your email to her and include this stuff, saying that you appreciate she's been working hard and explain your angle, too. No one's ever completely wrong, and if your shared goal is not to have angry kids, then it should be doable.'

'If I'd known you were a doctor of philosophy, I'd have spoken to you earlier. Now, do you know anything about rashes?'

It's been a good afternoon even though we never reached further than Wisbech. I park up and help Gary out. Even so little effort has worn him out. He stops before opening his front door.

'Thanks for a lovely day at the seaside.'

'No worries. Perhaps it's time both of us created a life, as opposed to wandering through it and complaining when nothing happens. It's funny, but I often think that's what the prisoners do, but I'm just as guilty of it.'

'We'll do something soon. I'm pooped, but I feel more positive. I need a plan and if I push myself, I can have a future too. Cheers again.'

He gives a tired wave and disappears through his door. I return to my house and smile at the cleanliness as I walk inside. Abi always used to say what a nice sensation it was to get back to a clean and tidy home.

There's very little food in the cupboards, so I have a tin of spaghetti hoops in a bowl. I turn the computer on and start writing that email. It's hard, though, when my mind keeps wandering to events in the prison. I remember Tara's strange word for a sex offender and do a Google search. A hebephile is someone who is attracted to pubescent children. I shiver at how confused those girls must have been in Lavinia's warped world. I eventually finish the email. My finger hovers over the send button. It's only Tuesday, and I said I'd wait a week. I wonder if she's thinking of me. I click send. The speed of her reply will be the proof I need.

49

I'm on another early, but I press my alarm before it goes off. It's funny how I always blamed the kids and their strange nocturnal habits for my tiredness, but they aren't here and still my mind whirs in bed, which prevents me from feeling rested. The girls on the wing flicker in and out of half-dreams in much the way some of the male prisoners did when I was working with them. Jeez, what a job.

The fridge is now empty, although I find a Twix in the freezer compartment. That sneaky wife of mine must hide them in there to stop me eating them all as soon as I see them. I put it in my bag with what appears to be a thousand-year-old apple. I could drive to the prison, then go straight to the supermarket after work, but driving is a lazy habit to get into, so I jump on my bike and pedal hard.

I can hear the squeak of Fats's bike before I see him as I wind through Moggswell Lane. I cruise next to my red-faced friend.

'Looks like Hitler could do with some Vaseline,' I say.

'That's right, sir. Would you rub some on him for me?'

We chat and cycle. Fats says he gets a lift from Braddock most days and he's been eating unhealthy meals around his house too. Apparently, Braddock used to be the chef at a top London hotel. It's funny who ends up in prison. The catering industry is notorious for its unpredictability, so we have a few officers join after getting laid-off from closed pubs and restaurants. To their surprise, they often stay.

'Braddock said he'd cook me and his sister his speciality on Friday night,' says Fats with a big grin. 'Beef Wellington. I can't wait.'

'Cool, sounds odd, but can't be bad if he was a top chef.'

A current of jealousy runs through me and I'm unable to resist a little jab.

'Is Lena going too?'

Fats goes even redder, which is a slightly worrying puce colour.

'I bet she'd love to get out,' I continue.

'She's not a big fan of rare beef.'

We reach the bike sheds and Fats gives me a strange look. I'm a great judge of expression, but I'm not sure if it's shame or guilt, or something else.

'I probably won't go,' he says.

I enter the houseblocks with Tex, who's with me on duty this morning. We're a bit early, so I sit next to her in the hub and listen to the youngsters telling jokes and pulling each other's legs. They are all so young today that Tex and I could be their parents looking on with affection combined with irritation at the noise.

The SO on shift is a strong woman in her early thirties called Liz Breakman, which is apt because I expect that is what she could do. I worked with her loads on the male side, where she was a real asset. One of the inmates nicknamed her No-nonsense Liz.

She's the polar opposite of Nasima concerning her personal life, having married a short bloke in the Offender Manager Unit. She has a photo of her family in the desk drawer, which she takes out when she starts her shift and grins at during the day. Her husband walks around with a chilled and contented expression on his face, so it's good to see evidence that some people are happy. Tex, on the other hand, looks devastated.

'What's wrong?'

'Did you hear about Rose-Marie?'

I shake my head.

'She had complications during the abortion and wouldn't stop bleeding. They think she had some kind of stroke last night.'

'Poor thing.' I think about it for a few moments. 'If you look purely at the facts, as long as she recovers, it could be better for her.'

'What?'

'Well, she's due out Friday, so we might as well release her now as she'll be in hospital for weeks. I doubt they'll let her go without a place to live. They may even be able to arrange proper support for her.'

I receive another strange glance, which is tricky to decipher. It's probably disgust or sorrow at my heartlessness. I traipse after her to unlock the wing, wondering what the hell is wrong with me, but it's not easy to forgive Rose-Marie for what she's done.

The wing is very quiet. They've all heard about Rose-Marie, and only about half come out of their cells at unlock. While Tex is doing meds, Red and Laurinavicius start fighting outside the servery in front of me. It's a brutal, desperate, nails-flailing, teeth-bared, vicious fight to the death, but conducted in near silence. I put my arm around Red's waist, pick her up, and spin her around.

'That fucking Russian is dead,' she screams.

I carry her to her cell and push her in. She is a similar weight to my eight-year-old, Tilly.

Red drops to the floor and begins a terrible wailing. I lock the door. Laurinavicius has vanished by the time I get back to the servery. I look up and see her cell door quietly close and decide I can't be bothered with the paperwork.

At 8 a.m., Billie arrives at the office while I'm eating my Twix and filling in the ACCT books. We have nearly half the wing under regular observation, and all of their anxieties have been exacerbated by the news of Rose-Marie's troubles. Billie, however, waltzes in as though she hasn't a care in the world. Her hair is even blonder and her tan is a deep rich mahogany. She's starting to look as if she doesn't belong here until she picks up my last chocolate finger, puts it in her mouth and mimes giving it a blowjob.

I gasp at the cheek of it but find it hard to stop staring. Only the phone ringing distracts my attention. It's Breakman from the hub. I expect bad news, but she just needs a favour from Tex or me. Unusually, she asks me to come to see her as opposed to telling me straight away. I chuck Billie out of the office, telling her to keep the Twix. I get the third stare that I can't decipher in as many hours from Liz when I arrive at her side. There's no calling this SO ma'am —even the prisoners call her Liz.

'What's up, Liz?'

'I need an hour of your or Tex's time for constant obs.'

I feel the colour run from my face. If a prisoner is put on constant observation, it means they are immediately likely to self-harm or try to kill themselves. It's usually because they have lost their minds or because they've done something so terrible that the pain of living is too much for them.

I've only done it once before. The elderly man in question had strangled his wife to death. Every time he was unrestrained, he smashed his head against the wall. I went home covered in blood. They had to sedate him in the end. Breakman's asking for an hour, but if the inmate is awake, it will feel like a year.

'Who is it?'

'Phillipa Kennedy.'
'What's she done?'
'Killed her child.'

50

Breakman gives me a tired shrug.

'I wouldn't fancy it either,' she says. 'But the rest of the shift today are young. I don't want them to go through it, and, before you ask, I'm doing an hour myself this afternoon.'

People naturally believe that if someone starts acting crazy, they get taken straight to a hospital to be looked after and treated. If only life worked like that. Many of us live such isolated existences, struggling by on our own, that there's no one to notice when the wheels come off the rails. Sometimes we're a long way from the track before anyone else realises. The first to know are often the police, and that's usually because a crime has been committed.

Unless the offender is completely insane, they have to go through the rigours of the justice system. That's overnight in the police cells, before being presented at magistrates' court, who, in this case, would send them straight to prison. Prison officers aren't trained to deal with this kind of thing. You just get on with the job whoever arrives and deal with any conflict. If you stay in the role long enough, you learn to process what you've seen and heard. Or you try to forget.

I consider Tex's history and her current mental state.

'I'll do it,' I say to Liz.

After leaving the hub, I shout through the wing gates to Tex, who's still doing cell checks, that I'm at a meeting for an hour. It's a strange walk, out of the houseblock into the bright sunshine, and to the relative darkness of Healthcare. I let myself in and stop at the first cell in the single corridor. There are thirteen further rooms on the right-hand side. This one is like a goldfish bowl. Inside, a thin, pasty, sickly inmate in prison greys lies on her bed fiddling with an e-cig. Braddock sits on a plastic seat in front of the large window with an orange ACCT book on his lap and a pen in his hand. He gives me a pained expression. It seems they've been pulling mature officers from all over the prison.

Oscar One, MacStravick, is in the office talking to a female officer when I present myself. The healthcare officers tend to be time-served after they've had enough of the wings. That experience stands them in good stead on the rare occasions that something like this occurs. They'll have done many sessions with the lady already.

'Thanks for doing this, Dalton,' says MacStravick.

'No problem. Is she violent?'

MacStravick looks to the other officer, who replies.

'No, she's quiet and withdrawn. Doesn't seem to know where she is. The doctor's been in with her loads. He's hopeful he can get her into a secure hospital in a few days, but he says she's relaxed now.'

'What did she do?'

'We haven't probed too deeply. A delivery driver found her little son naked next to the bins at her house. He rang the police, and she went wild and attacked them when they kicked her door in.'

'And she's relaxed after that?'

'The doc says she's had a schism of some sort to cope with

what's happened. Her life outside isn't real any more. She thinks she's at a confusing hotel.'

A young police officer, because that's what the response drivers usually are, would have discovered that small body and their life will never be the same again. I suspect mine might not be either unless I manage to find some empathy to bring to this experience. After how I feel about what Rose-Marie did, I'm not ready to stare at someone for an hour, judging them.

'Can I sit in there with her?' I ask.

MacStravick considers it for a moment and then smiles.

'Sure, good idea. Keep the door open though.'

I leave the office and walk to Braddock, whom I pat on the shoulder. He hands me the book, then moves faster than I've seen him do for years as he gets out of Healthcare. I pick up the chair and move it into the cell, where I place it against the window. The woman fails to register my presence, so I sit down and fill in the book to say I've taken over.

'Hi, I'm here to keep you company.'

She doesn't say anything or look at me for the first fifteen minutes. The only sounds are her sucking on the e-cig, which doesn't appear to be charged, and the scrawl from my writing. It already feels as though I've been in here for a couple of hours.

'Do you get on with these e-cigs?' she asks, causing me to jump.

'No, not really. The real thing is better, but much worse for you. Like many things in life.'

She considers that for a moment, scrapes her hair back behind her ear, Billie-style, and carries on puffing. I lose all track of time. She's well spoken and despite looking fifty, sounds closer to thirty. The room smells strongly of urine. Another ten minutes pass in a glacial manner.

'You're right,' she abruptly says. 'Bad things sometimes feel good.'

A tendril of fear tightens around my heart. I don't want to have any kind of conversation about what she's done.

'My first name is Jim, but people call me Dalton here. You're Phillipa, aren't you?'

She nods.

'That's a nice name.'

'Thank you.'

'Do you enjoy this warm weather?'

A small up-tick at the side of her mouth. 'No, too hot.'

And that's how it goes. Trite questions from football to ice hockey, and cooking to gardening. As she talks, I can see her teeth are dirty and her fingernails are bitten to the quick. I steal a peek at my watch after what feels like many months have passed and see I only have a few minutes left. I hear the sound of approaching boots.

'Why am I here?' she suddenly asks.

I struggle for a few moments.

'So we can look after you.'

'But why?'

'Some people need looking after.'

'I think I'd like to go.'

'You'll be able to leave soon, when we have everything in place for you.'

For the first time, her head turns to me and our eyes connect. Someone taps on the door.

'I'll take over now, Dalton,' says MacStravick.

I keep my focus on Phillipa.

'I've got to go now, Phillipa. Mr MacStravick here is going to make sure everything's all right.'

When I stand, she jerks herself upright, but doesn't say anything until I get to the door. I pass the pen and book over to MacStravick.

'Dalton,' she whispers. 'Thank you.'

I nod and leave at the speed Braddock did. Outside Healthcare, as if to expel something rotten from my core, I release the longest, slowest, deepest exhale that has ever left my lungs.

51

When I return to the houseblocks, Myerscough is locking Billie behind the wing gates. He looks sicker than Phillipa in Healthcare, while Billie appears angry. I begin to suspect that there might be something weighing on Myerscough like a bad diagnosis.

'You all right, mate? Just doing quarter days now?'

Dark eyes stare back at me.

'They put a call out over the radio for me to report immediately to Healthcare. That can't be good news.'

He's correct to be fearful, while naïve Billie is annoyed at having her morning outside cut short. I'm tempted to let him go there unsuspecting. I want to forget the experience myself rather than implanting it in my brain by talking about it, but I can't do that to him.

'It's a nasty one. Keep chatting to her and tell her we're doing the best we can for her. I wouldn't get involved in any specifics.'

He frowns. I nod and walk towards the hub. Breakman beckons me in.

'I'm afraid there's more terrible news, Dalton.'

'Bloody hell. Now what?'

'Rose-Marie's died in hospital. I just found out.'

I immediately look to the wing, where I spot Tex taking delivery of some tea packs from Tara and Kitty. They're all laughing.

'Shit,' is all I can come up with.

'Yes, I know. Can you do lunch and lock up on your wing by yourself? I'll come on and help for roll count. I'm aware how involved Tex was, so I'm going to send her home.'

'Sure.'

'Okay, ask her to get her things and come to the hub straight away.'

I leave the hub and let Tex know. She's not stupid and is already crying by the time I open the gate to let her off the wing. Tara watches her leave. She's not daft either.

'I take it Rose-Marie didn't make it,' she says.

'Keep it to yourself. You know what will happen when people find out.'

'Your secret's safe with me, Dalton. In fact, all your secrets are safe with me.'

I squint at her expressionless face.

'What does that mean?'

'You seem very pally with Damage. Is she getting to you? I warned you about her.'

'Don't you have any work to do?'

'I'm warning you again, that's all. The reception orderly has just returned and told me that the witch is back.'

'Who is the witch?'

'Zelda. She's been given an eight-stretch with a deportation order. Women only receive time like that for violence or something very serious, so be careful of her, too.'

Lunch goes smoothly, but Red doesn't collect her food. When I open her door, she's still kneeling on the floor in the same spot I left her in at breakfast.

'Red, come on, get up.'

I help her up and she turns to me. Her eyes are bloodshot and her face seems to have collapsed. Slowly, she reaches out and puts her arms around me and pulls me into the tightest hug I've experienced, as though she's trying to climb inside me for safety. I return it in kind. There's no sexual intent, and I need it as much as she does.

'What's wrong, Red?'

'I just miss my three little boys.'

Red is nineteen.

Breakman comes on the wing for bang up. I'm barely functioning after everything that's happened today. Breakman doesn't appear much better. Red is at least lying on her bunk when we reach her. She stares impassively at me.

'Red,' I say. 'I'll get lunch cover to look in on you over the next hour, okay?'

'Thank you, sir.'

Laurinavicius frowns defiantly at me from her bed when I crack her door for the head count, but it's obvious she's been crying as well. When we return to the hub, Peabody is on lunch cover. I give him the full update.

'Christ,' is all he says.

While we wait for the roll to clear, Breakman says she'll see every inmate on an ACCT book individually after lunch and let them know about Rose-Marie. I'm glad I'll be out of here in a few minutes. I feel like sprinting to the gatehouse. The emergency in-cell telephone rings. Breakman picks it up just as 'the roll is clear, both sides' comes over the radio. I stand and start shuffling out with everyone else seemingly desperate to escape.

'Dalton.'

I stop, sigh, and turn.

'It's W1-17, she's left her ID card in your office after being in the gardens. Be a sweet and drop it off.'

Shaking my head, I head back to the wing. I can't see her ID card on the table or hanging up with the keys, so I return to Billie's cell. I open the door to see her standing in front of me in functional underwear, but it would be impossible for anything to detract from such perfection.

She grabs my belt buckle and pulls me in with the same hunger that Red did, but there's no yearning for comfort, only lust. She pushes the door shut behind me. I'm too battered by the day's events to resist and half-heartedly return her pressure, but in seconds my body responds. She undoes my zip and quickly frees my penis. In another second, it's in her mouth. I put my hand down to push her head away, but instead I run my hands through her hair. I forget to listen out for the wing gates clanging or the sound of approaching feet, not caring even that there's a slit in the curtain. Heaven doesn't hold such concerns. I finish fast and Billie swallows. She rises with an intense smile, then kisses me gently on the lips.

'You can fuck me any way you want, but I don't have very nice underwear.'

I look in her eyes to see if she's joking, but her expression is plain. My brain is stunned by what I've just done. As I step out of the cell and push the door shut, I notice Billie's ID card resting on top of her pillow, where no one could miss it.

52

I leave the wing thanking God that Billie's cellmate, Zelda, is back today. I try not to think about the guilt as I cycle home, but it's difficult. What the hell am I doing? But even when I feel disgust at being so weak and treacherous, my body responds in a different way. When I reach our street, I knock on Gary's door to see if he fancies going for a drive, but no one's in. I get in my car and drive to Serpentine Green shopping centre where there are plenty of shops to distract me, and I can buy cheap alcohol from Tesco.

I browse in a sportswear shop and check out the footwear, but my trainers are okay for the moment. Tesco supermarket at Hampton is massive, so I stock up on everything that's been depleted in our house. It takes ages because I don't know where anything is. I find myself in the clothes section and wander to women's underwear, feeling as though everyone in the store is taking sneaky glances my way.

On the end of an aisle is a lacy black bra and knickers set. Apart from having smaller boobs, the model on the label even looks like Billie. I moisten my lips as I reckon Billie would look better in them. Imagine if I took them into the prison for her, and it was a random staff search day. It would take some explaining. I'd have to say they were for me. Shaking my head, I retreat out of there and grab a pack of work socks from the men's section.

Two and a half hours later, I arrive at home and haul my stuff into the house. I open a can of lager even though it's warm and guzzle it immediately. And then another. It's not until I'm nearly sick on the third can that I stop. I drink fast after I recover, knowing I have an eight o'clock start tomorrow, but if I pass out before 6 p.m., hopefully I won't be over the limit in the morning. After I've chinned the eight-pack, my brain still won't give me any peace.

I attempt to watch a film on Channel 4, but I can't concentrate and stagger to bed. When I close my eyes, a carousel of women rotates through my mind. There's Abi shouting, Kitty frowning, Tara laughing, Tex crying, Red howling, Billie teasing, and Rose-Marie dying. And their eyes are all looking at me.

I grab my phone from the bedside table and check for a reply from Abi, but there are no new emails.

53

I wake up tangled in my sheets and drenched in sweat. It takes about thirty seconds for me to be able to focus on anything. The alarm buzzes and immediately elevates my headache to biblical. There's no way I can drive, so I lurch to the shower and keep the water on for thirty seconds after it goes cold.

Just before I leave, I check my emails. There is one from Abi. I make a cup of strong coffee, take a big breath, and sit down to read it.

Hi, when you get paid, please transfer £100 to my account because the kids need a few things. A

I lean forward, eyes wide, and scroll down for the rest, but there's nothing else. She's clearly seen my long email because she replied to it. I expect to feel angry, but I just feel sad.

What are my children doing? Who's looking after them? Do they miss me? It appears that Abi has moved on very quickly. Was I so easy to leave? She was probably considering this move for years.

I have to fight for my children though. How can I best stay in touch with them? Even though I'm angry with Abi, I need to remain polite. She is the link to my kids. If they are in a different country, she is the only person who will be able to allow us to have a relationship.

I involuntarily snarl at the thought of Abi dating again and bringing another man into Ivan's and Tilly's lives. Children adapt fast. I'll give Abi a few more days to respond, then I'll ask her to ring me. If she gives me her parents' address, then I can send them a present or perhaps a letter to Tilly and a funny picture to Ivan. God. I'm sure I appreciated them when they were here and spent lots of quality time with them, but with all the madness floating around in my head, it's hard to remember.

It's another effort cycling to work. I'm tempted to cycle into the rowing lake instead of alongside it. I have an eight 'til-five shift, which means I'll probably not be on a wing. It's a pity, because I could do with a day sitting in the office with my forehead resting on the table.

When I get to the gatehouse, I see I'm free flow officer in the morning and education officer in the afternoon. The first involves escorting prisoners around the prison and is a relatively cushy number. On the male side, education duty is stopping fights and preventing smoking in the toilet. Both are forlorn tasks. I expect it to be easier over here.

Despite the fact I'm hanging, the morning passes quickly. Free flow is miles better than with the men, where it generally involves a lot of arguing. The females are less abusive and more rule-abiding. After the workers return to the wings, I help out in the med hatch as there is no GD today.

Tara comes off her wing for some paracetamol.

'Headache?' I ask.

'Yes, probably a spot of nerves. Even though I've only been here for ten weeks, it feels strange leaving. I always think I have a big sticker on my forehead when I get out that says *I've been in prison*. I should buy a T-shirt with it on, so no one's in any doubt.'

'A lot of people will miss you. You're almost like a mother to some of these, which is a little odd seeing as you're one of the youngest and most definitely the smallest.'

'That's why I'll never want any kids of my own. There's already plenty who need a mum and haven't got one. Will you miss me, Dalton?'

I look down at her as she looks up at me. We have a moment of real affection. She's so positive and full of energy, but her faith in other people has been ruined. She should have been able to count on that Lavinia woman after all that had happened to her, but instead she was just taken advantage of. I hope Tara learns to trust again.

'I will. There's something lovely about you. I give you nine out of ten.'

'Why only nine?' She beams.

'Everyone lies in here, one way or another.'

'I haven't lied to you.'

She looks genuinely upset.

'You've served ten weeks of a twenty-week sentence. You don't get time for prostitution, because it's pointless. The courts know that now and will fine you and offer intervention if you are inclined to accept it. Therefore, something aggravated your case enough for you to receive a custodial sentence.'

She clenches her fists at her sides and stares at me so hard that I'm not sure what she's going to do. Instead of her getting angry, though, a tear bursts from each eye and they stream down her cheeks.

'I'm sorry.'

'It's okay, you don't have to tell me.'

'I know, but I want to. It was a knife. The police caught me soliciting and gave me a warning, but when I spoke, they became suspicious of my posh accent, so they searched me, thinking I was selling drugs.'

'I assume it was for protection, not extortion.'

'Yes, it was pretty obvious what I had it for, but it's still dangerous. If you're angry and you can get your hands on a weapon, you're going to use it. That's when people die.'

'That's not a whopper, so you can be a nine and a half.'

'True, but the funny thing is, I even lied about what Kitty was in for. I said she's in for theft.'

'And she isn't?'

'Well, in a way. It was street robbery. It's a much more serious offence.'

'Isn't that the same crime Billie's in for? Was that Lavinia like a modern-day Fagin?'

Tara cries again, but this time through laughter. She stops herself by looking around and puffing her cheeks out.

'Did Billie explain her role in her robbery?'

'She said it was her partner's idea, and she tagged along.'

'Brilliant. You are a muppet, Dalton. I bet she also got you with the dry hand thing?'

My eyes narrow.

'I knew it!' Tara laughs. 'Billie doesn't have a skin condition. She puts her hands in bleach, which makes them red and sore. If you men haven't got the communal brain cell for the day, you fall for her sob story. Have a look in her cell.'

Tara is still chuckling as she leaves the med room, but the next inmate knocks her over. It looks deliberate. Tara gets to her feet and stands up. It's Billie's padmate, Zelda. She only has a vest on her top half and Tex was right, her arms are scarred. That's not unusual in here, but hers are uniform, as though they were done carefully and deliberately.

'Watch where you go,' says Zelda. She bares her teeth and drags a thumbnail across her own neck so hard it leaves a vivid red line.

Tara doesn't look at her, but instead turns to me.

'Talk to me this afternoon because you might not get a chance before I leave tomorrow. Don't forget.'

Zelda ignores me, gets her meds, puts it in her mouth and walks out of the room without taking any water.

'Oi, get back here!' I shout.

Zelda carries on walking to her wing, where Sheraton is holding the gate open to let the inmates on and off.

'Sheraton, shut the gate.'

He does, just as Zelda reaches him.

'Open,' she demands.

Sheraton points in my direction. I catch up with her.

'What's going on, Zelda? You know you have to drink a cup of water.'

Her eyes widen and blaze. It's a raw, personal anger, which I haven't experienced on this side of the prison. She forces her gaze away, turns and rattles the wing gates with fury.

'Okay, that's a warning. Do it again and you'll go on report.'

She clangs the gates again. There's no point in talking to someone when they are that cross, so I'll get her at bang up. I nod at Sheraton to allow her back on the wing. The rest of meds is without incident, so I return to Whisky wing.

Tex and Sheraton are doing roll count, so I let myself in their office and fill out the warning form. When I open Billie's cell, she and Zelda are on the bottom bunk. Billie's arm is around Zelda's shoulders; Zelda glowers at me.

'Here's your warning, Zelda. Don't repeat what you did today.'

'Come on, Dalton,' says Billie, mischievously. 'Screw that up. I was just telling Zelda how you've been looking after me.'

My eyes are drawn to the shelf in the corner where I can see my tube of cream next to another similar, besides two bars of Dove moisturising soap. Billie follows my line of sight and sees what I'm frowning at. She winks at me as I slam the door shut.

54

It's lasagne for lunch in the work canteen and I eat my bodyweight of it. I think of the small portion the prisoners receive. Afterwards, I can barely keep my eyes open in the hub. I'm tempted to have a power nap in an empty cell, but I doubt I'd wake up. My afternoon shift is so quiet in Education, I'm almost dozing on my feet. Only two teachers have classes, and one of those finishes early. The clearing of the final teacher's throat as he makes himself a coffee wakes me up where I've fallen asleep, face down on a desk in the staff office.

I recall my conversation with Tara and log onto a computer. I'll check her record first.

Tara Prestwick. AKA Ruined. Twenty weeks for possession of a bladed article. She could have got four years, but the judge obviously believed her claim that the knife was for protection. Sending her to jail was clearly a message to her about the seriousness of carrying a weapon. If she gets caught again for the same offence, the courts will slam her. But who's to say Tara didn't intend to use it for darker purposes?

Sue Halliwell, who is the ginger-haired girl, AKA Red. Two

years for aggravated burglary. Shit. That is nasty. It basically means she broke into someone's house with a weapon of some kind. To get two years at her age would indicate it wasn't her first similar offence.

Kitty Monroe, AKA Broken. Two years for street robbery, which also suggests it wasn't her first time, either.

Zelda Tiozzo, AKA The Witch. Eight years for conspiracy to supply class A drugs. Deportation in process. God, no wonder she's in a foul mood. She'll spend at least a year in one of our jails and then it's arrivederci! Italian prisons are a far cry from luxury, unless your idea of a good time is eight to a cell and twenty-three-hour bang up.

Laimutė Laurinavicius. AKA The Russian. Six months for threats to kill. That's not the biggest surprise.

Rose-Marie Nelson. I can't access the file. It has 'deceased' written in the notes, which seems incredibly impersonal for someone whom I'll never forget. Perhaps one day, I'll write about my experiences here. Rose-Marie shouldn't just be a statistic. Tex and I will light a candle for her.

Billie Harding, AKA Damage. Two years for street robbery. I take a note of the date and flick back to Kitty's conviction. It's the same day. So, Kitty was Billie's partner in crime.

Mihaela Ion. Twenty weeks for pickpocketing.

Ana-Maria Breban. Twenty weeks for pickpocketing. I read the details. Apparently, they were made to work as pickpockets by the people who brought them to the UK from Romania. That's two more people that I've misjudged over here.

Jessica Smith. The girl who sliced her own stomach. AKA Cut-up. Six months for multiple breaches of a restraining order.

Someone knocks on the outside door for Education. I open the barred gate and then the wooden door to find Billie in the green gardening trousers Myerscough found for her. The white T-shirt still gleams, but she has a smudge of mud across her forehead.

'Billie, what a nice surprise. I was just reading something about you.'

'Have I been nominated for an award?'

'Yes, it's the Biggest Liar Prize. You're the hot favourite despite considerable competition. Perhaps you could practise your speech now.'

'I need the toilet, Dalton. Let me in.'

'Speech first, please.'

'Okay, I lied to you. I really like you and I didn't want you thinking the worst of me.'

'And the moisturising thing?'

'I just wanted to see if you liked me, and you do. Now open up. I only got these trousers today.'

I let her in and she does a strange waddling run to the toilet. The last class finishes and they shuffle out. The English tutor is huge and hairy, and resembles a grizzled rugby player rather than an academic, but he thanks me for helping and leaves out the back way. I nip to the office to fetch my bag and to sign out of the computer. The toilet door slams and Billie comes and stands in the doorway.

'Better?' I ask.

'Much. My period is due tomorrow and I always get a belly ache the day before.' She looks up and down the corridor. 'Why's it so quiet?'

'Everyone's gone for the day.'

'Ooh.' She steps into the room.

'Billie, you aren't supposed to be in here.'

'Is there a camera?'

'Not in here, but there is in the corridor, so they'll know you were in here.'

'Chill, baby. It's not like they've got a guy studying one camera all day long. It's the same in shops. They only watch the recording if they hear about an incident. One kiss, and then I'll go.'

'No. No more kisses. I could get into serious trouble.'

'Come on, you bad boy. This might be our last opportunity now that my darling Italian chum is back. I know you want to.'

I do want to. I beckon her over with my finger. There's no chance of being discovered in the office. It hasn't got any windows, for a start, and there are double doors at both exits to Education, so I'd hear the jangling of keys before anyone was anywhere near us. I take my time and the kiss is amazing. We connect together so neatly, it's as though she were designed for me. She takes my hands and puts them on her breasts and I don't remove them. She finally moves a few millimetres away from my lips. Her voice is throaty.

'God, I fancy you so much.'

'Don't say that.'

'Did you buy me any new knickers?'

I shake my head.

'You're mean. Look, mine are terrible. They keep falling off.'

With that, she turns around and yanks her trousers and pants to her ankles in one swift movement. She pulls off her T-shirt, leans over the desk and arches her back.

'Fuck me, Dalton. Quick. This is our only chance. You said yourself you're returning to the other side soon.'

There must be a thousand reasons why I shouldn't do it, but unfortunately the strongest reason for doing it is that I want to. Her blue eyes stand out of her tanned face. They draw me in. Faced with this, I can't resist. No man could. I briefly think of my wife's cold email, then undo my belt. I slide inside her with no effort at all. Again, we fit perfectly.

'What about, you know?' I ask.

'I'm on the pill – besides, I'm due on tomorrow, so it's safe anyway. Just get on with it. Fuck me, sir. Do it fast and hard.'

I pound into her and try not to be too quick, but it's impossible. She whimpers and gasps, occasionally looking over her shoulder with her teeth bared. At the end, she turns and stares at me as I climax. Even though it was rapid, I can't remember sex ever being so amazing.

55

I let Billie out from Education onto Main Street and follow her to open the door back to the houseblocks. I watch her as she walks away. She stops after a few metres and turns around. The sun is lower and the tall buildings put her bottom half in shade. She looks so flawless that my breathing catches. She tucks her hair behind her ear again. I'm sure she does it because she knows I like it. And I do, I could watch her do it all day long. She stares at the floor, coyly, glances up and catches my eye, then runs to the houseblocks. I swear under my breath and walk to the gatehouse.

Myerscough is also leaving.

'Afternoon, Dalton. Sneaking out early?'

'I'm on an eight-five. No doubt you slip out early most days.'

'Perk of the gardens and everyone expects people of my age to be honest.'

'I've always said it's the quiet ones who get up to mischief.'

'I'd agree with that. Now, talking of sneaky, I'm overrun with eggs from all them damn chickens because liars keep saying they'll buy some and don't come to fetch them. Sound familiar?'

'Okay, fair cop. I'll drive in tomorrow and take a load home with me. How's that? What time should I pop over?'

'Are you still on the same wing as young Billie?'

'Yep.'

'Wander over after eleven, then you can escort her back to the houseblocks with you. Save my old legs.'

'Okay. How's she getting on?'

'Good. She's inclined to sit around in the sun, but she gets the work done. Chickens seem to like her. I like her, too, but she's not the innocent kid I thought she was, although none of them are.'

'You're telling me. She fed me a tale about the street robbery she was in for. Hinted it was her boyfriend's fault, but it turns out she committed it with a female friend.'

Myerscough freezes as he drops his keys down the chute. He swallows and his lips move, but he doesn't talk.

'You okay?'

'Yes. The little snake. She told me she was in for theft.'

'Well, I suppose it's still stealing. If any chickens go missing, I'd peek under her jumper.'

Myerscough blinks a couple of times and goes even whiter. He marches towards the scanners, puts his index finger in to open the glass panel and vanishes in a hurry. He doesn't look back.

I'm too tired and hungover to let his oddness concern me, so I drop my keys and radio in and check the detail for tomorrow. I'm on the wing with Billie again, or should I say Tex? I'm dreading it and looking forward to it in equal measure.

56

When I wake up, I feel a million times better than I did yesterday and wonder why I keep drinking so much. Gary popped over with a four-pack last night, but I only drank coffee. We had a good chat. It made me realise that I bottle everything up without man talk to discuss and resolve my feelings. I suspect alcohol is a release, at least for a while, but I'm just hiding from thoughts that need to be said out loud.

What was it that brought Abi and me together? We laughed about the same things. She loved the fact that I was forgiving of everyone's mistakes. The person I was hardest on was myself. It made me recall the moment she said that she wanted to marry me because she knew I would never give up. I hate the thought of being a quitter.

It's also true what Gary said. When you're a parent, your eye has to be on the children. Abi, in particular, rarely stops to consider her own needs. Her focus is on keeping the house clean, and ensuring the kids feel loved. They're the most important thing to her. Ivan can be exhausting to look after. Is it reasonable for me to expect her to finish all that, then wait in full make-up and seductive clothing for me to get home from work? Do I return from the prison, shower, and put my best shirt on? Although, an email responding to mine wouldn't be that much hassle. She's probably already registered the kids at that school in Spain.

Gary did ask me a horrible question: What are the names of your children's friends?

I could only remember one of Tilly's, but I knew Abi would know them all.

My family has only been gone a week, but it seems like so much longer. I never thought out of sight, out of mind would apply to my wife and children, but I'm struggling to think straight. It feels as if I'm single after Abi's chilly reply, but that doesn't excuse my behaviour. At least Zelda is back, which puts an end to any in-cell shenanigans. I'm not sure whether to tell Billie that there can be no more of whatever this is, or just to keep my distance.

As promised to Myerscough, I'm going to drive into work so I can take some eggs home. I wallow in bed for as long as possible, stretching and enjoying the freedom. When I can't leave it any longer, I sit up, but find myself distracted by the space that Abi used to fill. There are a few of her hairs on the pillow. Will her head ever lie there again? I can't even remember the last time we spooned, never mind went further. But if a man has needs, then so must a woman. What could I have done differently? Her needs might have been to feel appreciated or, better still, wanted.

I pull my uniform on and take the last clean shirt down. I need to put a wash on tonight. Downstairs, the kettle boils and I make a quick cup of coffee and add loads of cold water so it's drinkable. Even so, I burn my tongue as I really am cutting it fine. I have a fast glance at my emails on my phone and there is one from Abi. The title is 'Moving.' I see part of the first line.

I'm sorry it's come to this.

Great. I place my phone back on the worktop, walk outside and get in my car in a daze. It's a weird, light-headed drive to work. I'm guessing it's shock, because I don't feel cross. Perhaps it's panic. Maybe I've been expecting it, but reality has hit home. I've been casually thinking of the implications of them staying in Spain, but not fully comprehending that I will rarely see my children now.

When I arrive at the prison, I park in the far corner, open the door, and vomit dark liquid, which I hope is just coffee, over the tarmac. There's a bottle of water in the footwell, which is warm and old, but anything to quench the acid in my mouth. I get out of the car and a few drops of rain hit my face. The clouds above are black, rolling and threatening. I hadn't even noticed. The oppressive threat of thunder is in the air. It's about time this weather broke. Lennox arrives and screeches to a halt. She gets out of her car and sprints past me, laughing.

'Ah, Dalton. Feels like I haven't seen you for ages. I suspect you'll be with us soon anyway.'

I run after her.

'Why do you say that?'

'Your brother-in-law was at court yesterday.'

'Did they bring him back?'

'No idea. I was only on an early. Talks a lot of bollocks, that boy, so who knows what happened?'

There's a big queue of uniformed men and women at the gatehouse. Braddock is at the rear, shaking his head.

'What's up?' I ask him.

'The scanners aren't working properly. They won't recognise all the fingerprints.'

'Maybe some of us have been sacked, and this is the new way of finding out.'

'I wouldn't put it past them.'

'Hey, did Colt return last night?'

'Yes, and all his minions. Despite his bullshit about changing their pleas, they went guilty. The judge wanted pre-sentencing reports due to their ages. They'll be sentenced together in two weeks. Then we can get rid of them either way.'

A weight slides from my shoulders. I can cope with two weeks. After that, I'll be away from temptation for good. We receive our keys and radios, and I say my farewells as they split off to the male side. When I reach the houseblocks, the reception staff are taking that day's courts and releases. One of them is Tara.

She sees me and her face splits into a big grin.

'Dalton!'

She runs up to me and throws her arms around me, then her legs. I glance to the right where all the staff are staring out of the hub. Most are laughing. Tex is pretending to cuddle herself. The only one who doesn't look amused is Nasima. I decide I don't care and hug her back.

'Come on, Tara. I'll quickly walk you over. I've got three minutes.'

'Good. I thought I wasn't going to get a chance to talk to you, but I left a message with Kitty, just in case.'

'Sounds serious.'

'It could be.'

There are fifteen prisoners milling around. Most of them will be at court. You can tell the ones who are leaving because they're smiling and nervous with plenty of make-up on. The others are just nervous. I shout out to the officer who's escorting them.

'I'll get this door, you go.'

He opens the houseblock doors and marches off with the inmates trailing after him in a line like schoolchildren.

'Right,' says Tara. 'The rumour is that Zelda's got a weapon that she brought back with her from the other prison she was in.'

'Right, thanks for that. Why is that so urgent?'

'Duh, dummy! She's psychotic, and she's under Billie's spell. Jealousy makes people evil in here, and she's already an evil witch, so I assume the next step is murderous.'

'Okay, cool. I'll get her cell searched, but it's probably plugged.'

'Yes. You'll have to go diving for it.'

We laugh, both knowing that there's no way that would happen. They don't even do strip-searches on the women now without crystal-clear intel because the chances of finding anything are remote. The vast majority are compliant and the others have places we can't search anyway. Most of the females have histories of abuse and being strip-searched at what is already a stressful time can be incredibly traumatic. It doesn't seem to bother the men, unless they've tied a mobile phone to their dicks.

Tara smiles, but we're walking so fast, her little legs are close to running. She has a full pink tracksuit on and looks as if she's going on holiday.

'Look out for Billie, too,' she says. 'She always ends up in trouble, but she's just trying to make her way like everyone else. Being rejected and abused has made her clingy. She wants everyone to need her, then she wants to keep them close to her, even when it's bad for those involved. She likes you, we all do.'

'What made me so popular?'

'I've been considering that. In a way, when your adolescence is stolen, it's hard to grow up. We all daydreamed when we were younger about being part of a proper family. You're like a cool father figure. Many of us in here never had a dad about when we were growing up. So, we're still searching for him.'

'I'm only thirty-five.'

'That's old enough. Your problem, Dalton, is that you care, even if you don't want to. But that can be dangerous in here. Treat Billie as you would a Siren.'

'You mean like an alarm?'

Tara raises her eyebrows and lets her mouth drop open.

'It's Greek mythology.'

'Still don't get it.'

'The Sirens sang their beautiful songs and enticed the sailors onto the rocks.'

'So?'

'Like them, Billie's appeal is hard to resist. If you respond to the call, it will end badly.'

My face falls. Tara gives me a last hug, and a peck on the cheek.

'If it's too late, then stop it now. She just wants to be happy, but she probably won't do anything to hurt you. Remember that. And God knows how she got that chicken gig with her record.'

I merely nod.

'Laters, Dalton. I'll miss you.'

'I hope I never see you again, except perhaps to get my nails done.'

Tara smiles, but she's crying. She turns and runs up the corridor. I lock the door and plod back to the houseblocks, feeling like weeping myself. Despite Tara's kind words, I'm disappointed with myself. I don't know the rules over here. I've become unprofessional and everything I hated in a prison officer. Change has to start today, and that means talking to Billie.

When I return to the houseblocks, Nasima beckons me into the hub, which now has only her in it.

'Yes, ma'am.'

'Can you explain that?'

I slump into a seat and rub my eyes. I'm a skydiver hurtling towards the ground, knowing he left the chute on the plane.

'I can try,' I finally say.

'Go on, then.'

'We basically got on well. She told me she saw me as a father figure, which makes me ancient. Anyway, I liked her, and she didn't seem like a bad person. She's just a girl who needs kindness.'

'There are professional boundaries.'

'I know, or at least I did over the male side. Honestly, I haven't cuddled any of the blokes over there. But she was going home. She hugged me. What do I do? Yell "get off" in her face? Drop her? It's different here. These aren't wings full of violent villains, they're full of victims – you told me that. Nearly all of them have been exploited and abused and let down. They're broken and ruined.'

I stop when I say that and, before I know it, I'm laughing. Broken and Ruined. It's Kitty and Tara. It should be our jobs in prison to fix those who are sent here. Give them the tools and assistance so they don't come back. I understand the staff are trying, but as always it comes down to money. These girls need therapy and training, housing and education. If the government is struggling to house and help citizens and their children who don't have criminal records, then where does that leave people like Tara? They have no choice but to return to the life and circumstances that sent them here in the first place.

Nasima gets up from her seat and stares out at the prisoners as they begin queueing for their meds. She sits back down and takes a deep breath.

'Perhaps it's me who should apologise.'

'What for?'

'It's a tale of two jails. The male and female estates are different places, needing different techniques. You've been here more than five years, but nearly always on one side. In a way, you're institutionalised. I shouldn't have put you with the young offenders, who are our most troubled souls. They're children really, and it's natural to want to parent them.'

I give her a tired smile. 'It's crazy what a lot of them have had to cope with.'

'Look, Dalton. If you fancy a move to the female lifers' wing, you can go because we need to get Officer Healy off there.'

'Why's that?'

'One of the recently convicted women says Healy is the spitting image of her deceased husband. She has a picture of her husband in her cell, and it's true. I thought it *was* Healy for a spooky moment.'

'Ah, I see. So, she gets upset when she sees Healy on the wing.'

'No, she gets angry. It was *her* who killed him.'

I can't help laughing again. I'm definitely losing it.

'Sounds great, I'll take it.'

'Okay, good. I'll ring Details and swap you both after today. I'd better let you get back to work.'

'Cheers, ma'am. Appreciate the words.'

'Any time. I'm sorry, but you'll need to clear Rose-Marie's cell.'

She turns her chair around and moves her mouse to awaken her screen. I sit still for a moment with my head spinning, then walk onto the wing. The first person I see is Billie.

'Morning, sir.' She beams at me.

God, I'm going to miss her.

57

Tex is still visibly upset as she supervises breakfast. It's annoying that no one's cleared Rose-Marie's cell yet, and now it needs to be done today. There will be an inquiry into the end of her life because she'll be treated as a death in custody. Her possessions may form part of that investigation and they'll need to be handed over to a relative at some point, assuming anyone's interested. All this will drag the pain out for Tex.

Would it be better if someone who didn't know Rose-Marie well emptied her cell? Maybe that's the last kindness we can give her: to remove her things with respect.

I don't want to do the cell clearance, but I tell Tex to run the wing and I grab a thick plastic prison bag and get to it. The first thing I notice is how clean the cell is. With the men, you're usually tidying them after prisoners have been dragged to the block, and they're nearly always minging, the untidy state often matching their minds. But for people like Rose-Marie, who have lives that are beyond their control, sometimes keeping their cells neat is a way of trying to reclaim at least a small piece of it.

There are a few photos of babies on the wall that I hadn't

noticed before. Were they the kids she had to give up? You can tell the inmates who have support because their friends and relatives send in loads of pictures and cards, to let them know they aren't forgotten. The prisoner will cover the surfaces in them like wallpaper. Receiving a letter with home news might be upsetting, but the benefit of knowing that people still care outweighs the negative. The thought of meeting them again when you leave is what keeps many sane.

It's a gloomy day and I need to put the lights on. I try to be methodical, but it's hard not to think of Rose-Marie line dancing only a few days ago. She was still so young. Tears well up when I find a box that she's made out of matchsticks. It must have taken her ages, but time is a universal luxury here. In it are her special items. There's a lock of hair, a small plastic doll, some letters and a crucifix. I quickly put the box in the bag along with all her toiletries and food. I don't read the letters.

There's a knock at the door and I open up to find Billie outside.

'Yes.'

'Are you emptying her cell?'

'Yes.'

'She's got my shampoo.'

'Really? What brand is it?'

'It's a white and blue bottle.'

'Surely, if it's yours, you would know the make.'

Billie's vexed for a moment, then triumphantly says, 'Pantene.'

I look in the bag, which contains a bottle of Pantene, and pull it out.

'Okay, Billie. How much was in it?'

'What?'

'How much shampoo was in the bottle when you lent it to Rose-Marie?'

'I don't know, half?'

'Ooh, close! This is virtually full. Poor show, lying to get your hands on a dead person's property.'

'It was worth a go. She won't be needing it where she's gone.'

'Her family gets everything. Anything else? Shall I ring the mortuary and ask them to check her mouth for gold fillings?'

'Very funny.' She looks left and right on the wing before continuing. 'Hey, if I can get a bail hostel, I'll be able to leave on tag in a few months. We can hook up without worrying about what anyone says.'

My stomach lurches. I'd just been thinking that nearly everyone leaves. I hadn't considered the fact Billie might want to see me when she gets out. What the hell have I done?

'Billie, you know I'm married.'

'You were married yesterday, and that didn't stop you, now, did it?'

I shake my head as she saunters away. I feel sick but decide the best option is not to dwell on things. I put the shampoo bottle, which is actually only a quarter-full, back in the bag. Next, I count Rose-Marie's bras and knickers and place them inside. She was another inmate who could have done with some new ones.

I'm not sure if Billie meant to imply with her comments that Rose-Marie was going to hell or if that's in my own thoughts. A small part of me wants to think of Rose-Marie as a baby killer but I don't think that's fair. Although, it is difficult not to imagine the foetus as a small newborn. But it's also clear that society, or at least her position and decisions within it, had backed her into a corner where the only choices were too awful to comprehend. That's what I always say: prison makes little sense. You just have to do your best, bite down on the heartbreak, and try to survive.

I stop and relock her door to give Tex a hand with mass movement, which is when the entire houseblock heads off to work wing by wing, but we've only got a roll count of fourteen now. The two

Romanians agreed to their deportation to Romania, where they'll be allowed to be free. They'll probably be back in the UK within the month and returned here not long after.

'Commence movement,' comes over the radio. The girls gather at the gate and filter through. Some laugh, others are anxious and looking for threats that I can't detect. Billie is the last to leave her cell and has made an effort with her appearance. The other workers are drab in comparison and look as though they're going to work in an industrial laundry, even though that work's actually done on the male side. Billie could be heading to the make-up counter at Boots. Even her gardening trousers are ironed.

After the last worker has gone, I skip the morning meeting and head back to finish the cell clearance. It takes until eleven to clear out and mark down all of Rose-Marie's things, which is the time I said I'd see Myerscough. I leave the door wide open and ask one of the wing workers to mop the floor. Someone else will live there soon, thankfully unaware of their new home's history.

'Tex, I'm off to buy some eggs and pick up Billie. You want any?'

'Yeah, definitely. Get me two boxes. For some reason, I thought they'd taste weird, but they were so golden, and I got a double-yolker. He only feeds them organic stuff, so they should be miles more expensive.'

Smiling, I leave the houseblock and take the side exits to the gardens, which are at the back of the prison and are the most open part of it. A huge crack of thunder booms overhead. There are threatening black clouds sprawling across the sky, seemingly not far above my head. Getting struck by lightning would just sum up my day, especially if it hit me in the groin. My nostrils flare at the smell of violence in this place again, but this is nature's anger.

The garden detail rush by me with their heads down as giant drops of rain fall out of the sky. The supervising officer races past without looking up. I reach the big chicken coop. Even their tiny brains recognise trouble. They're scampering back inside as I open the door and find Billie. She's brushing the floor.

'Where's Myerscough?'

'In his office.'

'Are you finished?'

'Why?'

'It's going to hammer down in a minute. Everyone else has gone in.'

'Ten minutes.'

'Okay.'

I jog through the garden area. The office is on the side of the main prison and is more like a cupboard with a chair and a desk in it. A small room next to it has a fridge and a cabinet. Myerscough is just replacing the phone on its cradle. He leans forward and slowly closes his eyes.

'You all right?' I ask.

'I don't think I'm going to be.'

'What happened?'

'That was Oscar One. He wants to see me straight away.'

'What for?'

'He didn't say.'

'It'll just be a shit job.'

'No, he said to meet him in the HR manager's office.'

He rises from his seat, breathing fast, eyes flashing from side to side. I'm not sure I want to know, but can't help myself.

'Why? What have you done?'

'It's the kid, Billie. She was so keen and enthusiastic that I wanted her out here as much as she wanted to be. I just gave her the position without getting clearance, thinking I'd get it sorted in a few days. She said she was only in for theft, so I didn't worry about getting it. Then I liked her company here and thought nobody would notice anyway, but yesterday I had a look at her record.'

He shakes his head and pulls his coat on.

'It's my stupidity that Oscar One will want to talk to me about. I'd better face the music. Help yourself to eggs. There are loads in the fridge. It's a pound for a dozen now to get rid of them. Is Billie finished with her jobs?'

'She said ten minutes.'

'Okay, make sure you lock up here and she leaves her wellies. Wish me luck.'

I wave him off at the door, where I see Billie's pink trainers haphazardly dropped. If Myerscough has broken security protocol, then he'll need more than luck. I think of the sailors being lured to their doom by the Siren's song. I pull four boxes of six eggs out of the fridge, put them on the side and leave two pounds on the table in payment, even though I doubt Myerscough will be back to collect it.

The heavy raindrops are increasing in number, so I run across to Billy. A sudden gust of wind almost yanks the barn door out of my hand. I hang onto it and laugh at the vision inside. It's like a scene from *The Wizard of Oz* with chickens, straw and feathers flying about the place. The only thing that's missing is Zelda on her bicycle. A long roll of thunder echoes, seemingly just above the roof and I feel a sudden chill.

'Come on, Billie, quick.'

I take her hand and pull her out of the swirling dust and debris, locking the bolt on the door. It's so dark that it could be night time; even the prison floodlights are flickering on. The rain hammers down with an angry force, pounding my head, and drowning out other sounds. We run to the office. Billie laughs next to me as I frantically try to fit my wet keys into the office door lock. A massive flash of sheet lightning rips the sky apart and lights up the steel and concrete walls around us, followed by a mighty boom of thunder. Billie has her arms out, head tipped back, eyes closed.

'I'm still here!' she screams.

I finally get the door open and the gate behind it. Billie staggers in after me, resembling the world's prettiest clown as make-up pours down her cheeks. I'm soaked to the skin. We stare into each other's eyes, grinning, then crush our faces together. Micro-thoughts of my life before meeting her zip through my mind like the light show in the sky above, but they too are gone in seconds.

I force myself to step back, panting hoarsely.

'This has to be the last time,' I whisper.

She kicks off her wellies, pulls down her trousers and yanks off her wet shirt. No underwear today. She moves to the table and sits on the edge of it, legs spread, pulling me in. Not for a kiss, but to stare at me while she unbuttons my trousers. Intense, serious, dark-blue eyes, running with mascara, give her the appearance of an evil demon, but she's so beautiful, so perfect.

I stare up and down her body and take my time. If the prison director himself opened the door, I wouldn't be able to stop.

58

When we've finished, I've no idea if we've taken thirty seconds or ten minutes. Billie wobbles as she pushes herself up from the desk. She staggers over to the piles of clothes and pulls her cold wet shirt back on. Myerscough's pound coins are stuck to her bottom. They drop off as she bends over to pull on her trousers. She laughs.

'Are there any more up there?' I ask.

'I hope so.'

I can't help giggling too, as I zip myself back up and finally get my breathing under control. Billie scrapes her wet hair back and exhales. She looks like who she is: a young woman who ran with her lover through the pouring rain before making frantic, urgent love. I feel the same emotions on my face. We step outside and I lock the doors. I turn my head into the curtains of rain that are sweeping across the prison landscape, praying they will wash away the truth.

We walk back in silence, in the same way you stroll along the beach with the person of your dreams, both safe in the knowledge that this is what life is all about. I have to stop myself taking her hand.

The food trolleys are coming over as we reach the houseblocks. The torrential downpour soon has the orderlies soaked as well and we sneak in behind them. Kitty is with them and glances from me to Billie. She looks away, but she is smiling. The person who isn't smiling is Zelda. She waits at the wing gates. Billie takes our trolley and pushes it noisily to the servery, but Zelda's eyes are on me.

Lunch is a blur, as is roll count. I grab the security seals from the office and fill in the paperwork for Rose-Marie's property. I tie the seal on and carry the big plastic bag to the hub. Tex can't look at it. Nasima stares at it with pity. It's not much to leave behind.

'Take Rose-Marie's belongings to Security, please, Dalton. You can go straight home afterwards.'

I squeeze Tex's shoulder and get out of there before I can think about what I've done. The rain has dropped to a consistent rhythmic pattering as though it could continue forever, but I can't feel it now. The strong wind blows me across the sterile area to the admin block as if with a purpose, and I trudge up the steps.

I stare at the guy in the security office. He's glancing back at the big television behind him that flickers through the view from the security cameras around the perimeter. I lick my lips and place the bag on the empty table next to him. He glances at me for a second, then tells me to put the bag in the corner. I leave with haste. There's only one other person in the queue at the gatehouse. It's Myerscough, who also looks as if he's had an emotionally exhausting day.

I wait until we're both outside and trudging towards the car park. The eggs I bought are still on his desk, long forgotten.

'What did they say?' I ask.

'Suspended, but it's over.'

'How come?'

'She's got violence on her record. There was an incident when she was eighteen with a knife. There are all manner of tools in the gardens. Anything could have happened. They've more or less said if I leave quietly today, they'll pay me until the end of the month, and just put the error down to getting a bit old and forgetful.'

'It seems a harsh way to go after all the years you've given this place. One mistake and that's it.'

A strange expression comes over his face, which he quickly stifles.

'It could have been worse,' he says. 'Even though this place has taken everything.' He scowls at me. 'Security had one of those forms sent to them that allows the prisoners to grass on each other. It was signed with a single letter – Z. It's jealousy, plain and simple, but I can't have all the prisoners working out there.'

Outside, he forces himself to walk fast to his car and I watch him go. Just before he gets inside his vehicle, he glances back at the prison for one final look. I follow his eyes. With the sinister, swirling clouds of black and grey behind the high buildings, the prison makes me think of a Victorian mental asylum rather than a place for rehabilitation. But maybe that's the truth of it.

59

I drive home drained and tired, but not feeling particularly guilty, which surprises me. It doesn't get much more stupid than shagging a prisoner. Maybe there's a hint of relief that it won't be happening again. I analyse that for a few moments and then the shame arrives. It's not just Abi I'm letting down, but the kids too. It's a massive risk to take as well. Am I going out of my mind?

The officers who end up on the other side of the bars themselves are those who bring drugs or phones in for their lovers. Many of the prisoners attempt to seduce the guards on purpose and have no remorse when the officer loses their job or worse. I wonder if that's Billie's motivation.

I'm with the lifers now, anyway, and Zelda is back, so I should have little to do with either of them. Deep down, though, I don't regret it. I know on my deathbed, hopefully in many years time, I will remember that moment in the rain and be grateful. It was the most exhilarating experience I've ever had, all with the thrilling risk of getting caught.

I pause and reconsider. What about the births of my children? To be honest, they weren't exhilarating or thrilling. I felt nervous, helpless and scared. Those feelings remained to some degree until they could talk, which was a while with the boy. It's funny to think my children are my finest achievement, when all I did was some grunting, followed by a bit of back-rubbing nine months later.

Yet, they have given my life meaning. They've made it solid and real. I'm beginning to see that instead of them unsettling my equilibrium, they are actually what anchors me. How can I have been such a fool?

It's strange how connected I feel to Billie, but I must finish it. I won't have that many shifts before Colt's back at court. Will Billie be mature enough to handle rejection? She could cause trouble for me. God, what an understatement that is. But even parked outside my house, I'm thinking of her and how I would like to do it again, just one more time. I shake my head and get out of the car.

As soon as I enter my kitchen, I remember my family, who used to live here. I understand that once you have children, your priorities change. If you are a decent human being, you put your life aside to raise them because they're too young to do it for themselves. They are your responsibility. Although what can I do if fucking Abi has given up on me? I remember the email from her.

I turn our laptop on because I hate reading small writing on tiny phone screens. It's Tilly's laptop, really. I'm surprised they didn't take it, seeing as they aren't coming back. The email is surprisingly long:

I'm sorry it's come to this, but I suppose we can't help where we are. I have spent the last week looking for someone to blame. To start with, it was you, and then it was me. But it's not either of us really. It's life, and you're right. That's what I gave up on, not you.
I've been completely honest with my mum and dad about our situation and they both laughed, which was a surprise. They said nearly all parents go through a *similar stage*. A lot of their friends split up in this

period, believing life would be better, but it wasn't. Some realised this quickly and got back together, for others, it was too late, and they regretted it.

My dad wanted me to move out to Spain because he suspected you were beating me or cheating on me, because I seemed so unhappy. He feels terrible now, because he realises that, without grandparents, we're missing a vital support. A night out, or even a few hours' peace here and there, could make all the difference to our relationship and therefore our happiness. But not only have they been absent physically, they have been distant mentally, which he says is going to change.

The children miss you so much it breaks my heart even though Ivan has been more settled out here. He loves Paps and Mops, as he's nick-named them, and trails around after them. Tilly has missed Karen, Rebecca and Jolene, her three amigos.

So here goes. I want to move back home. I'm sorry it's come to me asking, but I feel I have to because of the way I left. My parents have helped me see that this is just a tough stage of life, which we'll get through. And probably, when we're out the other side, we'll look back on these years when the kids were young, and we'll miss them. As long as we stay together. Soon enough, it'll just be you and me, and that's what I want.

The children and I are booked on a flight that lands at three next Friday. My dad said he'll pay for a taxi to ours, but the kids would like it if you met us at the gate. I know I would too. Tell me what you think.

All our love

Abi, Tilly and Ivan.

For a few seconds, my heart stops.

60

My brain struggles to comprehend what I've read. I pace the house, hustling up and down the stairs, but it's no use. There's a tightness in my chest that I've never felt before; not even the time I put on riot gear and charged in first at twenty armed prisoners who'd barricaded the library. There's a flashing in my eyes. I pull on my running clothes, open the front door, and race down the road.

I don't care where I'm going; I have to run. Hurtling along the bus route into Orton Goldhay, I charge across the road, where I am rewarded with blaring horns and angry gestures. I run towards Hampton, sprinting alongside the queueing traffic. I tear by the fields, through housing estates, past pubs and shops. And still I don't tire. If it's still raining, it doesn't register.

Then, in an instant, the energy vanishes from my body and, like the controlled demolition of an old cooling tower, I lean to the side and collapse over a low wall into a bush. Lying there, in a hydrangea, I struggle to get my breathing under control and my heart to calm down.

A few minutes later, I drag myself up and crawl onto the pavement. I haul myself to my feet and look behind me. The owner of the bungalow stares at me in horror from her doorway as I slouch away from her garden, wisely choosing not to approach me. I walk home, slowly.

When I make it back, I think I've been burgled as the front door is open. Gary is sitting on my car bonnet. He also looks a little as if he's been in a wet bush with his dirty baggy jeans and holey jumper, but he's smiling.

'Did you get any?' he asks.

'Get any what?'

'I assumed that with you leaving the house that fast, someone must have been giving something great away for free.'

I give him half a smile.

'Rough day?' he asks.

'You could say that.'

'I kept an eye on your door for you. A repo man turned up, so your TV's gone, but the police said they'll come back later.'

I can't summon a grin.

'Want a beer?' he asks. 'Need to chat about things?'

I stand there in front of him, arms hanging heavy by my side.

'Sure.'

By the time we're slumped on my sofa with a cold one each, I've started to rationalise everything. I still need to talk it through with someone to help straighten it out in my head, but I can't tell even him the complete truth. Gary seems relaxed around most topics, but what I've done is unforgivable.

'Gary, can you keep a secret?'

He smiles, but then sees my lack of one.

'As long as it doesn't involve children, I can. Actually, maybe not animals either. Sorry, go on.'

'You know I said Abi left and was thinking of staying in Spain.'

'Yes.'

'Well, I got an email saying she's coming back, she's sorry, and she wants to try again.'

'That's brilliant news. Isn't it?'

'Yes. It would have been even greater news if I hadn't had sex with someone else while she's been away.'

His mouth slowly opens, and quickly closes, but his eyes crinkle, then he's laughing. I can't help joining in.

'Well, you were on a break,' he says. 'Or at least she was. That was quick work, though. She's only been gone about a week. It would have taken me that long to shave my entire body and buy some acceptable underwear.'

'What do I do? Surely I don't tell her?'

'Who's the girl? Are you still seeing her?'

'It was a one-off, and I won't be repeating it.'

I try to swallow my beer, but it stays in my mouth when I realise it was at least twice depending on how you count these things, and I almost have to spit it out. How am I going to feel lying to Abi?

'I wouldn't tell her, then. It won't help. She hinted that she would probably stay out there, so it's not like you were doing the dirty while you were together.'

'That's a very reasonable position to take, Gary. Although I'm not sure your wife, or mine, would see the facts in the same way.' I take another large gulp of beer.

'Hell, no,' he says. 'If my wife heard I said that, I'd be dragging a cross up the hill behind you.'

I spray a mouthful across the room.

61

I sleep surprisingly well, although the run probably helped with that. I've got my first weekend off in ages and have been looking forward to a lie-in, but dark thoughts gather, so I rise and get on with the housework. Abi moaned that it never ended, and I can understand that now.

My stomach rolls every time I think of Abi coming home. My hands alternate between clammy and cold, so I keep myself busy and spend all afternoon doing the little jobs that I've been putting off. There's a hole in the shed roof, our bedroom needs painting, and three doors need glossing. I even go to Stanground Carpets and buy a roll of their cheap, hard-wearing rental carpet to replace where Ivan decided to do his painting. The fitter is free on Thursday, which is just in time.

It's midnight when I'm finished, but, without alcohol, sleep is impossible. I have two bedfellows when I retire: guilt and remorse. They are relentless in their need for attention. I get up at six and go for another jog, which helps empty some of the worry. I had better email Abi back today and tell her I can't wait to see her, but I need to make sure I word it right.

At 10 a.m., there's a knock at the door. It's Fats, holding a deckchair, and Lena.

'We're off for a walk to feed the ducks, or a trundle, if you prefer.' She smiles. 'Fancy coming?'

'Okay.'

We take the quick route down through the underpass and Lena gets a beer can caught around one of her tyres. Judging by the piles of litter, it looks as if we missed out on a party here, but the revellers have gone now.

At the pond, Fats hands me the deckchair and pushes the wheelchair over the grass. He then lifts Lena out as though she's a child and carries her to the water's edge. I think he's going to lob her in for a moment, until I realise the deckchair is for her. Fats and I sit on the bank next to her in companionable silence.

'The kids and I like it here. Look, they've still got ten chicks,' I say.

'It's ducklings if they're ducks,' says Lena.

'Would it be wrong to picture Chinese food right now?' asks Fats.

'Very,' Lena and I reply in unison.

'It's a lot more peaceful without the kids.'

'Is it weird having children?' asks Fats.

'What do you mean?'

'You know, always putting their needs before your own, doing something for them when you'd rather be doing something else. I've never considered having any. I want to travel all around America. They're the only people in the world who understand my portion sizes!'

Fats and I chuckle until Lena comments.

'I'd like one in the future.'

I can't help another frown, which she sees. She barks out a laugh.

'Oh my, I thought you were weird the other day. Now I realise what it is. Do you know something, you men have the tiniest of brains?'

'What did I do?' asks Fats.

'Dalton thinks we're a couple.'

'Really?'

'Yes, because you didn't tell him any different.'

'Ah, I guessed he wasn't happy about me liking Braddock's sister.'

'I dread to imagine what happens in that prison with you two eggheads running the show.'

I look from one to the other. Brother and sister. How could I not have realised? A little giggle pops out, which sets Fats off. Soon, we're all laughing so hard that Lena nearly unbalances her deckchair.

We stay for an hour and it feels good. I sense I have something important growing with them both, as well as with Gary, that I didn't have before. I know having friends will help when Abi gets back. Even so, it's strange to not have realised they are related, especially when they're so similar. My radar has been off concerning many things lately. Back home, I go to bed early but still don't sleep. My thoughts return to Billie, not my wife and children. What kind of man am I?

62

I crawl from under my duvet at 6 a.m. for a drink of water. There will be no sleep until I reply to that email. The watery eyes, dark circles, and sagging face of the man in the mirror is unrecognisable. Luckily, I've only got an afternoon shift today, so I return to bed. I eventually get up at eleven. I spend half an hour deliberating about what to say, eventually emailing her back saying I'll be waiting at the airport and I can't wait to see them all. I sign it with all my love, feeling treacherous as I hit send.

The weather is mild with a warm breeze, but I drive to work. I'll definitely miss the convenience of having the car to myself when my family return.

At the gatehouse, I check the detail and can't believe it. They've still got me with the YOs. I stand in line waiting for my keys and radio, knowing that I have the same hangdog expression that I used to have when I was on the male side. Peabody and Sheraton are behind me. I remember when I saw them laughing in the queue before, when they must have been new. After only a few weeks in the role, their haunted faces now match mine.

When I open the door to the houseblock, Billie and Red are on the other side of it. They shouldn't be out of their cells at lunchtime and it's too early for them to have any kind of visit. Billie's been crying.

'What's up?'

'We're being transferred to Styal,' says Red. 'It's bullshit. My new trainers were supposed to come this week. After three fucking months. There's no way I'll get them now.'

The big SO from Reception, Odom, comes up behind them.

'Come on, ladies. Your chariot awaits.'

Billie's eyes meet mine for a second and she starts crying again. I hold the metal gate open for them. Billie puts her hand on my arm as she walks past and then she's gone.

I have mixed emotions in the hub. There's sadness obviously, but also a lorry load of relief. Nasima ignores the detail and sticks me with the lifers. The atmosphere on the lifer wing is different. The crackle of energy and instability that dominated the YO landings has been replaced by an air of sorrow. I recognise two of the women from the news.

Some prisoners are sentenced to six months and break down with the knowledge that they will miss their kid's next sports day. But it must be a whole lot different if you're found guilty of killing someone and know you're going to miss the whole of your children's lives. Most of these inmates are mothers. If there's no family to take their children and the kids are young enough, they'll be adopted. Otherwise, they get fostered. Knowing you are responsible for that must be a desperate thought to take with you to bed each night. It's a testament to the human spirit that people can endure it. Most find a way to survive, as long as they know that, one day, they'll be free. It helps to be with other women in the same position.

I'm letting an inmate off the wing for a healthcare appointment when Zelda comes to the gate with a mop in her hand.

'Guv, open cleaning cupboard.'

'What do you want to go in there for?'

'I take Tara's hub job.'

'Yeah, okay.'

The cleaning cupboard is actually a room the size of a small windowless bedroom in the corner of the houseblock where the mops, buckets and heavy electric floor polishers are kept. I unlock the door and flick on the light. When I turn, Zelda has twisted the mop, so it's diagonally across her chest. She growls and shoves it at my chest. It's so unexpected that I lose my balance and fall backwards, ending up sitting in one of the big buckets. Then I remember Tara's warning.

Zelda's weapon seems to be the red handle of a screwdriver. It's only when she presses a switch and the metal piece shoots out that I see my predicament. My face is at her waist height and the point is near my eyes. The end of the screwdriver has been sharpened, so it glints even in the false light. The corners of her mouth come up in a grin, and she pulls her arm back.

A shadow appears behind her and Zelda strains. Then her chest juts out as her arm is pulled behind and twisted upwards.

'I'll have that,' says Kitty.

She wrests the weapon from Zelda's hand with brute force. Zelda tries to push past her, but Kitty has her up against the door with her hand around her throat. Zelda strains for a moment, then her eyes widen in terror as she realises that Kitty is too strong. I scramble out of the bucket to my feet and edge past them, desperate to get out of the room. At the door, Kitty holds my stare.

'Give me a minute, then come back and lock it,' she says.

She shoves Zelda further into the room and the door gently closes behind them. I don't know what to do. The toilets are opposite, so I let myself in and splash water on my face. Kitty could be murdering Zelda in there, but, Christ, I could have been killed in there too. I leave the toilets and see Zelda limping back to her wing, looking as if she's fallen down a flight of stairs. I check in the cleaning room, but it's empty. Kitty has gone and so has the screwdriver.

63
JUNE

I'm at Arrivals in Luton airport with a dry mouth. Their flight landed an hour ago. My mind wanders to the prison even though I'm nervous. The rest of the week has gone by in a blur. The lifer wing is just what I needed. It's deathly quiet on most days. The prisoners are pretty decent and completely the opposite of the murderers on the male side. Over there, the prisoners have often killed for little; money usually, or just because they were angry at a real, or even a perceived, slight.

Nearly all the women inmates have killed their husband or boyfriend. They may well regret the crime because of the impact it's had on their lives and therefore their children's lives, but mostly they couldn't take any more and so the crime was inevitable. I don't probe too deeply, but, more often than not, there seems to have been years of abuse prior to the act itself and some would argue their actions were completely justified.

I've never really considered the fact that decades of abuse can cause women to snap and kill their husbands. The more I chat to them, the more I understand that it's not just the violence. They were also kept without money or friends, because their partners controlled every part of their lives. The children were often caught in the middle, and this fact was often what kept them in a different kind of prison.

Like Rose-Marie's, these women's choices were terrible, but in their cases the fault was not their own, until they finally lashed out. Killing can never be the answer though. With dad dead and mum in jail, it's hard to argue the children will be in a better place.

A bloke next to me at the gate looks equally nervous, but he has flowers. Great, I never thought of that. I contemplate nipping into Marks & Spencer, but I see Abi as the doors open and people flood out. I'm near the back of the waiting throng, but I'm taller than everyone in front of me.

Abi looks refreshed and tanned. She has a white dress on and a simple gold chain around her neck. Her hair is up the way I prefer it and I get an unexpected rush of affection and attraction for my wife. It feels strange to say so, but I like it. Tilly sees me first and points me out to Ivan. They both start running and burrow through the small crowd to get to me.

The overriding emotion I felt at both their births was relief. There was none of that instant connection that I'd read about in Abi's books. Perhaps that was because I hadn't carried them. All I did was fire the starting pistol. But I feel it now. It's a tidal wave and overwhelming. My children hang onto me and I kneel to stop myself falling over. I kiss the tops of their heads, smell their hair, their necks. It takes them thirty seconds to loosen their grip. I could stay like this for hours.

I have a sharp stab of guilt for what I've been doing and thinking since they've been gone, but I push it away. Abi stands three metres from us, looking awkward. I stand up and open my arms. She comes over and joins our group hug. She feels the same, smells the same. We connect like we used to. My family is back.

64

It's been nearly a week since Abi came home. I've worked long shifts every day, but I've got an early today. Surprisingly, there are fewer ACCT books on the lifers' wing. The inmates seem to have switched themselves off to feel less. Each day is the same and therefore nothing to get up or down about. Many have triggers though, such as their child's birthday or even their wedding anniversary, where we are extra vigilant.

Most of the women are in their mid-thirties or older. They support each other, which makes my role easier. Without the violence of the men, or the drama from the kids on the YO wing, time drags a little. The only excitement I had this morning was hearing two of them in the shower together. I coughed outside, hoping that it would shock them, but one of the cheeky cows popped her head out and asked if I wanted to join them. I instantly thought of Billie and left them to it.

I'm back cycling to work again, but before I go home at lunchtime, I stroll over to the male side to see Colt. It's hard to remember Wyatt now. Braddock told me he's at court tomorrow. I pop my head into the male hub to tell them I'm going to have a chat with Colt, but it's Fats on lunch cover, so I take a seat.

'The wanderer returns,' he says. 'Are you here to see the demon?'

'God, are you calling him that now?'

'Yeah, he's got toothache. It's made him worse.'

'Can't he get Gronkowski to knock it out?'

Fats laughs. 'You'll never believe this, but him and Colt are friendly now. They run the servery. Don't have no grief, ever, with them two giving out the food. It's a shame that he's going.'

'Don't worry, I'll be back to mess everything up for you.'

I leave him chuckling and go to Colt's wing. When I reach his cell, I tap my keys and open the panel. I realise I don't do that on the female side. There, I usually knock and wait for a few seconds. Colt is pacing up and down like a tiger in a tiny cage. I find myself slowly opening the door.

'Bruv,' he gasps. 'You got to get me into the dentist. I'm dying here.'

'You don't want to visit the guy here. He'll only whip the tooth out. You'll be gone tomorrow, get it sorted then.'

His face screws up. He gingerly rests his hand on his chin and plonks down onto a chair.

'Did you bring me any goodbye cake?' he asks.

'Yeah, but Fats just ate it.'

He attempts a grin, but grimaces instead.

'Hang on,' I say.

I leave the cell, lock the door, and stride to the staff room. Lennox drinks peppermint tea. I'm pretty sure it's supposed to help toothache. I grab three tea bags and a blue plastic prison mug and make a brew. When I return to Colt, I hand it to him.

'Did you piss in this mug?'

'Idiot, it's peppermint tea, which soothes toothache.'

'Yeah? Nice one. I owe you. Anything, man, say it. You sorted me out in here.'

I nod, not imagining ever needing his help. When I get back to my bike afterwards, I realise I'm nibbling my nails, which is something I haven't done since I was a child. Maggie has agreed to pick the kids up from school today. Abi is going to the supermarket this morning, buying some wine, then cooking a meal for the two of us. I'm a bag of nerves for my afternoon date.

When I arrive at home, Abi opens the door in the same white dress she bought in Spain, which I admired, and she has her hair up like when we got married and has drop earrings and high sandals on. She looks stunning. Chanel No. 5, her favourite scent, wafts over me as she approaches. Abi gives me a slow kiss, then passes me a glass of wine, which I down in one when her back is turned.

I feel rather underdressed in my uniform, so nip up the stairs to our bedroom. My wardrobe contains very few decent clothes and I'm still in my boxers, looking for a nice shirt, when Abi arrives at the door.

'There's probably not much point in putting anything on just for me to take it off.'

She sounds confident, but she doesn't look it. She undoes her dress at the back and it falls to the floor, revealing matching bra and pants in a very similar design to the ones I considered buying Billie. I smile reassuringly at her because I know she's self-conscious about the loose skin on her tummy after having children.

Making love to Abi is so unlike what I did with Billie that it could be a different act. I know Abi so well from all the years together that it's easy to please her. However, after so long without any close contact between us, we have an attack of the giggles when she's on top so Abi rolls off and turns over. She has tan lines where she's been sunbathing. Her white boobs, and her white bottom, which is still firm from running, jiggle provocatively as she kneels in front of me.

As I pick up the speed, a nasty thought materialises in my brain. Billie. When I had sex with her in Myerscough's office, she was as brown as a berry, but she didn't have tan lines on her top half, only her bottom. How can she have been sunbathing topless?

I begin to lose rigidity. Removing the thought from my mind is near impossible. It takes ages before I finally finish, by which time I'm sweating like a racehorse and Abi is howling like a wolf.

Afterwards, as she lies in my arms, she strokes my chest and tells me how wonderful it was. I am an absolute bastard.

65

FOUR WEEKS LATER

Colt went to court that Friday, and the judge sentenced the whole gang to eighteen weeks' imprisonment. That meant, with time served, he only had five more weeks to do, so I had to stay on the female side as they decided it wasn't worth moving them. Without Billie in the prison though, it wasn't a big deal. I have a week left now. I've got the hang of things over here, even though there are still some horrifying sights. One woman on my wing had been cutting her arms and inserting paper clips into the wound. Another ligatured herself with a bra, but managed to press the emergency button before she passed out.

Since Colt had more time to serve, I checked and found out the dentist's waiting list was six weeks. I had a word and got Colt put to the front of the queue. It seems my corruption has no end. My home life is much better. Abi runs three or four times a week, even if it's just for a quick one. I help out more, even if I'm tired.

Red returned to HMP Peterborough for her dad's funeral. She said she barely knew him but fancied a day out and the chance to see her sisters. I laughed my head off when she got brought back before the wake. These YOs pretend to be street smart, but they have no idea how the world works. I suppose most children haven't.

They shipped Red back to HMP Styal a few days later. I couldn't help asking her how Billie was getting on.

'Shit, man. Damage runs the show.'

I can believe it. Billie pops into my head from time to time. I daren't go out to the gardens, because I'm struggling enough to not keep recalling that moment. It's Billie I'm thinking of when the houseblock gates clang open behind me and I see her. I wonder for a moment if I created an apparition, but it's definitely her.

My stomach lurches. Whether through shock or happiness, I'm not sure. She walks past, only giving me a brief, disinterested glance.

When she leaves for meds later, she returns via my wing and shouts my name through the gates.

'Dalton, nice to see you again.'

'You, too, how come you've come back?' I shout over to her.

'Local visits.'

'Ah, okay.'

I leave the conversation I'm having with Sheraton and wander towards her, feeling uneasy. If you get transferred to a prison a long way from home, then you're allowed to come back once a year for visits. Styal is nearly three hours away. It makes me wonder why they shipped her so far. That sounds an alarm almost as loud as the lack of tan lines.

'Can I ask you a favour?' she says.

'Sure, if you answer a question for me.'

Her eyes narrow slightly, but she nods. 'You go first.'

'Last time we met, I noticed that you didn't have any tanning lines on your top half. Could you explain that?'

Billie's blue eyes drill into mine. I can definitely detect a new edge.

'That weird screw let me sunbathe topless.'

'What?'

'Well, in my pants actually. Dirty old git. Although he never touched me, he used to leer at me with his hands down his trousers. I didn't really get why Tara's men pay when there's no touching, but I do now. I should have asked him for money, but I was just pleased to be with the chickens. I hear he's been sacked?'

'Well, suspended. You told him that your offence was shoplifting, so he didn't get you cleared for outside work.'

'Ah, well. It was good while it lasted. Makes me worry for the chickens, though. I dread to think what he did to them when he was on his own.'

Jesus. That explains it. There's a camera right at the edge of the prison that's hard to pick out. I only know it's there because it stopped working one evening when I was doing nights. It points all the way down the gravel track that separates the inner and outer wall, but it picks up the gardens. I bet they studied the recordings after they realised Myerscough hadn't followed protocol. They rightfully have suspicious minds in Security. I should think they choked when the camera showed a near-naked Billie sunning herself.

'What did you want to ask?' I say.

'I have a problem. Something's come up and I need two hundred quid putting in this bank account.'

'What? I haven't got that kind of cash hanging around.'

'I need it, Dalton. Anyway, I thought you loved me. It's important.'

'I can't do it, Billie. Sorry.'

'If I'm stressed because of money, I might forget to keep my mouth shut about dirty middle-aged prison officers who take advantage of innocent young prisoners.'

And with that, she slips a piece of paper between the bars.

'It's in the name of B Harding. I wouldn't ask if I had any other way.'

Billie disappears fast. I fold the piece of paper and put it in my pocket. What am I going to do? I stare through the gates. I didn't realise that Kitty was mopping near us. She finishes and walks past with her head down, but she has a knowing look on her face.

66

If the sign of a great establishment is returning guests, then we must be doing something right, because later that afternoon we have another visitor. This time it's Tara. Kitty comes to the lifers' wing and lets me know. Kitty's changed so much now, from her clothes to her weight, her confidence, and even her personality is sneaking out. It's crazy how some people thrive in the dark.

I suppose nothing can hurt Kitty here. She flourishes on the routines and the rules. There are no adults intent on taking something from her that she might never recover. She has her friends close by. Like a delicate flower, all she needs is some space to grow without interruption.

When the inmates are all behind their doors after bang up, I nip onto the induction wing, where both Billie and Tara are located because they have just returned. They give the new arrivals single cells if possible when they first get here so people can get their heads together. I don't want to talk to Billie so I shall keep well clear of her now. There won't be any real emergency, she'll just be after money, and I suspect if Myerscough had hung around long enough, it would have been him feeding Billie's bank account. But I like

Tara. I can tell a decent person when I see one. I knew Billie was trouble. Perhaps that was half the attraction.

Peabody is on the wing. He looks as happy as I feel.

'Just having a word with Tara, mate.'

'Okay, the roll is in, so make sure you slide the bolt across.'

I give him a dirty look. Cheeky twat, telling me how to do the job after he's been here five minutes, but he's away with his thoughts.

I knock, leave it for a few seconds, then open Tara's door. She's lying face down on the bed. Her shoulders are heaving.

'Hey, Tara. What the hell happened?'

She turns to me and sobs. Bleary eyed, and without make-up on, she gets up and throws herself into my arms. I feel the tears soaking onto my shirt.

'I've made such a mess of things.'

I stroke her hair. After a minute, she settles a little and steps back. I smile at her.

'Surely it's not that bad.'

'It's worse. That woman named me Ruined, and that's what my life is. That idiot who lets me stay at his house for free went through my room and found my bank card with all the money I'd saved. There was ten grand. I was halfway to my target. He'd been caning the card while I was in here.'

'Did you leave the pin, then?'

'No, it was hidden at the back of my knicker drawer, so he must have been looking at my underwear. The sneaky, perverted old twat's been doing contactless with it so no one looked at my name on the card. When I checked my balance, five thousand was left, and there were hundreds of little debits, mostly at the local shop.'

'Bloody hell, that is sneaky. I take it you became upset.'

'Dalton, don't make me laugh. I went fucking nuts, but I'm not a violent person, and look at the size of me. I just started kicking him in the shin. Do you know what he did?'

I shake my head.

'He rang the police and said he was being assaulted. I kicked the copper when he turned up, too. They wanted a statement from my so-called friend, but he'd calmed himself. Told me he would repay the money, and the police that he didn't want to press charges.'

'Ah, but you'd already assaulted the policeman, thereby breaking the conditions of your licence, and so they recalled you to prison.'

'Correct. The fuckers drove me straight here. I'm five grand down and back for at least a month. I'm never going to get my salon. I know it.'

'Don't be daft. You'll get there. I bet they only give you fixed-term recall, which is fourteen days. If he pays you back fast and you start working again, you'll soon be on track.'

Tara takes a deep breath, then another.

'He's not going to pay me back, is he? Fuck it. I don't care any more. I give up. I'll be a prisoner to my past whether I'm inside or on the out. There's no point struggling.'

'Tara! Don't stop trying.'

'Why? You might believe I'm a nice girl, but I'm not. I'm rotten, through and through. Do you think I started off with dirty old men? I was just bright enough to see an angle in that seedy world. I'm so worthless I can barely bring myself to look in a mirror.'

'It's okay to make mistakes. You're Tara now. A good person, with people depending on you. You're the most respected person here.'

'I've destroyed my self-respect, my soul. Without that, what's the point?'

'Please, don't think like that.'

'Just leave, please. Thanks for coming by.'

She sits back onto the bed and rolls away from me. I ponder saying something else, but she'll need to get her head around what's happened.

'No problem,' I say. 'I'm here for the rest of the week, then I return to the male side, so we can chat again before I go.'

She turns around with a serious expression.

'Before you go, Kitty told me about Billie. I warned you, didn't I? If you've got a brain, it must surely live in your underwear.'

'I know. I messed up.'

'Trust me, you aren't the first. That's Billie's curse. She's beautiful and sexy, but she wants what she can't have. I bet she wanted to see you when she gets out.'

At my silence, she shakes her head.

'Everyone who fucks with Damage, in whatever way, learns to regret it. All three of us have learned to look after ourselves, but if you cross her, she will be utterly ruthless. She even scares me when she's like this and won't listen to reason. It's good that you're going back over to the other side.'

'Is that why they call her Damage, because she does some?'

'Oh, Dalton. Damage is what they call her in prison. That title suits her here, so she allows it, but it's actually a bastardisation of what Lavinia called her.'

'I don't understand.'

'If you want Damage's real name, you need to put a "d" on the end of it.'

67

I close Tara's door and slide the bolt across. Who the hell have I got myself involved with? Broken, Damaged and Ruined. It's like the unholy trinity. On the male side, I never got attached to anyone. There were quite a few cons who I enjoyed talking to. One of the funniest guys I've ever met was an arsonist. But I always kept them at arm's length.

I think that's largely because most were guilty as charged. Young men do daft things. Some men never grow up. Others are hungry for power and wealth but won't put in the hard yards to attain it legally. You don't accidentally rob a bank or forge notes and identities, so I rarely felt sorry for anyone on the male side. There is the odd badass female gangster on the female wings, but they are few and far between.

Here, most of these women have been wronged first, often terribly. Not many of them have gone out with the intention of breaking the law. Of those that do, they are often stealing to feed and clothe their kids. Or they're hooked on drugs before they're even adults. Help is scarce; therefore they live their lives in circles. Round and around, in and out of jail, drama upon drama, crisis after crisis, and their horizons are forever bleak.

As I reach the hub, the roll clears. I go inside to get my bag and find Peabody, with a face of thunder, and Nasima waiting for me.

'Take a seat, Dalton,' says Nasima.

My face burns hot, which I try to hide by grabbing a chair from the corner.

'Right,' she says. 'I'm not accusing you two of anything, but I know you've spent time with Harding. I'm moving that girl upstairs until she returns to Styal. I can't say why she's back, but it won't be for long. She's absolute poison. We've already lost one officer because of her. Her friend, Prestwick, can go up with her. Now, is there anything either of you wants to tell me?'

Peabody and I both shake our heads. Neither of us is convincing.

'Get out of here,' says Nasima.

We walk to the gate together in silence. It looks as though Peabody made the same mistake I did. That's why he asked to leave the YO wing when I first came over here. But it was too late. She'd got her hooks into him, as she has me. If she's tapped me up for cash, then he will have been pressurised too. Both of us are trapped. At least Peabody has the excuse of being new.

When we get outside, I notice Myerscough's SUV in the corner of the car park. I tap on his window.

'Hey, are you back?'

'No, I came here to return my uniform and ID badges. It's over for me.'

'Are you going to be okay? You aren't having silly ideas?'

Myerscough smiles. He looks old in civilian clothes and kind of droopy. I didn't think people still wore those pink and grey golf jumpers.

'No, I had a few bad thoughts, but I've got a plan. Many years ago, after a holiday there, I had a dream to live in a sleepy town in Portugal, learn Portuguese, drink wine, maybe even help out at a restaurant. I don't know where those hopes went to. My wife left me somewhere along the road, and I barely noticed. I was as lost in this sorry place as the people I was locking up. But I'm free now, and so I'm going to go to Portugal. I want open spaces and honest folk. Spend enough time in a place like this and you start to suspect that everyone you meet is lying or after an edge.'

'Good for you, mate. Send me a postcard.'

'Like in *The Shawshank Redemption*? It's a nice thought.'

He rolls his shoulders. I won't be getting a postcard. I see what's changed in him. He's relaxed. We carry this prison on our backs, even when we aren't here, but he must feel weightless now.

'I made a mistake, Dalton. First one I made in all that time, and I don't know why. I hope you believe that.'

'Put it behind you. Chase your dreams.'

'I will do. My brother's lending me his campervan and I'll drive all the way. That's something else I've wanted to do. They let me go because I told them everything, so you've got to be careful. They're on the warpath, Dalton, and they have your name.'

'What the hell did you tell them?'

'They asked me who suggested Billie work with the chickens.'

'And you fingered me? Cheers, mate.'

'I didn't have to. They already knew.'

68

As if my day wasn't bad enough already, when I got home yesterday, stressed to the eyeballs, the kids were at Maggie's. Abi was waiting for me with her hair up and those earrings in again, when all I wanted to do was lie on the sofa. This time I finished quickly. Must have been the worry. Abi asked me if I was okay afterwards.

Last night, I played with the children for ages. Ivan's a little calmer now, but he still gets angry very fast. I thought of Tara when he kicked me on the shin for not concentrating on the jigsaw we were doing. It only had nine pieces. Tilly is growing up. She got a phone when she was in Spain to stay in touch with her friends. It must be ever so sticky because she can't seem to put it down.

I had another night of tossing and turning. At 3 a.m., I accepted I have no choice but to give in to Billie's demand. If she told anyone about us, my life would be over. I'm on an overtime afternoon shift, but I'm leaving early because I need to visit the town centre and pay the money into Billie's account in cash. There's no way I'm transferring the funds from my own bank and leaving a record.

'I'll be back at seven-thirty. Don't worry about tea,' I tell Abi as I leave.

'Wait a minute. Can I have a quick word with you? I didn't realise you were going in early.'

'Yeah, I want to catch up on my personal officer comments. I'm miles behind.'

Abi comes and stands in front of me and puts her hands around my neck.

'I just wanted to say I appreciate your efforts lately. With the house and with all the hours you're working, we should have a bit spare hopefully, so you should treat yourself to something. Maybe that leather jacket you wanted. Hopefully we'll be able to go on holiday next year together.'

I manage to maintain eye contact, but it's hard.

'We'll see. There were a few bills for the car that I had to sort out. You saw the oil leak.'

'Well, anyway. Do what's necessary. I trust you to keep things ticking along. Love you, Jim. I'm glad you wanted us back.'

I leave the house fast, with the fake smile stuck on my face. Cycling to town, I work out that I'm about to give Billie two entire days' wages. When I arrive outside Santander Bank, I put a baseball cap on and a pair of sunglasses, even though it's an overcast day. The only way I could look more suspicious is if I had a bag with swag written on the side. I insert my cash card in one of the machines in the foyer and watch two days' toil and trouble churn out in the form of ten twenty-pound notes. Then I join a slow-moving queue, in which I sweat profusely. The transaction takes thirty seconds when I reach the front and I spend the time waiting for an alarm to go off.

At the prison, the detail at the gatehouse tells me I'm on the lifers' wing on my own. There must be staff shortages but it's fine by me because I don't intend leaving the wing in case I bump into Billie. I've got four more days including this one, then it's over, and I'll be back to somewhere I know. When I get in the hub, I see I only have a roll of twenty. I check the movements book and Nasima was good to her word and left instructions for Tara and Billie to move up to houseblock two first thing this morning. Odom's the SO this afternoon, covering for Breakman, who is off with stress.

Midway through the afternoon, there's a clanging at the gate.

'You got one on, Dalton,' shouts Odom.

I lock the office and walk to the wing gates. Odom is standing next to Zelda. I open my mouth to complain when I remember I told nobody about our little meeting in the cleaning cupboard, so she's just a con with a long sentence. I did exactly what I picked Tara up on. She didn't drop Lavinia in it for the things she did to them, and I didn't report Zelda. If you don't report crimes, they can come back and bite you on the arse.

There aren't enough women with life sentences to fill the lifers' wing, so they'll sometimes send over prisoners with five years or more on their sentence. Zelda now qualifies and has just turned twenty-two. Happy birthday. If you put short-termers in with the lifers, they drive them mad with constant talk of the great things they'll be able to do when they get out. It makes those with decades to serve murderous or suicidal.

I nod at Odom and he shuts the gate behind her. She looks warily at me. An inmate clears her throat as she comes into view on the other side of the gates. It's Kitty. Zelda stares at her for a nanosecond before looking down.

'Are we cool?' I ask Zelda.

'Yes, I'm sorry,' she replies.

I wasn't expecting that. Kitty smiles and leaves us to it. I stick Zelda upstairs in a spare single. The lifers don't get locked away during the day except for an hour at lunch, because that really would be inhumane. All they want is to keep busy. Just as I'm leaving Zelda, I stop.

'Zelda, why did you attack me?'

'Damage possessed me. I lesbian back home, but never feel like that for someone. I changed, but she's gone now.'

That's another tortured soul on Billie's count. She obviously doesn't know that Billie is back here. I decide to try to get to know her more.

'You have unusual scars on your arm.'

'Yes. I very stubborn. Bad men do this to me.'

It's another harsh truth about how humans can treat each other. It's the tip of the iceberg, too. To think we call most of our planet civilisation. The rest of the shift goes smoothly until late afternoon, Billie appears at my gate. She looks around before talking.

'Thanks for the money.'

'How do you know I put it in?'

'Phone banking, innit. Now Tara's back, the bank is the only person I've got to ring on the prison phones. I knew you would, though.'

'Why aren't you upstairs?'

'Not missing me, Dalton?'

'I'm busy. Where are you going?'

She takes a few steps away from the gates before whispering words that chill me to the core.

'I've got a healthcare appointment for a pregnancy test.'

69

I practically have to peel my hands from the bars, long after Billie has backed away and left. On my own, I'm too busy to look out for her returning from Healthcare. Is she messing with me and it's her idea of a sick joke, or a way of being in control? If that's the case, it won't be long before she's after more money. What the hell have I done?

I spend the rest of the shift wandering the landings trying not to think about the consequences of Billie being pregnant. Even if she is, it can't be mine because she was on the pill, wasn't she? She was due on the next day, though, and had the telltale stomach ache to prove it. Which means that any baby must be someone else's. I can't help the ridiculous feeling of having been cheated on.

I don't need help at bang up with such a low roll. Even I can count to twenty-one. Zelda's is the last occupied cell. She's waiting immediately behind the door, which would normally make me jump. But I only have one thing on my mind. Her hand shoots out.

'I do it for you. You victim, too. We learn, uh?'

'Eh?'

She hands me a folded piece of A4 paper. She looks vulnerable and very much her twenty-two years. I take it from her and realise I never really considered the possibility of Zelda's innocence. Is that some unconscious bias because she's an immigrant, or just because she gave me death stares?

'Thank you.'

'No, I give you thanks for not telling anyone what I tried to do to you. I no forget. Maybe one day I protect you.'

I open the piece of paper and it's a picture of a field of sunflowers in front of a row of tall green trees. There's a farm building on the right with two big stick people and two littles ones next to them. It's childish, not much better than something Tilly might draw. I look up and spot the pack of felt-tip pens on Zelda's table. The prisoners will do anything to busy their minds. Anything to keep the darkness away. I've spent my shift walking around the wing trying to do the same thing.

'It's lovely, I appreciate it.'

She speaks slowly, emphasising each word.

'It is my family farm. To think, I could not wait to leave.'

She half smiles and I see a girl sitting on the back of a cart pulled by a horse, swinging her legs with her sister, as they trundle along a dusty lane towards a setting sun. What is Zelda's story? She's a thousand miles from home and doesn't seem the type to set up a business distributing class A drugs all over the United Kingdom. Did she want to get involved, or are her scars proof she had no choice? The lies and the truths seep into your bones until you never know what to believe. It becomes easy to think the worst of everyone. Your humanity is just another possession that the prison wants to steal from you.

I lock her door and slowly scrape the bolt across. Do the people inside these cells ever get used to those noises? When I reach the hub, everybody else is sitting in a circle with their roll counts in. I almost stumble on a piece of rucked-up carpet, but no one laughs.

Odom's face is grim. I'm glad nobody is looking at me when I fill the form in, because my hand is shaking. Roll twenty-one. One on, Zelda. I deliberately stand opposite Peabody and two up from Odom. If he wants to see me, he'll have to lean forward.

'Listen in, you lot. I'm sure you're aware Harding is back. Rumours are floating around, so we might as well discuss it. She's pregnant. The nurse confirmed the test today.'

There's an audible gasp from everyone except Peabody and me. If there was still any doubt of who else was up to no good with Billie, there isn't now.

'We need to find out who's responsible,' continues Odom.

'Did she get pregnant in this prison, or HMP Styal?' asks Sheraton.

'We don't know which, but she's not been gone long, so we can only think it was here. I am able to confirm that it wasn't me.'

Thank the Lord for Odom's sense of humour. We all laugh and it breaks the tension. I put my hand up.

'She must have an idea of how far along she is, and who did it. Didn't someone ask her?'

'Yes, many have,' says Odom. 'Ms Harding refuses to say anything. She said she'll tell the director, but he's not in until tomorrow morning. I assume he'll talk to her first thing and then there'll be a meeting with everyone. Shit is going to hit the fan. Somebody in here won't rest easily tonight.'

He's right. I don't sleep a wink.

70

I lie in bed staring at the ceiling all night until the alarm goes off. It seems a long time ago that Gronkowski provoked the same feelings of anxiety, but then I was scared for my safety. Now I fear for my freedom. Abuse in a position of care is a serious crime, punishable by imprisonment. Judges make examples of people like me. Billie's pregnancy is an aggravating factor whether or not the baby is mine. I'd be lucky to only get two years.

I allow myself an incredulous smile. Imagine the conversation with Abi. Sorry, love, while you were away, I kind of lost my marbles a bit and had sex with this young girl in the prison. She's pregnant but it's not mine.

Today could easily be the worst day of my life. Wouldn't Billie know she was pregnant because she would have missed a period or two? Although you hear lots of stories where women go into labour not knowing they were pregnant. Would she have had sex with me knowing she was carrying someone else's baby?

When it's time to leave for work, the kids are watching TV. I give them the biggest hugs and tell them I love them more than anything. It's only now that I realise it's the truth, and not just something you say when you're a parent. I've felt like this for years and, in the chaos of my job, not even noticed that I can't live without them. I take my time saying goodbye to Abi as well. The second you're about to lose something is the moment you understand its worth.

'You okay? You look rough,' she says.

'Cheers. I just wanted a snog before I go.'

'I haven't brushed my teeth or washed my face.'

'I don't care.'

I pull her towards me. She struggles for a bit, but then melts into my arms. When we separate, she blushes.

'Lucky you're going to work, or you'd have matrimonial duties.'

'I'd have liked that.

'Maybe later.'

I step from the house knowing that if my name is pulled out of the hat at the meeting, later could be a long time to wait. I'd be arrested at work, in the police station overnight, and the magistrates would be asking for my plea tomorrow morning. If you want to get a third off your sentence, you need to admit your guilt straight away. They might even jail me immediately while they wait for probation reports with a custodial sentence inevitable.

I cycle off into the morning sunshine. It doesn't feel like a day to lose your liberty. Exhaustion makes it seem as if my bike's in top gear, even though I'm in the lowest. For the first time in our prison careers, Fats cycles past me.

'Hey, Dalton! Where you been?'

'Three days to go, then I'm hopefully back in your loving embrace.'

'I'm not sure there's room with Braddock's sister in there.'

'You old dog. Got your feet under the table, did ya?'

'That's right, sir.'

'She looks very similar to Braddock. Do you like him too?'

'Shut it, Dalton. I'm in a good mood and I've been dieting. It's not easy, and it makes me weak.'

'Made much progress?'

'Yes, sir. I've sneaked under twenty stone.'

I laugh and he does too. It's another reminder of everything I've put at risk by my stupid actions. If I'm found guilty, I'll lose his friendship as well as the respect of every person who works in that building.

Why did I risk so much? It's as though what happened with Billie was years ago and a different me. Billie's hardened demeanour since she returned makes her feel like a stranger now, when before I thought we had such a strong bond. Have I just been an old fool? I never for a moment thought she was shagging someone else, especially bloody Peabody.

'How's Lena?'

'Good, good. She got that position she went for and loves it. A guy there asked her out for a date this weekend, so she's all nervous and excited. Life's great, man. It's funny how quickly things can change.'

How right you are, Fats, I think, as we reach the prison.

After getting a set of keys and a radio, I trudge down to the security door and press the button. Nasima has arrived at the same time and walks through with me to the houseblocks. I'm so nervous, it's an effort to focus on what she's saying.

'You look rough,' she says.

That's exactly what Abi said.

'One of the kids keeps having nightmares, so I haven't slept for days.'

'Nobody tells you about that at the baby shower.'

'No, it seems there are lots of surprises in store when it comes to parenting.'

How easily the lies come. I used to have pride in my honesty.

The director is in the hub when we arrive. He has a quiet chat with Nasima, then both of them leave and walk upstairs to what I assume is Billie's cell. At seven-fifteen, we all unlock. Nasima hasn't returned. It's Tex and me on the wing today. I can't remember the last time I spoke to her.

'Hi, Tex. How are things? I don't think I've seen you since you went on holiday.'

She pauses before opening the wing gates, then shrugs.

'I suppose they call it a nervous breakdown. A mini one, maybe. I couldn't get out of bed for days, but I gradually improved last week, so I'm back. It was all of that stuff with Rose-Marie, you know, one thing too many. So, they stuck me with the lifers today, so I don't have to look at her cell.'

I put my arm around her as we walk to the office.

We get breakfast done and send the workers off at mass movement. Then we head to the hub where Nasima and the director are waiting for us. I can feel my knees jellifying. When I open the hub door, there's also the head of Security sitting on one of the chairs. Everyone else filters in. Peabody is last. He is so white, I can see blue veins in his forehead. When the director starts talking, a thin trickle of sweat runs through Peabody's sideburn and down the side of his face.

'Right, this is an extremely serious situation. It reflects very badly on the jail. We need to handle this sensitively and sensibly. I've spoken to Harding this morning and asked her how far along she suspects she is, but she said she can't be sure. Do we think she is telling us the whole truth?'

He directs that to Nasima.

'Maybe,' she says. 'A lot of these girls don't look after themselves, however, Billie is always very in control, so I'd say she's messing with us.'

'You may well be right,' said the director, 'because she has hinted at the man responsible.'

He scans the circle of people looking at him. Even the innocent hold their breath.

'I told her to name him outright, but she refused. She believes she was as responsible as he was and didn't want to dirty his memory. All she would say was, why do you think he killed himself?'

The air is filled with whispered swear words and the name Sandringham. The mystery of why Sandringham drowned himself is over. I picture his beautiful bereaved girlfriend who still works in the prison. Billie's poisonous reach is endless.

'Quiet, please! Ms Harding, however, has said very little on the matter. Her Home Detention Curfew date is only a month away. She says if we get her out then, and find a place for her to live on tag, she'll leave quietly and not tell a soul.'

The director stands quietly to allow this information to sink in. I can't help but smile, which I cover with my arm. It's a huge relief that I'm not responsible, and judging by Peabody's flushed face, he feels the same.

But the gall of Billie! She knew she was pregnant before she came back and she let me stew. She must have blackmailed Sandringham, and done the same thing to Peabody and me. Maybe even Myerscough, too. Now she's doing it to the director. She is front-page news if this gets out, which she knows. I hear the director's leaving next year. I bet he'd rather this didn't come out before then.

'Rest assured,' he says, 'there will be a full internal investigation, but if the prisoner wants to keep it quiet, we will look to respect her wishes. I will need to speak to the Home Office and the police, obviously. A crime has been committed here. Whether it's in the public interest to drag Sandringham's family through a public hearing is debatable. Especially if Ms Harding refuses to cooperate. We can't force her to tell us anything. After all, she's the victim in this.'

My eyes widen at that. I catch Nasima looking at me. I give her what I hope is a reassuring smile.

'Anyway, be on your guard today. This news will spread like wildfire in here, and I've no idea how the inmates will react. It's possible someone out there knows a different version of events. The gossip may force them to reveal their hand. Others might be angry or it might stir up troubling memories. Every ACCT book should have a meeting this morning. I knew Officer Sandringham well. My thoughts are that he wouldn't seek out this clandestine affair, but we don't know that for certain. If she did seduce him, it's possible she did the same to others, so be alert. Does anyone have anything to add?'

I look around the room, shaking my head. When I reach Nasima, she's still staring at me.

71

During the rest of the shift, Tex is quiet and distant. After dinner, I push the trolleys back to the kitchens with Kitty, who's becoming a great orderly. I suspect nobody would risk messing up her floor. When we return to the hub area, Billie is wandering around as though she's in a shopping mall.

'What are you doing down here?' I ask.

'Looking for you. No one dare tell me off now. I thought I'd tell you that because of the pregnancy, I've had to have a sexual health check.'

At my horrified face, she presses her advantage.

'I don't want to catch that HIV thing again, cos that was really nasty.'

'Back upstairs, immediately.'

I grab her arm and march her to the stairwell, but they are locked at this time of the day. I open the door and gesture for her to go up the stairs.

'Hey, take it easy. I'm pregnant.'

'Back to your wing, please.'

'How did you feel when you found out it was Sandringham's? Relieved, or maybe a little sad? Our kids would be gorgeous.'

'Billie, stop it. Can't you see how destructive your behaviour is? Look at the lives you're wrecking.'

'I didn't tell him to kill himself, did I? I didn't even know I was pregnant then. It's a bit weird to think when you and me were doing it, I already was. Anyway, I'm glad I bumped into you. I want a necklace. One of those locket ones, which you can put a picture in. Not too expensive, but something nice. Something around fifty quid should be fine.'

'Billie, you're off your head. I'm skint.'

'Fifty quid won't kill you. I just need something to remember you by. I'm never coming back to this place again. I know everyone says that, but I've been talking to Tara and Kitty. We're going to pool our money and save for that salon. Tara will run the business cos she's the smart one, but we're all going to work there and be normal. I'm having a kid now, and there's no fucking way I'm putting it in harm's way by returning to jail. Tara and Kitty think the same. Birdies salon, open soon!'

She's grinning, but I just point up the stairs.

'Cheer up. Look, I've pulled this out of an old Argos catalogue. It's less than fifty quid. You've got off lightly. Didn't you get to have the best sex of your life with me? That's cheap at the price you're paying. Bring it in Friday. Isn't that your last day?'

Jesus Christ. How the hell does she know that? I frogmarch her up the stairs, open the door at the top of the stairwell, and usher her through.

'This is the last thing, Billie. No more, okay.'

She spins around and blows a kiss at me.

I close the door. Instead of going down the steps, I sit on the first one. That's the problem with blackmailers. They don't stop. Will I ever be free of Billie?

I focus on only being over here for two more days after today and stomp down the stairs. Odom's coming into the houseblock with a prisoner in tow. His eyes light up when he sees me.

'Good timing, Dalton. We're flat out in Reception. Here's a new arrival. Can you house her on the induction wing? She'll need a single cell.'

He hands me her file, then turns to the inmate, who has a haughty expression on her face as if she's never been anywhere so foul in all her life.

'Thank you for your patience, Ms Burford. Please follow Officer Dalton, we'll have you sorted in no time.'

I walk over to the induction wing gates and open them. Sheraton is working the landing and I find him in the office.

'Hi, Sheraton. Give this lady a penthouse suite.'

Sheraton looks at the whiteboard behind him.

'Can you stick her in twenty-three for me, mate? I've had to nick someone for smoking.'

'Okay, follow me, Ms.'

I glance down at the front of the file to see her name. Lavinia Burford. While I walk up the stairs, I ponder how many Lavinias I have met in my life. Was Burford the surname that Tara mentioned when she told me her story? This woman is the right age as well. I resist the temptation to look inside the file for her index offence. The reality of what's happening to her has hit home as we walk along the line of grey metal doors. She stares at each one in horror.

'Do you have any possessions with you, Lavinia?'

'No, I came straight here.'

All she's clutching is the prison toiletries pack and some sweets that they give you on arrival. Her clothes make her resemble a headmistress from the sixties. Straight from court in non-court clothes can mean only one thing. She's been picked up, charged, and the magistrates have declined bail. They tend only to do that for serious cases, or ones where women or children may be at risk.

I open the door of twenty-three. She stands in the entrance as if she's in a cowboy film checking whether she'll take the room.

'It's disgusting in there. Show me another.'

It's been a long day.

'Madam, there are two ways that you can enter the cell. The best way is to walk in.'

She holds my glare for a few moments, then strides in and turns around to face me with her chin raised.

'I can't stand to be here.'

I step into the doorway. It's a foul cell with a strong smell of faeces. I'm tempted to slam the door shut on her, but my professionalism, the little I have left, resurfaces. She is still a human being.

'Lavinia, it's bang up in twenty minutes. Just get your head down. You'll have induction in the morning, and all will be explained to you then. I'll tell the officer that you want to clean the cell in the morning. Doing that will make it all feel a bit more normal. Are you going to be okay?'

She turns her nose up again but keeps her gaze a foot above me.

'I suppose I'll be fine.'

'I'll leave a message for the night staff that you're new to this sort of thing.'

She nods, while blinking repeatedly.

I close the door and return to Sheraton.

'She seems lovely,' I say to him. I fill in his obs book: one on. 'I'll put her in the movement log.'

'Cheers, Dalton. Mental day, huh?'

'Aren't they all?'

I open Lavinia's file as I leave the office.

Lavinia Burford. Offence: rape of a child under thirteen. I walk away shaking my head with my slow footsteps echoing miserably around the quiet wing. Kitty is outside the gates, not even pretending to mop. Her eyes are blazing and her top lip has curled back into a snarl. The woman who should have looked after them, but didn't, is here for justice. I fear that Kitty will take it upon herself to dispense it.

72

The next morning when I wake up, bright sunlight streams through the window. The usual bird chorus is absent. I stretch and yawn, but I'm not tired. Missing all that sleep must have finally caught up with me. The children aren't at school today due to a teacher-training day, and I can hear them laughing and giggling with the odd shout through the ceiling. I'm sweaty after a warm night, so I nip into the shower and put it on cool. Thirty seconds is enough and Abi will have her hot water.

When I wander downstairs, the kids squeal happy birthday at me. With all the drama, I'd forgotten.

'We thought you were never going to get up,' says Abi.

She comes over and gives me a big kiss full of real affection. Ivan walks over like he's handling a bomb and solemnly presents me with a parcel. I take my gift to the kitchen table where my breakfast has been laid out. Hmm, I haven't eaten Coco Pops since I was about ten, but birthdays are always a good time for change.

I open Ivan's present. He's drawn me a picture, which Abi has framed. There are two big people in front of a house; one who resembles the elephant man, and the other in a dress who is as wide as she is tall, and two little kids holding hands, who look like penguins. I think of Zelda and feel my eyes well up. Ivan has kept just out of reach though, so I blow him a kiss.

Tilly stands next to him, takes one of Ivan's hands, and passes me her present. She's drawn us all on the beach on a towel. On close inspection, I can see she has drawn me and her next to each other and we're holding hands. Tears pour down my face.

As it's my birthday, Abi insists I have the car to go to work. She says that's my present, but then she lifts up a carrier bag, which contains five neatly wrapped gifts. They're little things: a box of Maltesers, a bell for my bike to replace the one that Ivan broke, a new leather belt, a joke book about middle-aged men entitled *Has Your Man Turned into Mr Grumpy?* She also hands over a portrait of me.

Abi went to art college after school, but struggled to find work in that area. When we met, she'd already given up on that particular dream, but she's found the time to do something special for my birthday. It's a picture of me looking straight ahead. My face fills the whole page. It's impressive and the detailed lines and shading must have taken many hours.

'I had plenty of free time in Spain.'

'It's fantastic.'

'I know.' She giggles. 'I used the photos on my phone to copy from, but I loved doing it. These last few years, I've really forgotten who I am. I basically gave up on everything, but I'm no quitter.'

I said almost the same words while she was away. She pulls me into a strong hug. She didn't quit on us in the end, and this is her way of trying to make things work. But I hate the picture. My eyes are dark and shrouded, but instead of the mystery Abi deduces, I see guilt.

I drive to Argos on the Maskew Avenue Retail Park. There's a big sign out the front saying spend over fifty pounds and get 20 per cent off. I walk in and flick through a catalogue. The best bit about my birthday is that it's five days before my wife's, so I never forget her date.

Billie's locket necklace is forty-five pounds. On the same page is a spinning ring that catches my eye. It's silver and brass, classy, and only twenty pounds, which means it's practically half price with the discount, but I can't help feeling terrible buying Abi a lesser present than my blackmailer. By the time I've paid and they've fetched the jewellery, I'm nearly late. I race to the prison and park up, then sprint towards the gatehouse. When I push open the door and approach the scanners, there are two men and a woman from Security waiting for me.

73

MacStravick, who is Oscar One, is also there, and he steps towards me.

'Come through the scanner, please.'

I feel like dropping my rucksack and sprinting away, but I don't have anything on me, or do I? Heat rises in my cheeks.

'Pass me your bag. Follow me.'

I hand it over, then follow them along the corridor. The changing room has the SO from Security in it. Peabody is in there having a pat-down search. Opposite is the chill-out room, which they have also commandeered. There's another security guy waiting, wearing blue plastic gloves. MacStravick passes him my bag, which he opens and slowly begins to remove everything.

'Ready for a search, Mr Dalton?'

MacStravick examines my face, while one of the other officers gives me an extremely thorough rubdown search.

'What's this for?' I ask.

'Just a random check,' says MacStravick, with a little shrug.

The way Security works is they build a picture from all of their sources of intel: phone calls, overheard chats, incoming and outgoing mail that they read, CCTV footage, and obviously from the inmates who grass people up. Some information won't be true and will be the result of sour grapes, jealousy, or even deflection. But if Security have reached the point where they're searching me, then I've figured repeatedly in their intelligence gathering.

'What are these?' asks the bag searcher.

'Presents. It's my wife's birthday in five days.'

The man looks to MacStravick, whose eyes have narrowed. He takes hold of the two sealed packages and opens one. It's the ring. He checks under the soft packaging before handing both items back to the searcher. He smiles at me, but I feel uneasy.

'Come up to the office with us. We'd like a little chat,' he says.

I follow him and the security SO up the stairs, through the admin block, straight into the HR manager's office. Mrs Kelly is expecting us there. She's a pleasant, warm woman, but she isn't smiling. There are three seats facing one other around a table.

'Thank you, Mr Dalton. Please sit.'

'What is this?' I ask, as I take the chair which is clearly for me.

'This isn't a formal interview, more a fact-finding mission. I'll be taking notes for my benefit, but there won't be a record of the meeting. If at any point this becomes more than a chat, I will explain the procedure. Do you understand and are you happy to continue?'

She interviewed me when I applied for the job. She was a lot jollier on that occasion. My collar is shrinking by the second. If I say I'm unhappy, or want the union in here, I might as well admit to my guilt.

'Is there anything you'd like to tell us?' she asks.

'About what?'

'Your wing.'

'Not really. It's quiet and a bit boring. I'll be pleased to return to the men.'

'You find the young offenders boring?'

'I'm on the lifers' wing now.'

I resist a smile as the wind leaves her sails. The security SO's face reddens.

'What can you tell me about Billie Harding?'

'Not much. She's quite volatile. Typical YO.'

'Do you get on with her? Do you like her?'

'Billie has her moments and can be funny at times, but she's a little damaged.'

I watch her pause, then look at MacStravick. Something unsaid passes between them. He takes over.

'What is your opinion of Officer Peabody?'

Ah ha. Does this mean they don't have anything concrete on me?

'He has his moments, and he can be funny at times.'

All three of them stare hard at me. I stare back. MacStravick stands.

'You may go. Thanks for your patience.'

I manage not to blow out a long breath. Instead, I rise, grab my bag, leave the room, and return to the gatehouse toilets. I sit on one of the seats for ten minutes trying to centre myself, before getting my keys and radio. As I stroll over to the houseblocks, I accidentally break my earpiece ramming it into the radio. When it's not plugged in, everyone else can hear the radio chatter from Comms, but I can't be arsed to go back as I'm late already. I press talk and hold the radio to my mouth.

'QP, this is Officer Dalton taking call sign Yankee Seven.'

'Officer Dalton, Yankee Seven confirmed, please acknowledge First Response, over.'

'Confirming First Response.'

When I reach the houseblocks, all the prisoners are queueing at the wing gates for work. Nasima beckons me towards the hub.

'Take a seat, Dalton. Tex can do movement to work.'

I sit next to her, with my heart racing.

'There's something going on around here, and I don't like it. You got noticed on the male side for all the right reasons, but here it's the opposite. You're too close to some of the prisoners. Your lines have become blurred. Tell me what's happening.'

'Nothing. I'm out of here tomorrow. Hopefully I'll never be back.'

'And why's that?'

I pause, realising I have my foot millimetres from a tripwire.

'Prison doesn't make much sense on either side. It's inhumane to lock people up all day and night for so long without hope, especially if you give them nothing to do but watch TV. But at least on the male side I understood the punishment aspect of it. The men knowingly did wrong in most cases and deserve to pay the price. It doesn't feel as clear-cut as that over here. Most of the prisoners on this side are crying out for help, but will never get any.'

Nasima stares out of the window of the hub, then presses the talk button on her radio speaker.

'Commence mass movement to work.'

Suspicious eyes return to me.

'Well,' she said. 'You wouldn't have been allowed in the jail today if they'd found anything, so let's make your last few days quiet ones.'

I nod and stride to the door. Before I can escape, she sneaks a jab in.

'Dalton, Peabody has resigned. I'd have prosecuted him, but they've let him go.'

'Sorry to hear that.'

'Is it a surprise, though?'

'Nothing surprises me about this place.'

'They're watching you, too.'

I'm unsure how to respond to that, so I just leave. Other than doing the daily cell checks, I spend the rest of the day sitting in the office. Tex knows something's up and leaves me to it. She works hard doing everything that needs doing while I stare at the wall.

It's late afternoon when I hear the gate being rattled. I look out of the office and see Billie waving at me through the bars. Tex is upstairs, so I nip over to Billie.

'Look, you need to get away from here,' I snap at her.

'Where's my locket?'

'I have it, but I can't give you it.'

'Why not?'

'They searched me on the way in.'

'Well, hand it over if you've still got it. They won't be searching you on the way out.'

She's got a point.

'There's another thing,' she says. 'I need another two hundred pounds.'

'What the hell for? I paid you.'

'I've worked out how much I need for when I get out, but someone's let me down.'

'No, I don't have it.'

'I know, but you will on payday.'

'Why will I?'

'I've got eyes. I can see who's always here on overtime, but I have a gift for you too.'

'What?'

'I don't have Hepatitis or AIDS, or whatever the fuck they call it. Your wife will be pleased, or do you use condoms with her?'

I flinch at the risk I took. Billie presses on.

'You met me months before you thought you did. I remember you in Reception the night I came in. You looked at the red marks on my arm like I was scum. I was one of the two who you called junkies when Kitty was kicking off in Reception.'

I close my eyes as I picture the wretched girls who they brought in with Kitty. They looked so worthless that I never gave them another thought. Now look where we are. One of them is blackmailing me at work. Not in a million years could I have imagined the situation I'm in now. Has she used me to take revenge?

'You know nothing about me, Dalton.'

'I know you're damaged. Go on, piss off.'

'No, you had yours, and now I want mine. You have to pay. They'll chuck me out of here with sixty quid. How am I going to get a cot, or baby clothes, or everything else with that?'

'The council will help you.'

'Screw the council, you'll help me. The need to provide for my baby will mean I don't give a shit about your future.'

Billie snarls the words, but she's started talking louder. I look behind and see Tex walking towards me.

I glance across at the hub and spot Nasima watching us.

'I haven't got enough to give you,' I whisper to Billie.

'Compared to me, you have plenty. You have a house, a car, a bike, furniture, and probably a big fucking TV. I don't even have a place to stay.'

My radio crackles. We both look down at it.

'Personal alarm. Personal alarm. Officer Thrapston. Last known location female education department. First Response, please attend. This is a code red.'

Billie and I stare at each other. Education is where they do induction for the new arrivals. Lavinia will be there, and so will Tara.

'Shit, Tara, oh, God!' says Billie, stepping away from me with her hand to her mouth.

I unlock the wing gate and yank it open.

'Go, Dalton. I have the gate,' says Tex, who's now reached us.

I sprint to the houseblock exit, passing a confused-looking Kitty, arriving at the door at the same time as Sheraton. I open the houseblock door and he unlocks the gate behind it. Nasima runs out of the hub and shouts to us.

'Go, I've got them.'

We run to Main Street, through the doors, pound up the steps, and unlock the door to the education department. I hear shouting and crying coming from inside. A throng of milling prisoners with anguished faces are on the other side. When we open the gate, a surge of female bodies presses towards us. There's no stopping them. They shove past us, over twenty of them, and stream onto Main Street. The last one to go is Tara. For the first time since I've known her, she doesn't look at me.

'Leave them,' I shout to Sheraton. 'They'll be stuck on Main Street. The cameras will pick them up.'

I grab my radio and press talk.

'QP, Officer Dalton, First Response at location. Prisoners have left Education and are in Main Street. Put a freeze on. Send an officer out from Healthcare or the gym. Do not allow the inmates to leave. I repeat, do not open the doors back to the houseblocks and do not let industries release any of their workers.'

We stride along the corridor, checking left and right in the rooms for evidence of what's happened. Thrapston is standing outside the toilets surrounded by vomit on the floor. I'm not sure if it's hers or someone else's. She points to the toilet door. Her mouth moves, but her words are mumbled. I push the door open. There are three cubicles. All of their doors are shut. I can smell blood in the air amongst the foul stench of human waste. The first two cubicles are empty.

I approach the final door and there's the tip of a shoe visible underneath it. It's the type of footwear that looks out of place here. I nudge the door open slowly with one finger.

Lavinia is fully clothed on the toilet. She's sitting peacefully with her eyes closed. There is a large pool of blood beneath her, and the handle of a red screwdriver sticking out of her neck. I remember Tara's exact words: 'If you're angry and you can get your hands on a weapon, you're going to use it.'

74

Sheraton arrives next to me. He inhales sharply.

'Bloody hell. Is she dead?' he asks.

I know from experience that liquid spreads fast, but this is a huge puddle. There's no chest movement. I pick up a wrist and can't find a pulse. She's cold and strangely firm to touch. It's obviously a crime scene, so I don't want to move anything else, but I have to make sure. I tread in the blood and put my fingers against her neck. The skin is cool and lifeless.

'I'm afraid so, let's back out of here.'

It's obvious who did it. When we step outside, MacStravick has turned up ahead of two nurses. They all look at me hopefully, but I shake my head. They cautiously walk through the toilet door. MacStravick comes out shortly after and takes some deep breaths.

'What happened?' he asks me.

'I don't know. We're First Response. Thrapston was on duty here. That body sitting in there has been dead a little while. Long enough to cool. Judging by the shock, Thrapston must have gone in to see if anyone was in the toilet, or maybe a con or teacher told her someone was missing. You need to ask her.'

We find her in the office and on a seat with her head between her legs. She's been sick again. MacStravick crouches next to her.

'Talk to me,' he says.

She tries to explain, but through a lot of tears and dribbling, so she is impossible to understand. I tap MacStravick on the shoulder.

'Are all the prisoners on Main Street still?'

'Yes.'

'I'll get a piece of paper and take their names and locations. We'll need to speak to them before they return to the houseblocks. Or at least escort them back and lock them in their cells until we have time to interview them.' I point to the camera at the far end. 'Ask Security to look over the recording straight away. It's a bit of a distance, but you'll be able to see who went in that toilet this afternoon after the deceased did. Whoever killed her will be on there.'

He nods at me and gives me a cautious smile. I'm not telling him how to do his job. Even if you've been doing this for decades, you never lose the shock of a violent death and your brain still needs time to adjust. Sheraton's face tells me his stomach hasn't had time to adjust.

'Come on, Sheraton. Let's get the last few inmates outside and start organising them.'

At that point, Victor One, who oversees the Oscar One level of management in the prison and is basically in charge of the whole place, arrives. She has two managers with her. They rapidly take control.

Three hours later, it's time to go home. All the officers sit in the hub staring at Victor One. She stares grimly at us.

'We've identified twenty prisoners who visited that toilet after Lavinia Burford went in there. However, only five entered within ten minutes of the victim going in. They are the prime suspects. Their names are Goshawk, Shaw, James, Prestwick and Bragan. I need volunteers to stay and ferry the inmates backwards and forwards to the police interviews, which will be taking place up in Legal Visits.'

Half of the officers put their hands up; mostly the youngsters who don't have children to get back to.

Victor One stares at me.

'How about you, Dalton? You were the first on the scene.'

'I was second after Thrapston. All I saw was a cooling body. Whatever happened did so long before I showed up. I'd stay, but a friend has the kids and I need to pick them up on the way home.'

'Fair enough. Good work organising the prisoners afterwards. All of you have done well with what must still be an incredible shock. A murder within these walls is rare. However, the pathologist mentioned something we hadn't considered.'

She waits until she has our attention.

'He said the angle of insertion of the screwdriver is unusual for an attack. It was probably a left-handed person, perhaps a strong individual, because the weapon might have been pushed into the neck. There was little room to swing it due to the side wall of the toilet. He also mentioned just now that it could have been a self-inflicted wound. That would be a grim way to commit suicide, but not impossible. What was she in for?'

'Hang on, sir. I'll check,' says Sheraton.

While he taps away, I frown. What happened to clever Tara? Why do something so stupid and so serious? Lavinia's game was up, but now so is Tara's. There will be no Birdies salon now. Not for about fifteen years, anyway. She might get that as a minimum if she mentions the abuse she suffered at the hands of Lavinia.

But it's not just Tara's dreams going up in smoke. Kitty and Billie will lose an ally and possibly the only consistent positive influence that they've ever had. All for revenge. Kitty must have kept that screwdriver and given it to Tara. If I'd reported the attack as I should have done, that weapon might have been found. At the least, they'd have transferred Kitty and Zelda out of here. Then nobody would have died today.

I stoked them up too, by saying they should have reported Lavinia's crimes at the time. By not doing so, she was free to stay out there and abuse other children all over again. In some ways, I put that screwdriver in Tara's hand.

'Rape of a child under thirteen,' says Sheraton.

There's a sharp intake of breath.

'Okay,' says Victor One. 'It's possible that she'd kill herself. Many have suicidal thoughts after being caught for a crime like that and can't handle the shame of being exposed. Is anybody aware of anything that might confirm or deny that? Who spoke to her? What was her state of mind when she came in? Does anyone know a reason why any of those five women mentioned earlier might want to kill Lavinia Burford?'

A heavy silence fills the room. Officers shuffle their feet; others stare around as though waiting for someone to reveal a secret. I raise my hand. My voice is quiet.

'There's something I should tell you.'

75

All heads in the hub swivel towards me. My brain is scrambled with the events of the last few months, but my conscience demands I say it.

'Go on, Dalton,' says Victor One.

'I was here the evening she came in and I put her away. She was in shock. Lavinia was a posh, reserved woman who couldn't begin to comprehend this place, and she was guilty of crimes against children. She was furtive on the wing, looking for dangers she knew would eventually come. I reckon it was suicide.'

'What makes you think she might take her own life?'

'Well, as I was shutting her in, she said that she wouldn't be able to stand it here.'

There's another murmur of surprise.

'I hope you documented the conversation,' she says.

'Yes, she'd have had first night observations anyway, but I had a word with the night officer and told him to look in on her much more frequently than once an hour.'

'Did you put it on the handover sheet?' she asks.

'Of course, ma'am. I'm a professional.'

There are a few chuckles. To her credit, Victor One knows where the file is for the handover sheets. She pulls it out and finds the most recent entry.

'Yes, Dalton, your comments are here. The officer on duty last night has noted the inmate told him she would pull his tongue out if he didn't stop turning her light on. Actually, that doesn't sound like a defeated person.'

'No,' I reply. 'But if she'd decided to kill herself, she may have felt it was okay to be as rude as possible. What was the worst that could happen? With a hefty sentence, she may well have died in here anyway.'

I'm in too far to reveal that Lavinia used to look after Tara many years ago. If they search back that far, then so be it, but I won't point them in that direction.

'Fair point. Right, Dalton and the rest of you who aren't staying, off you go. We'll be busy in the morning, too, so if you're in, be prompt.'

Already, I can feel the pressure of tomorrow. As I walk towards the exit, my lies stalk me like a physical presence. Driving home, they will box me in like a too-big passenger, and later, they will be pressed against my side in bed. As Comms clears me through the sterile area door, I find MacStravick and the security SO waiting for my arrival at the gatehouse.

'Quick word, Dalton.'

I follow him to the chill-out room. He gives me another of his cool looks.

'I just wanted to check that jewellery after all,' he says.

Handing him my bag, I decide this moment sums up life. It's a game of half-chances, where coin tosses can mean death and incarceration, or they lead to a lucky escape. I could have given the locket to Billie, but I didn't. MacStravick smiles when he sees everything is as it should be and disappears, leaving me to put my stuff back inside the rucksack.

I think of what kind of birthday I've had. My prison life has taken a body blow as my home life has dragged itself from the canvas. It'd be nice if they were both great at the same time. I consider my decision to muddy the water around Lavinia's death. I suspect Kitty, Tara and Billie felt jail wasn't an appropriate punishment for the lifetimes of suffering that Lavinia had caused. Instead, the girls passed judgement and Tara carried out the sentence. That can't be right, but some people are evil. They'll never stop.

Will Tara keep quiet when they question her? I can't help smiling as I pull up outside my house. It doesn't do to underestimate clever Tara. She's ruthless. I feel daft for doubting her intelligence and stupid for dismissing her conviction. Of those five who went in that toilet after Lavinia, little Tara is the last person they will suspect. If Billie or Kitty had been in the frame, they'd have been arrested by now.

The girls' failure to report Lavinia all those years ago may have meant she could continue with her sick ways, but the fact they didn't raise their hands back then also gives Tara a way out. The police will look for motive, but they might not delve too deeply to see the connection because of who she was, especially if they suspect suicide.

I hope Tara gets out soon. I reckon, given half a chance, her business will be a success, and Billie and Kitty can be part of it too. Then they might actually find some peace. Perhaps Lavinia's death can be the end of that chapter, maybe even the book. It's time they started a new one where the past is forgotten. But we will all have secrets to keep.

76

I'm woken up at 5 a.m. by Ivan poking my forehead.

'Daddy, me cold,' he says.

Without thinking, I hold open my covers. He's only ever got in once before and he didn't stay long. This time, he snuggles in and his breathing settles. Mine does the same. A flash of light wakes me. It's Abi, taking a photo of Ivan and me cuddled up. Abi shows me the picture and a slow wave of deep satisfaction comes over me.

'Sleeping in late again, eh?' she says. 'Take the car and fill it up with petrol on your way home. We should head to the countryside tomorrow for a picnic. Have a family day out. It's supposed to be warm this afternoon and glorious tomorrow. Can you get a message to Wyatt to come and see me the moment he gets out? I need to apologise for not visiting or supporting him.'

I am tempted to say it's him that needs to do the apologising, but I don't mention it and instead just nod. I slide away from Ivan so he doesn't wake up and sneak out of bed. It's funny how little has changed, but how everything seems different since Abi came home. Maybe the world can be a better place if we try to be kinder and more thoughtful to each other.

I only have an eight-to-five shift, so I get in early. The detail says I'm GD for the day, which means I won't be able to dodge Billie on a wing if she sneaks downstairs. I could go upstairs and say goodbye to Tara, but, with suspicion hanging over her, I'd better not. That only leaves Kitty, who is brushing the floor around the hub when I open the houseblock door. It looks like she's trying to dig a trench, rather than collecting dust.

There's only Nasima present when I step inside the hub. She appears to wish her shift were finishing as opposed to just starting.

'Morning, ma'am. Am I GD?'

'I'm not sure—we've had two personal alarms go off on the male side, both on Charlie wing. The ambulance has been called. Can't you hear it on the radio?'

'I don't start until eight, so it's still off.'

'It's just what we need after all that shit yesterday.'

'By shit, do you mean murder or suicide?'

'Between you and me, Dalton, they haven't got a clue. The police questioned the five prime suspects, but they more or less shrugged and said it wasn't them. The other fifteen said they saw nothing. Nobody knew who she was, but apparently Lavinia appeared on the local news yesterday morning. Perhaps that triggered her to end it. She had very little to look forward to.'

'I suppose they'll investigate the crime scene for prints and DNA, which might help.'

Nasima laughed. 'I pity the poor folk who have to investigate in there, because they'll find evidence of about three hundred women. I heard there were partial prints on the weapon, so I'm guessing that if they are the victim's it's suicide, if they aren't hers, then murder.'

'Maybe someone else gave Lavinia the weapon and said use it, or we will.'

Nasima sat on her seat and drummed her fingers on the table.

'It's your last day today, isn't it?'

'Yes.'

'I'd like your opinion on a few of the inmates, if you don't mind.'

I get the feeling that whether I mind or not is irrelevant, so I'm relieved when her phone rings.

'Saved by the bell,' she says with a wry smile.

'I'm going to collect my bits and bobs from the wing office.'

Nasima nods and answers the phone.

'Shit,' she states. 'How many?'

I scoot out of the hub. It's probably best I keep out of the way in case they're searching for volunteers for something nasty. Tex is in the office with Sheraton. She beams when I knock on the open door.

'Ah, Dalton. Last day for me as well. I'm back to Mother and Baby. A whole load of newbies started their officer careers today, so things will be back to normal for us. We've got four of them on this afternoon.'

She steps around Sheraton and we hug like old friends, even though I still know very little about her. I shake Sheraton's hand, but he's distracted by his radio. I still haven't turned mine on.

'What's happening?' I ask him.

'Barricade on Charlie wing. The command centre has been opened.'

'Who's barricaded?'

'Two guys who are being transferred up north. They've taken another prisoner hostage. Said they're going to execute him.'

Even though it sounds terrible, it doesn't shock me. It's all I've known since I started this job. The prisoners won't really kill him, they just don't want a transfer miles from their families. Compared to HMP Peterborough, some of the Geordie and Scouse prisons are madhouses, so I can't blame them.

'You should volunteer,' I say to Sheraton. 'Get your ears wet. They'll be looking for a team of men to go in.'

'No, thanks. The ringleader is Bart Langley.'

'Ah!'

Langley is reputed to be a professional cage fighter, even though I couldn't find any sign of a public record online when I looked. He was padded up with his brother when I left the male side and Bart was actually the smaller, more reasonable one of the pair.

I open the drawer of the cupboard and clear the few belongings that I have in there. It's just a few pens, a mug with *Toy Story*'s 'Woody' on it that Lennox gave me for my last birthday, saying that I looked like him, and my black notebook. When I pick the latter up, a small piece of paper drops out. There's a drawing on it. BiRDies is written in black writing, and in a line below each capital is Broken, Ruined and Damaged. The big letters have been highlighted in pink with exclamation marks around them and reminds me of the film *Cocktail*. How the hell did they get that in here?

I stroll off the wing, looking up and down the landings. It has never felt like a prison on this side, even though the building is virtually identical. Perhaps that's a reflection of the people who are forced to live here. The women might be prisoners, but most try to pretend they aren't. I lock the gate and walk towards the hub, where Nasima is gesticulating on the phone.

'You off today, sir?'

I turn around to see a sheepish-looking Kitty.

'Yes, last shift. Will you miss me?'

'We all will, sir.'

She's clearly got something on her mind as she stands there with her head bobbing from side to side.

'Spit it out, Kitty.'

'Do they know what happened to that woman?'

I contemplate doing the right thing and saying who knows, but I'm already in way too deep.

'They think it could be a suicide. As long as nobody's prints turn up on the screwdriver, whoever did it might get away with it. But whoever did it should consider themselves very lucky and change their lives accordingly. Their friends should also feel grateful.'

Kitty beams at me. She's not quite ready for a hug, though. I think of Ivan. Kitty sticks her fist out and we do a little bump.

'Good luck, sir, and thanks for everything.'

Nasima's knock on the hub window grabs our attention. She beckons me in.

'Well, there's a barricade with two inside on Charlie wing. They've decided to go in. They're looking for enthusiastic men and women to put a hand in the air.'

I suck the air between my teeth.

'There won't be too many keen if it involves the Langleys.'

'I told them both of yours were up.'

'You're very kind.'

'It's a chance for you to show them who you are.'

'The Langley brothers?'

'Yes. Get over there as fast as you can. They're fetching the shields and riot gear now. Don't worry about coming back today. You'll have paperwork until Christmas when that door opens.'

'Okay.'

To leave like this is an anticlimax after everything that's happened. I look down the landings and see the wing officers locking up the last few stragglers before work. It's quiet, but not too quiet. Just relaxed and calm. I wonder what else I'll miss. I give Nasima a nod.

'Thanks for your help, ma'am.'

'You too, Dalton. Take your knowledge and experience with you and spread the word. You've done your best, and that's all we can expect from anyone.' She reaches over and shakes my hand. 'But we both know it's time for you to go home.'

I sling my rucksack over my shoulder and leave the hub. After a final glance and a quick sniff of the air, I hustle over to the men's side. At least I won't have to risk hearing Billie's demands for another two hundred pounds. As I'm approaching the male houseblocks, a young lad is escorting Colt and his gang across to Reception to process their release. Judging by his shiny boots and starched trousers, the officer must be a new guy. Colt sees me and peels off.

'Jimbo! Here to say goodbye! Nice one.'

'Yeah, I wanted to make sure you'd gone. You were getting too comfortable here.'

'True dat.'

'And go and see your sister.'

'Laters, bruv. Call me, innit.'

The new officer has caught up with Colt.

'Excuse me, sir, you need to come along with us,' he says to Colt.

Colt and I share a moment. The newbie sounds eerily similar to C-3PO. Colt leans into the officer's personal space.

'Or what, super screw? I'm a bad man. You're going to have to wrap me the fuck up, cos I is free. Get me?'

Colt turns and winks at me, then trots off after his mates, who are lounging at the doors to Main Street like some kind of boy band from the back streets. I'll be amazed if they aren't all in here again within six months. In fact, the only one who probably won't be present in the prison is that new officer, if he's smart.

I open the houseblock doors and chuckle at the heady smell. Home indeed. I walk to the hub.

'Where the fuck have you been, Dalton?' says SO Bowell with a grin.

'I was just with your wife.'

'Well, it's a credit to you that you've survived the experience. Get suited up, we're going in when you're ready. Want to lead?'

'Hell, yeah!'

I stride to the manager's office where we usually suit up. Fats and Lennox are in their underwear.

'Did you bring any oil, Dalton?' says Fats.

'I always carry my special recipe.'

'Gross,' says a laughing Lennox.

Chuckling now, I drag off my clothes and pull on a boiler suit. I put my boots back on, then shin and elbow guards, and a stab vest. Finally, the helmet and thick gloves go on, and I'm ready. Bowell walks in with another new officer holding a camcorder aloft.

'Okay, team,' says Bowell. 'Team one is Dalton, Fats and Lennox. They'll take point and aim for the bigger brother, Clay. Team two is Atkins, Taufel and Garvey. Hit the other brother but be aware it will be a mess in there. If you find yourself on the wrong man, don't worry. Grab an arm, head or leg, and hold on. Smith and Warren are back-up. If you get injured, roll away. I'll send Smith and Warren in after ten seconds anyway to secure their legs.'

He pauses and looks around the room into each of our eyes.

'These guys are strong, but together you are stronger. Visors closed. Let's go.'

We hustle out of the office into quiet. The male prison is locked down. We double past Braddock, who is swinging on the wing gate that he's opened for us. I give him a thumbs down as I pass.

'Flatulence,' he shouts. 'Doctor signed me off.'

I line up on the right of the door with Fats and Lennox behind me. We form a V: me at the front with one of them on each shoulder. I raise the shield. Taufel's team mirrors ours on the other side. The two brothers are in a big cell, but there still won't be much room in there, and the doorway is only wide enough to let one in at a time. If they've got a weapon or anything to throw, the first person in will swiftly discover what it is.

Bowell looks at me. He has his key out ready and gives me the nod. He opens the door and I charge in with an almighty roar. Clay steps forward and hurls a pool ball, which pounds into my shield. Another one thrown by Bart ricochets off the top of my helmet. I pitch the shield at an angle and stab down towards Clay's groin. Fats yells at the top of his voice and Lennox's banshee cry rings in my ear next to me. We thump into the growling prisoner and slam him against the wall. Nasima was right. This is where I belong.

77
FOUR MONTHS LATER

I double-check the figures are correct for the wings. It's lunch time bang up in an hour and I need to get out on time to pick up Ivan and Tilly from their grandparents. Abi's parents moved back last month and they've been a great help, despite her dad's battle with cancer. That's what made him change his mind about everything. When the end is in sight, money and opinions matter little, you just want to be with the people you love. I guess he'll have to put up with me at the same time.

They tried to get back in touch with their son but he wasn't interested in maintaining ties. Wyatt will be able to add that to his list of regrets later in life.

Lennox enters the hub.

'Those two from Alpha who went to court are back on the wing, boss,' she says.

'And Halifax, the hospital escort?'

'No word. He was having some piles removed, so he'll probably be a while.'

We both grin. Halifax is inside for breaking his partner's arm. Last time he was in the prison, he'd broken her nose.

'Let's hope they forget the anaesthetic.' Lennox laughs.

Our eyes meet for that extra moment that means you're either good mates or attracted to each other. Fats reckons she only bought me that Woody mug because she fancies old people. She leans over me to look at the details and I get a waft of perfume and feel the heat from her proximity. She doesn't need to be this close, so maybe he's right. But I'll take friends. There'll be no more mistakes. I have too much to lose.

The hub phone rings.

'Senior Officer Dalton speaking.'

I listen for a minute with my chin lowering to the floor.

'You are shitting me,' is all I can eloquently manage.

I listen further, still stunned.

'Okay, I'll get him out. We have time if I bring him down myself.'

I gently place the receiver in its holder. In the last six months, I've aged little, yet I've changed plenty. Now I'm mature enough to understand what maturity is, I'm surprised by how wrong I was about it. Experience and common sense are not about knowing everything, maturity is actually understanding that you don't know everything, and you never will. Mistakes will happen, and you will always judge people wrongly. It's called being human. Knowing that, and acting accordingly, is what makes you a grown-up.

I leave the hub and lock the door behind me. I reach Delta wing, where a few of the inmates are lounging with their arms through the wing gates. On this side of the jail, if a new officer tells them to shift, the prisoners will say no and they'll need to be threatened. Previously, if I'd told them to move, they would have done so grudgingly. With my shiny red badge, I don't even say anything. They disappear with a look.

'Gronkowski,' I shout down the landing.

He pops his head out of the servery, smiles and walks towards me. How his T-shirt hasn't split apart Hulk-style, I'll never know. A couple of the YOs stare at him in awe despite the apron looking small and effeminate on him due to his size.

'Yes, boss. Have you come for lunch? Good range today, some of it warm. Maybe even meat in meat pie.'

'Tempting. Are you still saying you're innocent?'

'Of course. I am no killer.'

'I have news.'

I search his face for signs of deceit or suspicion, but there has never been any since that incident where he smoked spice and attacked us. It turns out he was a prison officer back in his home country. That was how he knew the rules here, whereas I'd automatically assumed he'd been on the wrong side of the bars. I'd also suspected he was guilty of the crimes he was charged with.

'As you know, the girlfriend of the man who died in your case had regained consciousness but remained semi-vegetative, but she's talking now. She has given the police a description of the man who battered her and killed her boyfriend.'

Gronkowski raises his chin as if to take a blow.

'It sounds exactly like you. Strong, maybe six-feet tall.'

He looks baffled for a moment. I continue.

'Perhaps a bit less. Slim, probably a teenager, and Asian.'

His lips twitch and he shakes his head repeatedly. He walks backwards, then forwards, then back again. With his huge arms held out to the side, he bellows, 'It is over? I can go?'

'Yes, the police have dropped all charges against you.'

'Oh, God. My baby, my girlfriend.' Tears pour down his face. He steps towards me and pulls me into an embrace that threatens to snap my neck like a chicken bone. 'Yes, yes, yes!' he bellows at the ceiling, causing everyone to come out of their cells.

'If you pack your stuff quickly, I can get you down to Reception before bang up.'

'Screw my stuff! These guys can have everything. All I want is my freedom.'

'Well, you'll need your ID card and you should take the photos your girlfriend sent in of the baby for you, and her letters.'

His enormous smile of complete joy shines from his face like a holy light in this dark place of despair. He pelts down the wing, people scampering out of his way, and leaps up the steps to the top landing, where he punches the air, Rocky-style. I walk along the landing as he disappears into his cell. All the usual goons are hanging over the balconies, trying to look cool or hard, but even they are smiling. Gronkowski was one of the good guys. Who'd have known?

Gronkowski appears two minutes later with a full carrier bag and runs down the top landing, high-fiving laughing cons on the way. At the gate, Scranton comes out of the laundry room, hands in his trousers pockets, and sneers at him.

'Pissing off, are you? Great. There are too many Russians around here.'

Gronkowski turns to me.

'Do I have ten seconds?'

'Take as long as you need.'

Gronkowski drops his bag and shoves Scranton back into the laundry room. The door closes. Eight seconds later, Gronkowski reappears alone and rubbing his knuckles.

'Worth it?' I ask.

'Totally. I no get in trouble?'

'No, it's slippery in there. He should be more careful. Scranton may be a dick, but he's no grass. He knows the rules.'

I walk Gronkowski off the houseblock. A few of the officers wish him well when I say where he's going. We walk along Main Street. I can't help smiling at the energy glowing from him. At the doors to Reception, I stop before I let him through.

'Why did you attack our staff that morning?'

'I am sorry. That is why I knock Scranton out. He gave me spliff. I very upset because I innocent and have baby. It too strong, full of madness, but I smoke it all thinking it stop me acting like asshole. Then remember nothing. Wake up with sore biceps and bad head. Will you accept my apology and tell others?'

'Yes, of course. Everyone makes mistakes from time to time. It must be nice to leave this place. But it's hard to think that you've been locked up here for so long when you didn't do anything wrong. The fact you handled it so well is impressive. It's tough to live in these conditions under any circumstances. Although I sometimes wonder who has it worse in here: the officers or the prisoners.'

'Then you crazy. You get to sleep with nice pillow, see your woman, eat steak.'

'Yes, but this place has a strange effect on me. My presence still lingers here, even when I'm at home.'

Now it's Gronkowski who studies me.

'That is why you are good man. Everyone knows that, even if they not want you knowing. By the way, Gronkowski is pronounced with a v, like in kovski.'

'Really? Why didn't you say?'

He laughs as I unlock the door.

'It not important compared to rest of nightmare.'

We lock hands at the reception desk and I leave, smiling. Didn't Peabody say something similar when we got his name wrong?

When I get back to the houseblock, lunch and meds are under way. In the hub after the roll is in, we shake our heads at Gronkowski having spent around six months in jail for a crime he didn't commit. What happened to being innocent until proven guilty?

I drive home in my old car. Abi has a posh new Audi, which her parents bought her so she and the kids have something safe and reliable to pootle around in. We could have paid a deposit on a house with that money and got something cheaper, but I think her father wanted to see them in it now he knows his time might be short.

One of my hub caps came off on the parkway last week. I had to pull over and run across four lanes of traffic to reclaim it. It's lucky her dad wasn't driving past, or he'd have been tempted to aim for me.

When I reach the house, Abi is at the door chatting to one of her friends. I park up and walk towards them. At first, I don't recognise the woman Abi's talking to, but then she flicks her hair behind her ear, which shows her pregnant bump, and there's no mistaking Billie.

78

I stumble as I step towards them, causing Abi to look up.

'Did you come home via the pub?' She laughs, but the smile slips from her face.

I don't know what to say, but Billie turns with a huge grin.

'Hey, Dalton. I was just telling your wife we used to work on the same wing. You remember that favour you offered when I said I was moving? Well, I've found a place and need a hand.'

I nod at Abi. 'Give us a minute.'

I let out a groan as Abi stares suspiciously at me and shuts the door, leaving Billie staring lovingly my way.

'What are you doing here?'

'You've got something of mine.'

'What?'

'My locket.'

'You came here to get that?'

'Yes, I want it. Besides, it's not like I have a busy schedule.'

'It's in my car.'

I walk back to our parking space and sit in the driver's seat. The chain and locket are hidden in a small storage compartment. Abi loved the spinning ring that I got at the same time. I remove the little box and give it to Billie, who's standing next to the car.

'I'll also be needing that money,' she says.

'Billie, I haven't got it. Look where we live. We're not rich.'

Billie crosses her arms over her bump and taps her foot.

'You are compared to me. You've got a home, a wife, a car. I have a bedroom in a bail hostel with three smackheads. You're pretty fucking rich from where I'm standing.'

'You said that first amount was the last.'

'Yes, but that was before Peabody did a runner. He even moved house, the wanker. My kid needs a cot, a basket, new clothes, nappies, cream, the works, and he's getting it.'

'It's a he, then?'

'Yes, they told me at the hospital.'

Suddenly, I think of Rose-Marie and what she did when backed into a corner.

'The money's not for an abortion, is it?'

'Are you kidding me? I want this baby. I've wanted to love someone that's not going to reject me ever since I can remember. Now I finally have that chance.'

My anger vanishes at that harsh truth.

'Why don't you ask Sandringham's family for help?'

She snorts air up through her nose and forces it back out.

'I didn't tell anyone it was his. They might want to get involved and I don't want that. I'll raise it my way.'

She pauses and lifts up the right leg of her tracksuit bottoms. A plastic monitor, about the same size as a man's sports watch, is around her ankle.

'To be fair to the prison, they got me out on tag, so I'll keep to my side of the bargain. I have to stay in the hostel from 9 p.m. to 6 a.m., or I get recalled. When the baby arrives, they've found me a room in a place which just has young mums in it. Sounds wonderful, doesn't it? Please help me, Dalton.'

'I can't.'

The hard look that she returned from HMP Styal with appears again.

'You have to. This is definitely the last time. Tara's got a job at Amazon. She tried to return to her old career but couldn't do it. Said she thought of you.'

I can't help smiling. Good for her.

'Did she get her money back from that bloke?'

'I went around to see that dirty old twat who nicked her cash. Gave him the word. He's up to date now. Kitty has a position lined up at a factory for when she gets out. It's some kind of rehabilitation thing. We're going to be fine, but I need a little handout now. Don't forget, you were in a position of responsibility. I bet female prisoners are always flirting with the officers, even the old ones. If you don't want anyone to find out about your lack of control, or how you forced yourself on me, then get the money out and ring me on this number by tomorrow.'

She passes me another piece of paper. Then she fiddles with the phone in her hand, holds it up and takes a photo of me.

'For my locket,' she states.

She fixes me with her stare for a final time, then walks away to the end of the road. There's a big lad, wearing a leather jacket, sitting on the street sign watching us, who looks vaguely familiar. When she reaches him, she stops to talk. They both look back my way. Just behind them, Colt walks around the corner, holding hands with a blonde girl. He gives the lad in the leather jacket a filthy glance, then walks towards me.

I turn back to my house, where Abi is staring out of the kitchen window.

79

When I open the door, Abi is waiting behind it.

'That looked cosy. What did she want?'

My brain whirrs like a spinning top.

'She lent me some money to get my car fixed while you were away, and she wanted it back.'

'And?'

'I didn't have it on me, and she got arsey when I said I'd give it to her tomorrow.'

'Does she still work at the prison?'

'No, she left to have the baby.'

'She seemed very angry.'

'She also wanted to borrow extra off me, but I said I had none to spare.'

Abi's frown softens. 'Why?'

'Well, she isn't working, so how's she going to pay it back? We need that money to put towards a new house.'

'So, she helps when you need it, but then you do a credit check when she asks you for a favour. How much did she want?'

'I owe her a hundred, and she wants another hundred.'

'Jesus, can't you give her fifty or something?'
'I guess.'
'You need to get changed. We've got guests for tea.'

I groan. I'm not in the mood for Colt. The doorbell rings while I'm climbing the stairs. I put a clean shirt on and return downstairs. There's loud talking and laughter coming from the lounge. I open the door and Colt is sitting on my sofa with Ivan on his lap. Next to him is the blonde-haired girl, who is dressed like a hippy and looks about seventeen. Tilly is staring at her as if Elsa from *Frozen* has turned up in real life.

'Jimbo!' shouts Colt. He manhandles Ivan off him, which would usually make Ivan angry, but he doesn't seem to care. Colt glances back at the girl. 'Elizabeth, this man saved my life. Thank you, Jim. Really, you are a great guy.'

There's something dodgy going on here. Colt sounds funny.

'It's fine, Colt. You're family, after all.'

I attempt a smile, but Colt leans in.

'It's Wyatt. No more Colt, okay?'

'Dinner's served,' shouts Abi from the kitchen.

'Ooh, super, I'm starving,' says Elizabeth, beaming at Wyatt. 'Show me the way, honey.'

Wyatt beams back at her. I have an urge to vomit. Abi has cooked baked salmon, which I'm not keen on, but it's Wyatt's favourite. She serves him first, too.

'So how did you two meet?' Abi asks Wyatt.

'A bloke at the prison told us about this course on training to be a chef. They had some spaces for people who've been in the nick.'

'And you're on the course as well, Elizabeth?' asks Abi.

'Call me, Liz, please. Wyatt insists on calling me Elizabeth. He says I'm posh.' She titters, sounding very posh. 'And yes. The course isn't just for people like Wyatt. I'd love to be a top chef even though Daddy isn't keen, but I know my own mind.'

Talk about opposites attract. I can tolerate love's young dream, but I don't want it putting me off my food. I zone in and out of the conversation, thinking about Billie. Do I give her the money? Who knows how many times she's going to come back? I need her out of my life for good.

After dinner, Liz gets dragged into the sitting room to play Connect Four with the kids. Wyatt wants a smoke, so I go outside at the same time and ask him to go for a walk.

'Nice girl, eh?' he says.

'Yes, she doesn't seem the type to like gangsters. Is she mad, or drunk?'

'Very funny. I was nervous at the start of the course, but I didn't want to mess it up, so I cut the attitude. We were sat together, and she's all chatty and confident and sexy. Anyway, I keep quiet and she asks if I fancy a coffee afterwards. Now we're tight. I'm in love, man.'

'What of your lovely friends and the gang?'

'Fuck you, Dalton. Time to grow up, innit.'

'What about that gun tattoo?'

'She loves it. All chicks do.'

I laugh and squeeze his shoulder as we walk.

'Who was the bird outside staring at you, the one up the duff?' he asks.

'A girl I know from the prison.'

Wyatt laughs.

'You old dog, Dalton. Don't worry, I owe you, so I won't say anything.'

I stop walking.

'Wyatt, this needs to stay between you and me.'

'Swear down, homie.'

'I may have got a bit too close to her, but now she's threatening me, saying she'll tell them I did things that I didn't. Even if she's lying, I'd lose my job.'

'Ah, gotcha. She's tapping you up for cash. Is it your baby?'

'God, no.'

'Cool. Then it's easy. You can't stand for any of that bullshit, she'll never quit. Meet her somewhere dark and strike back, hard. Tell her next time, she's a dead 'un.'

'Oh, yeah, great idea. She's pregnant.'

'Fuck pregnant. That ain't for you to worry about. She's extorting you, that's on her.'

'I should just pay her one last time and say that's the end of it.'

'Bruv, they don't stop. Nip it in the bud. I tell you, give her a quick jab, so she knows you're serious. Then forget about it. She ain't going to the cops.'

It hasn't taken Wyatt, or Colt, long to slip back into his street identity. I only see pain ahead for Elizabeth. I remember the big lad that was waiting at the end of my road.

'Did you know that lad in the leather jacket she was with?'

'Yeah, that's Bumpy. Used to be one of my crew, but he was too mental, even for me. He pounded the steroids in prison and since he got out. He's tripping now. Owes me money, though. Mugged me off when I asked. I've been too busy with Elizabeth to catch up with him. She says if I go back to jail, it's over, so I ignored him. But I can't let Bumpy owe me. All I've got is my rep.'

'Is he violent?'

'Shit, man. Very. Anyway, the girl. Arrange to hook up tomorrow night. Somewhere out of sight where you won't be disturbed. Don't mention me, but I'll come with. She'll bring Bumpy for protection, but they won't know I'm gonna be there. I'll lay it on him, and you can lay it on her.'

I don't know what to say. He's right, though, about part of it at least. She'll never stop. Wyatt's left jail, but he remains a prisoner to his reputation.

'Okay, I'll see if she wants to meet tomorrow night at eight. There's that wood under the parkway near the Gordon Arms pub. There are no lights nearby. I'll let her think I've got the money.'

'Sweet. I'll come here at seven-fifty. Give me a buzz if plans change. Remember, Dalton, you're in the jungle now with the rest of us. You eat or get eaten. You live, or you die.'

80

I ring Billie from the garden while the others have dessert and ask her to meet me at the wood tomorrow at eight. She quickly agrees and hangs up. Wyatt and Liz leave soon after. Abi listens to music while she tidies. I tell her I'm knackered and will turn in myself after putting the kids to bed. That will give me time to consider what I'm going to do. Tilly is almost asleep on her feet and gets into bed on her own while I deal with Ivan.

'Hurry up with my story, Daddy, or I'll be snoozing,' she shouts from her room.

'Don't go yet, Daddy. I've had a lovely day,' says Ivan, as I stand to leave him.

His hand comes out of the cover and holds mine as I sit back on the edge of the bed. His speech and tantrums have made significant progress in the last few months. He's still a little different from the other children, but that's fine. I love him the way he is, which makes me angry at myself for the things I did. When I check on Tilly, she's fast asleep. I have so much at stake.

Looks like another night of no sleep. Relying on Wyatt to get me out of this mess doesn't seem sensible, but what else can I do? I can't go to the police, and if I call Billie's bluff, my life could implode. She's sure to tell Abi. She might even get that Bumpy to take me out. It's unbelievable. All those years in the prison and I was never really scared. But now I'm terrified and in desperate trouble, and I brought it all on myself.

The night is long and restless. I understand the women in jail are often victims before they are villains. But Billie's behaviour is criminal and there are no excuses. She knows exactly what she's doing. I judged her and Kitty's street robbery to be an opportunistic crime through necessity. Who's to say they didn't plan it? In fact, I might have guessed that Kitty was the driving force, but all bets are on Billie now.

Lavinia wasn't an idiot. When she named them, she was simply describing them. Those three girls are broken, damaged and ruined. Is Billie a monster, beyond redemption? If so, what does that make me?

After rolling around for hours, I get up and revisit the kids' rooms. I even stand next to Abi in our room and think of everything we've been through. She has a part-time job now at the dry-cleaner's and the kids are settled at school. We're finally building a deposit for a house of our own. Yet, Billie could blow it all apart.

It's my weekend off and we've been keeping Saturdays as family time since Abi came home, although she works in the morning now. What I hate most about this whole situation is the lies. I'm forced to lie and lie. The web of deceit gets heavier and more complicated. Surely, it will soon collapse.

Eventually I give up trying to sleep, and watch TV until everyone wakes up. Just before eight in the morning, Abi sweeps around the house kissing us.

'Bye, bye, bye.' She laughs. 'Looking forward to movie and pizza night later.'

I see her out. She has a spring in her step as she walks down the road. Her new role is only fifteen hours a week, but it's an escape from being a mum. In the future, she wants to go back full-time somewhere, or train to do something in teaching, maybe even art. I've been so focussed on my career and job that I didn't notice our children have deprived her of both. I close the door and look at my watch. The future starts tomorrow, when all this is done.

Ivan is having one of his spiky box days, as Tilly calls them. It's as if he's surrounded by a force field and you can't get anywhere near him. By eleven o'clock, he still hasn't said or eaten anything.

'Come on, guys, let's go to see the ducks. They'll be flying away soon to somewhere warmer.'

I read online that ducks like lettuce, and to use it instead of bread. We have some old iceberg lettuce, so I grab that and we set off. It's the kind of day I hate. Mild, but not a pinch of blue sky anywhere. Just a steady sheet of grey and the occasional drop of rain, which does nothing to disperse the close feeling. We head hand-in-hand towards the underpass, with me thinking it's not even midday yet, so it should be safe enough.

We're through it and heading up the concealed slope when three lads come around the corner. One wears a big leather coat and has white hair. It's bloody Bumpy. They stop in a line and glance at each other. I feel the children's hands tighten in mine. I look behind me, but my options are limited with two kids in tow. The three boys, and that's all they are, stride towards us.

'We forgot to bring any money out with us, and we're thirsty,' says Bumpy.

I'm not sure how to play this. I'm not even certain I could take him on one-on-one. He has the thick, heavy-set build of someone whose punches will be sledgehammer blows. The other two are thin and weedy, but they all have the dehumanised expression that only marijuana or spice can produce. I take deep breaths without appearing to do so.

'I have nothing on me. We're just out for a walk.'

'Still got a phone, haven't you?'

'Not with me.'

'Bullshit, who comes out without their mobile? Maybe this will help your memory.'

He reaches behind him and pulls out the scariest-looking blade I have ever seen. It's like a weapon from a martial arts film. He points the tip straight at my face, but his eyes clear slightly as he peers at me.

'I know you?'

Bumpy saw me in uniform. That's all people see. I regularly walk past ex-prisoners in normal clothes when I'm in town and don't get recognised.

'No, I don't think so. Let us go, please, my children are scared.'

'They should be scared. Phone and money, now!'

Ivan has seized my leg with an iron grip. Tilly is quietly crying and has grabbed my arm with both hands.

'Come on, Daddy, let's go,' she whispers.

She tries to drag me backwards, but it's not easy to walk with Ivan attached to me. Bumpy moves the knife point in a tight circle. His eyes have emptied of any emotion.

'Wait a minute,' says the taller of the other two lads. 'Come on, dude. The kids are roaring. Let's chip off.'

'No, I ain't leaving without something.'

I hear screeches behind me. It's two young men on mountain bikes. Bumpy still has his knife out in front of him. He moves the tip, so it's directed at the new arrivals. The cyclists look at each other, then one of them gets his phone out and points it at the action. Bumpy and friends are too caned for rapid thinking. Eventually, Bumpy realises the implications of having his picture taken.

'Get that phone,' he shouts.

The three of them chase after the cyclists, but they're ready. They flip their bikes around and race off. I pick up Ivan,

'Run, Tilly, as fast as you can.'

Tilly's no runner, but she tries hard. Protecting your family gives you extra strength. I grab Ivan, pump my legs while holding him in front of me, and we are rapidly away from the scene. We do a wide circle, but soon have to walk. I put Ivan down, but he refuses to let go, so I give him a piggyback as we skirt around through the posh area next to our estate. The shopping centre is quiet. I check my bank balance to see if my wages are in, but they aren't. I have eighty-one pounds left. Then we quickly run across the busy road, not keen on taking another underpass.

The children are subdued when we get back to the house. I set Ivan up in the lounge with *Danger Mouse* and a bag of crisps. Then I start tidying up. Tilly follows me the whole time without saying anything. Finally, she tugs on my shirt.

'Daddy, who were those people?'

'They were kids, messing around.'

'I was really scared, and I want to live somewhere else.'

'Me, too, baby. It's okay, they've gone now.'

I hug her back, knowing it's more lies.

81

Abi returns from work with two frozen pizzas for tonight. We go for a drive to Ferry Meadows and walk around the lake. Abi mentions the kids are quiet, but I don't give her the complete story. Tilly tends to talk to Abi about things that have bothered her during the day at bedtime, so it will definitely come up. She knows not to go down that underpass. It's further proof that I need to get my family out of here to a more peaceful place. That is my focus but it's a tough mountain to climb with house prices going up faster than I can save.

The children perk up with an ice cream, but the first real flame of anger ignites in my head. I'm sick of people taking the piss. This world is tough enough as it is without people taking advantage of others. It makes me want to hit back. I never used to be able to understand the violent crimes that the men had been sent down for. But I'm learning. Wyatt's world is ruled by the strong and the ruthless. It's my fault that I've become immersed in it.

Later, I put the pizzas in the oven. I struggle to force a single slice down, with my mind on the excuse I need for popping out. My stomach is focussed on tonight.

'I fancy a couple of cans, Abi. I'm going to nip to the shop in a bit. Do you want anything?'

'Get me a big pack of Walker's cheese and onion and I'll pinch one of your beers. Is that why you've been quiet?'

'You got it. One-track mind.'

'Can I have some beer?' asks Tilly.

'Me, too,' says Ivan.

'Looks like it's beers all round.' Abi smiles.

I walk upstairs, dreading what's about to come. How nice would a few cold drinks be, slumped with the kids in front of Saturday night TV?

Wyatt is outside as promised, which is a relief. I pick up on his focus and try to draw on some of his strength. It's funny how people have a prison persona. He's back to acting like Colt.

And it's not just the inmates who change. The officers are different inside, like Tex, or others who become caricatures of their normal selves. I suspect at least Braddock's mum calls him by his first name.

Behind those walls, I'm Officer Dalton, a man worthy of respect. But out here, I'm just Jim the dad and husband, with two young kids, a wobbly marriage, who's pushing forty with a lot to lose. A person who has been backed into a corner as Rose-Marie and so many others have been in the past. And that's when poor choices are made. Choices that can be life-altering, but right now I'm just tired and want it to be over.

Colt and I stride out of Malborne, through the village, and turn right on Oundle Road. The cloud cover and intermittent showers make for a dark night, but the wind has picked up and the drops have more venom. Occasionally, the moon peeks into view and adds an eerie glow to everything it touches.

As we approach the entrance to the wood, Wyatt pulls his hoodie up. He's dressed all in black and appears older than his years. We step through a small opening in a fence and edge carefully along the path between the trees. The moon is out and we can see where we're going, but as soon as it disappears behind the clouds only a few metres of the muddy track are visible ahead of me.

We stand still for ten minutes, ears straining with the rustling sounds around us. A gust of wind howls through the branches above and speckles us with water.

'Screw this, Jimbo, they aren't coming.'

'Yeah, let's go. I need a few beers.'

We turn to head back the way we came when we hear distant cursing behind us. Someone's approaching from the other side of the woods. I can see a bright light much further up the path, bobbing and weaving, then disappearing. The ground down here is treacherous when it's wet and big holes quickly fill with water.

Wyatt reaches inside his coat. He takes a handle out that doesn't look dissimilar to the one that Tara used on Lavinia. This weapon, however, has a button, which Wyatt presses. A wicked three-inch blade flashes out. He presses the button again, and it vanishes.

'Here, Jim. Have this. I'll take care of Bumpy, but the girl is on you. Finish it now.'

He steps off the trail and behind a tree as total darkness falls once more. The people approaching are much closer, and soon they stand in front of me. Billie looks tiny with Bumpy's bulk behind her. He points the phone torch at the floor, which casts us all in strange shadows.

'Did you bring it?' she asks.

'I told you, I don't have that kind of money.'

'That's a shame, Dalton.'

'I hoped you'd reconsider.'

She seems so calm. How dare she mess with my life? Why do people think they can get away with this kind of thing? Do they simply assume that most people won't resort to extreme violence, even when pushed? I unzip my coat.

'What are we to do?' she says.

'I did bring you something.'

A twig snaps next to me, causing Billie and I to flinch, whereas Bumpy lowers into a crouch. In the quiet, it sounded like the crack from a gun. Wyatt steps into view as though the forest has released a creature from the netherworld. Bumpy's torch beam moves up Wyatt's body to his shrouded face. Wyatt peels back his hood. The beam wobbles. Wyatt holds his own phone up and the weak light from the screen shows Bumpy frantically whispering to Billie.

'I've been looking for you,' says Wyatt.

'I'll get you your money, I have some now,' gasps Bumpy.

'It's too late. That's not going to repair my reputation.'

The light disappears from Bumpy's torch as he spins on his heels. Then we see it waving through the trees and bouncing around. We can hear him crashing through the undergrowth as he flees the scene. Billie steps out of the way as Wyatt scrambles after him. Billie and I study each other as the shouts disappear into the wood.

I reach into my back pocket. Billie's quick. I'll give her that. The pain is equally rapid. I look down and see a small black handle sticking out of my left-hand side. My grip weakens and the four twenty-pound notes, which were the remaining balance of my current account, slip from my fingers.

'Oh, Dalton. I'm sorry, I...'

I try to talk, but only a wheeze comes out.

'Bumpy told me you'd have a weapon and to use one first. I thought you'd gone for it.'

'Ah!' is all I can manage.

She looks down at the knife handle. Her expression registers that her prints are on it.

'Please, say you were mugged. You'll never hear from me again. We're even now.'

She whips the small knife out, which blurs my vision with agony, almost causing me to faint. She puts it in the side pocket of her coat. After picking up my money, she grabs my left hand and holds it over the wound. She places her other hand against my cheek, then she's gone.

I've watched movies where people get shot or stabbed, then stagger and drag themselves for miles to safety. Until this evening, I imagined that was possible, but it isn't. Not for me. My eyes begin to close.

A cool breeze rustles the branches. It chills the sweat that covers my body, except for where the sticky warmth runs down my left hip and leg. My left hand rests on the hole in that side, but it lacks the strength to staunch the flow.

Twenty metres away, through the treeline, occasional cars roar past. I blink back tears. Perhaps, there is still a chance. I manage to shuffle forwards through the damp leaves, gasping through gritted teeth. A sharp, intense spasm in my stomach forces me to arch my back and look skywards. Through the canopy overhead, the moonlight bathes me. I sense part of me drawing upwards, and my face relaxes.

My weak legs give way, and I slump to my knees, then topple forward over a felled trunk at the side of the path, but any pain has left me now. As my vision blurs once more, there's no rush of reminiscences or regrets. Instead, the faces of my children appear in my mind, memories from less than an hour ago. I told them that we would always be a family. Instead, I will die alone in the mud.

And it's no less than I deserve.

82

NEARLY A YEAR LATER

My life has changed. That night gave me the motivation to escape from the trap that I was in. I lay there in the wet and cold, desperately trying to stay conscious, hoping Wyatt would return. He did, just as the ambulance's sirens approached. Wyatt ran out to the road and brought them back, possibly saving my life in the process. I lost nearly five pints of blood. Luckily, the only organ damaged was my small intestine, which they stitched up in a four-hour operation. Wyatt disappeared because the paramedics rang for the police.

They questioned me afterwards. I told them I'd heard something strange in the woods as I walked past. When I went to investigate, a man pulled a knife on me. It was too dark for me to see his face. They asked if I'd seen anyone else as a woman had rung 999 for an ambulance but not left her details. I said that Wyatt had heard my cries for help, but I didn't know his name.

Abi believed my story and was heroic in her response. She kept things ticking over and made me realise how lucky I am. Sometimes, adversity reminds you of what you have.

I had three months off work. It was heaven. When I returned,

I'd been gone from the prison environment too long. I had softened and found the constant aggravation too personal. A few weeks later, I finished my shift and knew I was done. My sentence was over. I slid my keys and radio down the chute that evening, then threw in my ID card and my tie for good measure. I rang in the next morning and said I'd simply had enough. They were fine and thanked me for my time. As you can imagine, that sort of thing happens a lot.

I'm now a team manager at IKEA. The money's the same, the stress is different, and no one's died yet. But this story isn't a fairy tale.

Wyatt didn't catch up with Bumpy that night, but he swore he would. I told Wyatt I was worried that Bumpy might realise he could blackmail me about what I did with Billie, even if *she* didn't want to any more. Wyatt said he'd sort it, and I didn't tell him not to.

Wyatt's good behaviour was short-lived. Around the same time as I was starting at IKEA, Wyatt was starting a one-year stretch for assaulting a policeman. Despite what she said, Elizabeth visits him. Must be that tattoo.

Abi also went to see him. He gave her a cryptic message to pass on to me: *No more bumps in the road.* Sure enough, the next week's local paper had an article on the overdose of a Stephen 'Bumpy' Frisk in HMP Feltham. He was a big lad, with white hair, who was serving a two-stretch for street robbery in an Orton Malborne underpass. The post-mortem showed the presence of a toxic combination of many drugs, no doubt procured from different people. I suppose you could call it a team effort. Bumpy's body was found covered in bruises, which were unexplained.

As for the other guys? Sheraton moved to the male side shortly after I left. He didn't last long and now works as an estate agent. The rumours were that Peabody broke immediately under questioning and confessed to an inappropriate relationship with Billie, which didn't progress to sex. The fact he asked for a transfer away from the wing after the incident with Gronkowski helped save his hide and they let him resign. He works for the same company as Sheraton and they live together. I bet they wake up with a smile, as I do, safe in the knowledge that their jobs are no longer life and death.

I bumped into MacStravick in The College Arms in town. He told me that the police at a holiday compound in Portugal received reports of a pervert near the pool. They arrested a man who was found with a telescope in his campervan. His mobile phone contained thousands of images of young women in bikinis. Myerscough had a massive heart attack while he was being questioned. Upon hearing the details of his demise, his ex-wife revealed she had left him years before due to his obsession with young women.

I heard the prison attempted to contact the girls who worked with him in the gardens to see if there was any inappropriate behaviour, but nobody wanted to get involved. Despite what Billie thought, at this point in time, none of the chickens have been offered counselling. Myerscough's post-mortem revealed significant heart disease. Stress might have been a factor.

Fats remains in jail. He's engaged to Braddock's sister, Emily, and they're planning a quiet wedding. Lena went on that date with the man from her new office. The guy turned out to be the owner of the company. She moved into his house a few months ago when Emily moved in with Fats.

Apparently, Odom and Nasima were dating each other all that time. The guy in the photo frame was Odom's best mate at school, who died in Afghanistan. Nasima was that man's sister. Nasima and Odom are both managers in the prison now.

Braddock and Tex still walk the landings. You could say they are the beating heart of the place. Perhaps, one day, they will find each other.

Lennox left the prison service to join the police. Occasionally, I catch her racing around in a first response vehicle. She looks the business and always waves.

Gary and I are close. His back prevents him from doing much, but he reads more and involves himself in the world when possible. He insists he's now a better husband. We both laugh when he says that.

At odd times, I wonder what happened to the girls. I'll never forget them. The only one I know of is Red. She was found dead in a squat with a syringe in her hand. She never saw her boys again, and she also didn't see her twentieth birthday.

Abi, the kids and I are moving house today. Her father's cancer wouldn't be thwarted, but he left us the money for a deposit and then some. The removal van is arriving at ten this morning. Abi is insisting that our place is scrubbed clean despite us leaving and I've learned not to argue about those sorts of things. I tell her I'm going to get a bottle of bubbly for when we're moved in tonight.

It's a glorious day at the end of autumn. I step out of the front door and glance up at a vast turquoise sky where huge, billowing, pure-white clouds stretch as far as the eye can see. It's time to say goodbye to this area and its memories. I walk down the path to the underpass where Bumpy liked to operate his business. The council has painted it again, but it's still a foreboding place.

I reach the wood and wander through. It's been dry for weeks, and, in the sunshine, it's peaceful. I stop where I almost died. Billie thought I was about to stab her, but I'd pushed Wyatt's hand away when he'd offered me the weapon.

Before I started on the female side, I couldn't understand why officers could be corrupt, or how normal people might hit out, or even kill, but life is rarely straight forward. Events have a way of sweeping you along. Sometimes all you can do is look back.

At the shop, I find a bottle of Prosecco that hopefully won't remove the enamel from our teeth and I join the queue. There's a girl at the front with a pram. She looks classy and poised in tight black jeans and a short red leather jacket, but then drops her purse and wobbles on high heels as she retrieves it. She scoops her hair behind her ear as she rises. I'm tempted to shout out, but I don't.

I watch her leave and think of that thunderstorm.

After paying, I step outside and pull my shades down in the bright sunlight. Billie is sitting on the wall, pushing her pram back and forwards. My heart betrays me as it speeds up.

'Hey,' she says.

I stand in front of her, but don't feel any malice. All those events seem so far away, and it's good to see her. I raise my sunglasses.

'Hey,' I reply.

We stare into each other's eyes for a while, but it's not uncomfortable.

'Thanks for ringing for the ambulance,' I eventually say.

'Thanks for not telling the police I stabbed you.'

'Does that make us quits?'

'Completely.'

I should walk away, but I want to hear about the others, and I hope that Billie's okay.

'Is Birdies open yet?'

'No, but it will be. Tara got the go-ahead two months back. She found a place in Whittlesey. We're moving there and living together. It's a start and it'll be good to leave Peterborough behind. Kitty and her are there at the moment, cleaning and painting. My shared house for new mums is just behind the Botolph, over there. I have one more week left. Junior, here, started crying, so I went for a walk to get him to go to sleep, but he's wide awake now.'

I smile at her. She's calmer.

'I stopped for some water,' she continues. 'Get this, though. Kitty has a boyfriend, and she's passed her driving test. She's so different.'

'That's great news. I'm pleased for you all. And good for Kitty. How about Tara, is she dating?'

'No, she has no interest. Maybe one day, but I doubt it.'

They're such complicated women. The simple, terrible truth is that Tara killed someone. Dress it up how you like, but only a certain kind of person drives a sharp object into someone's neck without any immediate provocation. It's murder. Perhaps she always carried a knife with the intention of using one. Tara is a bright girl. I guess she knows what she's capable of. Therefore, I suspect she's decided to only ever be with people she trusts or awful things are likely to happen.

If Abi is the victim in all this, then Tara is the tragedy. And I really liked her.

Billie clicks her fingers in my face.

'Earth to Dalton. I'm still looking, though.'

She beams at me and my body tingles in response. It seems what's broken can be fixed, while others can be ruined forever. The truth is we all get damaged as we go through life. Perhaps the answer is to keep trying and focus on not repeating your mistakes. It looks as if Billie has learned that lesson.

'We talk about you a lot,' she says.

'Really, why?'

'Tara says that people like us don't have many strong male role models in our lives. I reckon she means that most of the men we know are wankers.'

It's hard to disagree with that. I've been carrying what I did with me like a cloud full of rain. Some days, it's heavier than others, and I don't think I can hold it in. Surely, I'm not someone to be admired or even respected. Working on that YO wing has rocked the foundations of what kind of man I believed I was. I hope that I will learn to cope with what I've done and become a better person. We all deserve a second chance.

I crouch next to the buggy. The baby has the same deep-blue eyes as Billie.

'What did you call him?'

'I named him after his dad.'

'Sandringham is a bit of a mouthful.'

Billie's eyes crinkle and she laughs. The baby turns his head towards me and I stare at the dimple on his cheek. Billie crouches besides me and whispers what I already know.

'His name is Dalton.'

83

I shoot upright. Billie stops laughing, but she has an amused air.

'You said you were on the pill, and that you were due on.'

'I would have thought you'd know I can't be trusted by now.'

'Jesus, Billie. Why?'

She stares down the road for a few moments, then shrugs.

'Do you know what? I'm not entirely sure why, but when I was with you, I felt as if I belonged. That I was worth something. Do you understand? I was where I was supposed to be. I feel like that now when I'm with the baby.'

'Oh, Billie.'

'I think you and me shared a perfect moment.'

'Did you share one with Sandringham and Peabody?'

'Ooh! No need to get snotty. I didn't have sex with them, just fooled around. It was a bit of fun, and I knew they'd bring me things. I liked the control I had over them and it made me feel good. But you were different. It was like I was under a spell.'

'Sandringham killed himself.'

'I know. I only realised after I'd left the nick that I was partly to blame.'

'You also said I was a middle-aged loser who works in a prison.'

She grins. 'I have poor taste. Come on! I was just trying to hurt you because you hurt me. I'm damaged, remember?'

Despite her brutal take on life, I can't help a small smile sneaking onto my face.

'I'm sorry, Billie. I should have known better.'

She stands up.

'Don't be stupid. I'm as much at fault as you are.'

'I should have been looking out for you, not sleeping with you.'

'Yes, and I lied because I wanted you. I couldn't stop thinking about you. I still can't.'

There's a pause while we look at each other.

'And what do you want now?' I quietly ask.

'Nothing. I have enough. Go back to your family. I know what happens when families fall apart, so I would never break up yours. I'll be fine. I don't need your money any more. I have friends and a job. We can even live above the salon. I finally feel like I belong in this crazy world. The anger and desperation I felt has left me, and I'll always have a part of you.'

She steps towards me and gives me a gentle peck on the cheek.

'Don't be too hard on yourself, Dalton. We both made a mistake. Occasionally, though, good things happen because of them.'

My eyes drop from her face to the locket necklace that I bought for her. No wonder she wanted it, and I'm glad she has it. She grabs the handles of the pushchair and raises an eyebrow. I move out of the way. Billie pushes the baby around the low wall, then walks down the street with her head high. Little Dalton stares at me as they pass by.

I step over the wall and watch her. I'm not even sure what to think. How do I deal with knowing I have another child out there? It doesn't seem as if we've done a terrible thing, so I must be as deranged as Billie is. How would others judge me? Is Billie a bad person? Am I? Or are we merely people, rolling with the blows?

Sometimes, when you're lonely, or you feel that you've been let down, it's easy to reach out and take the wrong hand.

As Billie disappears into the distance I want to run after her. I even think we'd be happy together, at least for a while. But I've already flown too close to the heavens. Halfway along the street, she suddenly stops. A breeze tugs at her hair. She stays like that for five seconds, straightens her shoulders, then carries on pushing. Was she my prisoner, or did Billie make me hers?

I let out the breath I've been holding and walk the other way. The girl I fell in love with was called Damage, and I'll never forget her. That person has gone now, and part of my heart leaves with her. But my life and my future are at home.

MESSAGE FROM THE AUTHOR

Thank you for reading *Prisoner*. I worked both sides of HMP Peterborough for four years. I learned a lot during that time, and I hope by reading this you will too.

There's a bit of me in Dalton, but he's taller and thinner than I am. I didn't have sex with any of the prisoners either. Although, every year, prison officers get caught crossing that line.

The newspapers and the entertainment industry give you an impression of prison that is far from correct. Our jails are desperate places and a long way from the holiday camps that they are portrayed to be. Within those walls are people who struggle, and some of them are men and women like you and me.

The concept of a prisoner is an interesting one. There are the obvious definitions, such as a person being punished for a crime or confined during a war. You could even be reading this book behind bars. But it also means a person who feels confined or trapped by a situation. People are prisoners to their beliefs, their feelings and their commitments, sometimes even their health. You could say this describes life in general and we often flourish under our obligations. However, these restrictions can be tough to endure, especially if there is no end in sight.

I quit the jail over five years ago and yet most of the time I still see myself as a prison officer. When you work in a place like that, even after you leave, part of you is left behind. I'd say the prisoners feel the same way when they step outside for what they hope is the last time. But you also take something with you. Once you're free, at least for a while, it's much easier to spot the beauty in the world when you've seen it at its ugliest.

Recently, there's been an outpouring of support for our emergency services and healthcare staff in our changing world, and they all deserve it. The police and NHS in particular have many tough days at work doing jobs that at times must seem impossible.

Yet, when there is applause for these brave souls, few consider those who toil behind high walls. Unless you've been in one of these places, you wouldn't understand their disturbing world. Short-staffed prisons are full of some of the most damaged and violent people in our society, all day, and every day. Often, prison officers work the wings alone.

I was one of them, quietly lining up at the gatehouse, waiting for my keys and radio, steeling myself for the day ahead. Sometimes, now, I feel as if I have been released from a long sentence. Or, perhaps, that I escaped.

Sadly, people like the Sandringham character in this book, and others whom I worked with, do not.

The emotional toll of a job like this is a heavy burden, which can become intolerable. Winding down in a healthy way is hard. Mistakes are made. People explode under the pressure, while others silently fall through cracks.

You won't find many news headlines about what goes on inside these institutions because the government keeps it that way. Therefore, very few are aware of the horrific, devastating, traumatising incidents men and women behind bars cope with on a daily basis. That applies to those on both sides of the cell doors.

In fact, prison officers are often portrayed as knuckle-dragging authoritarians or uncaring tyrants, when many of them are not much older than those they are trying to control. Often, the staff are just youngsters who are thankful to have work. They soon realise it's no ordinary role, because prison officers deal with a part of our society that's almost a secret. And they will see things they can't forget.

They will become heroes, and nobody knows.

MORE FROM ROSS GREENWOOD

We hope you enjoyed reading *Prisoner*. If you did, please leave a review.

If you'd like to gift a copy, this book is also available as an ebook, digital audio download and audiobook CD.

Sign up to Ross Greenwood's mailing list for news, competitions and updates on future books.

http://bit.ly/RossGreenwoodNewsletter

Why not explore the DI Barton series:

ABOUT THE AUTHOR

Ross Greenwood is the bestselling author of eight crime thrillers. Before becoming a full-time writer he was most recently a prison officer and so worked everyday with murderers, rapists and thieves for four years. He lives in Peterborough.

Follow Ross on social media:

- twitter.com/greenwoodross
- facebook.com/RossGreenwoodAuthor
- bookbub.com/authors/ross-greenwood
- instagram.com/rossg555

ABOUT BOLDWOOD BOOKS

Boldwood Books is a fiction publishing company seeking out the best stories from around the world.

Find out more at www.boldwoodbooks.com

Sign up to the Book and Tonic newsletter for news, offers and competitions from Boldwood Books!

http://www.bit.ly/bookandtonic

We'd love to hear from you, follow us on social media:

facebook.com/BookandTonic
twitter.com/BoldwoodBooks
instagram.com/BookandTonic

Printed in Great Britain
by Amazon